THE HEIRS OF THE ARCTIC

Also by Aslak Nore in English translation

The Sea Cemetery

Aslak Nore

THE HEIRS OF THE ARCTIC

*Translated from the Norwegian by
Seán Kinsella*

MACLEHOSE PRESS
QUERCUS·LONDON

First published as *Ingen skal drukne*
by H. Aschehoug & Co., Oslo, in 2023
First published in Great Britain in 2025 by

MacLehose Press
An imprint of Quercus Editions Limited
Carmelite House
50 Victoria Embankment
London EC4Y 0DZ

An Hachette UK company

The authorised representative in the EEA is Hachette Ireland,
8 Castlecourt Centre, Castleknock Road, Castleknock,
Dublin 15, D15 XTP3, Ireland (email: info@hbgi.ie)

Copyright © 2023 H. Aschehoug & Co. (W. Nygaard)
English translation copyright © 2025 by Seán Kinsella

This translation has been published with the financial support of NORLA

The moral right of Aslak Nore to be
identified as the author of this work has been
asserted in accordance with the Copyright,
Designs and Patents Act, 1988.

Seán Kinsella asserts his moral right to be identified
as the translator of the work.

All rights reserved. No part of this publication
may be reproduced or transmitted in any form
or by any means, electronic or mechanical,
including photocopy, recording, or any
information storage and retrieval system,
without permission in writing from the publisher.

A CIP catalogue record for this book is available
from the British Library.

ISBN (HB) 978 1 52942 454 6
ISBN (TPB) 978 1 52942 455 3
ISBN (Ebook) 978 1 52942 457 7

This book is a work of fiction. Names, characters,
organisations, places and events are
either the product of the author's imagination
or are used fictitiously. Any resemblance to
actual persons, living or dead, events or
particular places is entirely coincidental.

1

Typeset by Jouve (UK), Milton Keynes
Printed and bound in Great Britain by Clays Ltd, Elcograf S.p.A.

Papers used by MacLehose Press are from well-managed forests and other
responsible sources.

*This book is dedicated to
Kjetil Anders Hatlebrekke (1970–2023)
and other veterans who fought for Norway and paid the price*

"To betray, you must first belong."

Kim Philby

Prologue
ARCTIC GRAVEYARD

Longyearbyen

In the high Arctic the year only has one day: the sun comes up once and goes down once.

Sunset in October lasts almost a week before darkness descends for the winter.

In Longyearbyen it had been night for only a month. Owing to the wind chill, the temperature of minus 11°C was closer to minus 19°C. Out of the November darkness of the Advent Valley a light appeared, faint at first, then growing gradually brighter until a headlight became visible.

The witness who had first raised the alarm – the owner of Casa Polaris, a holiday cabin situated on a slight slope above the flat valley floor – would later say it was the jerky, erratic light that had first caught her attention.

Governor Robert Eliassen had just finished his working day following a meeting with the pastor. He was a burly police officer in his sixties who had got the job after a long, successful career in the police and security services in northern Norway. Wearing a trapper hat and wind mittens, he had just set out on his snowmobile on the 300-metre stretch back to the governor's estate.

The pastor had wanted to discuss the graveyard on the slope towards the summit of Plåtafjellet, where the permafrost was slowly forcing all the coffins up out of the earth. Everything buried on Svalbard came up again sooner or later.

The pastor had shown him an article in the international media about it being "forbidden to die" on the archipelago. An exaggeration perhaps, but the place was no "cradle-to-grave" community, as Eliassen was fond of saying.

Svalbard was not a place to be born or to die.

Contrary to what most visitors assume, the name Longyearbyen has nothing to do with the seasons at 78 degrees north. The appellation is not related to the polar night and the midnight sun, those phenomena in the outermost regions so fundamentally at odds with our common human categorisation of reality – the sun rising in the morning and going down at night – that they can induce madness, delirium or cause one to be bitten by the so-called "polar bug", which renders life on the mainland empty and meaningless. No, Longyearbyen is named after an American miner.

Eliassen had almost reached the governor's estate, a cosy yard surrounded by red wooden houses that stood in stark contrast to its futuristic neighbour, the governor's administration building. "Darth Vader has landed in Longyearbyen" was how one foreign reporter had described it. Another wag had observed: "What may be considered fantasy and science fiction in other places is social realism on Svalbard."

At that moment Eliassen heard the whine of an engine and saw a snowmobile burst through a snow bank at speed before coming to an abrupt halt in the yard.

"Hey!" he called out, dismounting and running the last few metres over to the vehicle.

Atop the snowmobile a thickset, bearded man was sitting almost rigid before, with what appeared to be a strenuous effort, he rose from the seat and collapsed in the snow.

Hypothermia, Eliassen quickly concluded. Years in the Arctic had not only made him adept at avoiding the condition himself, but also to see when those with less experience of the region had not managed to adequately protect themselves from the cold.

He tried communicating in both English and Russian but failed to illicit a response. As he made to take hold of the man by the shoulder, the Russian mumbled something.

"Don't . . . don't touch!"

His eyes struggled to focus on the governor.

"Medical care . . . emergency . . ."

"I'll get you medical help, of course I will," Eliassen said. "But you can't lie here. You risk freezing to death."

It was as though the man pulled himself together. "P-p-poison," he said.

"What?" the governor replied.

"Poisoned," the Russian whispered in English, in a low, rasping voice.

Robert Eliassen stood up and took a step back. Had he touched the man lying on the ground in front of him? No, but he had been a hair's breadth from doing so. He took out his phone, called a number and described the situation in a few brief words to A & E.

"Who are you?" Eliassen asked.

"My name . . . is . . . Colonel . . . Vasily . . . Zemlyakov . . ."

"Where have you come from?"

"B-B-barentsburg."

"My name is Robert Eliassen and I'm Norway's chief official here on Svalbard," the governor said with authority.

The Russian convulsed, ending up on his side with his head in a little snowdrift. Eliassen could see blood beginning to trickle from his nose and mouth.

"The ambulance is on its way."

Several things were clear to him. Firstly, this man was fatally ill. Secondly, if the Russians had poisoned him, God alone knew if he too was in danger.

A poisoned Russian colonel on NATO territory was an international incident. In Brussels such an occurrence could be characterised as a *chemical attack*. Eliassen shuddered.

"Governor?" Zemlyakov whispered and pointed in the direction of the Advent Valley. "Falck?"

"Falck?"

Governor Eliassen stared at the man in front of him. He was of course aware of the Falck family's business activities on Svalbard. They had held mining rights there since 1916. Furthermore, Hans Falck, the celebrated doctor, was an old acquaintance from the 1970s, back when Eliassen was busy keeping communists like him under surveillance.

"What do you mean?"

"Falck have a foundation and a company . . . SAGA."

"And?"

Zemlyakov coughed up blood.

"We have someone on the inside of SAGA."

"Who?" the governor asked.

Just then the ambulance arrived and two people in hazmat suits carrying a stretcher rushed over. They gently lifted the Russian and placed him on the stretcher. Zemlyakov turned his head as they were about to place an oxygen mask on him. He gave Eliassen an entreating look.

"Someone in the family . . . you'll get the name . . . in exchange for my protection."

He passed out. The ambulance drove away.

Robert Eliassen switched off the ignition on the snowmobile. Silence fell. He stood staring at the Opera Mountain on the far side of the fjord. In the darkness it resembled a theatre stage with the lights off. A mole inside the Falck family?

He took out his phone and rang the doctor on call.

"I need to question the Russian," Eliassen said, "as soon as possible."

"I'm afraid that'll be impossible," the doctor answered and drew a deep breath. "The patient died in the ambulance. There was nothing we could do."

PART I
ADVENT

1

330TH SQUADRON

Norwegian waters, northern Norway

The rescue helicopter, a Sea King, lifted from the helipad as though being hoisted and paused several metres above the ground, swaying in the wind, before tilting its nose slightly downward and flying out over Vestfjorden.

The message had been concise: Russian trawler north-west of Sortland. Captain acutely ill.

Hans Falck, seated at the back of the aircraft to the right of the rescue swimmer, was wearing a signal-red survival suit with wool underneath, and had a three-point seat belt fastened. Sleet lashed the window. There was a strong headwind; the cabin shook, causing the tightly packed medical equipment to rattle. It was the final day of the crew's current stint on emergency standby.

Below he could make out the strait between Bodø and the high peaks of Landegode Island. Although it was early in the morning, the November light was so dim that the cabin was bathed in dusky darkness.

Ever since he was a boy and his uncle Herbert had shown him the stuffed polar bear at the Svalbard office of the Hanseatic Steamship Company, Hans had been drawn to the north. For him it was akin to a law of physics, like gravity bringing an object to the ground. All the memories of this part of the country lay hidden deep within him, in the same way people carry their lost youth or the reminiscence of an old flame. The air could conjure it: the dampness by the coast, the dry, freezing conditions on the plateaus inland. Or the rugged, endless landscapes covered in snow, illuminated by the Northern Lights in winter and bathed in eternal sun in the summer. The northerners' warmth and friendliness reminded him of the people in the Levant.

"Doctor Hans," Giske, the rescue diver, said. The confident young western Norwegian took a slurp from a cup of instant soup and looked nonchalantly out at the storm. "Wasn't it down there that the Hurtigruten ferry with those relatives of yours sank during the war?"

Hans stared pensively down at the spumy whitecaps in Vestfjorden. The shipwreck had led the Oslo branch of the family to deviate from the direct line of descent in the Falck family. The biggest of their many lies.

It had also been in these parts, during a seminar in Trollfjorden, that Siri Greve had come to him with a copy of Vera's will.

Greve had offered him and his branch of the family control of a company worth twelve billion kroner, a non-profit foundation, and perhaps the most attractive piece of private property in the country. M. Magnus had been on at him a lot lately. "You have to exercise your rights, claim what's yours," he insisted.

Of course, Hans could offer good reasons for not having taken up the fight. That his radical conscience stood in direct opposition to the Falck fortune. That his idealism was incompatible with modern private capitalism. That his place was in the field and not in some rose tower at Rederhaugen.

For him, saving one life was saving the world.

He could say all this, and those listening would be lost in

admiration, as they always were when he spoke, whether that was around a dinner table, after receiving an honorary degree, in a Lebanese refugee camp, or at a public meeting in northern Norway called to fight the closure of a local hospital.

They would all sit spellbound.

In the eyes of the world, Hans was the exemplar of a man of action. When the alarm went, when the bombs were falling and people were in distress, no one was on the scene quicker. It was a drug. But when family relations became difficult, Hans buried his own secrets below layer upon layer of work.

The Sea King helicopter shook violently just as the contours of the Lofoten Wall, shrouded in storm clouds and low fog, emerged below him on the left side.

Like Hans, Giske the rescue swimmer had that resting-pulse composure that seemed so alien to civilians, who were afraid of even slight turbulence on a commercial airliner. That type of thing had never scared Hans. It was the silence he feared – the stillness after an agonising conversation at the dinner table, following the exposure of infidelity.

They had flown above the rugged, mountainous islands in Vesterålen and were headed out over the endless Atlantic when the pilot's voice came over the headset.

"Five minutes to reported position. Giske, stand by for descent to boat."

Hans spotted the trawler first: a blue hull below a black winch with the bridge towards the bow and a broad stern, high and rigid, like a factory at sea. Maybe thirty metres long, although it was difficult to gauge for sure. A blast of wind lifted the helicopter into an updraught and back down into an air pocket, like a ship at sea. The diver stood up and made his way to the open hatch with a swaying gait. An icy wind hit them. The navigator had got to his feet and was beside him.

"We're in position," the pilot said, with that forthright, almost nonchalant voice that was the mark of a safe pair of hands in rough weather.

"Any update on the captain's injuries?" Hans asked. "Alcohol poisoning?"

"They seem quite stressed," the navigator said. "If I had to guess, I'd say it's something acute and painful."

"Giske, prepare for descent," the pilot ordered.

The navigator and engineer double-checked that the rescuer was secured. Grasping the bar above the hatch with both hands, Giske leaned out and allowed himself to be lowered in the wind. Snow blew into the helicopter, heavy flakes melting on the thigh of Hans's red survival suit. The rotor blades made an infernal racket.

After what felt like an eternity, the rescuer eventually reported he was on the deck.

"Status of the Russian?" the navigator radioed.

"They won't let me enter the cabin where he's lying," Giske shouted. "But from what I can gather, he's suffering intense pain in the abdominal region. Condition poor in general."

"You need to get him on the stretcher," the navigator shouted, "then we'll have a look at him up here and take him to Bodø."

There was crackling on the line and the sound of voices raised in anger.

"The Russians are refusing to let me take him," Giske radioed. "They think it's too dangerous, and he's in too bad a state."

"Then there's nothing we can do," the navigator said. "We'll bring you back up."

"Wait!" Hans shouted into the headset. "Giske, can you ask the Russians to have someone place a hand on his lower abdomen? Tell them to press down, no more than a couple of centimetres. Is he in any more pain?"

"Surprisingly little, they're telling me," the rescuer said after several seconds.

"Ask them to release the pressure with a swift movement."

The subsequent scream left no room for doubt.

In the cockpit, the navigator, engineer and Hans exchanged glances.

"I think we can save the guy," Hans said in a serious tone. "I'm going down."

The others nodded in silent agreement.

Hans linked himself securely to the line, stood up and took staggering steps through the swaying helicopter cabin over to the hatch. He clipped himself into the hoist harness. The navigator double-checked the attachments.

Then Hans swung out into the blackness and began to descend. The noise of the rotor blades mingled with the wind. Far, far below he could make out the lights of the trawler. He was so high up. The outline of the vessel came into view on the crest of a wave, seeming as motionless as a stranded ship at low tide, before disappearing down into a trough of white-whipped foam. He swung so far back and forth that for a moment he thought he would be hurled into one of the masts.

The wind was strong, but with the weight bag at the end of the guideline providing ballast Hans felt safe.

Now he could see the trawler clearly. A large, rusty beast.

Seven metres to go, five metres, three metres . . .

Down on the deck he released himself from the harness and began walking unsteadily. "What'll we do?" Giske asked.

"You wait here," Hans shouted. "I'll talk to the Russians."

Two Russian seamen approached him. In the wind Hans

shouted that he was a doctor and he had a suspicion of what was ailing the captain.

One of the Russians gestured and attempted a response. "Doctor OK. Operation here."

The other Russian took a step forward, as though to emphasise what they meant. Hans nodded and hurried up to the bridge, where he was shown to the captain's quarters.

The captain was lying on a stretcher on the floor. He was an athletic, muscular man in his forties.

Hans opened the medic bag and assessed what he had to hand. He held a scalpel up to the light.

"Really?" one of the Russians said.

A big wave caused the wheelhouse to shake.

"It's this or death," Hans said soberly.

He administered a sedative and the captain went out quickly. The crew continued to stand around them.

"I need someone to help me," Hans ordered, pointing at the seaman who seemed to speak the best English, before handing him a surgical mask and gloves. "You."

Hans began by cutting through the captain's shirt in the area between the upper pelvis and the navel. Placing a hand carefully on McBurney's point on the lower abdomen, he applied surgical spirit. Using the scalpel, he made an incision about five centimetres long, and while the seaman helped keep the cut open, he negotiated the muscle fibres until the peritoneum was visible. The ship continued to roll. Making a slightly deeper incision, Hans opened the peritoneal cavity. He stuck his forefinger in to locate the large intestine.

Below that the swollen appendix came into view. It was red and the shape and size of an earthworm. Hans drew it up, found the appendicular artery, then secured and ligated it, before cutting it and pushing the stump of the appendix back in. Then he closed the abdominal wall and the skin. The operation took only minutes.

"For the last time," Hans said, "he needs to come with us."

"He stays," the Russian replied brusquely. "Thank you, doctor."

On his way out, Hans grabbed the beaker he had placed the appendix in, putting it in a diffusion-proof bag which he then sealed.

The rescue diver approached him. "Well?"

"Should be OK," Hans answered.

"Fuck, some job," Giske said.

There was a crackle over the radio.

"Falck, Giske?" the navigator said. "We're running low on fuel."

The Norwegians made their way quickly through the wheelhouse, down onto the deck.

"We're ready to be hoisted up!" Hans shouted, his voice full of adrenalin.

The next second he sailed off in an arc over the gunwale, as the trawler rolled on a wave higher than any of the others.

Hans already understood. This would go wrong.

For a moment he had a sensation of weightlessness before he was hurled back towards the trawler and saw a steel mast growing before his eyes.

Because this was what he had always dreaded. Not death itself, but that concentrated fear of death, from the moment the free solo climber loses his grip on the rock face until he meets the ground, the second between the detonation of the roadside bomb and the blast it releases, the tenth of a second between the guillotine falling and it cutting the carotid arteries.

Then the curtain fell.

2

THE TIME FOR DECEIVING THE AUTHORITIES IS OVER

Rederhaugen, Oslo

One of the first things Sasha Falck did as the new director of SAGA was to have the statue of Big Thor, which had long adorned the large square lawn in front of the main entrance, pulled down.

To replace it, she commissioned a sculptor to make a bust of her paternal grandmother. The artist specialised in figures of strong females and, however unclassifiable she might otherwise have been, Vera Lind certainly belonged in that category. Besides her writing, which held cult status in certain circles, she had defied the male members of the family, at great personal risk, in order to tell the truth.

Sasha looked up at the bronze face. It was early morning on September 1. There was much to be done before the naming ceremony of *Falck 3* – a rescue boat the family business had donated to the Norwegian Sea Rescue Society – took place in the capital. After that, a reception was to be held at Rederhaugen. As director of SAGA, Sasha was playing a key role.

A cold winter rain was falling and raindrops lay like beads of sweat on the forehead of her grandmother's likeness. Sasha pulled the already damp scarf tighter around her neck and stepped over the low railing separating the gravel path from the lawn where the bust stood. *Vera Lind 1920–2015.* Sasha had of course considered an epitaph, maybe something from one of Vera's books, but the view her grandmother held of the inscription on the statue of Big Thor had dissuaded her. *"To live on in the hearts we leave behind is not to die*; more like 'His mortal remains have left us but his pomposity will live for eternity'," she would say with a scornful laugh.

The features of the bust resembled Sasha's own face: the pointed Roman nose and the high cheekbones, although the coiffed hair indicated it was modelled on an older version of her grandmother. The skin was smooth, as though after a facelift; the eyes had the vacant aloofness of a statue as she stared out at the horizon of the fjord. Grandmother pointed towards another reality, of art and passion, beyond the self-control Sasha always strove for.

It had all begun the previous year when Vera, at the grand old age of ninety-five, had committed suicide. Her will was nowhere to be found. Despite her father's warnings about not "looking under that rock", Sasha had begun probing into her grandmother's secrets. Her investigations had pointed her in the direction of Vera's manuscript, *The Sea Cemetery*, originally written in 1970. In it, Vera had used a journey on the Hurtigruten ferry and its subsequent sinking during the Second World War to tear down the image of Sasha's grandfather, Big Thor Falck, as a war hero. In reality, he had been a Nazi collaborator and a war profiteer. The manuscript had been seized and Vera had been placed under a guardianship order by her own son, Sasha's father Olav.

When Sasha finally found the will, she understood why the relationship between Vera and Olav had been so fraught. Her son had been the result of a love affair with a German soldier. Sasha and Vera's other descendants therefore fell outside the bloodline on which the Falcks based control over the family businesses and inheritance. With the stroke of a pen, her grandmother had, in effect, disinherited them. Sasha had burned the will. Even though the fear of this crime coming to light was still present, it grew weaker with every day that passed.

Sasha was making her way back towards the office when she heard a voice behind her.

"Alexandra?"

She stopped. Recognised the low, whispering voice and melodious north Norwegian accent of Martens Magnus. MM to his colleagues.

"You're not my father," she said. "Call me Sasha."

MM possessed the sort of anti-charisma which often characterised people who succeeded in the labyrinth of bureaucracy. He had divorced the previous year, a development that had brought him and Olav closer.

But although M. Magnus was Olav's confidant, that friendship was no obstacle to her father ridiculing him when his name came up in conversation with his children.

"MM would unplug his own mother from life support if he needed to charge his phone," Olav would say. But people listened to his advice. He was a person worth staying on good terms with.

A stocky man with rat-like features, he belonged to the type of former special forces officer that combined cynicism with vanity. Today he was sporting a black double-breasted coat over a burgundy polo neck, and a strong scent of aftershave lingered around him.

"We need to talk," he said in a firm tone.

Despite his flaws, when MM insisted on something, it was wise to listen. Sasha had appointed him head of SAGA's North Norway Division, a move that had drawn approval from her father. In the north all activity – property, ports, shipping – had far-reaching political implications. It was a game MM mastered better than most. Her own learning curve had proved steep, but with angels and devils like Martens Magnus on her shoulder she had come through.

"As you're aware, Sverre and the rest of the Afghanistan contingent are landing today," MM said, as they made their way down towards the pavilion.

"We don't have any contact," Sasha said. "Was there another reason you wanted to talk?"

Martens Magnus nodded. "I've just come from a meeting with, among others, public officials and the governor of Svalbard."

The story of the poisoned Russian colonel had caused a stir after the media had got hold of it some weeks previously. Longyearbyen society being so transparent, the inhabitants knew about every event almost as soon as it happened, and a possible chemical attack from Russia on sovereign Norwegian territory was not exactly a warning shot fired at a polar bear; it was international news. Governor Eliassen had been interviewed by *Der Spiegel*, the BBC and the *New York Times*, prime ministers had condemned, NATO had consulted and the Russians had denied.

"The results of the forensic examinations are back," MM continued. "They show Zemlyakov had a high level of ricin in his system, and that he died of septicaemia. This is the same highly toxic protein used to kill a Bulgarian defector in London in 1978, among others. But the time frame is important. Ricin will usually kill people within three days, so it's relatively slow acting. According to the post-mortem report, Zemlyakov had been poisoned at least twenty-four hours previously. And from the log of Russian shipping traffic we know he arrived on a Russian vessel that docked in Barentsburg four hours prior to the incident in Longyearbyen. Directly from a Russian base on Franz Josef Land."

Sasha thought for a moment. "So, he was poisoned on Russian territory?"

"Looks very much like it," MM replied. "Intelligence is of the view he planned his own escape to the West *after* the poisoning. He came by boat, stole a snowmobile in Barentsburg and drove to Longyearbyen, a trip that in darkness and without local knowledge took as much as three hours."

"I'm familiar with the route," she said.

"The fact the poisoning seems to have taken place on Russian territory is the reason for the relatively cautious nature of Norway's official response."

They had reached the shore at Øksevika. The low-lying clouds merged with the grey horizon.

"The colonel's last words," MM whispered, "were that the Russians had someone inside SAGA. In a central position."

She swallowed, nodding slowly. Then she picked up a flat stone and skimmed it across the water. Why this now? Just as she was in the process of putting behind her the shocking events stirred up by her discovery of Vera's manuscript and will. It had threatened to blow the family apart. Now her relationship with her father was on the mend, she was on top of things.

And now this.

"We have a strategy in place for the northern areas under your purview," she said. "How does this information relate to them?"

"That's precisely what I'm trying to ascertain."

She turned to him. "What are the security services saying?"

"What indeed. They're saying that equality, diversity and

inclusion are important and that the investigation mustn't clash with the holiday period. They're *looking into* the matter."

Sasha had met enough military types to know that they spoke about "the police", as in the security police, with a condescension that surpassed how the police referred to security guards.

"*The police* are competent technicians and undercover operatives," MM said. "I'll give them that. I imagine they'll turn up en masse to install microphones in the walls and monitor your phone, then send a few men later on to stake out the reception. But do you think they'll catch a SAGA infiltrator in that way?"

He shook his head.

"So what do you suggest?"

"Johnny Berg," he answered, without hesitation. His gaze was steady.

The thought of John Omar "Johnny" Berg had roughly the same effect on Sasha as when she stumbled upon online videos of daredevils balancing on the edges of skyscrapers and cranes: her blood pressure and heart rate went up, her breathing grew faster and her palms became sweaty. She tried to turn away but was drawn to what frightened her.

It was Johnny who had helped her find out the truth about *The Sea Cemetery*. He knew the *entire* truth.

The outsider, street boy, secret agent, lover, who, under the pretext of finding Vera's manuscript, had manoeuvred himself into the family before she herself had intervened.

"I'm not in touch with Johnny Berg."

Magnus sighed, with a little too much resignation for her taste.

"You should consider getting in touch. Berg could be a useful man to be on good terms with right now."

Sasha made no reply. She could not say what she was thinking: that even if contrary to all reasoning she was to heed her darker instincts, Johnny did not want to have anything to do with her. She had burned Vera's will before his eyes, then had him sent to prison. "Whatever we had, it's over," Sasha said, immediately regretting her choice of words. It sounded like a lover's confession.

"Berg is out of prison and is writing a biography of Hans," the officer said. "He's regained partial custody of his daughter. Things are going much better, by all accounts."

"The biography of Hans was a ploy to get inside the family," she mumbled, while trying to conceal her curiosity.

"At the outset perhaps, but now it's serious. Berg has a watertight reason to sit and work at Rederhaugen. Give him a desk somewhere. Let him find out who's leaking information to the Russians. And not a word about this conversation, do you understand?"

"Martens," Sasha said. "The time for deceiving the authorities is over. This is a job for the security services. If you ever drop hints abouts extra-parliamentary escapades under the auspices of SAGA again, I'll see to it you're placed under investigation – by the *police*."

"Alexandra," MM protested, before seeming to accept defeat.

"And one last thing," Sasha said. "If you mention Johnny Berg's name once more, I'll see to it you never set foot in Rederhaugen again."

3

NONE SHALL DROWN

Honnørbryggen, Oslo

Olav Falck arrived late at Honnørbryggen dock for the boat-naming ceremony, and as he sank out of breath into the place reserved for him in the first row, he noticed the seat was wet and water was soaking through the seat of his corduroy trousers.

Damn. A damp backside had a tendency to cause a cold, and colds at his age had a tendency to last forever.

"Your Royal Highness, members of the Norwegian Society for Sea Rescue, family and friends," Alexandra said from the podium as she looked out at the audience – from the princess, who was the patron of the lifeboat, to the retired politician who headed the rescue organisation, before her eyes fell on her father.

Sensitive as he was to the dynamics of power, Olav immediately recognised the new pecking order. What about *familia ante omnia* – family before all else? He himself had become a pleb. Only last week a receptionist at Rederhaugen had been about to stick a name tag on him, before Greve had rushed over to avert the indignity.

A red carpet at a right angle from City Hall behind them led to the dock, where *Falck III* lay floating on the grey-black surface. The rescue boat was large, that was beyond doubt. So large he wondered momentarily if the seabed conditions might be too shallow in here. From a structure astern with a roof big enough for a helipad, a walkway went to the wheelhouse towards the bow of the boat, with its high command bridge and a powerful mast on the roof.

His daughter leaned forward on the podium. "Who are we? Who are we as individuals and as a nation?"

Her rhetorical star turn, Olav thought, lines delivered for the first time at Vera's memorial reception. They had since become something of a credo for her mission with SAGA.

"We're a coastal nation," she continued. "My grandmother, may she rest in peace, came from Lofoten. She grew up with stories about shipwrecks, with wraiths sailing half-boats with torn sails, with the constant fear of drowning, of loved ones never returning. Naturally, this made the people on the coast particularly religious. Prayer houses were aplenty, superstition was strong. Life was predestined. One could die at any time. In 1861 it was reported that between 712 and 759 fishermen were lost annually. Annually!"

He could see more and more of Vera, of the storyteller, in his daughter. Whatever might be said about the rescue service's other donors, not many of them were gifted public speakers. She could hold the shipping aristocracy spellbound. Their own offspring were for the most part wastrels and party girls in London society, lacking any sense of history.

"We should therefore be grateful to those far-sighted people who gathered on a summer day in 1889 to establish the Norwegian Society for Sea Rescue. In my family we are proud and humbled to have played a part in that story by supporting rescue operations along the coast ever since we donated a wooden boat in 1916."

His daughter had realised the power that lay in a young

woman being versed in subjects his old friends spent their retirement studying: maritime history and genealogy.

"That lifeboat was named *Falck*," she said, "and it was followed by *Falck II* in the 1960s and 70s. *Falck II* was fitted with an echo sounder from a rescue vessel named *Skomvær II*, which was later passed on to *Sjøfareren*, as though to illustrate that rescue boats exist in an unbroken historical line – a tradition we are extremely proud to be carrying on with *Falck III*. As part of the centenary celebrations of the family's involvement with Svalbard, we'll be organising an expedition to the archipelago on this boat, prior to handing it over to the Norwegian Society for Sea Rescue."

Applause broke out. Olav shivered in the drizzle. Alexandra might be able to plot the Falck family's place in the maelstrom of Norway's history with a few elegant strokes of a pen, but did she have what it took when SAGA had to engage in realpolitik?

When his daughter succeeded him as CEO and chair of the board in the spring, he had sat her down to explain what the job involved, in all its technicalities. When he was finished, they had remained sitting in front of the log fire and he had fixed her with a solemn look.

"That was the official part of the briefing," he had said. "Because SAGA always has been, and must continue to be, a spearhead serving Norwegian interests, and ultimately safeguarding our freedom."

"We live in a democratic country, Daddy. One can't carry on as one likes," Alexandra had replied.

He had countered by telling her that that was exactly what SAGA was, a last line of defence for democracy when opponents were unwilling to accept democratic values and the rule of law.

Alexandra rounded off her speech with a surprise. "I've spoken about the ties between the rescue services and our family. We also have personal experience of tragedy at sea. The Norwegian Society for Sea Rescue's vision and motto is also our own: 'None shall drown'."

Applause rang out; a marching band came trooping down to the quay as the boat was festooned with balloons and garlands in the colours of the society.

What is this, Olav thought, a child's birthday party?

His suspicion was heightened when he caught sight of the vessel's godmother, a pale teenager surrounded by bodyguards and people from the royal household, who bestowed a name on the ship and her good wishes into a waiting microphone. She released the rope with the bottle and it smashed on the hull on the second attempt.

The invited guests clapped and the band played a musical salute.

"All we're missing now is paper hats and a cake with candles," Olav whispered to the man next to him. He did not laugh. No, Olav thought, this wasn't the place for jokes undermining the state.

"You must be proud of your daughter," his neighbour said.

He was, of course. At first, he had feared what all parents feared – crime, drugs, serious illness – and when they grew up without any of those nightmare scenarios occurring, a vague worry began to surface about them finding their place in the world. A feeling that lingered where the two other children were concerned: Andrea and Sverre had both yet to settle down and have children.

Olav had only been worried about Alexandra on one occasion: when she took off with that manipulating scalp hunter Johan Omar Berg. He had made his feelings known on that matter. Because he so seldom raised his voice at her, she had listened.

His daughter and Martens Magnus beckoned him up to the bridge. The captain was on hand to explain proudly that *Falck III* would be the largest vessel in the rescue service's fleet, and, along with the German cruiser *Hermann Marwede*, one of the world's largest rescue ships.

The princess got to try out a survival suit and, after some hesitation, jumped into the cold black December sea to enthusiastic applause before she departed.

The rain had got heavier; it was the kind of day that never grew bright. Olav stood by the rail as the boat moved astern between the City Hall jetties, then took off forwards at cruising speed. On one side the walls of Akershus Fortress rose up grey and unapproachable, on the other side the white roof of the Astrup Fearnley Museum curved downward into the water, like a capsized sailboat on the surface of the fjord.

A feeling of melancholy came over him, as it often did when he passed the school building where he had begun sixty-nine – yes, crazy to think – years ago. On the other hand: he might enjoy life as a pensioner.

"Olav," said MM, who had come up beside him, placing his strong hands upon the railing. "Did you hear about Hans?"

"What is it now? Has he been appointed UN High Commissioner for Refugees? Caught in flagrante with a young lefty politician?"

"We just received word that he's been involved in an accident. He's seriously injured."

Olav spun around towards the officer. "What are you saying? Where is he? In the Middle East?"

"No, the incident occurred on the Norwegian continental

shelf, outside Vesterålen, with the 330th Squadron. We don't have the details yet, but he's in a coma in the hospital at Bodø."

"Christ," Olav said. This was startling news.

Over the bow of the ship, the precipitous cliffs below Vera's old cottage came into view and, from behind the rock formations, the rose tower became visible. The boat slowed down and chugged calmly alongside the longest pier in Øksevika at Rederhaugen's southern tip. It was hard to comprehend. Hans Falck, womaniser, voice of the oppressed and saviour of disabled war veterans, the man with nine lives. Could he really be lying in a coma?

"Let's hope he pulls through," Olav said.

MM nodded. "Absolutely."

"You know, Martens," Olav said, leaning over the railing, "men like Hans, men with that ability to seduce people, are never as alive as when they're dead. You understand? Let's pray he survives!"

4

PUTIN IS THE WEST'S ONLY HOPE

Rederhaugen, Oslo

A taxi swung through Rederhaugen's main gate and glided slowly along the avenue of linden trees. The trees were slightly crooked from the autumn storms. Sverre Falck sat in the back seat. The dress uniform was making his thighs itch. The evidence of his service in Afghanistan dangled on his chest, along with a colourful salad of other medals. They had awarded him the Medal for Defence Service Abroad with a rosette, now pinned on his uniform, over his heart, for "bravery and courage".

The car stopped at the turnaround.

"Thank you," the taxi driver said.

"I'm the one who should be saying thanks," Sverre said, opening the door.

The driver looked at the uniform. "For the job you do, for the country."

Back straight, chest forward and eyes straight ahead. Wasn't that what the officer had drilled into Sverre when he was a young recruit?

Many had spoken ill of him and there had been no shortage of doubters prior to his posting in Afghanistan. His father, his siblings, fellow soldiers. But the fact was, to quote the group commander, "that sharpshooter Falck has, from an objective view, far exceeded expectations".

Head up, eyes forward. He had returned in triumph. He had used the time in Afghanistan to think. About how to obtain what was rightfully his. The top position in SAGA.

So why could he never quite rid himself of the icy breath from that black dog on his shoulder? Was it the remnants of his previous tours over there, the wires by the roadside, the blast, the whistling in his ears and the sand in his nostrils when the IED exploded? Or the terrified foreigners at the guest house they liberated from the terrorists, or the ghosts from the Hotel Intercontinental?

The memories merged, forming distorted faces, just as the twisted features of a troll sometimes appeared in a forest at night if one stared long enough at a tree.

Sasha was standing in the doorway welcoming people. The iron fist of jealousy gripped his heart. Once, when he was a boy, he had stood in that large doorway with his father. It was his place. The firstborn, in direct line.

"Stand with your legs apart, like a field commander," Olav had told him, patting his son on the head with those rough hands of his. They used to read about Charles XII of Sweden and Napoleon in the evenings. "You carry the general's baton in your bag, Sverre. Someday you'll be the one standing here."

He had always tried to please his father. Had followed the path he had plotted. The army, law studies, Afghanistan, the SAGA Group. Olav was never satisfied. "A man's life is incomplete if he has never experienced war, love and poverty," he used to say.

As if his father had experienced poverty. Or war. Sverre wasn't even sure if Olav had ever really loved anyone.

Eventually Sverre had had enough. The last time he had

been at Rederhaugen was the family council that spring, when the Bergen relatives and his own Oslo branch were to divide the inheritance. Sverre had wanted to sell his shares in the SAGA Group to the Bergen Falcks, something his father regarded as an act of disloyalty. The consequences of which now stood in front of him with outstretched arms.

"Sverre!" Sasha smiled, placing her dainty hands on his upper arms.

She looked older, or perhaps it was her style of dress.

"I've spoken to the chief of defence. The reports on you in Afghanistan are very good."

It was the sort of testimonial that should have filled Sverre with pride, but something about his sister's condescending, official tone ruined it. *Reports on you* – who spoke like that to their brother? She obviously enjoyed seeing him come crawling.

A cosy aroma of wine and cloves, mixed with the hum of voices and the clinking of glasses, met him as he stepped inside. Before he was halfway through the crowd of people in the foyer, he had already been offered a seat on the board of a foundation by some elderly Friend of the Armed Forces. He said hello to Olav's old secret weapon Signy Ytre-Arna, a seasoned political horse trader from the Centre Party with the notches of a number of ministerial posts and board seats on the belt around her not insubstantial waist. "Everything about Signy is big," Olav was fond of saying, "except voter turnout for her party."

Sverre excused himself and went to the bathroom. He threw some water on his face. Looked in the mirror. In his features he could recognise his pre-Marine Hunter Command self: the long nose with the pointy "falcon beak", the pale skin that bronzed in the summer, the small blue eyes that lent him a searching look. A face that before could be described as arrogant, but now had life experience etched into it, like a piece of antique furniture finally realising value.

He liked it. He was a different man from the one who had travelled to Afghanistan. On returning to the hall, he heard a voice: "Sverre!"

Andrea worked her way through the crowd, as tall and androgynous as before, although her dark hair had grown and was back behind her ears now. They embraced.

"You're the only person I'm happy to see," Sverre said.

His little sister left her hands resting on his shoulders, as though to make sure it was him. "It's good to see you, Sverre, I've been worried about you!"

Sverre assumed a more blasé air. "All good here at home?"

"Everything's alright. Alexandra the Great is ruling with an iron fist." She shrugged. "Been wondering if I'll do the same as you and sell my stake in this shit."

"Hold off on that, I haven't sold mine yet," Sverre said quickly. "I want to talk to you before we make any decisions."

As always during such receptions the foyer was abuzz with gossip and the pronouncements of armchair politicians.

"Did you hear that Hans is in a coma?" his sister said.

"What are you talking about?"

"An accident, in northern Norway. Marte and her brothers have travelled up."

What did an indisposed Hans mean for Sverre's own plans? Perhaps not a great deal, but Sverre was the one in the Oslo branch on best terms with the Bergenite, so this was bad news. Could he use it to his advantage?

He was waved over to a group of old drinking friends from the West End, who were in a heated discussion with a young woman.

"And you are?" Sverre asked, looking at her.

"Ingeborg," she said, revealing two dimples. "Ingeborg Johnsen."

The woman turned back to the conversation.

"You're obsessed with Islam," she said. "Do you seriously believe that a religion comprising a maximum of five per cent of the country's population – a tiny minority of which are in favour of political Islam – will introduce theocratic rule in one of the world's most secular and modern societies?"

"You're the voice of naivety!" said Victor Prydz, an old schoolfriend of Sverre's, a rentier and investor known for his deeply reactionary views.

"And because none of you see anything other than Islamification," Ingeborg went on, "you're blind to the real political threats to our society. The authoritarian regimes in the East, in China and Russia."

A blue handkerchief was poking up from Prydz's breast pocket. They always matched the colour of his waistcoats. He leaned closer to her. "We're on the same side as the Russians. We're both high cultures. Against the desert savages. Most people in the West have capitulated. Do you think people in Hungary or Russia let Muslims bully schoolkids who eat salami?"

"Salami!" she said scornfully. "You think this is about sausages?"

"It's a symbol of something bigger. In the East people are proud of their country. They're not ashamed of their own culture. Putin and Orbán aren't our enemies. Putin is the West's only hope."

Prydz turned to Sverre. "But look! Here's a man who's actually fought for the fatherland against the forces of Islam. What do you say, Sverre Falck?"

Previously, prior to going to Afghanistan, Sverre used to nod at Prydz's views. He too had been highly critical of the West's naive and failed integration policies. But something had happened.

"No one defends the fatherland; you defend your teammate. You'd know that if the draft board had found you fit for duty, Prydz," he now said. "I also have the impression that Islamism is on the decline."

"Exactly!" Ingeborg Johnsen said, looking at him with interest. "When future historians look back at our time, they'll be fascinated by how the wealthiest and most technologically advanced *civilisation* in 2016 was frightened of a bunch of scruffy extremists in the desert."

Prydz and the rest of his small flock slunk away.

"I hope I didn't scare off your reactionary friends?" Ingeborg smiled, when they were alone.

"Prydz doesn't mean any harm."

"No, like many on the far right he's so obsessed with Islam that he doesn't see who he's ending up in bed with. Putin is a megalomaniac fascist. If somebody doesn't put a stop to his imperialist ambitions in the Crimea, we're in trouble." She studied his uniform for a moment. "Medal for Defence Service Abroad with a rosette." She nodded.

"I didn't have time to change," he lied.

"Admit that you put on the uniform to impress the Friends of the Armed Forces," she teased.

He had primarily had the young women from the think tanks in mind when he put on the dress uniform. But he had not expected someone to be au fait with the details of the decorations.

Again this cheerfulness, this confidence. Most people are not present when they meet others; they are trapped within themselves or use others as a means to something else. Sverre Falck, pre-Afghanistan, for example. Which is why we are so happy when we meet someone who gives of themself, is able, in small glimpses, to display the spectrum that makes us human. Like Ingeborg did.

"Is this your first time at Rederhaugen?" he said, handing her a glass.

"As an adult. My mother knows Olav; I was here as a child."

Of course his father knew the Johnsen women. Their tentacles reached even further than his into the Norwegian social elite. "Would you care to see the building?"

She answered with a smile. As he led her through the rooms and down into the library, he thought about how different she was from his preferred type. Her hair was light blonde, like rye, and she was wearing a loud red jacket over a white blouse.

The lights in the library came on, one after another. The silence felt more intense after the din upstairs.

"Nice place," Ingeborg said.

Her gaze swept over the shelves before she turned to him.

"Where do you work?" Sverre asked.

In a voice not exactly seething with enthusiasm, she said that she was a researcher at NUPI, the Norwegian Institute of International Affairs.

He grinned. "Odd. Haven't I seen your byline in the newspapers?"

"I *was* a journalist. Nana likes to say that a person who quits journalism early on can achieve anything in life."

"OK," Sverre said. "Diplomatic recruit at the Ministry of Foreign Affairs?"

Ingeborg laughed and shook her head. "Such cheek. Have you heard of Pamela Harriman?"

He shook his head.

"The first time I heard of her was when Dick Holbrooke called her *the best US ambassador of the twentieth century*. So I googled her. I read that Harriman was considered one of the twentieth century's greatest seducers, with an endless number of rich and famous notches on her bedpost. She was known to undertake extremely thorough research: when she came on to men, she knew exactly what they wanted. And she used all these qualities when she became an ambassador. Think about it, Sverre Falck: the best female diplomat of all time was a socialite and a mistress. Thanks, but no thanks."

He liked her making fun of diplomacy, in the way you only could if you had the confidence from being brought up amid it.

"What are you going to be when you grow up, Sverre?" she said, running a slim forefinger along the spines of the books.

"Thought I'd just run the deep state," he said, shrugging.

"Sounds like you wish you were head of SAGA," she laughed. "I thought that position was filled?"

Sverre put on a stiff smile. "How about you?"

"I'm going to be prime minister," she replied, as though it were obvious, as if she was talking about one day inheriting the family home.

"The reception is over, prime minister," he said, looking at his watch. "When can we continue the revised budget negotiations?"

She laughed. "You're amusing, King Sverre. Who says we have to part company just yet?"

5

I COULD DO THAT JOB

Rederhaugen, Oslo

It was past ten o'clock when Sasha entered the old gatekeeper's lodge. It was quiet, only low voices coming from the girls' room.

"Mads?" she said, tentatively.

"You're late," her husband said, and kissed her.

She didn't reply, but pressed close against his slim, wiry torso. Even if she might joke about his midlife crisis, with all the hours lost to working out, she was grateful he was not letting himself go.

"A very long day," she said, her voice disappearing into his jumper.

The reception itself had passed off without any major scandals. Siri Greve had noted how the average age had fallen by at least ten years since Olav's last get-together. That comment had pleased her. The gathering had also been more international, but after the news about a mole in SAGA, Sasha was wondering if it was such a good idea to allow these foreign diplomats to roam around so freely.

The second secretary from the Russian embassy and the mining director from Barentsburg had both been there.

Sasha poured herself a glass of wine.

Mads studied her. "Any news on Hans?"

"Christ, no, not that I've heard."

She checked her phone. The last message from Marte said the family were up there taking turns to watch over him. They thanked her for her concern.

She rolled the stem between her fingers. "His condition is still critical but stable."

"Something else is bothering you, Sasha."

She sighed. She wanted to let him in on the secret about the SAGA informant. He was sure to have something sensible to say about the matter. Granted, MM had said it was to be filed under *top secret* but where were her loyalties to lie: to that northern rodent rather than to her husband?

No, but telling him would be a crime.

She lit a cigarette by the window and sat down on the sill.

"There's a draught," he said, but Sasha knew it was her evening cigarette he wanted to put a stop to. She pretended it was nothing and sat thinking about Hans. Checked a newspaper online. Nothing yet, but it was only a question of time before "celebrated doctor fights for his life" would turn up.

Did Hans know the truth about Vera's will? No, he couldn't. What would it mean if he died? It would, to all intents and purposes, solve several problems. But Sasha noticed how guilty she felt thinking like that.

That said, it was not an improbable hypothesis that Hans was this mole MM was talking about. Hardly any other Norwegian had fraternised with as many shady characters as he had. When the Maoist revolution had failed to materialise in Norway, Hans had spent his time with militant groups in the Middle East and at distant Norwegian outposts like Svalbard and Kirkenes, where close contact with Russians was almost unavoidable.

He could be the Russians' man and might have been so for decades.

But others could also have been. Sverre had demonstrated that he could stab the family in the back when he took the Bergenites' side last year. His closet narcissism and easily injured pride were probably born of a personality type a talent spotter in intelligence would look for when seeking out traitors. True, he had been in Afghanistan, but who knew what he got up to there? Andrea, for her part, was perhaps a little young, but she was also fundamentally disloyal.

Neither could lawyer Siri Greve be ruled out. She was not averse to putting her finger in the air to see which way the wind was blowing. "Greve should count her blessings she wasn't a lawyer when the Germans invaded in 1940," Olav used to say.

But what did a foreign power want with SAGA? A foundation with the stated aim of promoting its country and history could of course be of interest to an intelligence service. Or SAGA's geopolitical dimension as a spearhead for Norwegian interests. She would just have to ask the security services; it was their domain, not hers.

Her thoughts were interrupted by knocking downstairs on the front door, and a second later she heard her father's voice in the hall. "Alexandra?"

Her husband raised his eyebrows, smiled cautiously, then got to his feet and kissed her on the top of her head. "I'm going to bed."

Olav entered the living room. He had changed into his preferred outfit of a fleece and a pair of cords after the reception and he looked around nervously. Sasha offered her father a glass of wine which he duly accepted. He sat at the end of the table looking preoccupied.

"You're growing into the role," he said.

She nodded and mumbled a thank you. Her father obviously had something on his mind.

"Hans," he went on. "He's survived war zones, coups and revolutions. Imagine if it's the storms in northern Norway that get him!"

"What was Hans doing with the 330th Squadron?" Sasha asked.

"You tell me. A lot of people take more of an interest in their roots as they age. The Bergen branch of the family had close ties with northern Norway during the heyday of the Falck shipping companies."

"That was a long time ago."

"He was raised on stories about the place in the glory days," her father continued. "Later, after college, he went to the north. Lefty doctors in the 1970s did that sort of thing. But what do I know about his motivations."

Although narcissists like Hans were ostensibly easy to understand – driven as they were by fame and the admiration of women – there was something puzzling about him.

Sasha found herself wanting to talk to her father about the mole. Exchange theories about who it could be. When it came to qualified speculation over familial intrigues and political motives, no one was better suited than Olav. But MM had told her to keep the revelation under wraps, and if he got wind of her having spoken about it to her father, it would weaken her own position. She decided to wait him out.

"I get the feeling you want to tell me something," she said finally.

"Do you know who called me earlier?" Her father's face broke into a resigned smile. "Aunt Connie from Bergen. Do you remember her?"

It was a long time since Sasha had thought of her. Most families had a scold, and fortunately Connie Knarvik, scourge of any meeting she took part in, was the Bergen wing of the family's problem.

"She's a bit of a mess, isn't she?"

"You can say that again. The first thing she said on the phone was that she'd tried to call you five times, but that you probably didn't have time for *people like her.*"

"I never accept calls from unknown numbers."

"Then she told me she was getting in touch to convey her *condolences* on the passing of Hans. I calmly explained that I had spoken to the hospital in Bodø only minutes previously and that his condition was stable. Next she launched into a rambling monologue about how Hans had been dead to her for more than thirty years. Prattled on about everything from Vera's manuscript to her years in the Communist Party, about her childhood in Bergen and how she had lost everything. It's sad to see what prolonged substance abuse does to a person's cognitive abilities."

Sasha recalled that her aunt's drug abuse was an open secret even when she was young. That her parents and brother had driven around the streets of Bergen to get her into recovery and clean for Christmases at home.

"I remember her as a very beautiful, intelligent girl when she used to visit Rederhaugen in the 1960s," Olav said. "To think she would end up like this."

Sasha smiled mischievously. "You're getting sentimental, Daddy."

"Bear in mind that Connie is a shareholder in SAGA."

"Hasn't she always voted by proxy? Her two shares are equivalent to 0.2 per cent."

"Well," Olav replied, "Connie owns the Advent Valley property on Svalbard. It's basically none of our business . . ."

Sasha bit her lip. "I sense a *but* coming."

"When SAGA was established in the 1960s, Connie's father gave me a loan, a so-called *convertible* loan, which according to the deal could be converted into shares in SAGA."

"Can you elaborate?"

"Should Connie want to sell the property, which may have great geopolitical relevance in the Arctic nowadays, the sale according to the original contract will be converted into a stake in SAGA. Fifty shares, five per cent. And, believe me, she is not someone you want sitting with a swing vote in the front row at an AGM."

Her father fell silent and sat rolling the stem of the empty wine glass between his fingers.

"You seem worried, Daddy?"

"You know my views," he said. "Ever since SAGA was established, I've believed the sea to be a curse. This incident with Hans is the latest in a long line of accidents that have befallen our family at sea. It was a godsend we divested ourselves of the shipping companies. My attitude has always been that we should have solid ground under our feet. That's why I have serious reservations about this association with the rescue service. And expeditions to the Arctic, they're the last thing we need."

Sasha was beginning to feel annoyed by her father's attempt to override her.

"You're just being superstitious."

"There's more to the rescue boats than you think," her father continued. "Matters that have lain buried for decades and because of major political tensions in the Arctic can now come to the surface. And they shouldn't. Connie's property on Svalbard is also a part of this picture."

Exhausted after the long day, Sasha resisted the temptation to continue the conversation. Svalbard, again. Once more her mind turned to the talk with Martens Magnus. Might there be a connection to the mole? And if so, what?

Sasha saw her father to the door and out into the December darkness, then went straight to bed.

She fell asleep right away, as she always did, and when she awoke with a start at 2.23 a.m., soaked with sweat and her heart pounding, the dream was etched clearly in her mind. It lacked subtlety, but dreams often do, she thought, like an overly symbolic surrealist painting: the flames from the will set the curtains in Greve's office alight, rapidly spreading the fire that soon engulfed the entirety of the main building at Rederhaugen, the flames escaping through the windows and over the mansard roofs as she ran away from the heat and sparks, away from all that was theirs.

6

CITIES BEGINNING WITH B

Rana & Andenæs law firm, Oslo

Since the start of school in the autumn, Johnny Berg had agreed with Ingrid's mother that their daughter could stay at his place every other weekend, from Thursday afternoon until Monday morning. His apartment belonged to an officer attending a three-year programme at a training school in the USA, and was situated on Thereses gate in Bislett, not far from his daughter's school in Bolteløkka.

Ingrid was sitting at the kitchen table, talking about her upcoming outing to feed chickens at a nearby eco-farm at the weekend. A blue tram rattled past. Johnny could not get the previous night's telephone conversation with Jan I. Rana out of his head. Everything was ready, Rana had said. When he came to see him tomorrow, they would settle the last of the formalities. "Then we'll send in the cavalry to smash SAGA and the Falck family."

Initially, his daughter had been unhappy with her bedroom. But he had engaged the help of a female acquaintance and thanks to her it had been refurbished as an Eldorado of stuffed animals, maps and children's books bought at a flea market.

"When I was in first class like you are now," he said, "I put greaseproof paper over a map of the world so I could trace it."

"Ask me for the name of a city beginning with B, Daddy!"

To his delight his daughter had inherited his photographic memory and his interest in geography.

Johnny poured full-fat milk into his coffee. "Too easy. Give me a city starting with Q."

"Oh, come on." She thought for a moment before smiling broadly. "Quebec."

"Wow, you're good, Ingrid. A city in Norway starting with B."

"Bergen. Is that where we're from? We're called Berg."

He looked at her thoughtfully. "We can thank a man called Berg for that."

"Who was Berg? I want to meet Berg."

"A kind man. Who helped me when I was little." Johnny hesitated. "Unfortunately, he died before I was big, before I could thank him."

"Daddy," Ingrid said in a serious tone, "where are you actually from?"

That question had dogged Johnny his entire childhood. Norwegians born to immigrant parents hated being asked that. He did not know where he was from. Well, the trail led to Lebanon. While acting as Norway's chargé d'affaires, Bjørn Berg had taken him out of the country as an infant during the hostilities in 1982 and formally adopted him. But the diplomat had died in a traffic accident before he had time to tell the boy the full story of his origins.

For years he had been obsessed with finding out. He had learned rudimentary Arabic and scoured a certain city beginning with B to find someone who could help him, before the realisation sank in that nothing good could come of it.

The fact was he was Norwegian and recognising that was a relief.

They were late and they ran up to the school together.

Johnny kissed her goodbye and called out that he would collect her that afternoon. Dark December rain hung low over the city, but making his way down Sofies gate towards Bislett, Johnny thought about how life was better than it had been for a long time. It had more routine. He was exercising every day. Staying busy working on the biography of Hans Falck.

The one troubling thought was the meeting with Rana the lawyer.

The only bad habit Johnny did not want to kick was rolling tobacco. It performed a therapeutic function. He liked to think of rolling a cigarette as *mindfulness*, a calming ritual, and a substitute for the joints he used to smoke. And he needed to steer clear of *them*, he knew that.

So, after walking through the city centre, Johnny stood on the steps of the office of a law firm in Grønland, sprinkled tobacco into a Rizla paper, moistened the edge with his tongue and formed a perfect hand-rolled cigarette, which he immediately lit.

"John Omar Berg," Jan I. Rana said when he opened the door. The lawyer had shed several kilos. "Tobacco? I thought you said you lived a healthy lifestyle and were in great shape?"

"I *am* in great shape, Rana," he replied. "Haven't you ever heard of Jørn Lauenberg? Ran the fastest marathon on Norwegian soil. 2:12:58. A chain-smoking, beer-drinking Dane."

"If only we were all Danes!" Rana said loudly. "Come in, Johnny. I've rolled out the red carpet for you. You look good."

Since the last time Johnny met him, Rana had swapped cinnamon buns for carrots and sugary soft drinks for water. Otherwise, much was the same: the portrait of the king dominated the wall at the end of the oval table, the legal secretary was still white, and as usual Rana had a lot to say.

"How's the Hans Falck biography coming along?"

"He doesn't seem very interested in it these days."

It was Hans who had hit upon the idea that the only way to get close to the Falck family at Rederhaugen was to have a biographer hunt down all the stories about the scandals and infidelities involving himself. Even the Oslo Falcks, who never spoke to the press, had been willing to make an exception then.

That was how he had them swallow the bait.

It was a brilliant approach. The method could form part of the intelligence syllabus in the future. Johnny had steered Sasha into the hornets' nest around her grandmother's cancelled manuscript, *The Sea Cemetery*. But there had been an unexpected development.

"I became fascinated by Hans's life, for real. In a way it resembled my own. The thirst for adventure, the wanderlust. You can say a lot of things about Hans. But he's done a hell of a lot of good in the world, whatever the stuff we don't know."

"John Omar Berg, biographer," Rama said, shaking his head. "No offence, Johnny, but if you can write biographies, Norway is a ridiculous little place to ply your trade. Every dimwit in this country has an article about them in print in the national newspapers. As long as you're of average intelligence you can have your novel put out by a serious publisher. If you care to spend your teenage years in the youth organisation of a political party, you end up as prime minister. That's not how it is in larger countries. Take Pakistan, for example. Making the cut there takes some doing. All the politicians and top bureaucrats are educated at the best schools in England and the USA. In Norway there are too many positions and too much airtime to be filled, and too few first-rate minds to fill them."

"Norway has the best educated population in the world, but the worst educated elite," Johnny said.

Rana laughed. "You might expect the Norwegian system to work for the weak, which it does to an extent. But this country also creates outstanding individuals. We win ten times as many medals in the Olympics as Pakistan and India combined, our artists are world-class, and we have more millionaires per capita than the USA."

"You're guaranteed to get a newspaper to run an article on that," Johnny replied. "But something tells me you wanted to talk about something else."

"I want to talk about Olav Falck," Rana said. "About how his house of cards is going to collapse. You're the whistle-blower, Johnny. The man who makes it possible for us Norwegians to sleep soundly at night, the man left for dead in an extrajudicial conspiracy that can be traced directly back to Olav Falck, an ultra-shady one-percenter from the deep state."

"M. Magnus has contacted me," Johnny said. "He wants to apologise."

Rana interrupted. "He's full of shit. I've got the best journalist in the country lined up as a mouthpiece. Ready to go at fifteen minutes' notice. When he hears your tear-jerker of a story and gets it out there, the sympathy it generates for you will be enormous. And I mean enormous. You'll be Person of the Year, Johnny. While M. Magnus and Olav will be facing prison time."

"When you met me after Kurdistan, I was a wreck. I was bitter."

"And now you're not? Do I have to remind you of the last thing a Falck did to you? Sasha Falck stabbing you in the back and getting you arrested again."

Johnny's eyes drifted to the portrait of the monarch. "It

feels different. I have a job and a daughter. I can't face another round with Olav Falck now."

The lawyer sat for a long while, his head bowed and hands clasped below his nose. "I would ask you to reconsider that decision."

Johnny made no reply.

"This is a landmark case," Rana continued. "We have testimony and technical evidence tying Olav Falck, former minister of defence and retired chairman of SAGA, to a Norwegian intelligence agent. To you, Johnny. You were sent to Kurdistan to eliminate a foreign fighter and left hung out to dry when you were captured."

"Sorry, now's not the time."

Rana closed his eyes for a few seconds, opened them and leaned forward.

"This is much bigger than Olav Falck. Norwegians are adept at our national blood sport: chasing down a solitary idiot who has screwed up in some way. Norwegian bullfighting."

"Is Sverre Falck going to stand witness?"

The lawyer hesitated. "He's not answering my calls. I'm worried he may have had second thoughts over in Afghanistan. We're blind to injustices committed by the state. The state is benign, in our minds, our politicians aren't corrupt, our police are good-natured types who patrol the pedestrianised areas of small towns, our soldiers build schools for girls in Afghanistan, the bombs we drop on Libya are wrapped in velvet, our oil doesn't pollute. We're sitting here on a case that challenges that perception. Something that goes to the highest echelons of society."

"I support you, in principle," he said, "but I must think about my daughter. Sorry, Jan."

Johnny stood up. He felt uncomfortable and knew deep down that Jan I. Rana was right.

He switched his phone back on. The first thing he saw was a text message from a number he did not recognise.

Hi. My dad has been seriously injured on a mission with the 330 search and rescue squadron. He has been in a coma for the past twenty-four hours and is drifting in and out of consciousness. He mentioned your name when he came round. I thought you should know.
Marte Falck

Johnny stood in the middle of the throng of people coming and going in Grønland. Why had Hans mentioned his name?

Beirut, Baghdad and now Bodø.

Damn, what was it with cities starting with B?

7

THERE ARE WEEKS WHERE DECADES HAPPEN

Gimle terrasse, Oslo

Many romances take time to establish. The lovers hold hands while walking slowly out into the water. But there are also relationships – especially for those of Sverre Falck's age – where the pieces fall into place and everything happens at astonishing speed.

Because love does not follow a set dramaturgy. Logic and causality are extraneous. It suddenly becomes manifest, with a strength surpassing everything else life has to offer. Sverre realised that for forty years he had merely *existed*. But apart from the moments of combat in Afghanistan he had never lived. Not until now.

The weeks that had passed since meeting her were a fever dream: how Ingeborg and he had left Rederhaugen and wandered the dark, rainy December streets. Had they passed one another on those same streets before without being aware of it? They might have, and was there anything better than talking about how they had lived their parallel lives unaware of what happiness awaited them?

At the corner of Hafrsfjordgata and Drammensveien they kissed. Drunk and giddy, they had hurried up the streets to his old bachelor pad in the Falck building on Gimle terrasse, where they tore off each other's clothes, and he kissed her on the nape of her neck, her throat, her breasts, down over her midriff, before they disappeared into each other's bodily fluids and skin.

Those first twenty-four hours Sverre only left the apartment for champagne and takeaway food.

By the second day they had talked about moving in together.

On the morning of the third day Sverre asked if they should live happily ever after. When he reflected upon the general miseries of singleton existence and his previous "relationships" he could only shake his head in bewilderment. This was life. This was love.

"Time to celebrate our golden wedding anniversary this evening," Sverre said.

"Oh?" Ingeborg said, smiling.

"We've been together for exactly twelve days."

Wearing an army T-shirt in size XXL and nothing else, Ingeborg kissed him on the scalp. "My nana likes to quote Lenin: *There are weeks where decades happen.*"

"Wise woman, your nana," Sverre said.

Her grandmother, Wenche "Vesla" Johnsen, was a former social democrat politician, widely considered to be the "best first female prime minister the country never had" – a nonagenarian living legend who occasionally descended from the ivory tower of the Johnsen dynasty's multigenerational home on the edge of the forest in Årvoll to offer her opinion on matters under public debate.

What was most notable about the Johnsens – besides their preference for the folksy surname Johnsen rather than the well-respected Heiberg, allegedly to appeal to the social democratic electorate – was that their dynastic order was matrilineal. The men were witless. Lax, anaemic types afflicted by bankruptcies and a range of chronic fatigue syndromes, while the women seemed to be directly descended from prehistoric carnivores.

They must have had political EPO in their porridge up there. Vesla Johnsen had fought her way up at a time when very few women were in politics, before an old affair with a Russian diplomat with ties to the KGB put a stop to any ambitions of being prime minister.

Her daughter, Ingeborg's mother Britt Johnsen, had held a variety of ministerial posts, foreign minister being the most prestigious. At the tail end of her career, she had served as ambassador to Moscow for several periods, to the annoyance of the CIA, and this explained Ingeborg's polished Russian. Apart from these women, there was a whole host of Johnsen females to be found in critical societal roles.

Sverre knew all of this before he met Ingeborg; his store of knowledge concerning positions and networks in society was extensive. To say he could not have cared less about this would be a lie. For his part he had already begun to fantasise about a lavish wedding joining minister Ingeborg Johnsen and SAGA leader Sverre Falck in matrimony on the well-manicured lawns of Rederhaugen. It had to take place there. It would be an alchemic alloy of economic strength and political power.

Love, war and poverty. Soon he would have experienced all the ancient Greeks demanded of a man. Well, two of them in any case.

Sverre got dressed. "There's a Christmas party on Saturday week for all the relatives at Rederhaugen. I've said you're coming."

"Is that the done thing?"

"It's a pretty traditional gathering, and historically cohabitation has been a prerequisite for invitation."

"Perhaps we're not quite there?"

"No, but I was at dinner with my father and sisters the other day. Apparently, he's fallen head over heels for the widow of an old friend and spent December on a romantic trip to Paris and Rome. So, he wanted to 'relax the entrance restrictions somewhat' so his 'friend' could come along. If you follow."

Ingeborg went to the bathroom to clean up. She was going into the office today after a few days of "working from home".

As she was standing at the front door about to leave, he allowed himself to be amazed once more at how beautiful she was, her blonde hair still damp at the tips, her skin glowing and slightly flushed.

Ingeborg kissed him. "Then it's agreed. As a good social democrat I will be sure to familiarise myself with bourgeois etiquette before the party."

8

BURYING THE HATCHET

Akerselva, Oslo

For Johnny the next week revolved around Christmas preparations. Rebecca was away on a business trip, so he had ample time with Ingrid. He tried to do some work on the biography during the day but did not make much progress.

With his daughter, he went ice skating in Voldsløkka, made Christmas presents and read Astrid Lindgren.

One day M. Magnus rang again. Johnny could tell by the sound of his voice that his serene Advent was over.

The Syverkiosken was a dilapidated hot dog stand close to the River Aker. Johnny turned up just before the agreed time and offered a measured greeting as they took their place in the queue behind tradesmen and hipsters waiting to order from the friendly soul in the kiosk. MM's cropped hair disguised receding temples meeting atop a bald pate; his lined and tanned complexion suggested he spent a lot of time outdoors. There was a snus bulge under his upper lip.

"Best place to eat in Oslo," Johnny opined, ordering a wiener in a *lompe*, a tortilla-like potato cake in a bread roll, with jalapenos and crispy onion on top. They ate their meal standing at a corner of the kiosk, then MM suggested they walk north along the river.

The sky hung low and grey, as though waiting to discharge its load over the city. Perhaps, finally, in the form of snow.

The waterfall at Sagene roared powerfully, throwing up an abundance of spray. There had been so much rainfall that the walkway under the Ring Road 2 bridge was closed.

When they reached the flat stretch where the red-brick building housing Myrens Verksted and the rest of the old industrial area rose up on the right bank, MM said: "I'm sure you realise why I've got in touch, Johnny."

He made no reply but looked coldly at the officer.

"To be honest I've wanted to apologise for a long time," MM said. "You've been put through hell, there's no other way to say it, and I'm partly responsible for that."

Johnny remained silent.

Martens Magnus was the man who had sent Johnny on the last mission in Syria. Now it all came flooding back: not just the mission, the shots fired at the jihadist, the blood on the floor, the little boy with the teddy bear they had passed on their way out of the house. Not only that, the prison too, the orange jumpsuits, the smell of sweat, excrement and rotting flesh.

Johnny had spent almost a year in prison in the Middle East.

"What exactly do you expect me to say?" Johnny said. "That it's water under the bridge, that mistakes were made on both sides? Like when Heinrich Himmler wanted to 'bury the hatchet' at a secret meeting with an envoy from the World Jewish Congress in April 1945?"

"Murphy's Law," MM said.

"Sometimes peace isn't what's best," Johnny said. He felt mounting anger, unexpected rage from a hot spring that had long lain quiet beneath. "You're an agent handler, same as me. If there's one thing we don't do, it's leave the people working for us behind in the shit."

MM threw a small stone into the river. "I know what I say can't right the wrong but believe me when I tell you the apology is heartfelt."

Johnny made his way towards the edge of the rushing river, snapped a twig from a tree and dropped it in. The force that swept it along frightened him. For the briefest moment he thought about holding MM under the water until he lost consciousness.

"What do you want?" Johnny asked.

"It was Olav who wanted to leave you to rot," MM said. "Now his daughter has taken over. You know Alexandra."

They continued north, walking upriver. MM had the operational responsibility, but Olav was the one behind it. Or was he? It struck Johnny that this close-cropped northerner might be an éminence grise. Perhaps he was the one controlling Olav and not, as Johnny had taken for granted, the other way around. Information was a perishable commodity. MM had connections within both the Norwegian intelligence services and the special forces, as well as in government circles and SAGA to boot. An unusual combination.

In the context of SAGA Johnny was a peripheral figure. So why had Martens just felt the need to inform him about that power struggle?

"Alexandra Falck has donated *Falck III* to the Norwegian Society for Sea Rescue and is making speeches about the Arctic. How the areas in the north will be increasingly important now the ice is melting and the trade routes will open. Everyone wants their slice of the pie. But she doesn't have what it takes. What we need is leadership. *Clear* leadership." He uttered the words slowly.

"Can you be more specific?"

"The Falcks are sitting on what may well be the most

strategically important property in the entire Arctic. The Advent Valley, east of Longyearbyen on Svalbard, a piece of land roughly the size of Bærum county. It's a so-called claim area for coal mining, which according to the laws up there also grants the right to build infrastructure. Before the airport opened in 1975, the level floor of the valley was used as an airstrip."

"What's the problem with the Falcks sitting on the property?"

MM turned, exposing a row of yellow teeth rimmed with snus. "The owner of the Advent Valley is one Connie Knarvik, from another branch of the Falck family. She's an out-and-out mess. Was some kind of communist in the seventies and subsequently a junkie. Apparently now she's found God."

"Does she want to sell the land?"

"Yes," MM said. "The problem is that it would give her real shareholder's influence in SAGA, because any sale is tied to a convertible loan that Olav agreed to in the sixties."

"Why are you telling me this?" Johnny said.

"Because I have classified information to discuss with you."

Johnny could smell trouble. "And you trust me?"

"No, of course not," MM said, taking a document from a folder. "An NDA, stressing your legal liability should information be leaked. In addition, as a former member of the intelligence service, you are bound for life by the pledge of secrecy you signed when you joined. Have you been informed about the GRU colonel on Svalbard?"

Johnny had read about the case but knew only what was in the public domain.

"One of the things the press is not privy to is that Zemlyakov's last words concerned a mole. Inside SAGA and the Falck family."

For a moment Johnny was expecting an accusation to be thrown in his face.

"And it's for that very reason I wanted to talk to you, Johnny. Believe me, Alexandra Falck doesn't have long left. A majority on the board are in favour of her removal."

"What do you want of me?"

"I want you inside SAGA," MM said. "You'll have carte blanche. Because what I want you to do is give the tree a good shake. See what falls. Who the rotten apple in the basket is."

"Hmm," Johnny said.

"I've been trying to persuade Hans for some time."

"Isn't he in hospital in Bodø?"

"He's made a rapid recovery and is back in Bergen. We met yesterday. We're aware, of course, of Sasha's betrayal of you. We've agreed that Hans should replace Sasha as chair of the board. I'll take over as CEO of SAGA on an interim basis until a new candidate is found."

They had walked up past Bjølsen and come out onto the more level terrain in Nydalen. Everything had changed since Johnny had grown up in the area. A nail works had been situated there; later it had been the site of illegal rave parties, before industrial culture had become cultural industry, except of course for the Police Security Service, PST, which, oddly, had taken up residence at the top of a nearby hill.

"What do the Russians want with SAGA?" Johnny asked.

"That's your job to find out. But I think they want control of the property in the Advent Valley."

MM nodded towards the security service's headquarters. "You have the expertise to find out who's leaking information to foreign intelligence over at Rederhaugen. You're the best. PST are a mixture of cops of limited ability and politically correct political scientists. The lame and the blind. With them we run the risk of the case never being solved. And at worst, the situation will get out of control."

Johnny looked up.

Large snowflakes were wafting down from the grey December sky.

Finally, the first snowfall of the year.

9

HIS NAME IS JOHN OMAR BERG

Norwegian Police Security Service, Oslo

A snowflake landed on Sasha's nose just before she entered PST headquarters in Nydalen. The snow reminded her that she needed to buy Christmas presents. If the meeting up here did not take too long, she might have time for that.

"Falck?" a woman said.

Sasha stood up, they greeted one another and walked together up some stairs and down a long corridor. Line Mørk, her hair tightly swept back, had dark Mediterranean features under the heavy make-up she was wearing, far more than Sasha. From behind, Mørk had the physique of a swimmer, with slender hips and a V-shaped back ending in broad shoulders and long arms. Sasha, who had barely thrown a ball in her life, always found people in such good shape intimidating.

Mørk opened the door to a small room and motioned towards a chair.

"Thank you for coming," she said, in a soft, husky voice that instantly inspired trust. "A lot of people are alarmed when they get a call from us. I just want to stress that this has nothing at all to do with any wrongdoing on the part of you or your loved ones. This is purely a background check. Do you understand?"

Sasha nodded.

The officer recounted the events that had occurred on

Svalbard, without Sasha discovering anything that she had not read in the media or that MM had recounted.

"So, the first thing I'm wondering," Mørk said, and smiled pleasantly, "is of course if you have any idea whether there could be any truth to the Russian's claim: that they have people on the inside of SAGA and your family?"

"No," Sasha replied. "Obviously I've given it some thought, but any opinion I'd venture would be pure speculation on my part."

"Speculation," Line Mørk said, her voice soft. "Could you elaborate?"

Annoyed at being played so easily, Sasha decided to take control of the conversation. "I come from a large and . . . well-to-do family," she said, clearing her throat. "As you may perhaps be aware, deep divisions are not uncommon in such families. I could, for example, make insinuations against my brother, or Hans Falck, who has been at odds with my father for a long time. In many ways it's tempting to do so. But, as I said, it would be mere speculation. Instead, may I ask why PST is working on this?"

"Well, the tactical investigation itself is classified," the officer replied. "What I can say is that we're exploring the espionage claims of the Russian colonel on a wide front. Naturally we're aware that certain states – Iran, China and Russia, among others – are actively engaged in gaining influence in key industries and humanitarian foundations in the West. Typically, we'd be talking about so-called *agents of influence*, individuals who don't necessarily break the law, but who advance views in line with those states' long-term interests. To weaken Western democratic societies."

Sasha nodded.

"Alexandra. I'd ask you to reconsider the question. Has there been anyone in the past year who has demonstrated an unusual amount of interest in your family or the foundation?"

"There is one person," Sasha said, after a long pause, and looked over her shoulder, as though the very mention of his name was blasphemy. Why had she not thought of him before? Because what's obvious is often hidden amidst the clamour surrounding us. But a Russian spy?

"Johnny," she said. "His full name is John Omar Berg."

"What can you tell me about this John Omar?"

An hour later, Sasha set out into the snow, followed the crowd down towards the metro station and took a train heading west. Had she violated her own principle about not making insinuations? Well, maybe. But Johnny was not family.

She alighted at Nationaltheatret, walked past the Christmas market at Spikersuppa and continued down Karl Johans gate. Sasha had always thought that the city's main street resembled a pedestrianised street in a provincial city in northern Germany. Bremen, perhaps, or Lübeck.

She left the main street and cut diagonally across Nedre Slottsgate towards the central entrance to Steen & Strøm. The department store was filled with Christmas shoppers. Following the crowd past the perfume counters, she took the escalator to the oval atrium. She made one circuit of the floor housing the men's department. A Ralph Lauren shirt for Mads? Christ, what a soulless Christmas present.

Absent-mindedly, she weighed a grey lambswool sweater in her hands. That was when she caught sight of them: the hands, olive skin with visible veins. They triggered something in her subconsciousness. The same way people sense danger or desire before they can articulate it.

Sasha's gaze moved from the hands, up a dark coat, over a maroon flannel shirt and up to a face. She could feel the pulse by her ears, the sweat in her hands. Hoped the blush was not visible in the artificial light of the department store.

He looked stronger and fitter than the last time she had seen him. His hair was short and he was clean-shaven. But his eyes, those melancholic eyes with the long lashes that lent his face a feminine quality, the first thing she had noticed about Johnny, had not changed. They stood in contrast to the strength he otherwise emanated.

Maybe that was what Johnny was: one part man, one part woman. Androgyny. Much of what Sasha liked had that quality: the voice of Annie Lennox, the films of Tilda Swinton, the Neapolitan novels of Elena Ferrante. Her name, for that matter.

Or you could expand the perspective: for every portion of goodness, a portion of evil. A man who would sleep with her while wanting at the same time to destroy her family.

They took the escalators up one floor, making their way into the lingerie department. He ran his hands – those strong, narrow hands – along the racks of lace knickers and risqué corsets.

"M. Magnus is plotting to have you removed as chair of the board and CEO of SAGA and he's talking to Hans about taking over."

She felt her heart sink. "How reliable is the source?"

"One hundred per cent."

She thought for a moment, but none of the possible chess moves – Johnny casting suspicion on MM to strengthen his own cover, MM feeding Johnny the information because he knew Johnny would leak it to her – helped her out of the labyrinth.

"Why are you telling me this?"

"Because I don't like Martens Magnus."

How many times over the past year had she thought about it? Running into Johnny like this. She had even considered monitoring his movements to ensure it took place, like when she was a teenager and stalked celebrities. And now it had happened.

"This isn't a chance meeting, is it?" she said. "Nothing ever happens by chance with you."

"No," he said. "I followed you from Nydalen."

He turned and left.

10

ALMOND IN THE RICE PUDDING

Rederhaugen, Oslo

The Christmas shopping was out of the way, the last emails had been sent, M. Magnus had been summarily dismissed, and, as she lit the torches leading up to the house, Sasha's thoughts turned to the long-awaited Christmas break.

The Christmas party always took place on the last Saturday in Advent. A smell of Yuletide baking and saucepans with piping-hot *vin chaud* – hot red wine with sugar, orange, cloves and cinnamon sticks – permeated the rooms at Rederhaugen. Children ran breathlessly through the halls and hid in the building's many dark nooks. Outside it was snowing lightly.

No matter how tense the atmosphere between the Falcks in Oslo and Bergen was, an obligatory truce came into effect when Christmas rolled around. The two branches of the family had gathered every single year since the end of the war, the location of the party mirroring the changing balance of power. Throughout much of the twentieth century the Oslo contingent had made their way to Bergen, but, following the bankruptcy of the Hanseatic Steamship Company in the 1970s, the party had relocated to Rederhaugen.

In keeping with tradition, the Christmas tree had been cut down that same day in Falckeskogen, the forest between Heggedal and Dikemark. It was supposed to be pine, though no one knew exactly why. After it was felled, they ate pea soup and had a dram.

"I have something contentious to declare," said Andrea, who bore the main responsibility for the food. "Pork ribs beat mutton hands down."

"Careful, that's tantamount to drawing a cartoon of the Prophet," Sasha said.

"Nobody except sentimental people from the west of the country thinks cured mutton is fantastic. Strip it of nostalgia and it's bony and way too salty. A billion Chinese people and the French eat pork ribs. Tender as butter if you prepare them properly."

Sasha turned to a newly arrived couple. "Daddy," she said, kissing Olav on both cheeks.

"Is Sverre bringing along that Johnsen girl?" Olav asked. "Both the mother and the grandmother are formidable."

Shortly afterwards, Ingeborg and Sverre turned up with broad smiles and snowflakes on their shoulders. Olav focused on behaving courteously.

"Any Johnsen, or should I say Johnsen-Heiberg, is always welcome at Rederhaugen."

In the downstairs dining room, the Bergenites had made a noisy entrance and handed over seasonal delicacies from the west coast.

It took a few moments for Sasha to notice Hans approaching, stooped behind his children.

"Hans," she said, hugging him gently. She noticed the difference immediately. The accident had aged him. Slow movements had replaced his restless energy, his complexion was pale and his hands trembled as he placed them on her shoulders.

Sasha clapped her hands. "Time for rice porridge. A

marzipan pig for the one who finds the almond! It's strictly forbidden to say anything before everyone has eaten up."

The children, who had been sitting in an adjoining room watching cartoons, scurried in and lined up in front of the bowls, squinting and conferring to see if they could spot the almond in the glass serving dish.

Sasha took her time. With deft movements, she scooped small spoonfuls of the rice porridge from around the edge of the dish while slowly working inward, under the layers of sugar and cinnamon, without disturbing the melted pat of butter in the centre.

She looked around. Although the methods of eating varied – some preferred to stir the butter carefully around the cinnamon and sugar surface while others left the butter standing like a fountain in the middle – everyone sat in deep concentration, smacking their lips and glancing at one another, saying little. Who had got the almond? Sasha could not help but compare the party game to the hunt for the Russian mole. Was the SAGA informant sitting at the table?

Olav leaned over to Sasha and whispered: "There's something *up* with Hans today."

"Daddy, of course he's been affected by what he's been through, but we should be glad he's recovering so rapidly."

"I don't think it's just that," Olav muttered.

When Sasha signalled she was finished by clinking her plate, all eyes fell on her. "Could the winner please make themselves known?"

"It's me!" Ingeborg called out.

"The Johnsen family are known for their luck at games," Olav said, cheerfully. "My old uncle Herbert used to say it was never a good idea to play blackjack against Vesla Johnsen at the Soviet casinos by the Black Sea, because she always won, with or without the help of the KGB." He guffawed at his own anecdote. Ingeborg smiled politely.

As an accompaniment, Andrea brought in *rakfisk* with all the trimmings. The fermented slices of fish were accompanied by nutty-flavoured almond potatoes, sour cream with mustard sauce, raw onion and soft potato flatbreads.

Through the lively chatter around the table, Mads raised his egg glass of spiced aquavit and stared at Sasha for a long time. "The top job suits you, Sasha."

Later that evening, when the children had been put to bed by the nanny, the remaining guests repaired to the blue room on the top floor, where three Nobel Peace Prize recipients had spent the night. Bishop Desmond Tutu had left a handwritten note to say he had never had a better night's sleep than in the four-poster bed there.

Sasha tried taking the temperature of the room. Hans was eager to prove that a little time spent "on ice" in a coma could not stop him from partaking in life's pleasures.

Andrea put on a playlist. "'All I Want for Christmas is You' by Mariah Carey is the best Christmas song of all time. Miles better than 'Fairytale of New York'. That's been played to death."

"Any more incendiary opinions?" Sverre asked.

"Yes, as it happens," Andrea said, looking at each guest in turn. "Celebrating Christmas with the Bergenites is actually very nice."

The statement lifted the mood even more. Andrea pressed play. Music blasted through the room. People danced, Christian Falck with his wife, Andrea and Erik, even Hans and Synne swayed along. And of course, Ingeborg and Sverre. Her brother did his best impression of Shane McGowan, staring drunk and imploringly at his girlfriend.

Sasha sat next to Marte, who was rambling on about being curator of a culture festival in Kirkenes near the Russian border.

"Look at Sverre," Sasha said, a smile on her lips. Her brother's gruff, repressed manner seemed blown away by Ingeborg. "I'm happy he gets to experience this. Infatuation, love maybe, who knows?"

Marte raised her wine glass. "To love, Sasha."

"To love. I'm going to call it a night. Thanks for today, I'm so happy we can meet like this."

Sasha closed the door quietly behind her. The stairwell was cold and dark. Through the wall she could hear the music and animated voices. Life was not too bad, when she thought about it. The children were growing up, her father had settled into life as a pensioner, relations with Bergen were less strained now than in a long time, and Sasha found herself fantasising about going to bed with the man she had been married to for a decade. Life was actually pretty good.

"Sasha," said a voice behind her.

She had not expected to run into anyone out here now.

"I have something I want to discuss with you," Hans said, from the landing above.

She was about to say it could wait until tomorrow but something in his voice told her it had to be now.

Without saying anything, she waited on the landing below for him to follow. The light in the hallway leading to her office buzzed as she flicked the switch. Had she forgotten to close the window? No, then why was it so cold? Sasha deactivated the alarm. The office was tidy, all the work to be done before Christmas had been finished the day before. She stood by the window, looking out into the night, the darkness lightened slightly by the snow.

"I'm sorry I didn't have the chance to bring this up in private earlier," Hans said, taking a tentative step into the room before sitting down on the sofa and resting one arm along the back.

She felt a sharp twinge through her body. Her father was right; there was something up with him. Far off she could hear the music and voices. Perhaps he just wanted to confide in her. Hans was that type.

"So, what's left to do?" Hans asked rhetorically and answered his own question. "I thought about that a lot while I was lying in hospital. Was it all worth it, all the renunciations, all the travelling, all the rest of it? And what now, when I'm not able to do the only thing I've ever known?"

"Well?" Sasha said, waiting.

"So, I was thinking I need to move into a more hands-on role in SAGA."

"An exciting prospect," Sasha said. "I think having you as part of the team would be excellent. You have something the rest of us don't."

Hans Falck was a living legend, more famous and celebrated than the rest of the family put together.

"The point is," Hans continued, producing a sheet of paper and holding it up in front of her, "that in accordance with Vera Lind's will I intend to prioritise those who are direct descendants of Big Thor."

Silence.

"Sasha?"

In a sense, the apocalypse struck exactly as she had imagined: with dizziness, tunnel vision, hearing loss and the floor disappearing from under her.

It was completely quiet in the room. What did this mean, for the companies, for the foundation, for the family and the properties?

Hans stared hard at her. "You, and Olav before you, have run SAGA like a criminal enterprise beyond parliamentary control. I'm thinking of the Johnny Berg case, among other things. I was the one who got him out of Kurdistan. And the fact that you also attempted to destroy Vera's will has not made me more inclined to compromise."

Sasha was speechless.

"Transferring ownership of the estate and properties is the simplest part," Hans said. "Here's a temporary writ. You have the Christmas holidays and the first few days of the new year to pack. The formal transfer of Rederhaugen takes place on January 4."

He placed the document in front of her.

"It's possible we may consider extending the rental agreement on Hordnes, if we come to an agreement. The Serious Fraud Office are paying close attention so I would strongly advise against moving any assets over the next few days. The jig is up, Sasha, and Vera's will is going to be executed. Are you going to inform Olav and the others, or shall I?"

She recalled an old Buster Keaton film, where the wall of a house fell over the comedian, who, thanks to an open window, remained standing, swaying in the ruins.

"This isn't over, Hans," Sasha said, her voice quavering. "This means total war."

"Merry Christmas to everyone at Rederhaugen," he said, and disappeared.

11

THIS IS A LOT TO TAKE IN

Rederhaugen, Oslo

Olav's phone rang just after midnight.

He had left the party early to go and see his "friend", the widow of the publisher Grieg. Olav had no qualms about making love in the bedroom of a departed friend; on the contrary, the territorial transgression provided an extra erotic stimulus. He was particularly pleased when she confessed that her sex life with her late husband had come to an end several years previously when his health had deteriorated.

The telephone continued to ring.

The only thing that bothered an old pessimist and cynic was the thought that life itself resembled love: you might suddenly lose it, plunge right into the abyss.

He picked the phone up before placing it back on the bedside table, turning to huddle against the warmth of the female body. The phone rang again. He did not answer it.

When it rang for the third time, he picked it up.

"Daddy," Alexandra said.

"Yes?" Her voice was strange.

"I have something important to tell you."

Olav swallowed. "Is it a matter of life and death?"

"No," she said. "It's more serious than that."

A few minutes later, as he walked quickly across the recently snow-cleared courtyard, he tried to think straight:

what his daughter had said sounded absurd, as though she were suffering from acute delusions. At the very least she must have been exaggerating. But why? Alexandra was not prone to catastrophising.

The snow-covered inclines around the main house at Rederhaugen sparkled in the light from the torches still burning.

"Alexandra," he called out inside the empty building.

After scouring the house, Olav found her up in the blue room. Glasses, leftovers and half-empty bottles lay scattered around the place or broken on the floor, and Alexandra – who usually never went to bed before she had cleaned and tidied up – was sitting staring apathetically into the fireplace.

If one believes the world is coming to an end, if one thinks every symptom of illness is a possible death sentence, then all news involving anything else is good news: that is, after all, the advantage of being a pessimist.

"We'll get through this, darling Alexandra, we'll get through it, just like we always have," he said in an attempted paternal tone – a mixture of authority and compassion – and kissed her hair as he rocked her head back and forth in his lap, just like he had when she was a child.

She still would not meet his eyes.

Olav moved to a chair beside her. "If we're going to solve this, you need to tell me what happened."

Finally she looked up, her eyes red from tears. "We can't solve this."

"Just tell me, dearest Sashenka. In as much detail as you can."

"I found Vera's will when I was searching for the unpublished manuscript," she said, mechanically.

Olav nodded. "Go on."

"That was last spring. Greve was in possession of it. I tore it out of her hands and burned it."

"Probably not such a good idea, no." He tried to maintain a calm tone.

"It was the only option I had. *The Sea Cemetery* contained an epilogue that was never published either. In the fifty years Vera had writer's block, she tried to write it. Oh, there's so much you don't know, Daddy."

He felt a mounting exasperation. "Then it's high time you told me."

"Vera was in love with an anti-Nazi German soldier."

"I've read *The Sea Cemetery*, damn it!"

"No, you haven't read this. The reason Vera was so traumatised her entire life was because she didn't manage to save her baby when the Hurtigruten sank."

Now Olav was starting to wonder if his daughter was losing her mind. "Well, I'm sitting right here, Alexandra."

"That's because you were born nine months after the disaster, Daddy! You're the result of a night Vera spent with Hans Otto Brandt, who was also lost that day. You were born in Lofoten in June 1941. Grandmother named you Olav. She kept you hidden for a number of years on Yttersia. And when she fled to Sweden in 1944 she registered you using the original birth certificate from July 1940, with Big Thor as the father. I'm sorry, Daddy, I know it's a lot to take in."

Olav had told his eldest daughter he had cried when she was born, but she had never seen him do it. But he wept now, sobbing quietly, his tears seeping through the shoulder of her white blouse.

"I'm thinking about my mother," he muttered. "How we never had this conversation. Isn't that always the way?"

Getting to his feet, he made his way over the teak floor to

the window. The sky had cleared. He stood looking at the stars for a while.

"I'm glad you told me this," he said quietly.

"There's more, Daddy."

Below him, outside, the last torch burned unsteadily down, soon to go out.

"Because you're not Big Thor's son, we're not direct descendants. Hans and the Bergen part of the family will inherit the businesses, and, as owner of Rederhaugen, Vera bequeathed that to the Bergen branch as well. That was contained in the will."

"Do you remember what I said to you that time you were going through my mother's personal effects at High Cliff before the funeral, Alexandra? That if you continued with it, then everything we'd built up could come crashing down!"

"Daddy," Sasha said, in a voice that mollified him, "I'll make this right, I promise you. If it takes me the rest of my life, I'll get back what they've taken from us."

12

THE SWIM LADDER

Oslo Fjord

There was no merry Christmas at Rederhaugen that year. The days between Christmas and the New Year were spent boxing possessions and packing them into lorries to be put in storage.

His entire life, Olav had feared the worst: nuclear war, foreign occupation, arson, rising ocean levels and the breakdown of civilisation. He was a man who rarely gave expression to his fears, but this was the stuff of nightmares.

It became clear to him that the worst *had* come to pass. The downfall of the family, which he had always feared, had become a reality. But finding out that the very foundations of his life were an illusion left him floored.

When the New Year arrived, he finally sprang into action. He wanted no unfinished business. Despite her promise to fight back, Alexandra seemed to be falling to pieces. First, he met Johnny Berg for a beer and the special of the day at Dovrehallen. They had a frank conversation, and when Olav eventually walked out onto Storgata, he did so safe in the knowledge that he had passed on Connie Knarvik's name and contact details to Berg. He had whispered that the tragic love affair she had had with Hans might be worthy of inclusion in a biography. But what he had actually done was play his last card. Perhaps Connie was the only person sitting on something that could incriminate Hans.

The following day he put the boat out on the water and invited M. Magnus to take a trip on the fjord.

Mist lay over the water as Olav manoeuvred the double-ender south from Rederhaugen. He had tied up the ear flaps of his fur hat like a Russian and stood leaning on the gunwale. Next to him, wearing an anorak and a woollen hat, stood the officer.

Olav pushed the throttle forward, feeling the boat accelerate.

"We'll head south," he said.

Magnus rubbed his palms together. "Christ, chilly today," he said, shivering, then slapped himself to keep warm.

Olav nodded in silence.

"I had some people look at the options open to us, after everything that's happened," MM said, gazing at the horizon.

"I see," Olav said.

"The point being that even if Vera Lind's will is valid, and all the indications are that that is the case, she cannot undermine the law by reference to ancestral line. Sasha and, indirectly, you maintain control of SAGA, although it's probably best to face the fact that Rederhaugen is lost. That's a simple question of inheritance."

Who the hell does he think he is lecturing me on this, Olav thought. It was as though his contempt for the man next to him was getting his circulation going again in the cold.

"Have you spoken to Hans since the accident?" Olav asked, in a mild tone.

"No, not in a long while. I should have, however. It's always interesting to hear what he has to say."

In the middle of the fjord, Olav put the boat in neutral. To the right, a couple of kilometres away, he could discern the coastline at Asker, and at approximately the same distance off to the left, the Nesoddlandet peninsula rose sharply up.

Olav made his way astern. His silence over the past week made people uncomfortable, prompting them to talk.

"If I were to give you a final piece of advice . . ." Magnus said.

By all means, Olav thought.

"It would be to attach Johnny Berg to SAGA. Keep your enemies closer and all that."

"Good idea!" Olav laughed and drew a hip flask from his jacket pocket. "But first a dip. Race you!"

It was a test of manhood he knew MM could not resist, and the old special forces soldier quickly pulled off his clothes to reveal his naked, white, muscular body before diving effortlessly out into the freezing fjord. Olav followed, feeling how the water initially paralysed him until he slowly regained control with deep, rapid breaths. He lay on his back, staring up at the pale blue January sky.

Martens swam in a fast crawl around the boat and came close to him, treading water. "You're well able for ice-swimming, Olav, I'll give you that. But it's fucking cold today. I'm freezing. Getting out."

"Sure," Olav said, still lying on his back.

MM took a few slow strokes towards the stern and gripped the swim ladder with both hands. But just as he shifted his weight backwards to hoist himself up, the ladder came away from its mounting and he fell back into the water. The ladder disappeared into the depths.

The boat bobbed white and frost-covered on the surface.

"Whoops, that's a bit of a problem," MM said, with the

composure of a special forces soldier, then propelled himself backwards to get a better view of the hull and see where it was best to climb up. "I'll use the aft bilge pump outlet."

He was referring to a small drain hole, perhaps the size of a fist, about a metre from the stern. Olav watched as he inserted his fingers into it, bellowing fiercely as he raised himself up, but the smoothness and outward curve of the hull scuppered his efforts. MM splashed back down into the water.

"Come here," Magnus ordered breathlessly. "I think the hull curves least amidships. I'll stand on your shoulders to get up."

What had seemed like a simple idea proved more difficult in practice. Olav could already feel his body beginning to stiffen from the cold, his movements turning tremulous, and when MM tried to position himself on his shoulders, he sank flailing below the surface. The boat that seemed small when one was sitting in it appeared enormous from down in the water.

"Come on, Olav!" Magnus shouted, desperation in his voice. "Use all your strength. We can't give up!"

But Olav just lay peacefully on his back, his winter-shrunken dick floating on the surface, his gaze fixed on the misty bluish-white winter sky.

He felt MM take hold of his head from behind and swim a few strokes towards the fibreglass craft. The former officer swam around and slapped Olav on the jaw.

"If we don't get out now, we're going to freeze to death!"

"It's strange," Olav said, in a voice that was completely calm, as though addressing no one but himself. "I always knew it would end in the water."

"Olav!"

"No one sells out my children and gets away with it." Olav could feel the paralysing cold being replaced by something else, the water becoming lukewarm like the tubs he had been bathed in as a child. "All that's left for me in this world is to help my children."

His eyes met MM's wide eyes and blue lips. And with an almost imperceptible smile on his face, Olav sank into the clear depths.

Not every man had the privilege of drowning twice.

13

MY GIVEN NAME IS CONSTANCE FALCK

Holmenkollen, Oslo

Olav Falck was not honoured with a funeral at the state's expense, but a curated selection of people from Norwegian public life were present when he was laid to rest at Holmenkollen Chapel, a dark-stained timber church set upon a hill at the edge of the forest next to the ski jump.

The church was filled to capacity, but Johnny nodded to the verger and found standing room at the back. The two branches of the family sat on opposite sides, divided by the aisle. When she turned her head, he caught sight of Sasha in the front row, flanked by her siblings. What was going through her mind now?

About a week had passed since that freezing January day when a boat and two ice-bathers were found drifting in Oslo fjord. Amid the murmuring of old men and the rustling of the funeral pamphlets Johnny could hear the whispers: "He died as he lived. Drowning after ice-bathing? It was too soon for M. Magnus but a pretty dignified way for a seventy-five-year-old to go out. A titan like Olav Falck wasn't fated to end up in nappies in an old people's home."

The service was held by a military chaplain named Aslak, a bon vivant and agnostic with whom Johnny had often discussed morality, philosophy and women late into the night under starry skies in Afghanistan. The president of the parliament spoke. A retired actor from the National Theatre recited a poem, a world-famous violinist played a Bach fugue, and a pack of soloists from the foremost boys' choir in the country sang "Å Leve det er å elska".

Curiously, no one from the family spoke.

Johnny stared at the rows of pearl earrings and bald pates wreathed with grey hair. During his peculiar meeting with the man lying in the coffin, a few days prior to the accident, Olav had pulled no punches. He had not expected any forgiveness from Johnny for his role in "the mission in the Middle East".

Olav had done what he thought was necessary and for the sake of the family. The real reason for the meeting at Dovrehallen was because he knew of a person who "could fill in some vital areas of Hans's biography if he wasn't cooperative", someone who had never spoken to outsiders. Olav made mention of "a tragic love story", but what did that involve?

Oddly, none of the other interviewees had mentioned Connie Knarvik. The first time he had heard of her was via M. Magnus. The combination of these two things piqued Johnny's interest. When he contacted her, she suggested the funeral as a meeting place. But where was she? As the coffin was being carried out and a procession of mourners formed after it, he noticed a woman fitting the description Olav had given him. Johnny slipped through the people filing behind until he was next to her.

"Connie?" he whispered.

She stopped in the aisle and placed her hands on his shoulders, oblivious to the procession.

"Let me get a proper look at you," she said in a middle-class Bergen accent, studying him. "It's really you."

What did she mean? Once she must have been very beautiful, but the wan complexion and wickerwork of tiny wrinkles at the corners of her mouth indicated a hard life.

Johnny began heading slowly towards the door as he spoke in a low voice. "I don't think this is the ideal place for our conversation today."

"Ugh, I can't stand this place," Connie said. "This church was set on fire by the same lout who burned down our church in Fantoft."

Our church? Strange way to put it. They emerged into the clear January air; the sub-zero temperature stung the nose, and the snow creaked underfoot. As the coffin containing Olav Falck was eased into the hearse, they left the procession and followed the path around the area where the ski stadium was situated.

"Thank you for agreeing to meet me," Johnny said. "I'm working on a biography of Hans Falck."

"Are you a Christian?" she asked.

What sort of opening question was that?

"I'm on the fence," he said.

"Pity, I trust believers."

She suggested walking up the steps of the amphitheatre surrounding the steep landing slope of the ski jump. Her breathing was laboured. Below them, the city revealed itself under a layer of winter fog.

Connie lit a cigarette.

She studied Johnny as she inhaled. "You're like the rest of them, fascinated by Hans, desperate to know who's hiding behind the mask. But one thing is certain, Hans should be kept away from any position of real power. He'll only destroy people's lives, like he destroyed mine with his lies and manipulation."

It was clear to Johnny that underneath the veneer of bourgeois breeding there lay something else, something dark and fierce.

"Is that so?" Johnny said, his expression sceptical.

"Young man," she said indulgently, "my given name is Constance Falck, just as yours is Yahya al-Jabal."

How did she know that? "But?"

"We'll get to that, young man. But you need to keep one thing in mind. I grew up with Hans. Later we fell in love, or at least I thought he loved me."

"Your name doesn't crop up when I speak to other people about him," Johnny objected.

"The reason for that will become apparent," she said coldly.

"I'm listening."

She sat quite still without saying a word. Finally she took out an unopened envelope. "A letter, returned to sender, dated 1976. I've never opened it since writing it nor shown it to anyone else. But in circumstances where Hans has inherited a billion-dollar fortune and one of the most prominent positions in Norwegian society, I don't see what choice I have. Regard it as a test; there's more where that came from. It's the beginning of a story about treachery and deceit. Hans betrayed me on more than one occasion. I've always had my suspicions he also betrayed his country."

24/8/1976

Dear Hans,

You called me from the Arctic last night. Although the line was bad, I knew straight away from your voice that it was all over. Our cause, the exposé, the revelation that would strike a blow for the oppressed and send shock waves from Washington DC via Oslo to Moscow. Our contribution to a different world.

It was finished, dead. But not only that. *We* were finished, too.

I've never been more in love with you than in the past few weeks. Your energy as we worked together, the look you gave me when our eyes met, the feeling that we could climb to cloud nine together and capture the moon, like Chairman Mao wrote. That nothing was impossible in this world. You had that quality. You have it.

Whatever the reason for your actions, now I've lost everything. I left my husband, cut all ties with my family, and joined the party for your sake. You might respond by telling me I'm a grown woman in a free country with responsibility for my own choices. All that is true. But you know very well that once one has known true intimacy in a relationship, one does whatever one can to make it last.

Or do you, actually?

I'm composing this in the apartment on Gimle terrasse. "The Falcks' divorce block," you once jokingly said as we drove past. I'm sitting in one of the corner bay windows. From here I can see out over the fjord in the direction of Rederhaugen. I'm writing. Writing is the only thing that offers me a measure of peace.

"We have the train come to our own garden," Father said, having declared that the Falck family do not go to the station to catch the train. Do you remember that? It's etched in my memory.

Of course, I was much too young to understand it then, but recently I've thought about how it was our outlook on life he was putting into words, a world view I would come to despise.

For us the earth was not in orbit around the sun. It was the other way around. The sun revolved around the family.

"But that's impossible," you objected.

You were a little boy back then, and you promptly launched into a story about a runaway train derailing, careening through the city streets, sparks flying below the carriages.

"Wait and see," Father smiled.

At that time, I had the impression you spent more time at our house than with your parents in Hordnes. You worshipped my father. Even though Herbert was your great-uncle, I think you wished he was your father.

To you he was like a superhero who had wandered out of the pages of a comic. You never tired of telling your friends about the exploits of "Uncle Herbert" as you called him: the mountains he had climbed, the freezing waters he had endured when his kayak capsized, the film stars and racing-car drivers he mixed with, the polar bears he had shot.

I was thirteen, three years your elder, and had shot up over the past year. Still, it was as though the rest of my body had not managed to keep up. When I look at pictures of myself from that time, it puts me in mind of a swaying, windblown tree of the kind that grows below power lines.

We had eaten supper when Father appeared in the kitchen.

"Are you ready?"

He was wearing a long, dark overcoat and a hat. As always there was something energetic about him, a mixture of warmth and vainglory, that coarse laughter and those brusque movements.

He led the way out through the conservatory and opened the door. The low evening sun in the glass cast its light over the bushes and leaves, damp as tears on a cheek.

"Blast!" Father cried out, smacking his forehead. "I forgot the documents I was to bring to Oslo. The train will be here soon. Hans!"

The two of you ran back while I stood waiting. Our house, a beautiful old brick villa, was set in parkland linked by paths, steps and avenues, and was built by my grandfather, Theodor Falck Jr, during the first golden age of the family between the wars.

It was one of the finest properties in Bergen.

You and Father arrived back, out of breath. The footpath continued before taking a sharp turn that led to the other part of the property, where the Hanseatic Steamship Company had their premises. Below, like a rift in the landscape, ran the railway line, flanked by a wall with a colonnade on the side of the tracks nearer the house.

Stone steps led down to the elongated hollow where the train line wound through the undulating landscape. You grasped tightly on to Father's big, safe hand. The steps went about five metres down into the hollow, and to the left of the tracks were cave-like storage bays supported by columns, in front of which a wooden platform had been erected.

Then the distant noise of the train could be heard, the hissing in the tracks, the hoarse howl of the whistle, the stubborn grinding as it braked, before it came to a stop, right in front of the makeshift platform.

"That's our private carriage," Herbert said, pointing at the rear section. "The train comes to us. Never forget that. Never listen to the naysayers, to the pessimists, the equality tyrants, the bureaucrats, the realists. With them life is boring. Without them everything is possible. You hear me?"

It was June, sometime in the 1960s, and the train rumbled through the deep valleys outside Bergen, climbing up towards treeless mountains, where snowdrifts lit up the pale summer night. Father told us about how he used to take the morning train to Finse when he was a boy, go hell for leather on skis to Ustaoset or Geilo, and catch the night train back to Bergen.

"Tell us about the polar bear," you said.

"Did you know they once found a polar bear by Vardø on the mainland?" Father replied, looking pensively out of the window. "It must have swum almost a thousand kilometres through the Arctic Ocean to get there. Impressive creatures."

"I mean *the* polar bear," you said. Although you had heard it before, you never tired of the story about the stuffed bear that had adorned the entrance to the Falck shipping company's branch office in Bergen city centre.

Father smiled. "Alright. This is the story of how Svalbard became Norwegian. The year is 1916. Together with a group of engineers, bankers and Arctic explorers, Theo has sailed across the Barents Sea and into the majestic Isfjord, where the ice has just broken up. Longyearbyen is a settlement of barracks and huts for hardy mineworkers. The director, John

Munro Longyear, has been locked in a dispute with the Norwegian authorities for the last few years. Longyearbyen has been left like a garrison town in the Wild West; only a small number of guards remain. The American miner is angry. The telegraph link he wants is to go through Finnmark on the tip of the Norwegian mainland. But the Norwegian government is refusing to allow the American to establish a link to the USA and has established its own instead."

"Do they run into polar bears there?" you asked impatiently.

"I'm getting to that," Father said, "but first you need to be aware of one thing. At that time, Svalbard was *terra nullius*."

"What?" you and I said in chorus.

"It means that no country had sovereignty over the area. Even though our Viking ancestors had travelled to that cold coast, which *Sval-bard* means, even though our hunters and trappers had explored the archipelago more than any others, we Norwegians had no special rights to the islands. Understand?"

He looked at each of us in turn.

"So Theo Falck saw his chance and asked the American if he was interested in selling up. The American was hesitant, wanted to know who the buyers were. Theo told him it was himself on behalf of a consortium. Together with the Norwegian state."

Father studied us both. "Without Theo Falck – your grandfather, Constance, and your great-grandfather, Hans – the mines would never have come into Norwegian hands. Do you grasp the enormity of that? The man who secured Svalbard for our country was a Falck."

We couldn't grasp it, of course. Father continued: "After properly celebrating the deal with the American mine owner in the mess hall in Longyearbyen, and when the ice east of Spitsbergen had begun to melt, Theo set off. The sea ice conditions on Svalbard vary greatly from year to year, and that year it was possible to sail along the north-west coast without any great difficulty at the end of June. They stopped in Ny-Ålesund and continued north, along a magnificent, frozen landscape broken up by mountains and glacial ice tongues winding into the sea. By chance, on the north of Spitsbergen, they encountered some hunters. Otherwise it was just a great nothingness.

"Theo and Adolf Hoel are heading for Kvitøya, 'White Island', in the far north-east of the Svalbard archipelago, a place few had travelled to since the Swedish explorer Salomon Andrée and his party disappeared in 1897.

"The ice often lies thick around Kvitøya all year round, but in mid-July they attempt to get to shore. The Falck vessel copes with the conditions and as they drop anchor they gaze up at the ice cap that covers the entire island and gives it its name. Using ropes they zigzag their way up the ice, and after three days they make it. At the highest point, Theo sinks down onto the ice. And says: 'I name this Falckejøkulen.'"

Father patted you on the head. "And, little Hans, this is when the polar bear makes his entrance. Because provisions begin to run low, they decide to travel from Kvitøya to an old Dutch whalers' station in the far north of Spitsbergen. They set a course for it, arrive, eat and then collapse early into the makeshift beds, fed and happy.

"In the dead of night Theo awakens. He looks around the dark room. The hatches are closed and he can barely see his hand in front of his face. From the other room he can hear the steady snoring of Hoel. There's a sound, but from where? It seems to be from the kitchenette. But how? All the windows and doors are closed and locked. A sound of movement across the floor. Followed by a racket from the kitchen cupboards. A chewing sound. Theo lies completely still in his bed. The room is sealed so the midnight sun cannot penetrate. Someone is eating their food. Someone is slurping and gnawing. Should he get up? Theo does not move. He is overcome by a fear unlike any he has ever experienced, fear of something beyond human, as though some creature is inside the cabin.

"The bedroom door opens; strips of light fall into the room. In the doorway the silhouette of an enormous creature comes into view, the midsection as wide as a horse's, hairy arms and legs thick as logs. Theo never sees the muzzle of the polar bear. The beast stands in the doorway. The gun is resting against the wall, too far to reach, and besides, it's dangerous to shoot a bear at such close range.

"He hardly dares move his eyelids. The bear takes a step into the room. This is the end, Theo thinks. I hope, at least, that Adolf Hoel makes it back so the Falck glacier can keep its name. He feels the big snout press against his thigh through the sleeping bag, can smell the saltwater, seaweed and wet fur of the animal. The bear goes on sniffing, moving up to his stomach. Theo lies motionless.

"Fight, flight or freeze they call it, and there's but one option here. The polar bear pauses at Theo's face. Light from the midnight sun is falling through the door the bear has broken open, shining further into the bedroom, giving Theo's face a yellowish tinge. He lies there, corpse-like, feeling the animal's tongue, rough and heavy, lick him across the face and lips. Theo lies still. Until the beast trots nonchalantly out of the room, out of the cabin, sated and happy."

"But," I said, perplexed, "why did they shoot it? I mean, if it left?"

"Because," Father answered, "it came back the next day, trotting towards them at speed as they were making their way to the Falck boat. They had no choice but to raise their rifles."

"How do you know it was the same polar bear?"

"Because when they cut open its stomach," Father smiled, "they found a tin can like the ones in the cabin. Not the contents of the can, no, the bear had eaten the whole can. No wonder it was angry when it came back. Theo brought it back to Bergen and had it stuffed. Do you know what a giant like that weighs when it's born?"

We both shook our heads.

Father lowered his voice. "Between 400 and 600 *grams*. About the same size as a packet of butter, a tenth the size of a baby. Not so strange that the bastard was hungry."

We went to bed in the sleeper carriage and didn't wake until we pulled into Oslo the following morning.

At the quay a boat was waiting to transport us to Rederhaugen. At the helm sat Olav Falck, who Father told us had served at the frogmen's school in north Norway, consequently acquiring that vague air of self-confidence from having made it through tough military training. Now he was studying law.

"You look fit," Father said, looking the boy up and down.

"Ice-bathing, running and circuit training," Olav said, with decorous modesty.

Even though Olav couldn't have been much older than twenty at the time, he had that quality characteristic of politicians and other prominent members of society when they're young: ever since he'd started to shave daily as a thirteen-year-old and spend Friday evenings in discussion with teachers who invited him to soirées, he had been indifferent to the lives of people his own age. It was as though he came from a different country from them.

After a trip across the fjord, the boat docked at the south of Rederhaugen. I hadn't been there since I was a little girl and was wide-eyed as the round tower came into view. We walked across an impeccably manicured lawn and into the cold, damp hallways, up a winding staircase. Our footsteps echoed.

Father and Olav disappeared into a meeting that was obviously important, while you and I waited outside. You, fuelled by the Svalbard story the day before, sat engrossed in a book on the same theme.

After an eternity the door opened. Father and Olav emerged with Vera Lind. She owned the estate at Rederhaugen.

Under Vera's careful gaze, Father and Olav exchanged a firm handshake.

Father looked at me and then at you. "Constance, Hans, come with me, please."

He led us out to the lawn in front of the main building.

"What is it?" I asked nervously.

Father always had a cheerful, carefree tone.

A crooked smile appeared on his face. "Ah, nothing of any importance, my dear Constance. Family matters. Olav has officially taken on the legacy of his father, my dear brother Thor. He and the other descendants here at Rederhaugen are going to sell their shares in the Falck shipping lines and the Hanseatic Steamship Company. That will mean greater control for your branch of the family, Hans."

You kicked at the stones on the ground, seemingly uninterested.

"But the point is," Father continued, "Olav is planning to use the money from the sale of the shares in the shipping companies to establish a company and a foundation. SAGA, it'll be called, and he strikes me as a man who may be able to make a go of it."

"Good for him," I said, and shrugged. "Has that anything to do with us?"

"Not in itself," Father said, winking in the way a person does when they have an ace up their sleeve. "What he was actually after was my property on Svalbard."

The name of the mythical islands made you sit up and pay attention. "When Theo Falck secured Norwegian ownership of Svalbard in 1916, he eventually came into possession of one of the most valuable pieces of land up there. The Advent Valley, not far from Longyearbyen. I own this through a company of the same name: Advent Valley Ltd."

"You didn't sell Svalbard?" you said.

Father patted you on the head. "No, my boy, certainly not. But through my company I have given Olav a loan. It's all rather technical, but it's a so-called convertible loan. It can be exchanged for shares in SAGA, should the company grow to be successful. I have secured your future, Constance. You'll also be well looked after, Hans."

"Good," I said, indifferent.

"I want to go to Svalbard," you said.

"And one day you will," Father replied.

But perhaps I'm getting sidetracked, because what I actually wanted to write about was us. Do you remember where it began, do you recall our hands touching in the darkness of the theatre?

Father had stepped down as director of Falck and was spending more of his time on boards in the fields of sport and theatre in Bergen. That autumn Den Nationale Scene had managed to bring a Swedish actor to the city in the role of Johann Faust in Goethe's classic tragedy.

The production was a sensation, and the day after opening night, Mother and Father invited the Swede and the theatre director to lunch at our home.

You were thirteen, I was sixteen, and I could tell you were looking at me in a different way from before. Over the previous year I had become very popular with the boys. No one had so much as looked in my direction, then suddenly I had a number of suitors. First in the queue was a boy in the same year as me named Mikael Dreyer. What he lacked in looks he made up for in wealth and education.

My mother had stars in her eyes when Ekblad, as the Swedish actor was called, turned up, hearty and vivacious. He filled the room with his enormous presence. Here was a true artist, known internationally, I thought, instead of the dilettantes who usually came to visit.

"How do you do it?" my mother asked, when we had sat down to dinner.

"Do what?" Ekblad smiled.

Mother picked up a newspaper with a review of the play and began to read: "*The legend of Faust is one of the most central myths in our culture, a shocking depiction of how human ambition and pride ends in tragedy.*"

I couldn't help leaning over to you and whispering: "Mother is crazy about actors like this."

Our eyes met and I noticed a slight flush in your cheeks.

"I so wish I had that gift," Mother went on. "I can't imagine being an actor. How are you able to show Faust's pain and the dilemma facing him in such a harrowing way?"

Ekblad smiled disarmingly, indulgent. "Well." He cleared his throat while rolling the stem of his wine glass.

"You do come from acting stock," Father said, obligingly.

Mother dug a little further: "It must be a gift you're born with?"

"It's just technique," Ekblad answered calmly.

After the caramel pudding you and I stood looking through the programme of *Faust*. I think we were equally fascinated by the Swede, who, becoming restless, went out to the terrace to smoke. You followed, with me in tow. The winter sun was shining low over the landscape.

"Were you serious?" you said to Ekblad. "About all the feelings you summon up being nothing but technique?"

The Swede looked at you, a mild expression in his eyes. "Oh yes. Theatre is technique and life is theatre. Will you attend this evening's performance?"

The look you gave him did not convey that was your intention. Ekblad said he had tickets for two front-row seats. "You look like an intelligent boy. Come along, bring a girl, and I'll show you what I mean."

"Who are you going to invite?" I asked when we were alone again.

You shrugged, and I regretted the question, because I knew you had never had a girlfriend, nor asked anyone out.

Then you paused and looked at me. "Will you come with me, Constance?"

I agreed, and Mother was over the moon that we wanted to see the play together. "Just promise to keep Constance safe from the attentions of any strange men," she said.

You promised you would.

And so it was we walked up the broad stone steps at the entrance to Den Nationale Scene that same night. You with your hair slicked back, sporting a dark suit with a blue tie, me alongside, taller, in a red silk dress, my shoulders bare beneath my coat.

In the foyer I took out a cigarette and lit it.

"Do you smoke?" you asked, eyeing the cigarette. "Can I have one?"

"No," I replied. "But you can have something to drink."

I went to the bar and came back with two glasses of sparkling wine.

"Cheers, Hans," I said.

By your reaction I could tell you had never tasted it before.

The bell rang and the performance got under way. Ekblad must have been stirred by the eulogising in the newspapers; he played the title role with a self-belief far surpassing the tragic Johann Faust's own. The audience sat spellbound as Mephistopheles tempted Faust from the path of goodness, leading him to seduce beautiful Gretchen. How I was gripped by her tragedy! When she drowned her illegitimate child, I cried. And as the consequences of the diabolical pact dawned for Faust, conveyed by Ekblad in a quavering monologue so not a dry eye was left in the house, Hasse Ekblad met our gazes in the first row, with two smiling eyes and a little wink, invisible to everyone else, but it opened a whole world view.

For you in any case, but I'll get back to that.

Life is theatre. It's simply technique.

At the break we sneaked more sparkling wine.

"You know," I said, laughing, and stroked your slicked-back hair, "being at the theatre with you is actually quite fun."

Slightly tipsy we staggered back for the second act and sank down in our chairs. The curtain went up. The armrest was narrow, and our forearms were touching in the darkness. Then I felt your fingertip, against my forearm, from my elbow to wrist, gentle movements like squiggles, against my skin. I felt a tingle through my whole body, and my breathing grew heavier.

After the performance we went out into the mild winter night. A star-filled sky lit up the mountains. We followed the streets towards the railway station. The buildings looked like they were moving and I could see you were staggering. We caught the last train back and walked towards the estate.

"I'm not letting you travel all the way back to Fana on your own," I said, with as much authority as I could. "You can borrow the guest room, I'm sure."

All was quiet at the estate. I unlocked the door. The rooms lay in darkness. On the first-floor landing we stopped.

"Thank you for tonight," I said. "It was really nice."

You mumbled something inaudible. We stood facing each other.

Then we kissed.

You stood swaying for a few seconds, as though stunned by what had happened. Then you dashed to the toilet, and the last thing I heard was you retching and the sound of sparkling wine coming back up.

The next time we met was at the church a week later, on Christmas Eve. The day every member of the Falck clan was duty-bound to attend Fantoft church. Just as few had their own station along the Bergen line, not all families could boast of owning their own place of worship, but Theo Falck Jr had purchased a dark-stained stave church in Luster after the First World War and had it transported in individual pieces to Bergen.

The church was a brisk fifteen-minute walk uphill. It was customary for the family to make their way to the service together on Christmas Eve after eating rice pudding. That day it was raining. Fog hung low over the hills. The family was stretched out across the steep slope according to age and levels of fitness. Ever since I was a child, the church at Fantoft had had an aura of something terrible, like a log version of a crumbling Gothic castle, always shrouded in mist, like the setting for entering into a pact with the devil. The stave church's splendour – the dragon-like sculptures projecting from the gables – was in contrast to its sinister surroundings: the naked trees, almost deathlike. The spires pointed towards the grey sky.

We avoided each other on the way up. What were we supposed to say?

In front of the church, people from Fana, all dressed up, wished one another a merry Christmas. All these families wore their surnames like discreet jewellery. I knew several of the children from school. I saw Mikael Dreyer, and Mother, who knew his family, hurried over to say hello. I shook Mikael's hand awkwardly.

"Fru Dreyer," Mother said to a subtly made-up woman around her own age, "I'd like to introduce you to Hans Falck."

"Is this the little gentleman who looked after Constance when Mikael was busy on Saturday?" Fru Dreyer replied.

I hadn't considered it, but I could sense the jealousy creep up your spine while the Dreyer family showered you with compliments. Meeting a thirteen-year-old who attended a production of *Faust* wasn't an everyday occurrence.

"You have to say hello to Mikael," I said. "We're dating."

Shortly afterwards the bells rang out for Christmas in Fantoft.

Over the next few years we didn't see much of each other, but I think Ekblad's words must have made a strong impression on you: that life was a theatre stage; that everything was technique and the best actors succeed. Sometimes, over Sunday dinners with Mikael, Father would mention your name. You were the apple of his eye.

"Hans says he's going to be an actor!" Father exclaimed. "He's going to ride through the desert like Peter O'Toole in *Lawrence of Arabia*, or like Clint Eastwood through the Wild West."

"Quite the character, this Hans," Mikael remarked.

I said nothing.

That was when Father cleared his throat and said the entire family had been invited to sail on *Christina O*, Aristotle Onassis's yacht. The world's richest man had always had a close relationship with Norwegian shipowners. "We're going to the French Riviera in the summer."

I glanced at Mikael. Being on a yacht with the family wasn't the most tempting thing in the world but maybe we could sneak a few days to ourselves in Antibes? We would soon finish high school and I was keen to practise my school French with him.

"That's a very enticing offer," Mikael said, "but there's one problem." Conventional as he was, Mikael explained that he had signed up to work on a cargo ship to Svalbard for the summer, as tradition dictated. He was to begin at his father's shipping company as soon as term ended. Father nodded; it was the same in our family too.

"Of course, you whippersnappers need to get some dirt under your fingernails and find your sea legs before beginning in the family shipping companies!" Father said.

I hid my disappointment.

Father turned to me. "If you need a chaperone, Constance, we can ask if Hans would care to join us?"

Mikael seemed relieved, scared as he probably was that I would spend the time with handsome, moneyed French boys.

We left as soon as the summer holidays came around. The marina in Antibes was seething with life. The low white houses stretched around the harbour like a perfect set of pearly whites; the sky was a hazy blue, the sea green. A Riva Aquarama with a teak hull and white leather seats brought us to the yacht, lying at anchor further out. I was wearing a navy-blue denim jumpsuit, black Sophia Loren sunglasses, and had my dark blonde hair up in a *choucroute*.

Hearing French everywhere made me happy.

"Everything sounds better in French," I said as Antibes's sun-bleached old town below the fortress disappeared behind us. "Even 'sauerkraut' sounds romantic."

"Do they have sauerkraut in France?" Father asked. "They'd call it *zzauerkkkreaut*, wouldn't they?" he said, in a hopeless attempt at a French accent.

"No," I said, stroking my braid. "It's called *choucroute*."

You were in the boat too, Hans. You were wearing an elegant blue and white striped *chemise*. Even though you still had two years of high school left, you had become a young man. Around us the world was in turmoil – in the US, Martin Luther King and Robert Kennedy had been shot; in Paris there were riots and a general strike – but it was as though we couldn't quite grasp all that: our world was too different.

After a few minutes over the hazy blue sea we could make out the silhouette of a boat ahead of us, far away at first, as though in miniature. We drew closer to the white hull. Our pilot slowed down. Only then did I appreciate the size of the vessel. The people walking on the deck or leaning against the railings looked like tin soldiers. The yacht had to be close to a hundred metres long, bigger than the coastal ferries of the Hanseatic. *Christina O* had been a frigate during the war, Father informed me, prior to Onassis purchasing her.

The pilot of the speedboat took my hand and helped me onto a gangway, then the others followed.

A liveried valet opened a hatch. We stepped into a stairwell. The room, easily three decks in height, had walls and tiles in creamy yellow, and a spiralling staircase with a navy-blue stair runner.

A female housekeeper led us down. The air was cool. The carpet absorbed our steps. The housekeeper informed us that the suites forward on the main deck were named after Greek islands – Ithaca, Crete, Santorini, Rhodes, Lesbos, Mykonos and Corfu – and were furnished and decorated by different artists. Then she nodded discreetly and was gone.

I got Corfu and flopped down on the cool white four-poster bed with my arms and legs spread wide. Mikael should be here with me, I thought. Or should he?

Down on the main aft deck I encountered two furious, barking miniature poodles. In the dining room the table was laid but no one was there. Where are all the people, I thought, as I passed a grand piano in a smoking lounge that led to a wide swing door to a mahogany deck with a swimming pool in shades of blue in the centre.

The guests were sitting on sunloungers and raffia chairs under parasols. The women were film-star beautiful. The men were ruddy and corpulent. On a small platform a band were playing coffee-table jazz. Waiting staff brought round refreshments on trays.

"Here he comes," I heard someone whisper.

At the end of the pool, by the doorway to the smoking lounge, he stood. The atmosphere among the guests altered immediately. People began to speak more self-consciously in lower tones.

He was wearing wide white linen trousers and a casual

white shirt, the top three buttons undone. The serious face had heavy, melancholic eyes. His hair was combed back. The fact that he was barefoot seemed to emphasise the elevated, almost religious aura around him.

"Aristotle Onassis," he introduced himself to each of us in turn.

"I'd like to humbly express my gratitude for the invitation," I whispered, and the Greek held my gaze.

Onassis smiled. "Without Norwegians, as my old friend Anders Jahre would say, I wouldn't have become a shipowner at all."

He made no mention of it, but I had heard rumours of an affair with a Norwegian woman in the 1930s.

Before long, lunch was served in the dining room. A sumptuous lobster was carried in, along with various fish dishes from the Mediterranean, colourful salads drenched in olive oil, a trolley of oysters, white wines from Burgundy and reds from Bordeaux.

I ate the lobster, served with mayonnaise and southern French *panisses* – fried chickpeas with the consistency of chips.

"You know that the lobster is a scavenger that eats its own?" declared a ruddy, loud and boorish Englishman, in conversation with Umberto Agnelli and Pamela Harriman. He was the son of Churchill. In another corner, Jackie Onassis was sitting with Rudolf Nureyev. The Aga Khan, Evita Perón and Frank Sinatra were also there.

These people made me feel insecure and nervous. But I could see that you loved it. Forgive the comparison, but it has crossed my mind that it was like a drunkard's first meeting with alcohol. For you this was like coming home. It was among these people you belonged. You were yet to turn sixteen, but maybe we both understood that the world of the rich and famous was your drug, your character flaw.

While we listened to the Aga Khan's monologue on the breeding of racehorses, a man came and gave Father a bear hug and spoke loudly in American-accented English.

"Herb! It's you. Been a long time. Damn good to see you!"

"Bill," Father said genially. "Imagine meeting here."

Although the American seemed inconsiderate and arrogant at first glance, there was something genuine about how he and Father spoke to one another that contrasted with the rest of the passengers' conversations.

"Bill Astor and I go back to the war," Father said proudly, placing his hand on the American's shoulder. "There are no bonds stronger than those forged in combat."

"We have met but you'd hardly remember," Bill said. "I was in Bergen in 1952; you were just a little girl. And this guy here . . ."

He pointed at Hans. "He was just a baby, so far as I remember."

The American nodded to Father and they withdrew to another lounge. It's strange to think about it now, Hans: although we didn't know it at the time, that was as close as we ever got to our big disclosure. The Norwegian shipowner and the American CIA man.

But that wasn't what I was planning on writing about now.

I remember going out onto the teak deck to stand at the railing and look out. The wind was warm, like from a hairdryer, with no cooling effect, and the water was azure blue.

"You look like your mother," said a French-accented voice from behind. I turned and saw a middle-aged man in a linen suit approaching, his hands in his pockets. Mother had whispered that he ran a multimillion-dollar luxury clothing brand. "My name is Jean-Baptiste, but please call me JB."

I told him my name, eyes cast downward at the deck.

"Might I invite you for a drink, in my suite?"

I felt fear in the pit of my stomach.

I didn't want to. I lowered my eyes again and stammered a *yes*.

He led me up a spiral staircase.

In his suite I just stood there, stunned by the luxury and overwhelmed by the feeling of having trapped myself in a corner I couldn't get out of.

"Are you interested in Greek mythology?" JB asked.

"It's fascinating," I said.

Taking a turn around the room, he ran a hand through his perfectly coiffed grey hair. He lit a cigarillo; the smoke lay like a veil between us. I could see that he was old and wrinkled. Would he have any appeal if he were a clerk in a provincial French town? Or a shifty nightclub owner on the Riviera, which was probably more believable? What JB had, I realised immediately, was a melancholic look about his eyes.

He asked me again what I'd like to drink.

"Lemonade," I heard myself say, in a mechanical tone.

He brought over two glasses, then put on a record, taking the opportunity to move closer to me on the sofa when he sat back down. Even now, many years later, I tense up when I think of his hand moving to the small of my back.

"You probably aren't aware," he smiled, "but your mother and I . . . Oh, my, she was fantastic . . . Henny, Henny."

Had Mother had a relationship . . .? I stiffened with fear. And realised at that instant that the protection Father could offer was worthless here. Jean-Baptiste couldn't have cared less about a small-fry *paterfamilias* from Norway.

"Nothing turns me on more than mothers with their daughters," JB said. "Would you like to . . .?

He leaned towards me, pushing me down. I can still feel his stubble against my cheek, his alcohol and cigarillo breath, and the rough, hairy hand he put up my dress and over my breasts, as he kissed the nape of my neck.

I bit him on the throat.

A hard, vampirish bite. I felt my teeth sink into his skin.

He let out a howl. Blood was trickling onto the white collar of his shirt and the linen suit. "*Sale pute!*"

I pushed him away, rolled off the sofa, got up and ran through the room. Maybe the door is locked, I thought in desperation. Spitting a torrent of obscenities, JB had got to his feet and was trying to get hold of my dress. I fidgeted desperately with the lock.

"*Arrêt!*" he shouted.

The door opened.

I ran through the corridors. Bumping into liveried servants and famous people. I ran onto the deck. Threw up over the railings. Lobsters eat their own. The Levant wind caressed my face. I called down to the pilot of the Riva moored alongside the hull.

"I can't be here anymore! Get me off this ship."

Then you appeared. You didn't say anything but seemed to understand what had happened all the same.

"I'm here," you said quietly. "Come on, we'll leave, find a hotel on the shore, far away from this boat."

We spent the next week together, Hans. You understood how things were with me, and the first day you left the small hotel room only to buy pastries and lemonade. Sometimes you read to me, but mostly you sat on the edge of the bed gently stroking me. You had grown up.

I was a wreck. And not only because of the French man and the decadence on Onassis's yacht. What was I going to do with my life? Ostensibly everything was in place. A man from the same background as me, with the right friends and a large villa not far from where I had grown up. Mikael was in the Arctic to become a man. Mother and Father seemed more concerned that my sudden departure from the yacht might preclude a possible repeat invitation.

You and I rented a car and travelled inland into Provence, past magnificent lakes and small villages where we ate rustic dishes and drank carafes of rosé. At night we lay curled up together, without it leading to anything more. One day the owner of a guest house told us about a narrow river that we could follow upstream. The pebbles and boulders were scorching hot from the sun. Cliffs hundreds of metres high rose up above us; sometimes the river widened out into small ponds where we could cool off.

Unabashed, we bathed naked in a deep pool in the river, before sitting on a rock in the sun. You were going on more and more about the radical students in the USA and Paris, a popular topic in the newspapers.

"So what do you think, Constance?" you said eventually.

I hesitated. "About what?"

You laid your head on one side. "You know. I have feelings for you."

"And I for you," I whispered, eyes downcast.

You moved closer and put your arm over my shoulder.

"You don't love him, do you?"

"Hans," I said. "Think about it. We have no future together. It's impossible. You've been brought up practically as my brother."

"Is that how you see me?" you exclaimed. "As your brother?"

"No, but it's how other people see it. There can't be anything between us."

Strange to think of it now, but perhaps there was some poetic justice to it: I was the one who let you down the first time.

The stave church in Fantoft was filled to capacity.

Arm in arm with my father I stared straight ahead, only glancing at the dragon carvings on the ends of the pews on either side of the aisle. So many people! Old friends of the family, new friends, Rieber, Kjøde, Dedichen, Mowinckel, Reksen, Friele, Mohn and all the rest who bore their privileged Bergen surnames as status symbols, as well as Vera, Olav and the others from Oslo.

Mikael was proud as a peacock standing there with the priest, his fair hair combed back with pomade and a suit that only fit if he held in his stomach. I was in white, my arms and legs bare, and in my hair I wore a wreath. And I was white within. I knew nothing. Mikael's eyes were filled with love, but I knew well that love was black or white as well as blind. Fundamentally ruthless, it is present or it is not, and where it is not to be found it can never arise.

The priest celebrated the mass. We exchanged our marriage vows and a kiss.

I struggle to describe my feelings at that moment, Hans, due to their absence.

We walked down the aisle as a married couple.

Then I caught sight of you. At the very back, standing in the colonnade below the organ. Your hair had grown longer since the French trip the year before and was down over your ears. Our eyes met. Mikael was oblivious. You stared at me, as though looking right through me, and shook your head, almost imperceptibly.

The church door opened and the May light dazzled us. The forest outside was beautiful, but as always had a tinge of something else, something darker. Water glittered in the distance.

Mikael kissed me and we drove off together, waving from an open-top car.

PART II
EAST OF ISTANBUL

14

SHERIFF TIRASPOL

Rederhaugen, Oslo

Hans Falck awoke with a start. The clock on the bedside table showed 3.03 a.m. and he felt wide awake, without knowing why.

He listened attentively. Stared up at the dark ceiling. The night, lit by stars and snow, sent a dull light between the gap in the curtains across the floor, up the wall and over the ceiling of the blue room. He had always just laughed when women he was sharing a bed with spoke about *sensing a presence*. Had they been right after all? No, this was more tangible. Cautious footsteps, like a child sneaking out of a bedroom at night.

Silently, he pulled the duvet aside, twisted his body and placed his feet on the rug beside the double bed.

The footsteps were coming from the library, next door to the bedroom.

Hans realised he should be frightened. Since moving into Rederhaugen less than a month earlier, he had got into the habit of setting the perimeter alarm, something he had never done at home. He gave a start. Had he forgotten to switch it on? No. Or? No. Why had it not gone off?

For some reason Theo Falck's old Purdey rifle had been left standing in the bedroom after the move. He could see the silhouette of the barrel in the corner, the Falck emblem standing out in the feeble light. Although deactivated, perhaps it might function as a deterrent? Besides, the butt could be used as a weapon. He moved quietly across the soft teak floor, held his breath, and took hold of the stock without a sound.

Fortunately, the door between the bedroom and the library was slightly ajar. With the butt in the pocket of his shoulder, as though this old conscientious objector was some kind of soldier, Hans used the barrel to gently push open the door. From the position in which he now found himself he was looking straight at the fireplace, with the Falck monogram on the chimney breast.

A bright light flashed through the room.

Like the flares in Beirut that night in 1982. What was this? Hans took a deep breath, felt his heart race.

There was no way back. He took a few steps into the room, switched on the light to maximise the surprise and roared: "Stand still or I'll shoot!"

The intruder, a short-haired man with an athletic build wearing an army-green beanie, froze. Hans still could not see his face as anything other than a silhouette. Pointing the rifle at him, Hans ordered: "On the ground, get on the ground, damn it."

The man knelt down with his hands behind his head. Hans prodded his back with the muzzle, unsure where this sudden militaristic confidence was coming from.

"Where are you from?"

The man made no reply.

"Russian?" Hans asked.

"*Nyet, nei,* no."

Hans tried to think. His entire life he had abhorred weapons and could count the number of times he had held one on the fingers of one hand. But he had had his fair share of being *threatened* with a weapon. Child soldiers in the Congo and jihadists in the Middle East. How did they do it? At a slight distance or with the weapons up close? For an amateur the muzzle against the lower back was the most unpleasant. For a professional it was an opportunity to resist.

"Where are you from?" Hans asked.

"Don't shoot!"

He pressed the muzzle harder against the man's back. "Where?"

"Transnistria. M-m-m-oldova," the man stammered. "Tiraspol. Good football team. Sheriff Tiraspol. Same name as on my hoodie."

"Who sent you?"

"No one. I've worked on your house as a builder!"

The man was lying, that was obvious. "No burglar takes photos of a writing desk. Who sent you?"

He pressed the muzzle so hard that the intruder groaned in pain.

The top drawer of the writing desk was half open. Inside, resting on a bed of purple velvet were the prizes and awards he had received during his career: honorary Kurdish citizenship, the Lebanese Order of the Cedar, an honorary doctorate from the American university in Sulaymaniyah and numerous other honours.

The situation called for assistance. Hans knew people abroad who could take care of it, but he needed someone right away, someone who could make this man talk. He knew one person who met all the criteria. A man he had met and become acquainted with during his trips to the Middle East.

Using one hand, he fished his phone from his pocket, searched for the number and called it.

"Hans?" answered the sleepy voice of a retired intelligence

man. "Been a while. Last time we spoke must have been before you went to pick up Johnny in the Middle East."

Hans stared down at the man on the ground. "I need help, HK. The details will have to wait. Can you get here? Now?"

The old man grunted something barely audible.

"A guy has broken in to Rederhaugen."

"Ring the police, Hans."

"You don't understand. He's not a burglar."

"How do you know?" HK still sounded unconvinced.

Hans pressed the muzzle against the man. "For God's sake, Hans Kristian! I have him here, he's lying on the floor in front of me! He's no burglar. Says he's Moldovan. No thieves take photos of a medal collection."

On the other end of the line, the old man sounded suddenly alert. "I'm on my way."

As he manoeuvred himself into a chair, from where he could still keep the intruder in his sights, Hans tried to think. These past few weeks, the blue room, on the top floor of the main building, had functioned as a pied-à-terre and a home office.

Hans had become interim chairperson of the SAGA Foundation following Olav's death. The somewhat archaic paragraph 8 in the rules of governance was clear on that: "In the event of the death of the chairperson or the loss of that party's legal capacity, the oldest board member will assume the position of acting chair until such time as an extraordinary general meeting has appointed a new board. The aforementioned general meeting must take place within the space of a maximum of three – 3 – months."

Hans had three months to secure control over SAGA. Tomorrow he was supposed to meet Sasha for a mediation meeting at BAHR, a law firm in Aker Brygge. He was not looking forward to it. The meeting would end in dispute. There was no other possible outcome. Not since he had claimed ownership of the properties, with Vera's will in his hand.

Hans's own entrance as chairperson had been discreet. Having taken over with the least possible fanfare, he had announced he was granting himself fifty days for an in-depth study of the organisation for which he now had overall responsibility. SAGA had issued a brief press release on the matter, but Hans had declined all requests for interview, pointing out that his was an interim position, in accordance with the SAGA rules of governance.

Now half his time as acting chair had passed. To say that Hans was residing in Rederhaugen would be an exaggeration. His partner could not abandon her hospital shifts at the drop of a hat, and little Per had just started kindergarten. Hans had dismissed her complaints about them being apart from one another as a "typical middle-class problem" and that had only angered her. The first load of his property and possessions had arrived from the other side of the country: the treasures from Bergen, among them the honours, which he had laid in the rose-painted desk in the library.

And now a man claiming to be from Moldova had broken in to photograph them. Who broke in to photograph a medal collection? And why?

15

HONORARY DOCTORATE

Rederhaugen, Oslo

Twenty-five minutes had elapsed after Hans's phone call when HK paid the driver and stepped out of the taxi at the fork in the driveway. The rose tower was illuminated by the snow and stars. Rederhaugen looked exactly as it had the last time he had seen it. When was that, actually?

Hans-Kristian Hatle had sworn to spend his retirement far removed from anything that smacked of the intelligence services. His husband, a quiet, unassuming man, a retired undersecretary in the Ministry of Culture who liked hiking and gardening, had set this as a non-negotiable condition. HK had, however, been allowed to busy himself with the sequel to *The Problem of Secret Intelligence*, an academic text on intelligence work which, to his great surprise, had led to invitations to conferences and universities all over the world.

He had just returned from a trip with his husband to the University of Florence, where he had been awarded an honorary doctorate. Not bad for a dropout from the faculty of theology. HK had discovered new sides to himself that marked him out from most others in the intelligence services: he dreamed of public recognition. The success of the textbook had made him aware he liked being lauded. It was a side to him that had always been there but was now becoming more prominent.

Operational service was out of the question, however. That was grounds for divorce. So why had HK slipped out of bed in their spacious apartment on Sorgenfrigata? He had told his half-awake husband it was to "help an old friend". An intruder trying to take pictures of Hans's medal collection. HK had dressed quickly while thinking about what that might mean.

An idea had come to him. He had carefully taken out his honorary doctorate medal and held up the bronze object. Pole Clement VI, surrounded by the words *Fiorentina Studiorum Universitas*.

Yes, this would serve his purpose perfectly.

At Rederhaugen, HK made his way quickly up the stairs until he came to what appeared to be a guest apartment on the second floor.

The intruder looked around forty, with short hair and several days' stubble flecked with grey, and was wearing a stained hoodie over a thin, narrow-shouldered frame.

He sat up and sent a few Slavic expletives in Hans's direction.

"What has he said?" HK asked.

"Very little. He doesn't have much English or German, but, like I said, he claims to be a Moldovan who worked as a builder here."

HK took stock of the situation. "I'd like to be alone with him."

Hans shrugged.

HK led the Moldovan into an adjoining room. He calmly made two cups of coffee and placed one of them in front of the intruder.

"Do you take sugar?"

No reaction.

"Name?"

The man said nothing.

"Whatever your name is," he said, with the forbearing look of a schoolmaster, "you and I are going to have a serious conversation."

"Andriy," the man said, adding in passable English: "My name is Andriy."

He asked how the man spelled it and was told.

"Sounds Ukrainian," HK said.

The man's eyes widened for a moment. "How do—?"

"You're going to listen very carefully, Andriy. I'm the kind of man who knows things. Shall we start from the beginning?"

"Lawyer," the man mumbled.

HK shook his head. "I'm going to keep you here until you tell me what I want to know."

Andriy looked at him, heaped more sugar in his coffee, and drank. "I . . . have lawyer . . . when speak with police."

The man looked down. HK knew he was conducting a simple cost-benefit analysis: what was most expedient? Keep quiet or yield to the pressure? For the most part, petty criminals were more afraid of the people they were working for in their own country than the Norwegian police.

"I know what's going through your head, Andriy," HK said after a long pause. "You've got a Norwegian detective sitting in front of you and soon he's going to put you in a holding cell for a couple of days. Then you'll probably be released and at the worst receive a short suspended sentence for breaking and entering." He observed the Moldovan. "If that's the case, then obviously it would be in your interest to keep your mouth shut about who sent you."

The man stared at HK with amazement.

"Your problem is that that isn't how this is going to work," HK continued. "I'm not going to let you go until you tell me what I want to know. No matter how scared you are of your employer, whoever that may be, I can assure you that my alternative is worse. Do you understand?"

The man clearly did not.

"I have a background in my country's *sekretnaya sluzhba* and at the moment I am working on a very serious case."

HK's knowledge of Russian was fairly rudimentary but the mention of *secret service* in that language caused the man's lifeless brown eyes to widen.

"Right now you're involved in a case that's a matter of national security," HK went on, "and that means the powers of *sekretnaya sluzhba* are broad. So I repeat: shall we take this from the beginning?"

"Police, I . . . talk . . . to police."

"Let's start somewhere else. You said you were a construction worker. Disorderly conditions in that business, aren't there? How did you end up here?"

For the first time, the Moldovan looked HK directly in the eyes. And began to talk. About coming to Norway to make some quick cash as an unskilled labourer. Working on line clearing in northern Norway.

"Line clearing?" HK asked.

"Removing trees and bushes so power lines can hang safely. Heavy work, we carried all the equipment to high ground where the work took place, we were a team, waded through snow in winter, no Norwegians want that kind of job."

After that, Andriy had gone to Oslo, where he found work with an Albanian painting and decorating company. One day when they were painting an office block, Andriy slipped on an icy scaffold and fell three metres to the ground, resulting in concussion and a back injury. Not being a member of the Norwegian national insurance scheme, he was required to pay the hospital bills, and since Andriy did not have the 30,000 Norwegian kroner his stay in hospital amounted to, the Albanians had paid.

But it was no free lunch. It meant, in practice, that Andriy had signed an agreement of indentured servitude, tying him to work indefinitely for the Albanians in order to pay off his debt. As often as he was able, Andriy went to the Salvation Army migration centre in Majorstuen, on the west side of the city, where he could get food and a shower, as well as chat and play cards with some compatriots.

Andriy paused. So far the tale had been easy to relate. It was a story about the bottom of the Norwegian labour market.

"A powerful story," HK said, leaning forward. "Was it at the Salvation Army you met the person who asked you to perform the break-in?"

The Moldovan did not reply but his hands were trembling slightly.

"I think we can arrive at a solution that satisfies the people you're working for, but in order for that to happen you have to tell me what you were trying to find."

"*Fotografiya*," Andriy said haltingly with Russian intonation. "He wanted me to take pictures, nothing else, I am no *prestupnik*, not spy."

"Who wanted you to take pictures?"

The Moldovan stared at him, clearly terrified. "Dangerous people," he whispered.

"What's dangerous," HK said calmly, "is getting mixed up in matters involving state security. You understand? What's his name?"

"He said I would get 10,000 kroner for the photographs.

We were to . . . meet . . . tomorrow . . . early at the Salvation Army . . . said if I did not, then Russia would come. They find me no matter what."

"Russia?"

"They find me no matter what," he mumbled.

It had started to get light outside.

"You're going to do exactly as I say," HK said, placing the honorary doctorate from the University of Florence discreetly among the other awards. "You'll meet them at the agreed time. But first you're going to take the pictures they asked you to take. Get out your camera."

16

A FUCKING FAMILY COUNSELLING OFFICE

Aker Brygge, Oslo

As Sasha followed the lawyers into the sunlit atrium of BAHR's offices on Tjuvholmen and was shown into a lift that took them to the fourth-floor reception, she thought of something she had read about Queen Victoria: the monarch had dressed in black from the time Prince Albert died until her own demise in 1901. That was forty years. How long would her own period of mourning last?

The sartorial expectations of mourners reached a peak in the nineteenth century. According to etiquette, the clothes for the first year, or, to be precise, the first year and a day, should be all black; after this time, dark shades of purple and grey, or lighter colours with black trimming, were deemed acceptable.

Two employees of BAHR, a man and a woman, came walking across the light parquet floor.

"Alexandra Falck? Welcome." They shook the hands of the three lawyers accompanying her.

"Welcome," the woman said. "We offer mediation to solve inheritance disputes before they end up in court."

Sasha looked down at the floor. What did they think this was, a fucking family counselling office?

The February light shone through a glass partition as in a

greenhouse, and they were shown from the oak-panelled reception desk to a sitting area with a sofa and chairs in Italian leather. Sasha walked to the glass wall, placed her palms against the window and looked out over the harbour.

Olav had drowned and the gates of hell had opened. Hans had acted swiftly over Christmas. After delivering his message about the will, and the writ, he had given the Oslo branch until just after New Year to pack their essentials and move out of Rederhaugen. The family had installed themselves in the old Falck apartment with its out-of-date wallpaper in Gimle terrasse. Feeling the eviction as keenly as Olav's death might seem heartless and distasteful. The death of a parent was one of life's great and unavoidable traumas. On a par with love's absolute best-case scenario: sitting grief-stricken and broken-hearted over the loss of a partner after fifty years together.

Now everything was fog, cotton wool and Seroquel, "the Rolls-Royce of sleeping pills", as a friend had put it. The days followed the same pattern. Images from Olav's funeral were fading for her, just as his face was slipping away. She could not remember the overcrowded benches, the priest speaking, people from the highest levels of society offering their condolences, the casket being lowered into the ground, nor the singing of the Sølvguttene Boys' Choir.

When she thought about it, grieving over Olav while mourning the loss of Rederhaugen was not unreasonable. A person's death weighed much more than the loss of a property, of course, but giving up Rederhaugen was like losing a vital organ. Hans's takeover was not like one life being lost, but several generations in one fell swoop. Besides, Sasha could not shake the feeling that Hans had caused her father's demise.

Since his death she had come to realise what a good friend Olav had been to her. It sounded strange, because had she not been the one who forced her father to step down as the head of SAGA by threatening to expose his abuse of power?

Friendship was a mixture of the intimate and the professional, of working towards a common goal. Many people had a different view, she knew that. Her old friends maintained a strict division between friends and colleagues. Friendship between friends was a closed bubble of secrets about abortions, infidelities, partners' impotence and similar information shared in confidence. The price of admission was total loyalty. That was the group's strength, but also the reason Sasha kept her distance from them, because there was something static and retrospective about her relationships with her friends. Nothing bound them together professionally.

What she had with Olav was both familial and professional. That was the reason the pain was so much greater.

Her world had fallen apart.

The room Sasha was led into resembled a courtroom, desks and chairs arranged in a horseshoe shape with a judge's seat in the centre. And that damned light plywood and those laminated surfaces to boot.

"This space is used for arbitration," said the male mediator, a chubby man in his fifties with curly grey hair.

Sasha looked at her three lawyers, who nodded. Their hourly rates were on a par with those of Premier League footballers or Tony Blair's fee as a speaker. Pondering that sort of thing felt inappropriate at such a time, but the fact was she was haemorrhaging money, leaking like the DS *Prinsesse Ragnhild* in 1940. If it went on like this, she would soon be broke.

On the side furthest from the door sat Hans, flanked by his lawyers, five of them in total. He looked over and their eyes met for a few seconds without either of them saying anything.

Soon after, Mads came bustling in, flushed and out of breath, wearing a tight-fitting ski suit, a gilet and a stretchy training beanie. He kissed her.

"Everyone here?" the chubby mediator asked with feigned cheerfulness, looking around the room. "The matter we'll be discussing today is the will of Vera Margrethe Lind."

Sasha knew the wording by heart: "The Falck family has always followed the principle of 'direct line' concerning the inheritance of family properties." She thought about the moment the sheet of paper caught fire: "Olav Falck is the son of the German soldier Hans Otto Brandt, missing and presumed dead following the DS *Prinsesse Ragnhild* shipping disaster. For this reason, neither Olav nor his descendants have any legitimate inheritance rights." Had she believed it would never be discovered? "As the oldest family survivor in direct line from Thor Falck, Hans Falck is therefore my rightful heir after my death."

"To be precise, we're going to discuss the validity of the will," the lawyer went on, "and to what extent this serves to determine ownership and control of the SAGA Group. First let's outline what we're talking about. SAGA is divided into a foundation and a commercial enterprise. The foundation is self-owned and as such is not subject to change with regard to any inheritance settlement." He surveyed the people assembled. "The commercial enterprise is a joint-stock company, owned in its entirety by the Falck family. At the annual meeting the shareholders choose a board, and the board is responsible for both the company and the foundation."

He began to list the shareholders in descending order: "Alexandra Falck, Sverre Falck, Andrea Falck – all with holdings of 220 shares each. Camilla Falck and Margot Falck have 110 shares each. Since both of them are minors, Alexandra Falck has power of attorney to manage their holdings until they are of legal age."

He surveyed his audience. "These shareholders constitute 880 shares overall, or 88 per cent. As for the remaining shareholders, they are, in descending order," the lawyer said, listing them slowly, "Mads Falck, 55 shares, Hans Falck, 55 shares, Christian Falck, 2 shares, Marte Falck, 2 shares, Erik Falck, 2 shares, Georg Falck, 2 shares, and Connie Knarvik, 2 shares. In total that comes to 1,000 shares."

There was little to say about the validity of the will on technical grounds. Nothing to indicate Vera as testator had been under any undue stress or that the witnesses had not met the necessary criteria.

Hans sat back with his arms folded, nodding as the lawyer spoke. Of course, Sasha thought bitterly, it's always the privileged who call for "calm" and "sense"; always the victims who are furious. Hans appeared older: his hollowed cheeks made his face look narrower.

Sasha's telephone vibrated. She took it out discreetly. A British number. She put it away again. Mads stroked her gently on the shoulder.

"I have some supporting material regarding the will," Hans said.

"Yes?" the mediator said.

"The only reason this came to my attention at all was due to a whistle-blower at Rederhaugen. In April of last year Alexandra Falck burned the original copy of the will we are discussing here."

Sasha felt like she had received a blow to the temple. How could they know that? Only two others had been there. Siri

Greve. It must have been her, opportunistic and cynical as she was.

She had not called Sasha since the transfer and neither had she dared show her face today. The bitterness welled up within her like the jealousy of a jilted lover. Siri Greve was Hans's right-hand woman now, as though nothing had happened.

Hans's lawyer added coldly: "Such an act is covered by paragraph 363 of the criminal code, which states that the unauthorised withholding or destruction of a document is punishable by up to two years in prison."

A new thought occurred to her: Johnny Berg had also been there. Maybe he was the one who had done this? It might have been both of them, all of them, the whole world was against her. She felt Mads's big hand on her back and an acute pain throughout her body. And the images in her head! Bredtveit women's prison. Romanian prostitutes sharing tragic confidences with her. Hurried conjugal visits with Mads in a room with stained sofas. Handwritten letters from the girls.

"However," the lawyer said, with poorly disguised indulgence, "due to my client Hans Falck not wishing to impose further stress on the family, he has no desire to report the matter so long as the proposals he has submitted, and any further submissions, are complied with."

It was blatant blackmail.

The mediator announced a break.

Outside, Sasha smoked three cigarettes in quick succession. Even Mads did not say anything. The British number flashed up on her display again. Probably a telemarketer. Sun lay over the fjord. At the tip of Tjuvholmen she threw up. Then they returned to the mediation.

The lead lawyer in Sasha's team began: "In accordance with the Inheritance Act paragraph 64, and I quote, 'a disposition is invalid if it involves use or destruction which clearly has no reasonable purpose', end quote."

"Your point being?" the mediator asked.

"A will which is clearly contrary to the ethical values of a society can be set aside," the lawyer continued, finally going on the offensive. "Particularly if it breaches fundamental human rights."

"It's difficult to see how 'fundamental human rights' have been infringed upon in the case of Vera Lind's will," Hans said sarcastically.

"Is it, though?" Sasha asked, meeting his eyes. "The idea underlying the will is *jus sanguinis* – or rights based on blood. Let's pursue that idea further. Olav, my father, may he rest in peace, was, according to Vera, not in direct line from Thor Falck. But Olav's birth certificate states that Thor is his father, as do the documents from the police in Jokkmokk in Sweden, dated April 14, 1944, the first time Vera was in contact with official registers after the birth. No matter what the truth may be about Olav's biological father, Thor Falck was his *legal* father."

The lawyers looked up with curiosity.

"Were we to take Vera literally in this case, then an adopted child in our family would have no right to inherit, because the adopted child would not necessarily be biologically in *direct line of descent* in the Falck family. But the law here is crystal clear. According to paragraph 24 of the act relating to adoption, the inheritance rights of the adoptive child follow the adopted parents, not the biological parents of whom they are direct lineal descendants. To assert anything else would be a breach of fundamental human rights."

Sasha had finally delivered a combination that put Hans and his team on the defensive. On the far side of the room they stirred uneasily and Hans conferred with his lawyers.

"Well?" the mediator said.

"Well," Hans said, his confidence and the colour in his face having returned, "I can assure her that my future transfer of SAGA will be based on the controlling interest, not on any particular interpretation of the will."

Good luck with that, Sasha thought. You have five per cent and I own almost forty-five. Taking Andrea and Sverre – although she had misgivings about him – into account, they controlled almost ninety per cent of the shares. Hans's declaration sounded so fanciful and foolish that there had to be something she was not seeing.

"Finally, the question of Rederhaugen," the mediator said, clearing his throat.

"The will is crystal clear in regard to that," Hans said. "Vera Lind owned the property. She left it to me. There will be no compromise there."

Sasha sank down in her seat. Maybe the women's prison was preferable, after all. Maybe she would end up saying it made her see the world in a new light, helped her take a hard look at the values she had previously held, be grateful for what she had. Everyone who survived cancer always said it was the best thing that had ever happened to them.

By the time the lawyers had moved on to outlining the property transfers, Sasha had had enough.

"Don't you realise that you've ruined everything, Hans?" she said.

Mads nudged her gently with his shoulder, and the lawyers on her side looked down, in discomfort, at the laminate tabletop.

"The will doesn't say anything about evicting us," she continued. "We could have found a way to solve this, together. Don't you understand what that place means to me? I went straight there from the hospital when I was born, at three days old, and, apart from my college years, have called it home ever since. I've lived there my entire life. I know every slab of stone along the paths, every hummock in the landscape, every creak in the parquet floor, all the rooms and all the tunnels, the cliffs and quays, houses and trees, lawns and groves, I know all of it so well it has become a part of me, an extension of myself, who I am, something I have tried to convey to Mads here, and not least pass on to my children, and you've taken all of this from me – from us."

She stopped talking as she felt the tears begin to well up. Hans sat pensively rubbing his chin.

Sasha stood up, gathered her things, put on her jacket and walked out without a backward glance. Mads came running after and tried to take hold of her but she brushed his hand aside. He pulled her close, she sobbed, his embrace was calm, powerful. They stood like that for a long time, at the tip of the peninsula, while the Nesodden ferry passed by below the grey-blue sky, and he did not say anything because he knew any words would be the wrong ones, that only silent proximity was the right thing now.

As they walked back her telephone rang and the display showed the British number once again. After staring at the screen for a few seconds she pressed accept.

"Alexandra Falck speaking?" a man said in English.

She confirmed it was.

"I'm calling from PD Assurance. Olav Falck was a client of our company for many years."

"I see," Sasha said. She had always taken for granted her father would have personal insurance.

"PDA specialises in life insurance for wealthy clients. Olav Falck had a policy with us. His papers contain a clause that all information will pass to you in the event of his death."

What was this?

"You'll shortly receive an email with instructions on how to log in and details of a simple security procedure. We'd appreciate it if you could provide us with the information requested so that payment can be made."

"Are you calling from Nigeria?" she muttered.

"I beg your pardon, madam? As you may be aware, life insurance payments are not part of a deceased person's estate. We would therefore like to inform you that the insurance will be paid in a lump sum very soon. The amount comes to 14,245,000 pounds sterling. Our deepest sympathies for your loss. Good day, Ms Falck."

17

A SIMPLE LAD FROM NYDALEN

Oslo city centre

The facade was richly decorated with wrought-iron balconies and arched and oriel windows. Johnny straightened the knot in his tie. The Norwegian Society, a gentleman's club, had to be the last place in Oslo where a tie was mandatory. He took the lift up to the second floor and stated his business at reception.

The first time HK had invited him here, Johnny had been a ravenous special forces soldier who, after a month of field rations in the Arctic, had consumed three servings of Biff à la Lindström for lunch. That was just after the old man had shown up at the Marine Hunter barracks to offer Johnny the opportunity of training within intelligence. Johnny's lack of refinement at the club had made the older man shake his head. That type of behaviour was all well and good for gung-ho types and other grunts, he told him. If, however, your job involved charming and manipulating people – especially foreigners – you had to be cultivated.

"Let me give you an example," he had said. "As a marine you had training in hand-to-hand combat. You know as well as I do you need to practise and repeat a method thousands of times for it to kick in automatically in a high-pressure situation."

Johnny had nodded.

"It's the same with etiquette," HK had continued. "Say what you like about the people here in this club. But notice how the manners, conversational eloquence and sense of decorum are invisible and assimilated."

"I'm a simple lad from Nydalen," Johnny had replied. "It would be like trying to teach a politician to dance tango."

Although it was almost fifteen years since that last meeting at the club, HK looked younger and in better shape now than when he had shown up in impeccable tweed back then.

He greeted him warmly, and quietly showed him into a salon dominated by paintings in the national romantic style, Persian carpets and miniature statues.

"I understand you've been working on the biography?" the old man said when they had sat down with a glass of white wine each.

Johnny recounted the details of his meeting with Connie and her portrait of the shipping nobility in Bergen during the first phase of the Cold War. HK nodded absent-mindedly, as though he had something else on his mind.

"A fascinating story, very interesting," he said. "I've also crossed paths with Hans in the last few days."

It had involved a burglar at Rederhaugen, looking for evidence of Hans's medal collection, he explained. Under improvised interrogation the man had put his cards on the table. In short, HK needed him tailed to find out who was pulling his strings. HK was not acquainted with many people who could blend in at the Salvation Army migration centre and he was wondering if Johnny might take on the job.

"You want me back in operational service?"

HK held his wine glass up to the light and examined the fingerprints on it.

"It's written in the stars that I'm going to fuck up and

you'll need to save me again. Even if Hans isn't taking my calls, there's a story there."

It was extremely bad timing for a mission right now. He had neglected to mention what Connie had promised, but her remark about his birth name had opened the lid on something that had been closed for many years.

"So you want to be an author? I seem to recall you were just a 'simple lad from Nydalen'. You know full well there's no such thing as a former intelligence agent. This isn't a discussion, not really. If you find the contact, I'll explain everything. But I can tell you now that this is a matter that may be very germane to Hans's biography."

The following day Johnny passed the crest with the motto "blood and fire". Inside the migration centre he glanced around. If the gentleman's club was *Upstairs*, this was definitely *Downstairs*. Most of the people sitting at the tables or standing in the coffee queue had to be Romanian Roma. Johnny was wearing an all-weather jacket with a dark hoodie underneath.

On active service his appearance had been a great advantage. He could blend in with a crowd across large parts of the Western world, from Brazil to Murmansk, without drawing attention to himself. He fetched a cup of black coffee from a machine, sat down at a table and dozed as though he had slept rough.

In his mind he had dubbed the man Sheriff Tiraspol, after the description HK had given him.

At one point an elegantly dressed woman, who he guessed was the manager, spoke to him in a language he presumed was Romanian. He held the coffee cup with both hands, as though to warm himself, and kept his eyes firmly on the tabletop. One advantage of the centre was that it was a low-threshold service for undocumented migrants, so he hoped to be able to sit in peace for a while before they began to pry.

Sheriff Tiraspol turned up just before noon.

Johnny had positioned himself so as to have a good view of any new arrivals before they saw him. The Moldovan did not appear to know any of the others sitting at the tables. He got a coffee and an open sandwich, glanced around anxiously and sat down. Johnny remained sitting back in his chair. Sheriff read a newspaper. From the tables around came cheerful-sounding chat in a language Johnny did not understand. The Moldovan's phone lay on the table in front of him.

After a few minutes a well-built, shaven-headed man with neck tattoos appeared in the doorway. He scanned the locale before making his way to the Moldovan's table.

The two men sat across from one another for a couple of minutes, each ostensibly minding their own business. Then the Moldovan began reading the newspaper again and the man with the neck tattoos picked the phone up off the table and walked out.

Johnny got to his feet as the door closed after the man. Outside it was cold and clear. He scanned the long blocks surrounding the broad expanse of Kirkeveien. As elsewhere in Oslo, the architecture here was undecided whether to belong to an elegant French boulevard or a concrete socialist provincial town. The mixture could conceivably be termed social democracy.

The man with the neck tattoos crossed the road and headed in the direction of the city centre, past Restaurant Mistral, before crossing the road and turning onto Neuberggata and continuing along it until, after a few hundred metres of a gentle upward slope, the road came to an end at a gravelled public square surrounded by bare birch trees.

Vestkanttorvet. Johnny had to smile. When he was growing up, this was the place where stolen goods were sold. If your silverware was pinched, you could usually buy it back from some shifty-looking character at the Saturday market on Vestkanttorvet a few weeks later.

It was winter and the market was closed. So far Johnny had seen no sign of counter-surveillance of any kind. The man with the neck tattoos continued across the empty square, now covered in a brownish mixture of gravel and snow, before coming to a stop and standing at the top of the steps at the square's eastern end. Johnny looked around. On the corner across the street from the steps, on the ground floor of a beautiful apartment building, there was a shop, an odd pet store he remembered having been into as a child.

He took a detour through the side streets so as not to be visible to anyone who might be watching and opened the door of the shop. The man remained standing at the top of the steps with a view over the square. He was no more than fifteen metres away. A strong whiff of animal droppings and a screeching cacophony from the birdcages hit Johnny as he stepped inside the premises. One wall was filled with aquariums, the other was entirely taken up by a cage the height of the ceiling. It was early and there were no customers.

"Afternoon," said the owner, a suntanned man in his fifties, eyeing the stranger sceptically – most of his customers were regulars. "Can I help you with anything?"

Johnny noticed the window behind the birdcage offered a view of the waiting man, who had lit a cigarette and was slapping himself to keep warm in the cold outside.

"My daughter is dreaming of a canary or a budgie for her

birthday. I don't know anything about birds, but do you think it's a good idea?"

"Can-a-ries. Niiice cage birds," the owner said with the sing-song intonation of someone from east Oslo, pointing at the cage while Johnny glanced at the man outside. No movement yet, but if he was standing there it must be because he was expecting someone soon? This assignment was routine; he missed the writing.

"The male is forever singing," the shop owner continued. "Easy to care for, kids love them."

He proceeded to describe the other types of birds, but Johnny had noticed movement outside and was finding it hard to conceal his impatience.

"Would it be alright if I filmed your birds, then I can ask my daughter which one she likes?"

The owner shrugged. Johnny took out his phone. The canary flapped its wings. He filmed, tapping the screen so the man with the neck tattoo was in focus. A cyclist wearing a beanie and a navy winter coat was approaching. The man with the neck tattoo raised his arm in greeting. They engaged in conversation. Johnny tried to zoom in but the picture grew fuzzy. The man on the bike was handed a phone and immediately disappeared.

Johnny waited a few minutes, thanked the proprietor, and left the shop.

18

TO HELL WITH SASHA'S COALITION

Oslo city centre

The covered courtyard between the old apartment buildings in the city centre was crowded. The scent of perfume and wine mingled with the smell of sweat and other body odours. It would be an exaggeration to say that Sverre was voluntarily attending the "alumni gathering" of Ingeborg's management network, but a good friend of hers who worked as a political adviser at the Foreign Office was present and was being touted as a possible ministerial adviser. That could clear the way for Ingeborg as her replacement. And was it not often the case, Sverre reflected, that men became an appendage to the social life of their women?

The leadership talents he had encountered so far were privileged and ambitious young people educated at elite institutions such as Oxbridge, the LSE and King's College in England, ENS or Sciences Po in France, and Ivy League universities in the USA. Their attendance at these places had often rendered them so tolerant that they no longer tolerated the intolerance of others.

They were children of the affluence that had marked the country since the millennium. Perhaps they knew deep down that it was drawing to a close, that the world was spinning ever more out of orbit – under attack from raging populists, fundamentalists and nationalists, all scaling the fortress walls of liberal society, and, perhaps more fundamentally, under attack by nature itself.

As for the SAGA conflict, he was lying low. He would let Sasha and Hans claw each other's eyes out.

Deep down he was conscious of the schadenfreude generated by Rederhaugen having come into the possession of the Bergenites. Not because he was glad on their behalf but because he associated the property with his own defeats and humiliations.

After Olav's death and the revelatory effect of falling in love, he had begun anew. No, it had started in Afghanistan. A clean sheet, *tabula rasa*. With the best parts of the old life intact.

Like all couples in love, Ingeborg and he had gazed into one another's eyes and vowed not to end up like everyone else. Like revolutionaries who promise their revolution will not lead to despotism.

The Crown Prince gave a short speech to the packed audience under the heading "The High North". The new leadership talents had already been on an information-gathering trip to the north. Because, as the Crown Prince said, the Arctic was the place where the challenges of our time were manifest, the place the ice was melting fastest and the major powers were increasing their military spending. Thus it was important, he stressed, to maintain a *low* level of tension in the *high* north, and looked at the audience contentedly after his apt wording.

Just then Andrea showed up, waved when she spotted him and squeezed her way through the crowd towards the corner.

"How did you get in?" Sverre asked. "Are you a leadership talent now?"

"Obviously." His little sister smiled. "I just don't make a big deal about it. Have you ever heard a really fit person brag about their step count?"

A leadership talent in early middle age turned to them as applause rang out. "Can you please keep it down?"

"Aren't you a little old to be a leadership *talent*?" Andrea asked. "You can be a talent until you're forty, after that you're a character."

The Crown Prince's speech was finished and as he was receiving a round of applause, Andrea poked Ingeborg in the shoulder and asked to "borrow Sverre for the evening. Family matters".

Ingeborg nodded with a smile and kissed him, saying: "Do what you want, darling. As long as you remember the trip to the cabin at the weekend."

They kissed goodbye. He and Andrea hurried out onto Tordenskiolds gate before turning onto Stortingsgata. A bitter February wind was blowing through the city streets.

"How's it going?" Andrea asked, lighting a cigarette as they walked between the parliament building and the masonic hall. "Like, really?"

Sverre did not answer. That things were better than he could ever remember was not something he wanted to say out loud, not even to his sister.

"Daddy," Andrea went on, as they began making their way through Kvadraturen, "how many times have I pictured the scenario where he meets a sudden end? The ice-bathing I had actually prepared myself for, it was so obvious that was when it might happen."

"He always forced me to bathe in cold water when I was small," Sverre said. "I've hated it ever since."

"An old, grandiose narcissist and mansplainer departs this life. So why does it hurt so damn much all the same, Sverre?"

"Father spoke about it once. How life was a lemming march towards the cliff, and when your parents die, you peer over the edge and realise you'll be the next to fall."

Andrea had booked a table at Engebret on Bankplassen, a traditional restaurant Sverre only frequented in a suit and tie at the annual Christmas meet-up with Victor Prydz and a few other members of the Oswald Spengler Society, as his old group of reactionary friends, united in their loathing of society's political and cultural decline, called themselves.

Engebret looked, according to Andrea, as a restaurant should, with the interior's warm reddish-yellow colour palette, the crimson carpeted floor, and thick white cotton tablecloths with crystal glasses and silver all neatly laid out.

They both ordered the Lofoten cod, with liver and egg butter, and a glass of Beaujolais.

"Have you spoken to Sasha recently?" Sverre asked.

Andrea shook her head. "Why do you ask?"

"Father's old holdings were the same as ours, right? Twenty-two per cent, which he managed to pass on to 'the new generation'. And that generation isn't us, sister, that's for sure. It's the generation after us."

"He talked about transferring his stock to 'the next generation' when we had dinner at Rederhaugen last summer."

"But I didn't understand the implications at the time," Sverre said, feeling how the thought upset him. "As Sasha has kids, and we don't, it gives her an enormous advantage in controlling SAGA." Sverre went on, gesturing. "If neither of us were to have children, then, hypothetically, Sasha controls forty-four per cent. That's the same as our holdings put together and she can use those to vote with at AGMs, until the children are of legal age."

Andrea stuck a floury potato into the egg butter and cod

slices. "When Sasha was head of SAGA last year, she was so busy that getting ten minutes alone with her felt like seeking a royal audience. Since Daddy died, she's been in the foetal position."

"On top of that," Sverre went on, "an insurance company in London got in touch with her. Regarding a payout for Olav. Of just under 150 million kroner."

"How do you know that?"

Sverre looked straight at his sister, who had finished her fish and was already looking at the dessert menu. "Because Sasha called me out of the blue the other day. She felt the sum should be divided between the three of us."

"You said no to fifty million in cash on my behalf?"

"That fucking patronising attitude of hers just made it worse. First you – and I – are passed over by Daddy while he's alive, Sasha being the apple of his eye. But it's hard not to notice how he's continuing to give us a raw deal *now he's dead*, don't you think? But you can probably get the money if you ask."

Andrea only picked at her layered apple dessert. "You're planning on turning it down?"

"I'm so sick of all the bullshit about *familia ante omnia*, the flat back four, how blood ties mean we must vote in a block at all costs."

His little sister nodded slowly.

"To hell with Sasha's coalition, that's what I say," Sverre continued. "She's always treated us like shit and this is the ultimate proof. You and I have more than forty-five per cent of the shares, as many as her. And we have something she doesn't. We have friends. If we join forces with Hans and the Bergenites, against Sasha, we'll only be a couple of per cent short of a controlling interest in SAGA."

Andrea raised her glass. "I like the idea. Cheers, brother."

19

OCULAR HERPES

Nydalen, Oslo

Snow cloaked the fortress walls of Akershus in white when HK picked up Johnny at Vippetangen.

"Good work the other day," he said in greeting, his hands on the wheel.

Johnny got into the passenger seat. Two HGVs with Polish number plates crawled in front of them up towards the intersection at Ryenkrysset.

"What's going on? Haven't you taken retirement?"

"I am retired," HK said, contemplatively. "My husband gave me an earful. Said he was disappointed in me. Over the promises I had broken. They can tell when there's a mission in the air."

"*They?*"

"Our partners, Johnny! We become different, preoccupied. Like we're being unfaithful."

Johnny made no reply. He could not remember his old boss ever making him privy to anything resembling secrets from his personal life. Times had obviously changed.

"Is that why you're confiding in me about your private life? It was years before I realised you were living with a man."

HK gestured behind. "That's Etterstad back there. It was the kind of place you got your arse kicked if you read books.

Growing up gay and liking books there in the sixties wasn't easy, Johnny. Spent years repressing the shame."

"Lady Writer" by Dire Straits was playing on the radio. Johnny nodded at what HK had said and turned up the volume. "People get older, alright. Start listening only to dad rock. View modern architecture as ocular herpes."

Newly constructed buildings rose all around as they drove through Økern. The grass of Skeid football club's old training pitch below Nordre Åsen had been swapped for an artificial surface. He did not like that either. They turned off the main road and a few minutes later the gate of the basement of the Police Security Service headquarters in Nydalen slid open.

"The police?" Johnny said, looking at the old man suspiciously. "What exactly did I take a picture of?"

"You'll get all the necessary information."

An athletic brunette with CrossFit biceps and the name Line Mørk displayed on her ID card welcomed them, led them into a lift, and showed them to a meeting room where an analyst was sitting.

"Glad you could make the time, Johnny," Mørk began. "We've been gathering intelligence against SAGA since last autumn. We've been wanting to talk to you about the Falck family for a while."

"Hold on a minute," Johnny said, his arms folded. "I was asked to take a few photos yesterday. A small, routine freelance assignment. Why would we talk?"

"This is purely a background conversation."

Although her grammar and pronunciation were quite proper, or perhaps because of that, Johnny picked up on an east Oslo sociolect.

"Isn't this what you lot call an *empowerment conversation*?" he said. In the army people used to laugh at police terminology. As though being summoned to the principal's office would convince terrorists to lay down their arms.

"You worked with Alexandra Falck last year. Why?"

Her voice was still silky smooth but Johnny had the feeling she suspected him of something.

"Revenge and nothing else," he said, holding her gaze. "I had good reason to believe that Olav Falck was responsible for the grave situation I was put in. When Hans Falck offered me the opportunity to pen his biography as a pretext, of course I said yes."

"You're still working on that book, I understand?"

He sighed and looked at HK, who nodded almost imperceptibly. Once more he related the story about how what had begun as a cover had turned into a real project.

"Before I say anything more, I'd like to know why you're asking me about this."

"You infiltrated the family in a professional manner," she said. "Naturally we've examined your activity, but I'd like to hear about it in your own words."

HK had been sitting quietly, observing the exchange. Finally, he leaned forward, placing his elbows on the table.

"You can speak freely, Line. Thanks to the late M. Magnus, Johnny is aware of the so-called Falck mole. Could you give him an overview of the situation?"

She nodded. "We investigated SAGA employees, researchers and all the others, in order to cross-reference them with Russian contacts."

HK leaned against the back of the sofa. "What did you find?"

"Well," she answered, "first off, let me say that Russian

intelligence often have a modus operandi. Their operatives are furnished with advanced cover stories they have spent decades cultivating, usually with real identities from a third country. A scientist from Mexico and a political scientist from Canada can both be Russian intelligence agents. We've taken a deep dive into everyone at SAGA without finding anyone fitting this profile. In addition to that, we've carried out several forensic examinations and covert searches. I can't discuss them in detail, but they did not yield anything new."

"And now you've looked at the video Johnny shot yesterday?"

A mugshot of a man with a round face below a dark mane of hair parted on one side, with close-set eyes and a heavy beard, appeared on the screen.

"This is a man operating under the alias Ruslan Boshirov. We think he's the one who received the photos of the medal collection at Rederhaugen."

"The Moldovan talked about Ruslan," HK said, scratching his beard. "At first I thought he was saying Russia, but he meant the name, and since you reported the find, Line, I've done some asking around."

This was HK's bailiwick; Line Mørk sat discreetly back in her chair.

"We've found something in common between Ruslan Boshirov and Colonel Zemlyakov on Svalbard," HK went on. "Both men were attached to Unit 29155."

HK cleared his throat.

"This group is largely a mystery to Western intelligence, but we do know it's composed of veterans from their wars. An elite unit working in sabotage and dirty work in the West. Poisoning, liquidating, you know. These are the people who get their hands dirty, so to speak."

HK had got to his feet and was wandering around the room.

"Yesterday I met the Norwegian Consul General of Murmansk. He had flown home with the sole purpose of alerting the authorities to a Russian they have staying in the consulate. A Lieutenant Medved. And which unit is he claiming to be a defector from?"

"Unit 29155," Johnny sighed.

"Correct."

Johnny knew only too well what was coming next. And sure enough.

"You're going to travel to Murmansk as soon as possible to interrogate him," HK said. "Best-case scenario is that this man is sitting on crucial information about the infiltrator at Rederhaugen."

Johnny looked at HK. "And life in retirement with your husband? What happened to all your promises?"

20

DO YOU LOVE HER?

Ringkollen, Oslomarka

The porch was covered in a metre of fresh snow. Ingeborg and Sverre spent a half-hour clearing a way to the front door. Out of breath and smiling, she beat the snow off the soles of her shoes and turned to him.

The cabin was situated in Ringkollen, in the forest an hour's drive from the capital, within skiing distance of Oslo for fit cross-country skiers.

They went inside. Everything about the cabin had an aura of post-war frugality. The simple, brown-stained facade with the small white window frames, the washbowls in the "bathroom", a cubbyhole adjacent to the narrow hallway, the woven rugs on the walls, the stove fireplace with the neatly stacked logs of birch behind, the bedrooms bare but for bunk beds, the gas stove, the empty buckets you fastened to a yoke to collect snow to melt. The walls were practically stained with social democracy.

Sverre lit the fire; it crackled and burned well. This was a place for winter.

Ingeborg pulled off her woollen jumper, turned her back to him and put on a plaid shirt.

While Ingeborg began chopping vegetables and slicing meat at the kitchen counter, Sverre took a wander around the room. Looking closer, he understood that the winter cabin did not belong to an ordinary family. Behind the crime novels for Easter reading, a few biographies and the obligatory memoirs of leaders from the golden age of social democracy were several rare books. He took out one by Vera Lind, signed "To my dear Wenche, a light in the darkness".

"Did they know each other?" Sverre asked.

Ingeborg looked at him with a little smile. "I think they were united by a common resentment. Ask Nana."

The photographs on the walls, similar at first glance to what was to be found in other Norwegian cabins – happy families in the summer and winter – revealed a host of brass even Rederhaugen could not match: German chancellors, NATO general secretaries, American secretaries of state. All relaxing in the modest surroundings of the cabin's porch.

Sverre stopped at one of the photos. It must have been taken on a warm summer's day, because Wenche, Britt, Ingeborg and some others he did not recognise were sitting out on the steps, squinting in the sun. Mads Falck was sitting with them.

A little fling, Ingeborg had joked the first time it came up. A *fling* hung up on the family wall along with James Baker, Madeleine Albright and Lech Walesa. Really? If it was true that Ingeborg brought fleeting dalliances up to the cabin, the huge significance Sverre had attached to his own invitation would be greatly reduced.

Ingeborg coarsely chopped carrots, celery and onion, put the vegetables in a saucepan along with minced meat and pancetta, and poured red wine over.

"Lasagne is the Labour Party of dishes," she said, concentrating, as she dropped a bay leaf into the saucepan. "This dish excludes no one, not ten-year-olds or pensioners. OK, so hipsters might turn their noses up at it. They eat green and vote for the Melon Party. Green on the outside, red within."

*

After a while they glimpsed the light of a headlamp through the windows and went outside. It had become colder. Their breath clouded the air. The trees stood silent and glazed. Britt Johnsen emerged from the darkness, wearing a red anorak with a hood, pulling a sledge with Wenche Johnsen-Heiberg on it.

"How I hate old age!" Wenche exclaimed. "Any wonder I can't find a gentleman at my age when I have to ride on a sledge to the cabin?"

Ingeborg hurried over to help the old woman up and get her inside.

Britt unclipped her skis and the belt she had been pulling with. She removed a Selbu mitten and held out her hand.

"There you are, Falck," she said. "Welcome."

Sverre shook her hand. "Ingeborg tells me you've been to our cabin at Ustaoset as well?"

"I have," Wenche said. "Though I wouldn't call it a cabin. It's an estate."

"Where's Dad?" Ingeborg asked.

"Lying flat in a dark room. His migraines are back. He needs rest."

Sverre recalled his father's words about the men in the Johnsen-Heiberg matriarchy. He offered them each a glass of red wine. While there was something theatrical and charming about old Wenche, Britt had the probing gaze of a schoolmistress, and Sverre's table setting did not escape it. With a silent shake of her head, she removed the red tablecloth, placing a narrow embroidered lace alternative over the rough wooden table.

Ingeborg's aromatic lasagne was taken from the oven and placed on the table; they helped themselves greedily.

With an unsteady hand, Wenche raised her glass of

reasonably priced Argentinian wine. "To Sverre Falck, he is most welcome!"

They all toasted. The women seemed famished and ate with great relish. Sverre made sure to take the pieces at the corners, where the layers of pasta and cheese had caramelised. They were the best.

"All suitors in the Johnsen family," Britt said in a serious voice, "have to perform something in the way of entertainment after dinner."

"What?" he gasped.

"You seem surprised."

"Er, no," he said.

Britt Johnsen smiled slyly at the end of the table. A disastrous one-star review was in the air. After what seemed like an eternity, when Sverre sat staring out into the room, he got to his feet. An acoustic guitar was hanging on the wall above a woven rug.

"I'm going to play a song," he began, the guitar on his lap, while he tuned it and looked nervously at the three others. The two older Johnsen women sat stony-faced.

"A song sounds . . . promising," Wenche said, and smiled.

"And the song," Sverre continued, his gaze fixed on Ingeborg, "is about wanting someone."

He began playing the chords of the Dylan classic, "I Want You".

Until then, his only other rendition of the song had been at an audition for the reality show *Idol*. Just as happened that time, the jury's initial icy condescension was replaced by mild surprise, followed by nods of approval.

He played the chorus twice and concluded by standing right in front of Ingeborg. "Honey, I want you."

She looked at him with an expression more amorous than

any Sverre had seen before. The older Johnsen women clapped loudly.

"You're going to sell out Oslo Spektrum," Britt said.

"Three Michelin stars, dear Sverre," Ingeborg declared, with a dreamy look. "Worth the trip here alone."

For dessert they had a simple chocolate cake and drank campstove coffee with a nip of spirits. Sverre felt on top of the world.

"Anyone want to smoke a cigarette with me?" Wenche asked.

"But you've quit," Britt said.

The old woman sighed. "Pah, at my age you enjoy life while you're still lucky enough to be able to. Sverre Falck?"

Wenche Johnsen was slightly unsteady on her feet and held on to Sverre's arm as they made their way through the cabin out to the covered veranda. They leaned on the railing and looked out. It was a starlit night. Her hand trembling slightly, Wenche gave him a cigarette. Sverre struck a match and cupped the flame.

"Do you love her?" she asked, inhaling deeply, then quelling a staccato cough as she exhaled.

"I've never felt this way before," he said in a solemn voice.

"Good," she said. "And dangerous. Love was what brought me down in the 1977 election. Old love."

The basic story was well known: as a young politician, Wenche had had a brief, passionate affair with the second secretary at the Soviet embassy, a man who rose through the ranks to become a KGB general.

"Did you love him?" Sverre asked.

"I was more *in* love than at any time before or since, that's true. But is that the same thing?"

As a candidate for prime minister, Wenche had held a big lead in the opinion polls prior to the 1977 election, before a series of articles about her relationship to a certain KGB general became public.

Nothing illegal was ever proven; the articles were a demonstration of ideological and sexual vilification. But the doubts about Wenche "Vesla" Johnsen's loyalty were sown. Her reputation was tarnished, the party's popularity dropped like a stone and she stepped down as leader in the wake of humiliating election results. The dream of being the first female head of state in the Western world was dead.

She was standing so close he could see how crystal clear her eyes were, and she whispered: "Ingeborg will go further than Britt, further than me, than all of us. You know, Sverre Falck, I've always suspected it was your father who ruined my career. How can I be sure you won't do the same to my darling Ingeborg?"

21

WE BELONG TO A DIFFERENT CIVILISATION FROM YOU

Murmansk, Russia

The state coat of arms, a lion rampant with axe in hand, decorated the entrance of the Norwegian Consulate in Murmansk, a white and bright green mansion one block from the main thoroughfare of Leninsky Prospekt.

Johnny pressed the buzzer. "I have an appointment with the consul general."

Initially, he had planned to travel on a diplomatic passport to avoid any problems that might arise in Russia. After reviewing the situation of the purported Russian defector with the consul, however, HK had decided that a visit under his real name would be counterproductive. It was guaranteed to draw attention from Russian intelligence: what was a man like Berg doing north of the polar circle? It might lead the Russians to the defector. So far, they had no indications that the Russians were aware of the GRU lieutenant holed up in the embassy.

So, Johnny had brushed the dust off an old identity. He was quickly granted a visa and passed through immigration in Murmansk without a problem.

Consul Haram came to the door to meet him personally and led him quickly through the reception wing and over to the private area of the residence. The diplomat was somewhere in his mid-fifties, with a bald pate and a circlet of short grey hair. He cast an anxious glance over his shoulder at Johnny as he patted a small husky pup that was running around the parquet floor in no particular direction.

"He's only four months old," he said, scratching the dog behind the ears, "but he'll bark if there are any uninvited guests, you can be sure of that."

"You think they'd dare enter? We are on Norwegian territory," Johnny said.

"Mr Whatever your name is—" Haram said in a superior tone.

"Johnny. Call me that."

"Johnny," the consul said, "if half of what my guest is saying is true, they wouldn't hesitate to burn the consulate to the ground."

"Have the premises been swept for bugs?" Johnny asked, looking around.

"Yes, there were some technicians from NSM here last week."

"Good. So, he's in the guest room?"

Haram led Johnny down a hall to a door, knocked gently on it and announced in Russian far better than Johnny's own that the visitor had arrived.

A racket, like someone rearranging furniture, came from behind the door; Medved had obviously barricaded himself behind a makeshift security set-up. After a little while, the door slowly opened a crack, a closely cropped head came into view, and a pale face poked out.

Johnny stepped inside and found himself in a utility room with sinks and appliances but without windows. In one corner lay a blue-striped mattress, neatly made. A forty-litre rucksack stood upright beside it. An orderly man, Johnny thought, a soldier.

Johnny offered Medved a cigarette, and the Russian almost pounced on the packet. "Consul ... will not ... let me smoke."

"I'll open the door to the hall," Johnny said.

The Russian offered him tea and dry biscuits while relating how he had wound up there. Being convinced the entrance to the consulate was closely watched, he had contacted Haram at a fitness centre. He had passed him a note saying he had more information about Zemlyakov's death on Svalbard and requested to be smuggled into the consulate.

So far everything he had said had checked out. Johnny attempted to get a read on the young man in front of him. He had a large, slightly crooked nose and deep-set eyes. Spoke surprisingly passable English. No more than twenty-five years old.

"We need to talk about Zemlyakov," Johnny said. "He had a rank far above your own. How is it you knew one another?"

Medved's gaze turned inward, as though he were remembering something. "I was assistant to Vasily Denisovich," he said, using the patronymic. "He was one of the best officers in the Russian army. A man of integrity. We came from the same place."

It turned out both had grown up in the gulag city of Norilsk on the Steppes, deep in Siberia.

"You know," Medved said, with the beginnings of a smile, "Vasily used to say that if you've experienced fifty-six below zero in Norilsk, then you are well able to handle military manoeuvres in the winter too."

Medved had been stationed with a regiment on the Kola Peninsula during his military service, and he knew the border with Norway well. "The fact is, it's not as hard to get across as you'd think. A sentry once told me the easiest place to sneak over was just north of Nikel. By Nordmo gård on the Norwegian side. Do you know it?"

Johnny shook his head.

Medved told him he had eventually applied to the 45th Guards Spetsnaz Brigade after two years studying political science at the university in Novosibirsk. His first experience of combat was against IS terrorists in the Caucasus and he also participated in the Russian annexation of Crimea, an operation the authorities still denied. His contribution and academic CV had caught the eye of someone at the headquarters of Unit 29155 in Moscow, and Medved was given the position of Zemlyakov's aide-de-camp.

Johnny sat listening to the amiable young man's story. It saddened him.

"In another life I'm sure you and I could have been friends," he said. "Like you, I have military experience, like you I've fought IS groups. But tell me something, and this is outside my remit."

The Russian nodded respectfully.

"Why," Johnny continued, "would an affable, intelligent young man like you enlist in such a unit, fighting for a world where all that matters is the survival of the fittest, where democratic rule is seen as weakness, and your country has the right to expand its borders by force?"

His little speech came as a surprise, to both men.

The Russian considered the question for a while before answering.

"There is one thing you must understand, my friend. I belong to a different civilisation from you. I was born in a superpower and grew up in a decade when my country was falling apart and there was hardship all around. I've seen Russia be built up again. That makes me proud."

Johnny stared at him for a few moments, unsure what to make of this statement. "Yet here you are," he said at length. "You've sought asylum in Norway and offered to disclose military secrets. What makes a Russian patriot do that?"

"When we were at our base on Franz Josef Land, east of Svalbard, the place where Zemlyakov was poisoned, the colonel told me he was unhappy. Unhappy that both the Kremlin and our armed forces were being taken over by mafia crooks, charlatans and dangerous extremists." Medved dropped his head. "They were the ones who poisoned him. People who didn't like that he told the truth."

"Who are they?" Johnny asked.

Medved launched into a description of a far-reaching conspiracy involving Duma politicians, the Russian Geographical Society and people from the secret deep-sea executive, who, according to him, were engaged in a bitter power struggle with Zemlyakov and other "true patriots" from Unit 29155.

"Upon realising he'd been poisoned, the colonel only had one choice. In Russia he was in effect dead already. He had to flee to Norway, and he managed to stow away on a freighter to Barentsburg, and from there to Longyearbyen on a stolen snowmobile. I think you know the rest of the story better than me."

"Colonel Zemlyakov spoke of a Norwegian mole," Johnny said.

The Russian looked at him without blinking. "He did."

Johnny stood up and paced the small utility room. "If you can't give me the name, I'm not sure how much I can do for you, my friend."

Medved shook his head slowly. "You know I can't do that before I'm in Norway."

"How can I be sure you know the identity of the mole?"

The Russian smiled wryly. "As Zemlyakov's aide-de-camp I was privy to many things." He drew a circle on a sheet of paper. "The Falck family, you know of them?"

"You could say that."

"Originally it was the SAGA Foundation that was of interest to Colonel Zemlyakov," the Russian said. "Influence operations against soft targets of that type in the West – media, foundations, think tanks – have yielded considerable success for us in recent years. When we understood that SAGA also had a strong operational arm, this did not diminish our interest."

For a moment Johnny thought the Russian was about to lay out details of his own exploits under the SAGA umbrella. How could he know all this? Because the Russians kept abreast of developments on the Norwegian side. It was well known.

"Where was the operational arm of SAGA active?"

The Russian shook his head with a smile. Instead of answering the question he said: "The colonel was very interested in Svalbard. He was looking for a way in. Eventually we found it. A member of the Falck family owns a large property in the Advent Valley near Longyearbyen."

First M. Magnus had brought it up, then Connie Knarvik. And now a Russian defector sitting in a room a little larger than a broom cupboard was talking about the Advent Valley.

Medved folded his arms. "Do you think it likely, from the information I've given, that I know the name of the individual in question?"

"I believe you," Johnny replied.

"Our people are meeting the SAGA contact in Kirkenes. Get me safely across the border and you'll have the mole before you return south."

*

In the darkness outside it had begun to snow, a light flurry. The temperature had fallen to below minus twenty. Heading in the direction of the high-rise Johnny presumed was the city's prestige hotel, he walked through Central Park and came out onto Leninsky Prospekt. The main street was decorated with lights and bordered with trees on one side. The sound of a trolley bus cut through the silence of the wintery streets.

He could discern the glow from the enormous illuminated Alyosha statue on a hill above the city: the soldier, defender, who guarded the city and country from danger. Johnny rolled a cigarette. He had the distinct impression that Medved had been telling the truth. How could they get him across the border? Could he do it by himself? He found a Georgian restaurant and ate alone.

When he returned to the consulate, Haram immediately ushered him into a bug-proof room.

"I've spoken to Oslo," he said. "We in the Foreign Office have responsibility for Medved. He's our concern."

"You know as well as I do that this is an intelligence matter. Give me an embassy car and I'll exfiltrate him tonight."

"That's out of the question," Haram said. "You don't even have diplomatic immunity. We've put together a plan for this. There was a message for you, by the way, from your superiors. You're to travel to Kirkenes in the morning. Unfortunately, for obvious reasons, we can't offer you lodgings tonight."

22

NORWAY'S ACTING MINISTER FOR FOREIGN AFFAIRS

Kirkenes, northern Norway

Hans was standing at the bow as *Falck III* headed up the fjord towards Kirkenes.

The temperature was minus 29°C. A dim glow was visible on the pale blue horizon, above the frozen hills and arms of the fjord, bare and barren like all nature north of the Arctic Circle.

The cold made Hans's nose hairs freeze, but it filled him with memories, good memories, just as charred lamb transported him back to the Middle East, and the familiar scent of an old lover's perfume carried him back to the past.

He felt his chest swell when he thought about what he had rehearsed to say to win over the people in Kirkenes. If Hans was addicted to something, it was certainly not to any substance. Nor was it to war zones or sex, as many would have believed. Hans was addicted to applause and admiring glances. His mind and body did not function without a regular dose of approbation.

They had sailed from Tromsø the evening before last, after Hans had met with representatives from the Polar Institute to discuss the upcoming Svalbard expedition and had given a rare interview, his first as chair of the board. Hans had scoffed at the ignorance and arrogance of "southerners" on matters relating to northern Norway. SAGA, under his leadership, had plans that would have a ripple effect across the entire region.

The weather along the coast of Finnmark had been better than feared, and when they began their approach to Kirkenes, *Falck III* was met by another boat with a local entourage.

The mayor was around sixty and was a short-haired, alert comrade-in-arms of Hans from the party, involved in almost every radical left-wing endeavour in the north. She had become somewhat of a media darling in recent years for her pronouncements about Kirkenes being set to become "Norway's Singapore" when the polar ice melted and the Northwest Passage became navigable for cargo to Asia. She did not mince her words.

Hans could never remember her name, only that the Oslo newspapers relished referring to her as "Norway's acting minister for foreign affairs".

Hans's fifty days of "wearing his thinking cap" were up. He had spent the journey north honing the SAGA vision for Kirkenes that would be presented during the Barents Conference.

That vision would strengthen his argument when the power struggle flared up before the upcoming general meeting. It had dawned on Hans that he had a real chance of winning a majority. Andrea and Sverre Falck, the latter with his partner, had come aboard in Tromsø. Although they had yet to talk specifically about voting, their presence was a very good sign. With the two of them on his side, as well as the smaller holdings of his own three children, they would have a majority. The smallest possible, but a majority, nonetheless.

The buildings in Kirkenes came into view between the hills. Rectangular blocks of simple timber houses, erected after the German bombing, lay as though in a deep freeze, hidden under metres of snow.

The gangway was lowered and they went ashore.

"Sergei is going to give a speech at Gratishaugen," the mayor said, looking at her watch.

"Sergei?"

"What do southerners call him? 'Foreign Minister Lavrov'? I'm going to say a few words before him, so we don't have all the time in the world. Shall we get going?"

The architecture was just as Hans remembered. No one could accuse Kirkenes of being a picturesque fishing village. The silo of the mechanical workshop cast a long shadow across the quay they were walking along. The low sun rose over the Arctic landscape, colouring it in shades of blue. The Scandic hotel was situated a few hundred metres to the east. A lecture on Sami culture was taking place within.

"If you only knew how much good political work gets shelved in northern Norway because of Sami sites of cultural heritage," the mayor sighed.

"You'd like a return to the policy of Norwegianisation?"

"Give over, Hans," she said. "I support Sami rights, of course I do. My husband comes from a Sea Sami background, my grandchildren wear traditional Sami dress on special occasions. But I'm also a diehard socialist. I want workplaces! Business development! My fear is that northern Norway, and Kirkenes in particular, will become one big folk museum of lavvus and reindeer hides, devoid of people. That would put Norwegian security in danger."

Just then a motorcade of dark cars pulled up in front of the entrance to the port. They hurried into the vehicles.

The green room of the auditorium was abuzz with excited chit-chat. Hans and Mayor Sibblund conversed with the

Norwegian VIPs while they looked over their shoulders for the Russians. They had discussed the VIPs in private beforehand. The foreign minister "thought Norway was the fifty-first state of the USA" and the county governor was "a reindeer thief and an alkie".

Then Foreign Minister Lavrov appeared, strutting across the floor, smiling and looking relaxed in a dark suit. He flirted with the mayor in the Russian manner, kissing her on both cheeks and complimenting her on the mint-green scarf she wore swept over one shoulder.

"It's a pleasure to be back in Kirkenes," he said.

"The pleasure is all mine, Sergei," she said, taking hold of his hirsute hands.

Lavrov promptly began to lament the sanctions the West had imposed on his country in the wake of the annexation of Crimea, or "the reunification", as he termed it.

"You'll have to speak to the foreign minister," she said, and nodded in the direction of the delegation from the Foreign Office.

A few seconds of silence hung between them. Then a broad smile spread across Lavrov's face. "I thought you were Norway's acting foreign minister?"

Hans was introduced to Lavrov. It took the Russian a moment to make the connection. "Ah, Mr Falck," he said. "The Russian Federation owes you a great debt of gratitude."

Hans bowed slightly.

"As you know," Lavrov continued suavely; he had a focused gaze and real presence, "we Russians are well acquainted with Norwegian humanitarian figures. Yes, just think of Nansen. Norwegian adventurers like Thor Heyerdahl have made a strong impression on the Russian people. I regard you as a man in that tradition, and of the same stature, Dr Falck."

Lavrov left to take the stage and deliver a brief official greeting in which he summed up the cooperation with Norway in the northern areas, which in Russia's opinion was characterised by respect and reliability, and where the "peace-loving, spirit of fraternity" stood in sharp contrast to the hostility and Russophobic attitudes spreading across more southerly latitudes.

Then it was Hans's turn.

"I was born in Bergen, a city I still love," he said. "But every time I come to Kirkenes it's as though I come *home*. I'm a Norwegian, my home is the coast, my home is the route the Hurtigruten ferry takes along that coast."

Malicious tongues might have objected that there were many places – Kurdistan, Lebanon, Lofoten, Bergen, just not Oslo! – that could make a sweet talker like Hans proclaim that he felt at home.

"We are all a product of family, of upbringing and of the experiences we have in life," he continued. "In the Oslo bubble they talk about multicultural Norway as though it began with the immigration there in the 1970s. As people in East-Finnmark, you – and *we* – are part of a civilisation comprising the indigenous peoples, the Samis and Kvens, and Norwegians, Russians and Finns, who lived together in a multicultural society long before the southerners in Oslo ever heard of such a thing!"

Some quiet sniggering but that was grist to the mill for Hans.

"How many people down there in Oslo, criticising us for maintaining relations with our Russian friends," he said, his voice louder now, "know about the Red Army liberating Kirkenes in 1944 and withdrawing trouble-free from northern Norway afterwards? How many of them have heard of

Dagny Sibblund, Norway's first female paratrooper, who parachuted into Kirkenes as a Soviet partisan?"

The people sitting in the front rows were nodding now.

"The world looks different up here. Kirkenes lies further east than Istanbul! What in Oslo is condemned as fraternisation and acquiescence is our way of living together!"

The tone had been set.

"But hold on, you're probably thinking, here comes Hans Falck's big speech about northern Norway as *a region with great potential.*"

He uttered this last phrase in an impeccable parody of the Oslo accent, to the amusement of the audience.

"I've heard the politicians' speeches, and they always say the same thing. What has Oslo done for Kirkenes? They've closed factories, put people out of work, always viewed our relationship with our sister nation across the border with suspicion. They've even tried to enlist people to spy, to the detriment of Norwegians trying do business on the Russian side."

He raised a finger. "We at SAGA ask what we can do for each other, specifically. And the answer is simple: Kirkenes is situated in the most exciting place in the country. You share a border with a superpower. You have an ice-free harbour, you are western Europe's most easterly harbour in an Arctic where the melting ice will open the northern sea route, cutting journey time to the enormous markets in East Asia by a third."

He paused. These were facts known to the people of Kirkenes and failure to follow them with something more concrete would render his words hot air.

"SAGA isn't here to spout platitudes. We're here to announce we have an already regulated area for a port and transport hub. Just a few kilometres up the fjord here, at

Slambanken, which Olav Falck had the foresight to buy for a song in 1993 when he was at the helm of SAGA. We're going to build a large harbour in partnership with other major players. But for that to happen, we're completely dependent on the politicians, the Norwegian Coastal Administration and the Norwegian Public Roads Administration coming to an agreement. And that needs to happen ASAP. We're tired of self-righteous, pedantic bureaucrats throwing spanners in the works and hampering the development of northern Norway."

A rhetorical pause followed.

"The knock-on effects of a new port in Kirkenes cannot be overestimated, not only for how many jobs its construction will create – carpenters, plumbers, engineers, the list is endless – but most of all for the potential impact this port could have over the next hundred years for Kirkenes, for Norway as an actor in the Arctic and, yes, for the whole world!"

Hans ended by saying quietly: "If this is approved by spring, I guarantee on behalf of SAGA that we'll break ground before the winter sets in."

He smiled at the audience. "My friends from Kirkenes, do we have a deal?"

"Yes!" shouted the mayor from the first row.

Thunderous applause.

"Who's going to celebrate with us tonight?"

More cheers. The only drug that really did it for him. This was his vice.

He had won them over.

23

BROTHERHOOD BETWEEN PEOPLES

Kirkenes, northern Norway

A huge unidentified flying object appeared in the Arctic night sky. Rectangular, illuminated and as large as a Zeppelin, it flew slowly in over the square in Kirkenes, where hundreds of locals and visitors had crowded in the freezing cold.

The temperature had dropped even further in the last few hours but the sight was so overwhelming that Ingeborg and Sverre forgot it was minus 29°C. He put his arm around her down jacket and they stared up at the sky.

"It looks like a fucking UFO," he whispered.

"Authoritarian regimes put on a good drone show, you have to give them that," Ingeborg replied.

The serried rows of lights began to ascend in sync, like a Hollywood spaceship. The next moment they formed a reverse pyramid, the tip so low that the spectators could almost reach up and touch it. Then they reshaped into a red star with a hammer and sickle in the centre. The entire spectacle was like a cross between the Northern Lights and soundless fireworks, lighting up the sky in bright colours.

A gasp arose from the spectators, angry shouts could be heard, and some people shook their mittened fists. Even for the Barents Spektakel culture festival, allowing Soviet symbols to light up the sky over Norwegian territory was a step too far.

But the next moment the red star disappeared. In its place the lights formed . . . what? The golden lion of the Norwegian coat of arms!

Cheers rang out in the square. The drones then formed words in Cyrillic:

ДРУЖБА МЕЖДУ НАРОДАМИ

"What does that mean?" Sverre asked.

"Wait and see," Ingeborg said, winking.

The letters changed:

FRIENDSHIP BETWEEN PEOPLES

Cheering erupted in earnest, and the drones formed the shape of a bird, a white dove, which gained height over the square, spreading its wings before disappearing over the rooftops, over the church, the war monument and the high-rise building that was home to one of the largest police stations in the country. Then it was gone.

Ingeborg and Sverre began moving towards a pedestrianised street off the square. When Hans had asked Sverre if he could – as an Afghanistan veteran – make a small appeal on veterans' affairs in front of the liberation monument, he had been quick to imagine it would be the talk of the town. But Lavrov and the other A-listers were of course long gone. His audience had for the most part consisted of surviving partisans, stooped and hard of hearing, who laid wreaths before shuffling off.

"The BBC wrote about Kirkenes being full of spies," Sverre said. "I see mostly pensioners with Zimmer frames here."

"That display reminded me of the last time I dropped acid," Ingeborg whispered.

"You're going to be prime minister," he laughed. "You can't be doing that sort of thing."

"A reactionary argument." She smiled. "Approval of those

drugs by the Institute of Public Health is just around the corner."

She looked at Sverre, her complexion flushed with the cold. "Why don't we take some psilocybin soon? You and I, just the two of us, go for a walk in the woods?"

Sverre let out a nervous laugh. "I'm a loyal subject of King Alcohol."

"I'm serious," she said. "It was good for me, and it would be good for you too."

"What does that mean?"

She put a bulky, puffa-clad arm around him.

"Sverre," she said, in a maternal, condescending way, "we all have our own stuff. Neuroses, traumas, things that afflict us. I have mine. But admit it, Sverre. You're in your late thirties, and before me you were a relationship virgin."

He was about to counter automatically, but felt the words cut like a knife. Ingeborg must have noticed the pain her comment caused because she promptly apologised. But the damage was done.

24

THIEVES AND DETECTIVES DON'T WORK WELL TOGETHER

Kirkenes, northern Norway

Travelling from Murmansk to Kirkenes was like moving from the land of the giants in Brobdingnag to Lilliput.

Johnny drove past the frozen lakes and the city came into view. The landscapes were the same: ice-free fjords and sloping, snow-covered hills with low Arctic forest. The architecture too was similar, in that it was rooted in the reconstruction after the devastation of the war, and the people were much the same.

Yet Kirkenes was a small town with only a few thousand inhabitants; Murmansk would be the second largest city in the country had it been in Norway. The trip there had flown by. He turned the car into the square, a place dominated by an enormous mound of snow about the size of the Great Pyramid of Giza, parked and hurried the two blocks to the low timber building that housed the Norwegian Border Commission. He had received word to get there as fast as he could.

Two border markers stood in the snow: the Norwegian, in yellow, with the state coat of arms engraved at the top, and that of the Russian Federation in red and green. Who was it that had told him the story about the Norwegian who, angered by the Soviet invasion of Afghanistan, had sawn through the

Russian one and carried it to a pub in downtown Kirkenes? It must have been HK.

Inside the building he said a brief hello to the border commissioner, an old staff officer Johnny remembered from Afghanistan, as well as to a man he did not know from the Police Security Service, the PST, before being led to a room behind the official offices of the commission.

Einar Grotle, old master diver and former colleague of Johnny, was sitting at one end of a table. His red beard was even longer than last time, and his tree-trunk arms were folded.

"Grotle!" Johnny smiled. "Hell, it's good to see you."

"Welcome to the White Room," HK said.

"The White Room?"

Line Mørk was also there. "We consider this to be the most surveillance-secure location in the town," she said.

"In Afghanistan and Iraq," Johnny said, looking at her, "our American colleagues often wondered why they faced so many roadside IEDs and we didn't. I told them they might want to consider not driving around the villages in convoys of armoured Humvees like elephants in a china shop, and start using rusty old cars, like the locals."

Line gave him a questioning look. "Your point being?"

"Sometimes the most vulnerable place is the safest, and vice versa."

"Brief status update," HK said, from force of habit in an officer's tone of voice. "This is an important week here in the town. Firstly, because the Barents Conference, at which politicians and other decision makers discuss the northern areas, is taking place today and tomorrow. Foreign Minister Lavrov has given a speech, as has Hans Falck."

He took a sip of his coffee. "Secondly, because it's the

Barents Spektakel festival of culture, where Norwegian and Russian artists come together. This means a lot of people are in town over the next few days. I don't know if any of you have been following the debate in the media, but there's currently some controversy about the extent to which the festival is serving to justify Russian imperialism, to paraphrase the former police chief of Sør-Varanger, now governor, Robert Eliassen."

He turned to Johnny. "You've been in Murmansk and met Medved. Can you give us a summary of what he said and what his situation is?"

Johnny recounted the story he had been told, about the relationship between young Medved and Colonel Zemlyakov.

"The Russian said plans are in place for a meeting with the SAGA informer. And that he knows who it is but isn't willing to say until he's on the Norwegian side of the border."

"Sounds familiar," HK said tartly. "A short update on communication with the public prosecutor."

Line began. "We placed Ruslan Boshirov under surveillance and he's also subject to communications interception, granted by the public prosecutor in accordance with chapter 17, paragraph 111 of the criminal code. We're also monitoring the second secretary of the embassy of the Russian Federation, who has diplomatic immunity. Both arrived in Kirkenes by plane from Oslo yesterday. The second secretary is staying at the Russian general consulate, while Boshirov is a guest at Scandic Hotel."

"What about surveillance of people on the Norwegian side?" Johnny asked. "I presume the public prosecutor knows this concerns a potential rendezvous?"

"The public prosecutor rejected that request," Line said. "Needless to say, that will change if and when we find out the name of the Norwegian mole. But for the moment no dice."

Of course they've no problems monitoring the Russians, Johnny thought. And it stood to reason they did not grant communications interception and surveillance of members of the Falck family. There was no probable cause, not in the legal sense.

"I don't think these steps are worth much," Johnny said. "The Russians take it for granted they're under surveillance anyway."

Line Mørk looked at him. "What do you think should be done?"

"First of all, get Medved to safety. That's the most important thing. But there's a question I haven't heard you or anyone else from PST ask about this case so far."

He lowered his voice. "Why? Why choose someone to betray SAGA and Norway? All I hear is talk about obtaining more court orders and further communication interception. But that's not how we're going to solve this case."

No one said anything for a while, before Grotle broke the silence. "Don't mind Johnny. He's gone from a promising talent to a grumpy old-timer without anything in between."

Line's tense face and twitching jaw muscles disappeared, and she broke into a sudden smile. "I think Johnny has a point."

"But you have to remember why the atmosphere is a little strained when we meet you lot, Line," Johnny said. "You're the ones who catch the crooks. We *are* the thieves. Your job is crime prevention, ours is stealing secrets. Thieves and detectives don't always work well together, do they?"

"I'll keep a close eye on Consul Haram," HK said. "We'll put together a team with responsibility for getting Medved to a safe location for interrogation as soon as he's across the border."

25

STRATEGIC DEEP DEFENCE

Gimle terrasse, Oslo

Sasha and the family sat down at the dinner table in the apartment in Gimle terrasse while the cod was simmering and the potatoes were on the boil. Mads plated up, adding carrots and parsley butter.

"Mummy, I miss living there!" Camilla said. "I don't want to stay here. I *hate* this apartment. Look at the walls, they're *dirty*. Look at the bathroom, it's *old*. The ring of the doorbell makes it sound like the people living here are a hundred years old. Are we, like, poor now?"

Her little sister Margot was an inquisitive, bookish eight-year-old, whereas Camilla, two years her senior, was a marked materialist, who loved make-up, shopping and luxury holidays.

Sasha hid her face in her hands.

"Camilla," Mads said sternly, placing his hand on her thin forearm. She tried to pull free but he held on. "I understand that you don't like this. It's been a big change for all of us. Sometimes life is not so easy."

"Whatever," Camilla mumbled.

"But I'll tell you something," he went on, his tone serious. "I grew up in a home a lot of people would have called poor. A 'persistent low-income household' is the term they use. It was just my mum and me. She worked double shifts, not to afford expensive holidays, but because she wanted me to dress like the other boys. So that we would have a proper home. We ate porridge for dinner because we couldn't afford anything else. If someone had called a huge apartment in the nicest part of Oslo, with a bathroom that needed doing up, 'poverty', then I would have given them a slap."

"What? Are you threatening me?" his elder daughter cried out dramatically.

"Camilla," Sasha said, "you know just as well as us that it's not a threat. It's a story that we could benefit from hearing."

But the ten-year-old ran from the room.

Mads said nothing.

"Camilla has begun . . . menstruating," Margot said, with a shrug.

Her parents looked at each other in bewilderment.

"Camilla's got her period!" Sasha gasped, panicked by the thought that her little daughter could, in theory, become pregnant. "Jesus, Jesus." She shook her head furiously. "She's just turned ten!"

"The average age girls first begin to menstruate has fallen by a couple of years since you were young, Mum," Margot said. "How much that's down to diet or to other factors is debatable."

"Professor Margot Falck," her mother sighed, "have you any other observations to make about public health or the world situation?"

"You two are always talking about Svalbard. I want to go there too!"

"We can probably do that at some stage," Sasha said absently.

"Svalbard is a special place," Mads said, looking at his daughter earnestly. "If the world is a mine, Svalbard is the canary. If something is wrong in Svalbard, it should serve as a wake-up call. When the ice up there starts melting faster, it's a signal as to what will happen if we don't take climate change more seriously down here. If powerful countries grow hostile and start an arms race there, that conflict will come here sooner or later."

Long before Mads had turned up as a suitor at Rederhaugen, after his studies at business school and his stint as a youth politician, he had begun his working life as a shipbroker, mostly in northern Norway. He had done the Russian course in the military, and conditions in the Arctic in the early 2000s, after the Russians had come through the chaos of the 1990s, had been akin to the Klondike. In the north there was talk of oil extraction, gas, cooperation across national borders. Mads had quickly made a name for himself. A background in politics lent itself to an understanding of geopolitics, and his education in business proved useful.

Margot was silent, her eyes downcast.

"You don't need to frighten her needlessly," Sasha said as their daughter darted into the bedroom.

"She can handle the truth."

Sasha poured wine into his glass. "You're right, I suppose."

No sounds came from the girls' room. They had no doubt disappeared into the virtual world. Sasha had tried to enforce a strict schedule for screen time, but, like so much else, she had let it slide and now the iPad had become a babysitter. A calm settled over the apartment.

"Cheers," Mads said, softly. "You're looking much better."

They spoke in low voices, as though in a church.

She drank her wine slowly. "Last week we passed the fortieth day since Daddy died. The flood in the Bible lasted forty days. Moses came down from Mount Sinai after forty days.

It's when the dead finally leave us, I've heard. Their soul stops wandering and departs this earth."

"And you believe that?"

She shrugged. "No. But imagine if it's true all the same, Mads?"

He rolled his impious eyes.

"Remember the evening after the *Falck III* reception when Daddy called in at the house? He went on about how the sea had been nothing but a curse on the family. How we should have dry land under our feet. I accused him of being superstitious."

She broke off.

"Your father wasn't a shipowner by nature," Mads replied. "Nor was he a fan of the Arctic. The reasons for that are extremely rational."

"He said there was more to the history of the rescue boats in the Arctic," Sasha said. "How things that had been buried for decades could come to the surface because of political tensions. He implied it was somehow connected to Connie's property on Svalbard."

She put her head in her hands. "Why didn't I ask him more about it?"

"It's always that way," Mads said, stroking her back. "But Connie Knarvik also affords a possibility, for us."

Sasha liked the rational politician-like calm her husband was displaying. Where nothing was personal, where it was possible to turn matters to your advantage, so long as you remained *solution oriented*.

"What about her?"

"The extraordinary general meeting," Mads said. "It's to be held next month?"

"That's right." Sasha nodded.

"We need to mount a strategic deep defence of your SAGA interests," Mads said. "The first line is of course to activate the old coalition with your siblings. If that works, then the problem is solved and Hans is out as chairperson. Have you spoken to Andrea and Sverre about it?"

She shook her head. "I offered to share Daddy's insurance payout with them. But they haven't responded. Not even with an offer of fifty million each in their laps."

"Hmm," Mads said. "If the worst-case scenario comes to pass and your siblings back Hans, I've calculated that his side would have the slimmest possible majority."

"Shit," Sasha said and noticed a creeping sense of panic. "Then we're screwed."

"No," Mads said calmly. "Because that's where Connie Knarvik comes in. You're going to use the money from Olav's life insurance to buy the Advent Valley from Connie in exchange for her support. You'll be getting the best property in the Arctic into the bargain. In such a scenario she'll have fifty-two shares, or five per cent, and hold the balance of power."

"How do you know Connie will support me?" Sasha took a deep breath.

Mads smiled with satisfaction. "I don't know that. But I do know who she won't support under any circumstances. Her loathing of Hans is hardly a family secret, is it?"

26

THE BORDER

Russian border, northern Norway

"Medved is en route over Kola with the consul," HK said.

He had brought Johnny and Einar Grotle down to the seafront. The temperature had fallen further. In the darkness the stooping cranes and winches were barely discernible.

HK slapped himself to keep warm and was constantly checking his phone.

"Why are they travelling so late?" Grotle asked.

"Technicalities, according to the consul, many arrangements to ensure a safe trip."

"I don't like it," Johnny muttered.

Up the hill from the water's edge was a four-storey building in yellow brick, oversized given the sparse population of the municipality. It housed the police.

"What will we do while the police are busy doing their thing?" Johnny asked, lighting up a cigarette.

"You two attend the reception on *Falck III* as planned," HK said. "I'll stay in the white room to monitor the consul's journey. There's nothing we can do on the Russian side anyway. When something happens, you'll have exactly two minutes to show up. OK?"

"What happens when Medved crosses the border?" Johnny asked. "Don't tell me the police get him first? The evening news and human rights lawyers will get wind of it in no time."

HK turned to him. "Don't worry. I've made a deal with the police. As soon as he crosses the border, we take over. Transport him to a secure location, lock the door and stay there until we get the name we need. So long as the police are the ones making the arrest, they're happy."

His stiff, elderly silhouette disappeared into the darkness.

Johnny and Grotle made their way up the gangplank to *Falck III*, the words "Druzhba Narodov – Brotherhood between Peoples" on a banner above them. Marte Falck must have persuaded Hans to agree to the festival using the vessel as a party venue.

The mess had been transformed into a Russian bar from the Cold War, where the guests had to change money to roubles to buy beer and vodka.

The bar bore the name "Boris Gleb", and the walls were draped in diaphanous chiffon, illuminated by soft red light. A bar counter had been placed at the end of the room, and Soviet rock from the 1980s blared from the loudspeakers.

"Impressive," Grotle said, raising his eyebrows.

Photographs in a display case explained the story of the real Boris Gleb, a legendary watering hole on the border that, for a period of fifty-nine days in 1965, was a crack in the Iron Curtain, where Norwegian sailors drank with Russians, before the Norwegian authorities decided enough was enough and closed it down. Naturally, fear of espionage was cited as the reason.

There were whispers in the corners that curator Marte Falck was drinking with her father and Andrea Falck, along with Ingeborg and Sverre.

"Berg!" a voice yelled from behind. "Good to see you."

Johnny turned to find himself looking at the face of salmon-farming tycoon Ralph Rafaelsen. He offered a subdued greeting and thanked Rafaelsen for the loan of the northerner's Exosuit, which he had used to dive down to the wreck of the *Prinsesse Ragnhild* the year before.

He thought Rafaelsen was an unpleasant character.

"What are you doing here?" Johnny yawned. "Joint venture with the Russians?"

"Ha, that's a good one," Ralph said loudly. "Hans Falck is the one who lured me here. Investment in SAGA may be on the cards."

Johnny scanned the overfilled rooms to see if he could spot any undercover police.

Still nothing from HK.

The people around him were becoming drunk. Ralph whispered for Johnny to follow him. They climbed some steep stairs to the bridge. The boat still smelled new up here. The voices and the music down below grew faint.

"These are the captain's quarters," Ralph said. Hans was sitting in the cramped cabin, with his family, some locals from Kirkenes and a delegation of Russians. A chef carried in canapés of crab and reindeer, along with liquid refreshments.

The mayor was present, of course. "I spoke to my contact in the public roads authority today. He gave me verbal endorsement for construction of the docks at Slambanken," she said.

Hans raised his arms in celebration.

After the food and some chat, one of the Russians stood up and introduced himself as the deputy foreign minister. Speaking in Norwegian, because, as he informed everyone, his father had been posted at the embassy in Oslo in the 1950s, he said: "Before we continue with the party, I'd like to make an announcement."

Johnny looked around. The police had supposedly placed a ring of steel around the town to observe any contact between the Russians and the Falck mole, yet here they all sat, fraternising almost openly in a back room aboard *Falck III*.

"We would like to thank you for inviting us, Herr Hans. On behalf of the government of my country, I have the honour and pleasure of announcing that you are to receive the award of the Russian Order of Saint George for your outstanding and unique humanitarian efforts over several decades, efforts that culminated in a heroic rescue on one of our trawlers before Christmas, a mission which nearly cost you your life."

Hans nodded, looking down at the deck in embarrassment.

"We will confirm later the time and place of the actual ceremony. Congratulations, you're a true friend of Russia and of the Russian people."

Johnny left the gathereing and followed a narrow passageway aft. What was this boat hiding? Finding a doorway which led to a steep ladder, he descended. He found himself on what must be the lowermost deck. It was dark. He shone a light at the bulkheads. A few cabins lay further along, their doors ajar. He opened the doors and looked inside. The cabins were new and empty. At the end of the corridor, directly ahead, was another door. Johnny pointed the light at the sign. No unauthorised access. He tried the handle. Locked, of course.

His phone rang.

"Get over here now," HK said. "We've got a problem."

HK was pacing the white room when Johnny entered. A map of the Kola Peninsula marked with the consul's route covered one wall.

"The last message we received about the exfiltration of Medved from Murmansk was from here," he said, tapping on the map with a pointer. "About thirty kilometres west of Murmansk. The road continues west until you reach the Pasvik River to the north of Nikel, the largest town here. From there it's about twenty-five kilometres north to the border station."

The two others, as well as a liaison from the Foreign Office, nodded.

"The consul promised an update on the situation when he was twenty-five kilometres from the frontier."

"How long is it since his last update?"

"Half an hour?" HK seemed worried. "Too long, in any case."

"There may be a simple explanation," Grotle said. "Engine trouble. Routine check. Something along those lines. Almost all unforeseen occurrences have explanations like that."

"I don't like it," HK said. "Ring the consul."

"He specifically asked us not to contact him en route," the diplomat said.

"Call on the secure line."

"We think the Russians have methods—"

"Just call," the old man commanded.

The Foreign Office man put the phone on speaker and placed it on the table in front of the others. It was picked up on the third ring. They could tell immediately from Haram's voice that something was wrong.

"Consul Haram, what's going on?" HK said, his voice hard.

"I'm . . . driving . . . towards the border," the consul said quietly. "Should be there in ten minutes."

"And the passenger?"

There was a pause; the only sound was that of the engine in the background. The consul was speaking hands-free.

"He thought it best if . . . we parted ways."

"Consul Haram, could you please express yourself in plain language?" HK yelled so loudly it surprised everyone around him.

"He asked me to stop. Said he was nervous, wanted a smoke. Then he just ran into the forest. He also nabbed my personal phone, the Russian one."

"Consul Haram, let's go through this again," HK said, trying to breathe calmly. "Can you tell us exactly where this happened?"

The consul explained as best he could where the incident had occurred.

HK ended the call without saying goodbye.

"Shit," Grotle said.

"I know where's he's headed," Johnny said.

The others looked at him.

"I don't know why I didn't think of it before. He was the one who told me. Said he knew of a weak point on the Russian side of the border just south of a place called Nordmo gård. Where the river is at its narrowest. It's only a hundred metres from Russia."

"Nordmo gård," HK said. "How long would it take us to get there?"

HK sped up the hill from Kirkenes. Johnny was in the passenger seat, while Grotle sat in the rear.

"Have you tried calling the consul's Norwegian phone?"

"Three times, went straight to voicemail, and I didn't leave a message. It's connected via Bluetooth in the car."

At the roundabout Johnny's phone rang. He pressed accept and put the call on speaker. "Hello?"

They heard only a humming. "Medved here," a voice whispered.

"Where are you?" Johnny asked.

No answer.

Johnny strove to speak clearly. "We're on our way to Nordmo gård, I repeat: Nordmo gård. Are you on the Russian or Norwegian side?"

HK followed the signs directing them to the border.

"The security zone is about one hundred metres ahead," Medved whispered into the phone. "A checkpoint with a tower and searchlights. Manned by soldiers. I can see them now."

"Is it possible to get past?"

"I think so. The next stage is sparse forest, then the first fence, then a zone with motion sensors, after that another fence. Then the river."

"The border runs through the centre of the river," Johnny said. "Listen carefully. You need to get across the middle of the river. The guards on the Russian side won't fire shots into NATO territory. We'll meet you on the Norwegian side. We'll be there in twenty minutes."

In the darkness outside, illuminated only by the snow, he made out the mining quarries. They looked like dark pyramids.

"There's something I didn't tell you," Medved whispered. "Colonel Zemlyakov wrote a document with accusations. Allegations of corruption by his enemies. And the name of the Norwegian infiltrator. Hurry."

"Good luck."

Dial tone.

After nineteen minutes the car turned into Nordmo gård. HK skidded the Land Cruiser to a halt.

"No, keep driving," Johnny shouted, "you can get closer to the river."

They continued along a snowy cart road and after a couple of hundred metres the tyres began losing their grip, eventually spinning without moving the car at all.

Grotle pointed down the road. "Let's walk!"

They were on a small spit of land and began running through a low forest of pine.

Exhausted, they came to a clearing of sorts in the darkness.

The first thing they saw was the snow-covered river. Beyond it, perhaps two hundred metres further, lay Russia.

Then they saw a figure run out onto the ice.

Medved was trying to zigzag. A line of Russian soldiers appeared behind him in the clearing.

Medved ran onto the river ice.

Johnny ran towards him from the opposite direction.

"Run!" he screamed. "One hundred metres and you're in Norway!"

Then Johnny heard two simultaneous shots.

Medved fell forward.

At the same instant Johnny became aware of a searchlight upon him and a voice over a loudspeaker.

"This is the border guard. Ten more metres and you will cross illegally into the Russian Federation. Halt, or you will be fired upon."

As Johnny came to a stop, he could see Medved lying face down. He was dead. Blood was seeping out into the snow around the body. Johnny looked around. A row of soldiers formed a half-circle around him on their side of the river.

He raised his hands in the air and slowly took a step back.

PART III
SHAREHOLDERS' MEETING

27

THE PORTRAIT OF OLAV FALCK

Rederhaugen, Oslo

As was often the case, the end of February brought with it a warm föhn wind and temperatures rising into double digits. Streams trickled, and grey, snow-pressed grass appeared on park slopes, patches flattened like hair that's been covered by a woollen hat. The inhabitants of the city began to behave like people from more southern climes, inhaling the unusually early blossom while strolling on gritted footpaths and drinking beer on balconies.

Sasha was no different, although her watchful nature meant she knew better. What was it Olav used to say? "Fifty per cent of all snow that falls in the forest falls after the first of March."

It was the type of cocksure and half-true generalisation of his she used to find exasperating.

Now she missed those utterances intensely. She had never thought so much about her father as after he died. He came to her every night and every day, his imposing figure casting a shadow over her field of vision. Daddy rowing bare-chested on the fjord on a summer day, Daddy striding slowly on skis over the mountain plateaus in winter, Daddy ringing to vent his frustration or chat about the new cabinet ministers being a bunch of brainless broilers, and that a long life had taught him that Norwegian winter was unpredictable.

And sure enough: March arrived with a half-metre of snow and minus temperatures. Winter swathed the city anew in its blanket. Smells disappeared, like food in a freezer, and sounds were muted, as though the snow came with earmuffs. One might almost suspect the involvement of Olav Falck from the hereafter.

Winter's lack of sensory stimuli should have been good news for Sasha, who was trying to wean herself off sleeping pills. But the scrape of the snowploughs against the kerb outside broke the monotone hum of the city night and woke her. She sat up in the bed, then got up.

Outside, it was still snowing, almost imperceptibly. On the veranda she lit a cigarette and stood looking out. In the line of sight above the bay of Frognerkilen, she could make out King Oscar's summer palace, with its bright circular keep which resembled the rose tower at Rederhaugen. A few hundred metres to the left lay the pointed pyramid housing the ship *Fram* and the history of Nansen, Amundsen and the other Norwegian explorers of the Arctic.

She had tried to get in touch with Sverre and Andrea. Neither of them had taken her call, but a couple of days later her little sister had texted: "I can manage without handouts from the money Daddy left to you alone. Do what you want with it. I'll be fine. Please don't contact me again."

It could only mean that the siblings' old voting block at the shareholders' meeting was no longer in place.

She heard Mads approach before he came and stood beside her. Her husband had been concerned about her dependency on sleeping pills throughout the winter. Easy for him to say, having experienced the catastrophe at one remove and being able to sleep as soon as his head hit the pillow.

"Go to bed," she told him. Usually that was his line.

"I wake up when you're not there. What's wrong, Sasha?"

"Ever since we lost the property," she said, "I've avoided looking in the direction of Rederhaugen, never mind going out there. It hurts too much."

He nodded.

She looked out over the city. "I think that stage is over. After grief comes action."

Mads squinted at the horizon. "Or acceptance?"

"What do you mean?"

"That you accept the new reality."

She spun around. Stared at him. "That'll never happen. Accepting how you feel doesn't mean you accept the outcome."

"Fair enough." He nodded.

"Will you come with me if I go there, Mads?"

"To Rederhaugen? Of course."

"I can't stand the thought of Hans making himself at home. Going there would be trauma exposure. The shareholders' meeting is happening soon. I want to arrive prepared. Want to have taken the place back beforehand. If you understand me."

"I couldn't agree more. But let's get some sleep now, Sasha."

"I mean we go out there now."

She flicked her cigarette, leaving a trail of sparks on the rooftops of Skarpsno.

Her husband shifted his weight as the objections ran through his mind: it's three in the morning. The girls will be alone. What on earth are we going to do there?

"Alright," he said, straightening up. "You and me."

They got dressed and slipped out, closing the front door without a sound. Neither of them spoke as they drove the Tesla through the quiet, snow-filled streets of the city and on towards Rederhaugen. Mads parked the car on a side road. She felt a mounting excitement as they neared the entrance. The falcon engraved on the wrought-iron gate, its dark wings spread in the light from the snow, as though preparing for flight. Mads tried the door beside the gate: locked.

"I handed over all the keys," he sighed faintly.

"I'm sure Hans has changed the locks," Sasha whispered. "Come on."

She took him by the hand, and they followed the fence to the left of the gate for a hundred metres or so, before coming to a snow-covered tangle of vegetation behind Knatten, the property's highest point, where there was a hole in the fence only Rederhaugen's cognoscenti knew about.

"It's big enough," she said, "but stay low so you don't rip your jacket."

"Sounds like you're speaking from experience."

"Listen to the expert," she said, and crept through.

Up on Knatten, they sat on a bench. All the buildings at Rederhaugen were in darkness. From where they were sitting, a well-trodden path wound its way down through the little forest and on to the main house past the crossroads. They set off, staying low and moving carefully, her leading the way. It was like being ten years old again, like the time she, Sverre and Marte played hide-and-seek in the snowdrifts at night outside the Hunting Lodge at Ustaoset. Marte had counted to one hundred while Sasha hid in a snow cave. Her big brother had placed a hard-packed block of snow in front of the entrance so she could not get out. Sasha had never been more frightened than when she was sitting in the darkness of that cave, her shouts absorbed by the walls of snow, like someone trapped in an avalanche, her worst nightmare.

Her brother had a dark side. That was the only time Sasha saw Olav lay hands on Sverre. Her father had been so beside himself with anger that he had pushed Sverre to the ground and pressed his face into the snow.

Sasha was by the side door when she heard it. Quiet, quick steps, lighter than those of a human.

She froze. Guard dogs rarely kill, she thought. Before she had any more time to think, an animal leaped on her and she fell to the ground.

The dog whined and licked her face while pinning her down with lean, strong forelegs.

"Jazz," she said fondly, rubbing her father's old dog behind his pointy black ears. She felt relief and the uncomplicated love only a dog could elicit. "You haven't forgotten me, Jazz. I haven't forgotten you either."

"I have to admit *I* had, with everything that's happened," Mads said.

"Jazz is a guard dog," Sasha said, letting him lick her face. "He doesn't belong in an apartment. Neither do we."

Mads helped her up and they stood by the wall.

"He's probably changed the locks," she whispered, "but I doubt he's changed the code for the alarm."

"And if he has?" Mads asked, dubiously.

"Then it will be my pleasure to be arrested by the police for visiting my childhood home."

As always, one window on the floor where the library was located was open. With Mads's help she pulled herself up. Stepping inside, she heard the low monotone beeping of the alarm. It sounded familiar. She tapped in the code. Held her breath. *System unset*, the voice said. Mads climbed in through the window. They tiptoed further inside while holding hands. The library atrium opened around them as they made their way to the centre, surrounded by a circular bookshelf. There was something unfamiliar in all the recognisable surroundings.

"Is it strange to be back?" Mads whispered, squeezing her hand tighter.

"Nice, more than anything," she replied, in a dreamy tone.

"What is it you want to do in here exactly?" he asked.

Sasha thought about Johnny Berg. She might have been able to find something if he was here; he had broken into Olav's safe.

"Come on," she said.

They slipped out of the library, went up the winding staircase at the base of the rose tower to the sitting rooms on the first floor, and followed the hallway decorated with dark oil paintings of Theodor Falck, Theodor Jr and Thor Falck. She gave a start when she saw Olav's authoritative face looking down at her. Her own portrait had been removed.

She put her hand over her mouth. She remained standing like that for a long time, as though frozen, with Mads's hand on the small of her back, until she tore herself away and walked over to a corner cabinet in gilded wood, where she took out an old bottle of Saint-Émilion. She opened it, poured two glasses, lit the candles in the candlesticks with her lighter, and gestured for Mads to sit down opposite her at the long dining table.

She raised her glass, first to Mads, then to the portrait of her father.

"Ah, now I get it," Mads said.

Sasha's reply was slow in coming. "I needed to come here. Win back Rederhaugen mentally. Recover what's *ours*."

She looked at him.

Mads drank from the glass, carefully as though it were

communion wine. "It's three weeks until the shareholders' meeting. Tomorrow we'll get to work."

"I have a meeting with Connie."

He sent her an encouraging look. "A face-to-face meeting is always promising."

"I agree," Sasha said.

"This is going to work out, you'll see. We'll win back control of SAGA," Mads said. "Then we can turn our attention to the fight for Rederhaugen."

Sasha looked down at the table, her gaze introspective. "Thank you, Mads," she said at length.

He straightened up. "What do you mean?"

She leaned across the table, almost extinguishing the candles. "For helping me," she said softly.

Familia ante omnia remained Sasha's only way to orientate herself in the world. Now it was Mads, the two girls and she herself who were the flat back four. Now it was the nuclear family against the other relations. Them against the rest of the world.

28

BRING IT BACK HOME

Rederhaugen, Oslo

For Sverre, the ski meet at Holmenkollen involved lying on the sofa with takeaway food watching the mass-start fifty-kilometre race on TV. He had no interest in cross-country skiing, but Ingeborg enjoyed watching it. She liked winter sports, knew the names of the competitors and was familiar with their strengths and weaknesses.

"Come on," he teased, still hungover after a serious session with Prydz and some old friends. "Worldwide, gay rugby is a bigger sport than cross-country skiing."

His girlfriend ignored his provocations. "Do you know what I like? It's the tactics at play, same as in the big bike races."

"Tactics . . ." he said, as a group of skiers raced up a slope for the final time. "The 'world cup' in cross-country skiing is basically the Norwegian national championship. No one cares other than Norwegians and a few doped-up Russians. The 'tactics' involve taking asthma medication and using the Oil Fund to wax your skis."

"You're not paying attention," Ingeborg went on. "Did you not see those oddballs from Central Europe and Canada break away from the main group on the first round? They looked like they would make it, but the group swallowed their lead." She pointed. "Now there's a new breakaway. They've already opened a big gap. And they're going to hold out right to the end. Believe me. That's what tactics and strategy are all about."

"Getting into breakaways?"

"If you take part in every attempt to get away from the rest of the field, you'll tire yourself out. It's about making the right choice. Picking the one that can hold out all the way."

Sverre sat in pensive silence as the lead group stayed the course, passed the finish line first and proved Ingeborg correct.

"And you?" he said. "Have you joined a breakaway?"

"I'm sitting comfortably in the main group." She smiled, her dimples showing. "Waiting for the right one. What about you?"

Yes, what about Sverre?

The following Monday he parked the car at the crossroads down from the main house and walked up to the headquarters of SAGA with his little sister.

"What do you think Sasha would say if she knew where we were?" Andrea said, glancing over her shoulder.

"She should have thought of that before."

He opened the heavy door with SAGA engraved on it and stated their business to the new receptionist.

Siri Greve came to the lobby to meet them, ushering them quickly down the hallway towards the office wing. She seemed stressed, Sverre thought; she was giving instructions to the new head of security, a provincial type, of limited intellect, an ex-policeman whose name Sverre could not recall, while she simultaneously conducted a conversation over the phone.

Greve ended the call and sighed. "Journalists, you know how it is . . . Sverre, Andrea, good to see you both."

He noticed how her smile touched the corners of her mouth but not her eyes as she looked in his direction. That pleased Sverre; a person trying to ingratiate themselves with you meant you were *someone*. Someone important. Because Andrea was only here by virtue of her holdings. Ingeborg had said as much and she was right. She was always right. He ran through in his head one more time the bullet points she had given him.

They continued through familiar rooms and into Greve's office. Marte and Hans were already there and greeted him in turn.

Being in the same room as Marte used to give him palpitations. They had had a secret relationship for many years. An affair entirely on her terms, meaning she got in touch when she was between men and left him out in the cold as soon as a new lover came on the scene. When her marriage to Ivan, a Russian conceptual artist, had closed the door for good, Sverre had been heartbroken.

But that was before Ingeborg turned up. Having her as a girlfriend was like a superpower, making him feel twice as strong.

"Good to see you again," Marte said. "I think the last time was in Kirkenes."

"My daughter is bringing her experience as a curator to her work at the archive here. She was recently interviewed by Italian *Vogue*," Hans said.

"Has Norwegian public life become a little too parochial for you?" Andrea smiled, giving her dark hair a toss.

"Great you both could come," Hans broke in. "Siri has been teaching me how to swim the crawl this winter. Fantastic feeling. I'm sure she could give the two of you some tips too. You'd be swimming across the fjord before you knew it.

Siri had a time of well under a minute in the 100-metre freestyle. Do either of you swim, by the way?"

Sverre shrugged. "We can stay afloat."

"Sorry, an inappropriate introduction, no doubt, given the tragic circumstances."

Greve leaned her toned, ex-competitive-swimmer-gone-ashtanga-in-her-forties body against the desk and sipped a coffee while staring at a wall dominated by the portraits of her father and her grandfather, August Greve.

"You're early," she said, turning to look at Sverre and Andrea. "It's three weeks until the shareholders' meeting."

Sverre had wondered if Siri would step down when Hans took over Rederhaugen and became chair of the board, but he soon realised that Greve's loyalty was first and foremost to the Falck coat of arms, not to individuals in the family.

"Text from Georg Falck," she said, after a glance at her ever-present phone. "As a shareholder he is curious as to whether pheasant will be served, 'as was the case during the extraordinary general meeting in 1976'."

"He's as smart as a handful of earth, that man," Andrea said. "Daddy called these old shareholders' meetings family gatherings. Old aunts sipping tea and eating prawn sandwiches while nattering about how far to the left society has drifted, and which of the heirs have yet to start a family."

She looked at Greve, then at Hans and finally at her brother.

"Father bought the small shareholders out in the nineties," Sverre said. "Georg is the last of them, along with Connie."

"You can reply that the menu will be exclusively vegan this year, in the interests of animal welfare and carbon emissions." Andrea smiled. "Georg is slightly to the right of Paul von Hindenburg in his political views, so he's sure to like that."

"Let's get down to business," Hans said. "I have the distinct impression that you both want to play a role in the future of SAGA. For my part, putting together a robust coalition of major stakeholders is crucial. I simply wish to know what you want in return for supporting my candidacy as chairperson."

He fell quiet. Andrea and Sverre looked at each other.

"I want to take over the archive," Andrea said.

Hans scratched his temple and glanced at his daughter.

"As I said, that position has been filled," he said. "Marte has already begun."

"I have an education in museology, am a professional curator and have a wealth of experience with exhibitions of various kinds, most recently the festival in Kirkenes," Marte said.

"That may well be," Andrea replied, "but you own 0.3 per cent of SAGA shares. I own 22 per cent."

Marte looked at her. "Finish your undergraduate degree first."

Andrea stood up. "Alright, Marte. I'll get back to my bachelor's at Blindern. But don't feel too bad if you're not voted in as chairperson, Hans."

Hans got to his feet and waved a dismissive hand.

"Wait, wait," he said, and motioned for Andrea to sit back down. "We can work this out."

In fact, he explained diplomatically, Andrea taking over the running of the SAGA archive was something that could be accommodated, but not until she had finished her degree. Most of the employees had a university education so it would not go down well otherwise. Marte could be promoted to vice-president of SAGA. Something she immediately accepted.

In the old days Sverre would probably have quoted what his father said about having *Vice-President* on a business card being the cynical leader's way of persuading a narcissist to refrain from demanding a pay raise. But Sverre knew better now.

Wait for the right breakaway.

"As for you, Sverre, I've been impressed by your performance in the last few months. I want you to take on M. Magnus's position, as divisional director for the northern areas."

Sverre thought for a moment. Sipped from the glass of water.

"Who are you planning on choosing as CEO if you're voted in at the general meeting?" he asked.

Hans hesitated before answering. "That hasn't been decided yet. But in my view the position in the northern areas is much more exciting. More operative. A good fit for you, Sverre. You know the military and understand geopolitics. You're a Falck."

Was now the time to challenge Hans directly? No. He leaned back in his chair. "Are there several candidates for chair of the board?"

Siri Greve and Hans exchanged glances. They obviously had bad news to relate.

"Well," Hans said, clearing his throat. "Siri?"

Greve picked up a sheet of paper and, in a toneless voice, read: "In accordance with paragraph 8 of the SAGA Foundation charter, which states that a candidate wishing to be considered for chairperson of the board must inform voters beforehand, I confirm I will stand as a candidate for the aforementioned post. Best regards, Alexandra Falck."

Had his sister risen from the dead?

Hans poured himself some coffee from a silver pot engraved

with the Falck emblem. Steam rose from the cup as he blew on it.

"It's to the point, anyway," Hans said finally. "Andrea, Sverre, she's your sister. Initial thoughts?"

Sverre remained sitting with his arms folded. Maybe his sister's statement of intent was not the problem it appeared at first. Maybe it was an opening.

"The voting blocks are similar in size," he said. "Andrea, myself and you in the Bergen branch can achieve a majority of a single share at the general meeting. So far as I understand, we have 50.1 per cent. Sasha has 49.5 per cent. Or 49.9 per cent if we include Georg and Connie's shares."

"Your calculations are correct," Greve said.

"You asked for my initial thoughts," Sverre said, looking at Hans. "Say what you want about my sister, but she's neither stupid nor naive. She figured out long ago that the old loyalty pact of block voting at general meetings is dead and buried. If she's standing for election as chair, she must have a realistic plan to win."

"But what kind of plan?" Hans asked. "Disregarding some highly unlikely scenario, like her convincing my sons to vote for her, it's a lock."

"There is a way," Greve said, mechanically. All eyes fell on her. "When Sasha was CEO, I passed on a message from Connie."

Marte and her father exchanged despairing glances. Hans said: "What did Constance have to say?"

"She wrote that she wanted to 'play a role in SAGA'. Sasha laughed at the thought at first. Then I told her about the property in the Advent Valley and the old agreement on the convertible loan."

Greve described the circumstances whereby Connie would

acquire a stake of five per cent. She did not expound further. The consequences were clear.

Yes, Sverre thought, growing exultant inside, this was the opportunity.

"I can take the job in the northern areas on one condition," he said, looking at Hans. "My first order of business is the purchase of Connie's property. We reintegrate the Svalbard estate into SAGA."

Hans shrugged nonchalantly. "Certainly. We reintegrate. Bring it back home. Has a nice ring. Sounds *Norwegian*."

Sverre's heart was pounding.

He moved to the window. Below him lay the tiled terrace covered in windswept snow, then grass further out, then forest and finally the sea.

You need to stay with the main field and bide your time.

This was the breakaway he had been waiting for.

29

TO BETRAY, YOU MUST FIRST BELONG

Bislett, Oslo

There were noises outside. Johnny woke with a start. The sun on Thereses gate was coming in through gaps in the curtains of the apartment in Bislett. The dust was dancing. A stabbing pain began in his frontal lobe, and it felt like a melted atomic reactor there was spreading its radioactive fallout to the rest of his head, with acid rain all the way to his fingers and toes. Someone turned a key in the lock. Immediately he was on his feet. What if it was the owner? Fuck. Or Rebecca and Ingrid? That would be disastrous.

It was HK. Johnny stopped in his tracks. As usual the older man was impeccably turned out in a half-open vintage navy Henri Lloyd jacket and a colourful cravat, the kind of outfit all the preppy boys Johnny despised wore in the nineties.

"You've been incommunicado since Kirkenes," HK said.

"Napoleon didn't answer letters for three weeks," Johnny said. "Know why?"

The old man made no reply.

"Because he knew that by the time he did write back most of the problems listed in them would have disappeared."

"Aha," the old man said, his gaze resting on the silver foil and a powder-dipped bank card, "so I was correct in my assumptions."

"Is this the annual intervention?" Johnny said, and drank a glass of water. "You're going to save me from self-destruction?"

HK did not answer, but shook his head as he opened the cupboard below the sink, took out a roll of black bin liners and tossed them to Johnny.

"Not only are drugs bad for the body and soul," he said. "That goes without saying, the stuff you consume in any case. No, it's that the experiences people have are so banal. Surely you've noticed that? When people are high they think they're privy to revolutionary insights about the world and themselves, but all they're uncovering is their own paranoia. Like that link you sent me at 4.49 a.m. last night . . ."

"What are you talking—"

HK stood with his hands behind his back. "You disappoint me, Johnny. Speedball with hash, cocaine *and* the University of YouTube is an extremely *unfortunate* combination. For, well, a man of my intellectual vanity, it's an insult."

What had he actually sent HK? Johnny was not sure if he wanted to find out.

"You can tidy up this pigsty on your own this time. I'm going to the shops. Roll call in one hour."

His authoritarian expression on leaving left Johnny in no doubt as to what he should do. Calmly and systematically, he cleaned the bathroom and kitchen with white scouring cream, before washing the windows and mirrors with newspaper and the floors with pine oil soap. HK was right, in many ways. Substance abuse was like workplace five-a-side football: exciting and dangerous for the participant, excruciating for spectators.

He had blamed himself for Medved's death. According to the people from PST who debriefed him after the events in Pasvik, the fact that contact was made over the phone was possibly the reason he was exposed. But then why had he taken the consul's mobile? That was immaterial, as far as PST were concerned.

In an attempt to turn his mind to other matters, he had rung Connie Knarvik and received a tongue-lashing in return. She had told him secrets which she had never shared and he had given her "the cold shoulder".

"I thought you were different, Johnny Berg," she had shouted down the phone, "but you're just another insincere, narcissistic asshole who's not listening."

HK arrived back on the dot at the time specified, gave the flat a once-over and nodded curtly. Then he placed a shopping bag on the kitchen worktop.

"You've earned a break."

Johnny sat on the windowsill and rolled a cigarette.

"Why did Medved change his plan?" Johnny said. "Why run from the consul when he was so close, in Nikel?"

"Panic?" suggested HK. "We're talking about a man who had been hiding in the consulate for several weeks."

"He didn't strike me as the panicky type," Johnny said.

HK stirred two saucepans. "Well, it might have been his plan the entire time. Let's say he's a pro. He figures being smuggled across in a car with diplomatic plates means being rumbled in some way or another. That his only hope lies in getting out when he's close to the border, legging it through the forest and crossing the river. Wouldn't you do the same, Johnny?"

Johnny dropped down from the windowsill, took out plates and cutlery and set the table. "We've been looking at this case the wrong way."

HK looked offended. "What do you mean?"

"I'm talking about the police investigation, and the

authorities believing it can be solved by putting Russian diplomats under surveillance."

"Placing Norwegian citizens under surveillance isn't that simple, Johnny. Public prosecutors, the media, jobsworths and law professors on Twitter all hold strong opinions on it. Democracy, don't you know. It's easier with Russians. There's reasonable grounds for suspicion by virtue of their nationality."

Johnny looked at him. "The Russians have killed two of their own to protect the Norwegian mole. First the colonel on Svalbard, then Medved. I think this is bigger than we've realised."

"I share that assessment," HK said. "But truth be told I'm getting fed up of finding you in the kind of state I found you in today every time you think things aren't going your way and you feel powerless. That can't go on."

"Is this where you fire me?" Johnny said, with an air of indifference. "If so, I can live with it. I die a little inside every time I visit PST in Nydalen."

HK slammed his fist on the table. Johnny gave a start.

"Shut your fucking mouth, you little ingrate. I've been looking out for you for fifteen years. Pleaded your case against all kinds of pedants. You may be an expert at stealing other states' secrets, but it's got to the point where I can't be bothered to defend you any longer."

Was that how other people saw him? For a brief moment Johnny imagined life without the old man's involvement. He would be alone. HK continued.

"It went wrong with Medved at the border, but that wasn't because of the phone call. And it doesn't make the mission we have any less important. On the contrary. We're investigating the Russians because we fear they're on the trail of something big. And that SAGA and the Falcks are the Trojan Horse."

HK got to his feet and improvised a dish from his beloved France. He had got hold of Tomme cheese from the Massif Central and used it to make *aligot* – a cheese-based potato mash he was planning to serve with sausages from Voss and a Rhône wine, which he now poured into a glass and handed to Johnny.

"Sorry," Johnny said, looking at his boss.

"Apology accepted," HK said slowly, "with reservations."

They ate in silence, and when they were finished, HK got up from the table and stretched his slim pensioner's body.

"You're not going back to Nydalen," he said, as though in passing. "I've managed to argue my way to our being allowed to set up a small group to work on this case. The way we want. Cort Adelers gate 17, the old apartment is at our disposal. We start tomorrow."

The relief Johnny felt came from deep in his stomach and spread outwards. It was like warming up after a swim in ice-cold water. It was a long time since he had felt like that.

"*Skål*," he said, raising his glass and smiling. "If I was gay and thirty years older . . ."

The old man waved away his gratitude.

"I think we began at the wrong end," Johnny said. "We've been wondering about the who, the what and the where, but not about the why. *Why* does someone become a double agent? What motivates them?"

The old man nodded. "What was it Kim Philby said? To betray, you must first belong."

"Poetic," Johnny said. "The more I've worked on Hans's biography, the more I've realised it's a story of betrayal. He belongs to the shipping nobility in Bergen, but betrays them. He's a member of the AKP, but betrays them. And most of all he betrays Connie. Hans systematically stabs everyone in the back on the way up."

"It is an interesting story," HK nodded. "But moving forward, I need you focused, ready to engage with more direct threats. You can write the book when we've caught the SAGA informant."

"Don't worry," Johnny said, "neither Hans nor Connie wants anything to do with me at the moment. By the way, what was that message I sent you last night?"

"It was a link to an obscure right-wing website." HK put his glasses on. "'In defence of Eurasian civilisation'. Ring any bells?"

"Not really." Johnny had no memory of it.

"I read it, and it was pretty strange stuff," HK said. "A travelogue from Hungary and Russia where the writer praises how Eastern Europeans are tackling 'the threat of Islam' and decries multicultural Western societies for 'digging their own graves'. Is that an opinion you share, Johnny?"

Johnny felt a chill, not so much at the content as the fact he could not remember sending it.

"Sorry," he said.

HK walked over to the sparse bookshelf and stood studying the spines of the books. "I reread the two best novels of all time a little while back. Retirement, you know."

"*War and Peace* and *Les Misérables*?"

"Good, Johnny – your mind and memory are still more or less intact. Do you know what a failed theologian finds at the core of those two works?"

Johnny poured more red wine into his glass. "That the West must never consider invading Moscow? That the world is an unfair place for the wretched?"

"I find mercy. Writers who tackle biblical narratives nowadays always do so with the Old Testament's stories. Crime. Vengeance."

He straightened up and grinned. "The God of the Old

Testament is a vindictive prick. In the New Testament, however, we find the Lord I once found, who shows mercy to all the children of man, whether they are deserving or not. That is Western culture's most revolutionary idea, that's what sets us apart. Mercy is what we're actually defending in our line of work. And mercy is what lies at the bottom of both *War and Peace* and *Les Misérables*. That's why those stories live on."

"Interesting theory." Johnny's eyes had begun to glaze over.

"You've done a lot of stupid things, Johnny," HK said, lowering his voice. "I'm showing you mercy by bringing you back in. Are you prepared to show others mercy as well?"

Show others mercy? Even by HK's standards this was an odd question.

"Ostensibly you began working with the Falck family to avenge yourself in Old Testament style, yes? I don't believe your motive was revenge. It was about what troubles you at the deepest level, Johnny. It was about finding out who you really are."

30

EVERYONE NEEDS SOMETHING TO BELIEVE IN

St Olav's Cathedral, Oslo

A sermon in a foreign language could be heard through the open door of St Olav's Cathedral. Sasha slowly ascended the steps. A Slavic language, Polish perhaps? The nave of the church had stained-glass windows at the apse, filtering the bright morning light. The service was well attended.

Sasha was in a surprisingly good mood. Things had fallen into place since Mads first suggested purchasing the Advent Valley property from Connie with Olav's insurance money, in exchange for her support at the shareholders' meeting.

"Nice of you to come, Alexandra," a voice whispered from behind her.

Sasha turned. If the phrase *a life lived* could be applied to someone, she thought, it was Connie Knarvik. Then again what was an *unlived* life? Her own prior to everything that had happened? Connie's tanned face had the wrinkled complexion of a chain-smoker, criss-crossed by a mesh of lines, especially around her eyes and mouth.

If there were levels to the school of hard knocks, Connie Knarvik, alias Constance Falck, would hold a doctorate. Even her name – the ultra-bourgeois urban Bergen surname being replaced by the common rural toponymic type – was marked by it.

"Aren't there a lot of people here?" Connie sat down on the bench beside Sasha as the faithful began leaving the church. "We can thank the Poles and the Vietnamese for creating a church so much more vibrant than the Norwegian state one."

Sasha was struck by Connie's voice, rough and hoarse, but with the sensuality and spirituality of a soul singer.

"Do you see St Olav's arm over there?" Connie pointed at a gilded hand, inside a golden receptacle. "Do you have a relic of your Olav, dear Alexandra?"

My Olav, thought Sasha, it sounded inappropriate, but Connie had a mildness to her voice that took the edge off such comments, like a priest or a spiritual yoga teacher. She shook her head.

"We don't have much time for relics in this country," Connie went on. "I thought about that when I was reading *The Sea Cathedral*."

"Cemetery. *The Sea Cemetery*."

"Of course. It was so important that you brought Vera's story to light. And that romantic meeting between Vera and Wilhelm in Nidaros Cathedral, *Cor Norvegiae*. I loved it!"

She was talking to Sasha like a passionate fan of literature.

"Vera was also a socialist," Connie continued, "maybe more broad-minded than us Maoists. But her heart was on the left. It wouldn't surprise me if with age she developed more of an interest in religion."

Sasha neglected to relate the uncompromisingly atheistic contents of her grandmother's suicide note, and merely smiled.

"There are many who believe that communism and Catholicism are at odds with one another, but just think of the relics from the communist leaders. Did you know that in the

1940s it wasn't uncommon for people to cross themselves before visiting Lenin's mausoleum in Red Square?"

"Maybe everyone needs to believe in the existence of something greater?" Sasha suggested.

"I think so," Connie said softly. "It often comes into my head when we're criticised for the things we did. For the Cultural Revolution, the struggle sessions and the cadre evaluations. We weren't perfect, of course, we made mistakes, lots of them, but we did so because we believed in a better world. It's important to remember that."

"What's a cadre evaluation?"

"The Workers' Communist Party's ideology was based on the idea that we would lead the masses during the revolution," Connie said, a flame of nostalgia in her eyes. "It no doubt sounds strange today, but we were an elite party, with highly educated members. If you wanted to become a cadre, a leading member, you had to face an evaluation. Pretty harsh assessments, overly sensitive types would no doubt say; not for the snowflake generation. But there was an element of self-criticism too, and that was even more intense. We wanted to rid our personalities of all bourgeois inclinations. Drive out all tendencies in that direction."

Sasha noted she spoke about the harsh climate of the 1970s with the same pride many women of that generation did, and which made them critical of the "overly sensitive" types who followed.

Connie sat with her eyes closed and her hands clasped. Then she turned to Sasha. "You wanted to speak to me?"

"As you know, I lost Rederhaugen and most of what we owned three months ago," Sasha began. "It was taken away from us by Hans."

Connie did not say anything, but at the mention of his name, her eyes flashed.

"He's a liar and a traitor," she said at last.

"I'm considering standing as a candidate in the election for chairperson at the general meeting. Standing against Hans."

"When does that take place?"

"According to the notice, it's nineteen days from now. At Rederhaugen. I'm working on putting together a coalition of shareholders to ensure Hans loses and we regain control."

"What can you offer?" Connie asked, her voice wary.

Was it money she wanted, or the sense of being important enough to determine the next chapter in the history of the family?

"To purchase your property," Sasha said. She had to convince her. "You'll receive cash; in exchange I'll get your votes."

Connie studied her with the look of someone who had been deceived on more than one occasion in life. "How much?"

"One hundred and forty million kroner."

She sat for some time, concentrating, the lines in her face seeming to grow deeper. "I don't like it."

"OK," Sasha said, "why not?"

"My father always said that the Advent Valley was the best piece of land in the Arctic," Connie said. "It's worth more than the rest of SAGA put together."

So essentially it was the money. Even though Connie did not own more than two shares in SAGA and probably lived on the wrong side of the city, Sasha would have thought she still had some remnants of sentimentality. After all, she was an old communist.

"One hundred and forty million in your bank account the day after the shareholders' meeting," Sasha reiterated. "That's my offer."

Connie began to get to her feet. "You think this is just about money. Come up with something better, then we might meet again."

She stood up and left.

Sasha remained sitting, deep in thought.

Connie had a reputation as a troublemaker. Had she said something wrong? Something that offended her? She sent a text to Mads. "We need to meet."

Upon leaving the church, she took a shortcut across St Olavs plass and walked past Blitz House, the old anarchist squat that had become a self-managed social centre. The building brought her own youth to mind, not that she had been a typical habitué. She had attended the nearby Oslo Cathedral High School, where the student body had been divided between preppy and alternative types, between quilted gilets and knitted jumpers, between yes and no to EU membership. As an Oslo Falck, there was little doubt as to which she belonged to.

Although a shrinking violet at school, she had sometimes gone alone to the dimly lit café in Blitz, secretly admiring the radical girls, who were often the children of Maoists. Loud, confrontational and unafraid: why was it so easy for them and so difficult for her? Perhaps by simply being a Falck, she now thought, one was fated to be in the crossfire – between left and right, power and rebellion, Bergen and Oslo, Olav on one side, Connie and Hans on the other.

Why was she thinking about that now? Because Connie had rejected her offer? One hundred and forty million and a raised finger to Hans: it was difficult to understand her thinking. Maybe the family whispers were true and she was unstable, mad. How was she going to get Connie on her side?

While exhaust fumes had coloured the snow in the city streets ash-grey, winter lay undisturbed in the palace park. She met Mads on the knoll by Frederiks gate. In front of the palace, guardsmen were marching.

"Bad news?" he asked, as they began to stroll.

He knew her well enough to know the answer.

Sasha nodded. "She thinks Advent Valley is worth much more."

Mads had his hands in the pockets of his winter coat. "What's your assessment?"

"I have no idea. But without her support we're far short of a majority."

Mads nodded pensively. "She may have spoken to people on Svalbard. There were some other Bergen heirs looking to sell a large parcel of land there a couple of years ago, with mining claims included. The state purchased it for 300 million, or so rumour had it. And that land didn't have anything like the strategic importance of the Advent Valley."

"We don't have more money," she sighed.

"There is one more possibility."

They came to a halt. He pulled her close, felt the warmth of her breath. "But before I say anything, I need to be sure you're ready."

She looked up at his broad jaw. "Ready for what?"

"For the gloves to come off. To do whatever it takes."

His jawline tightened as he said it.

"Go on," she said.

"Don't forget I was a shipbroker before I met you. I still have a lot of contacts in the north and east, where there may be interested parties willing to pay an even larger amount. Actors with deep pockets."

Sasha felt a creeping discomfort.

"But . . . the occupation of Crimea . . . the war in Donbass . . . Western sanctions?"

"Read the Svalbard Treaty. Then you'll understand that the Russians have the same rights there as other states."

"But selling to the Russians," Sasha said. "That wouldn't sit too well with most people in 2016, would it?"

"We're not going to sell; Connie is. We're going to *facilitate* the sale. We'll talk to people you know and trust."

"Who?" Sasha asked.

"I was thinking of Signy."

The thought of Signy Ytre-Arna, her father's crafty old ally, a former minister in the Centre Party who had gone on to serve as a board member for multiple international companies, gave Sasha a glimmer of hope.

"Signy is bound to be aware of the issues around this," Mads said. "Plus she knows SAGA and you personally. Say what you like about her, but she's no fan of Russian imperialism."

Sasha sensed some of the same excitement she had felt during her trip with Johnny Berg the previous year. Sensed the blood begin to flow a little faster around her body. Felt more in love with, no, that didn't sound right, felt more *attracted* to Mads than at any time since they became husband and wife.

Fear and excitement were hard to separate.

31

TINKER, TAILOR, SOLDIER, SAILOR

Cort Adelers gate, Oslo

Cort Adelers gate 17 was an unremarkable apartment building on the west side of the city. He let himself in and checked the postbox: nothing of interest.

Two tones of grey dominated the facade: dark cement on the ground floor and a lighter shade further up between the functional windows. A sign by the entrance listed the businesses floor by floor, the names generic enough to raise one's suspicion of them being shell companies.

Consult Service Ltd did nothing to buck this trend. According to another large sign in the lobby, the company was the sole occupant of the sixth floor, and, like a number of others in the area, it belonged to the service. Why here, exactly? HK had never got a good answer to that. He made his way to the top floor by way of the stairs, a habit he had formed in retirement.

HK was in a far better mood than he should have been, objectively. His husband had been extremely disappointed when he informed him one evening that their trip to London was cancelled. They had been planning on going together, but when Medved had been shot at the border, and HK had been hastily summoned by the authorities to remedy what the press were already dubbing "the spy war", it became obvious that the prestigious conference on "Intelligence Gathering and Methods in the Twenty-First Century" at King's College in London would have to take place without him. A shame, really: there had been talk of Cambridge University Press publishing his book and bringing it to a wider public.

Although every cell in his vain body screamed that he should do the opposite, although his husband urged him to cut back on work, he still prioritised it over everything else.

Maybe I'm an idealist deep down, he thought.

Or perhaps a thrill seeker who wasn't ready for the boredom of life as a pensioner and, like an old circus horse with the smell of sawdust in its nostrils, just did what he had to.

HK cleared away the cardboard boxes and opened the window to get rid of the smell of moths and stale air. Then he placed newly purchased bouquets of flowers in vases he found in the kitchenette at the end of the hall. A certain degree of comfort was important.

His office was set obliquely in a corner. Three other offices intended for Line Mørk, Einar Grotle and Johnny were situated in the wing that overlooked the adjoining street. The friction that had already arisen between Line from PST and the others from the intelligence service was as unavoidable as the major religions clashing over the Temple Mount in Jerusalem. The Police Security Service and military intelligence despised each other. They always had, irrespective of country or era. Only a bureaucrat could believe the distrust would be dispelled by a joint operations centre with the euphonious name *FEKTS*.

He liked Line. He wrote her name on a Post-it note and put it on the door of the largest office.

The operations room, situated in the middle of the office space, was hidden from view on all sides.

On the end wall he hung up four photos.

The first was a picture of Siri Greve in a dark jacket and a white shirt.

Beside it, he put up a picture of Sasha and Mads Falck.

Then one of Sverre Falck.

And finally one of Hans Falck.

HK took a step back, content with the visuals. Five individuals, five main suspects. There were others, of course, in and around SAGA and the Falck family. Everyone from Signy Ytre-Arna to Andrea and Marte Falck. But this was the core. You had to start somewhere. Now all that was missing was HK's group.

Well, and the Gospel according to Johnny Berg: *why*. HK stood studying the photos. Who becomes a double agent and betrays their country?

Half an hour later his three subordinates were in place. Line marched in wearing a broad smile and rosy cheeks after a morning of dead lifts and pull-ups, while Grotle teased Johnny about getting the smallest office.

"Welcome," HK said, when they had placed phones on a tray outside and taken their seats in the innermost room. "I won't waste time beating around the bush. This is just to say that the authorities are very concerned about the Russians' willingness to resort to violence. I refer of course to the liquidations of Zemlyakov and Medved. In my capacity as leader I've been tasked with putting together a group that you three are part of. Understood?"

The three of them nodded gravely.

"We're being granted considerable latitude, and the authorities want what the media are calling 'the spy war' brought to a quick conclusion. They recognise that there is a Norwegian mole. Our mission is simply to find this person. To avoid any leaks we'll be working independently of the other services. And we won't be interviewing any possible suspects for the time being."

He pointed to the photos on the end wall.

Line raised her hand. "Does that mean the state prosecutor is going to look favourably upon us using more – how shall I put it – rigorous methods in catching the Norwegian suspect?"

"Conceivably." HK nodded. "Yes, Johnny?"

Johnny was leaning back in his chair. "Our adversary is smart. We need to show greater intelligence. Use a chisel, not a sledgehammer."

"Can you elaborate?" HK said.

"Leaving aside the obvious motivation of money," Johnny said, "ideology is an interesting factor. Kim Philby rose to the highest echelons of British intelligence while acting as a Soviet spy and he was primarily driven by ideology. He believed the communist system was superior to Western democracy."

"But can we really picture a SAGA mole being spurred on in a similar way?" HK said, and cleared his throat. "The current Russian regime lacks the appeal the old Soviet Union had prior to its crimes becoming public knowledge, no?"

Johnny sat up straight. "To an extent. But Hans Falck, after all, does have close ties to Kirkenes, where, as we know, there are many people who sympathise with the Russians. But there's another interesting ideological dimension to consider. A few days ago, in a – uh – moment of weakness, I sent HK a link to an obscure far-right website, one praising Putin."

"You ended up at the horseshoe theory." Grotle grinned.

"HK couldn't understand why I'd sent it, and neither could I," Johnny continued. "Until I reread it. Because it did provide ideological grounds for entering into the service of the

Russians: only a strong, authoritarian leader can save the West from Islamisation."

"Idiots and crazy conspiracy theorists have always existed," Grotle objected. "Does this have anything to do with SAGA?"

"Possibly," Johnny replied. "The author, Victor Prydz, is an old schoolmate and close friend of Sverre Falck. An eccentric type. Social commentator and investor in various right-wing organisations. In his article he makes much of the fact there has been so little terrorism in Russia in recent years. I would counter by saying that if Norwegians were no longer allowed to think freely and needed to dismantle a free democratic society, in the Russian manner, to prevent terror or espionage – then I'd sooner live as a free person with a real but small risk of political violence."

"Ideological motivations are exciting, but the rather vague suspicion you've outlined doesn't exactly stack up to a court order," HK said. "Get on to the *why*."

"Delusions of grandeur and narcissism," Johnny continued. "Our own Arne Treholt, for example, thought he could play an important role in securing world peace and preventing confrontation between the USA and the Soviet Union. Treholt was a mid-level diplomat, from a small country. A double agent doesn't even need to see him- or herself as a traitor, and very often does not. The double agent is convinced that their role in *building bridges* is important, and – being a narcissist – that no one other than they can fulfil it."

"Good," HK said, before offering a recap so far. "I share your thoughts on the *why*, Johnny. We'll continue looking at that line. All the same, I think we need to consider more active measures."

"What might they be?" Line asked.

HK looked at her. "You work at finding a way into Sasha

and Mads Falck. When it comes to Hans and Siri Greve, I think that will prove difficult before the shareholders' meeting. Hans isn't even taking calls from his biographer."

"I can try again."

"No," HK said. "I want you to contact Sverre Falck."

Johnny looked uncertainly at the two others, then back at HK. "Really?"

"Sverre is an obvious suspect, and also one of the four who know SAGA best, after all, he was groomed to take over for years, and has a good relationship with the other three."

"Will I get in touch as Hans Falck's biographer?"

HK cleared his throat. "That's one possibility but not the best as I see it. Sverre Falck is a biddable boy and may have been instructed by Hans not to talk."

Johnny looked at him quizzically.

"You're to contact him as a *veteran*. You'll discuss the prospects of cooperating on issues relating to those who have served. Band of brothers, comrades-in-arms, that sort of thing. Call it whatever you like. One veteran picks up the phone when another veteran rings."

32

A SMALL PARTY HOLDING THE BALANCE OF POWER

Heggedal, half an hour outside Oslo

Mads just about managed to manoeuvre the Tesla up the steep sides of the valley towards Heggedal. He parked and Sasha jumped out. Although they were not far from Oslo, fresh snow clung to the pine trees covering the hills around them, in contrast to the fog in the lowlands, which lay like a blanket below. In Oslo it was raining.

Sasha checked the map on her phone. "She said it was here."

The silence was broken by the noise of a chainsaw cutting into a tree trunk. They looked questioningly at each other and began to walk in the direction of the sound. In a deforested patch, a person in a signal-red snow scooter suit and earmuffs was standing with their back to them. Beside them lay what must have been once a proud birch tree. Mads and Sasha moved in a wide circle around the person with the chainsaw and made their presence known when they were almost directly in front.

Signy Ytre-Arna put the chainsaw down and pushed up a pair of protective goggles. "Ah, look who it is!" she cried in a broad Sogn dialect, which after all her years in national politics had gained a touch of an eastern accent.

Although Signy had been one of Olav's most trusted board members and closest allies, it was unlikely she was dwelling on his death. No one could accuse her of being easily offended or *hypersensitive*. Signy was a former oil and energy minister from the Centre Party, a political animal who had taken on the bloated form of a large poultry bird, after a daily diet of political meetings for the past thirty-five years.

Sasha was not the least bit surprised that Signy Ytre-Arna chopped her own wood. Nor that this, to put it mildly, unusual woman in her fifties, who was on first-name terms with "Angela" and "Vladimir" and had sat on the board of Saudi Arabia's national oil company, now suggested they take a break there in the forest, where lukewarm coffee from a thermos was poured into two cups, and fingers of a Kvikk Lunsj chocolate wafer bar were distributed.

"Now," Signy said. "What can I help you with?"

"Well," Sasha began, "for almost a century the family has owned land close to Longyearbyen on Svalbard that includes a claim area for coal mining."

"Herbert Falck's old property in the Advent Valley. I know it, of course." Signy nodded.

"Then you're probably also aware that Herbert helped SAGA out in the 1960s with a loan which was convertible," Sasha said. "His daughter Constance – Connie – inherited the land, and now she wants to exercise her right to increase her share capital in the SAGA Group—"

Signy slapped herself to keep warm as she completed Sasha's line of reasoning for her: "And the fifty shares she's sitting on in SAGA hold the balance of power. I'm aware of the scenario: I often warned Olav about it when I was on the board."

"Really?" Sasha said. "Why didn't he do something about it?"

Signy shrugged. "I suppose he wasn't that worried. Connie

Knarvik was an irrelevant monopoliser of meetings and seeing as your family controlled ninety per cent of the SAGA shares, where was the risk?"

Signy looked at Mads. "Not to mention, Olav belonged to the same party as you. Historically the country's largest. That tends to affect your thinking. This idiotic notion of Olav's that only the two biggest parties count . . ."

Yes, ranting about the narrow-mindedness of small parties and their special interests was another one of her father's more foolish preoccupations. Sasha smiled sadly at the thought.

"What Olav was blind to was that the smaller parties can end up holding the balance of power and wield influence far beyond what their share of the vote would dictate. Just like my own party. Or Connie Knarvik."

Sasha nodded slowly.

"Why not just buy out Knarvik yourself, by the way?" Signy said.

"I tried," Sasha answered.

Mads spoke up: "If we manage to sell the Advent Valley land for the right price, we think Connie will support Sasha's candidacy at the shareholders' meeting. But we don't know. I've spoken to investment managers at Industrifinans, and to the Ministry for Trade and Industry."

"Industrifinans," Signy said, "are good if you want a better return on money that's been sitting in the bank gathering dust. But a sale like this is a few shoe sizes too big for them. Not price-wise but in terms of the geopolitical implications."

Mads gave Sasha a sideways glance. "And the Ministry for Trade?"

"The state," Signy said, with emphasis, "well, let's put it this way, slow help is no help. I think you're going to have to look elsewhere."

"We don't have much time," Sasha said.

"How much?" Signy said.

"Just over a fortnight."

Signy looked at her, shaking her head. "Forget it. These processes often take years."

"I know that," Mads said. "But no one thought we would wind up in this situation. First, Sasha's siblings unexpectedly formed a voting block with Hans and the Bergen branch. Then, against the odds, Connie turned down Sasha's purchase price."

It appeared Signy was thinking hard, because she did not refute the argument right away, as she normally would.

"Besides," Mads said, "there must be a way to fast-track a sale in, for example, Russia, if a property of such large political and strategic value were brought to their attention."

"OK," Signy said, "let me make some calls."

She stood up and walked in a zigzag through the remnants of the massacred birch tree.

"Who do you think she's ringing?" Sasha whispered to Mads.

"I don't know but I'd love a look at her contacts list," he said in a low voice.

From the edge of the woods they heard a loud voice speaking English with a heavy Norwegian accent. "Yes . . . hello . . . this is Signy Ytre-Arna calling . . . yes, yes, all good, cutting down trees in the forest . . . I have an urgent question."

She disappeared further into the woods, where her voice was no longer audible. To ease her nerves, Sasha lit a cigarette. Mads wrinkled his nose. She smoked it quickly and by the time she had stubbed it out in the snow Signy had returned.

"I spoke to a friend. A former member of the State Duma, also highly decorated as it happens – the only person to be awarded both the Hero of the Soviet Union and of Russia."

Christ, Sasha thought, what's she cooking up here?

"Anyway, Artur Aliyev is in St Petersburg until the day after tomorrow. He's going to receive you at the Geographical Society at 1 p.m. for a private lunch in his reserved room at the library. Do you both have visas?"

"That we don't," Mads said, smiling weakly.

"Well, let me see what I can do. There's no time to spare. Say hello to Artur for me."

She got up, put on her protective goggles and gloves and walked over to where she had left the chainsaw.

"I need to get to work," she said, starting the chainsaw the way other people start an outboard engine, "if I'm to make it to the palace for dinner!"

33

BETWEEN US VETERANS

Vippetangen, Oslo

Sverre looked down at the rows in the pyramid-shaped sauna at Vippetangen on the waterfront in Oslo city centre. Young girls sat perched below him. He drew up his feet and sat sideways on the wooden bench. Sure, he had put on a few kilos since meeting Ingeborg, but those calories represented pure joy.

He had met Johnny Berg twice. The first time was in Afghanistan many years earlier. The Norwegian army was small enough that the members of Sverre's sniper squad knew who the special forces and intelligence people were. Indeed, it was their civilian style that made them so recognisable. People like Berg had an aura bordering on the mythological in the military, because they did not give a damn about the rules others had to follow. The second time they had met was the year before, at the Marine Hunter's Shack in Ramsund.

Sverre checked his watch. Sweated. Where was he?

After Ingeborg had been passed over at NUPI, the pieces had fallen into place just like she and Sverre had discussed. She had been summoned by the foreign minister, who informed her that one of his political advisers had taken maternity leave and a position was available. Adviser was the least distinguished of the political appointments made by each government, below minister and deputy minister. It was often a low priority post for loyal youth politicians without talent. But if you played your cards right, it was possible to use the position as a springboard for loftier peaks.

Sverre did not doubt for a moment that Ingeborg would do just that.

At that moment Johnny appeared at the entrance below, with a desert-tinted year-round tan and a towel around his neck. He was slim and sinewy; Sverre had no trouble picturing him as a triathlete who concealed his six-pack beneath a suit and tie by day.

Sverre waved to him.

"Glad you could make it," Johnny said. He had a deep, sonorous voice and there was an intensity to his green eyes. As he laid his towel on the bench, Sverre glimpsed three diagonal scars across his chest and what had to be an old bullet wound in his shoulder.

"Nice spot," Sverre said, looking around.

"Heard you did a good job in Kabul."

Sverre nodded. He was a sucker for compliments.

"You see much of the lads from the sniper squad?"

Sverre hesitated. "Less than I had hoped. What about you?"

"I'm not really into sausage parties," Johnny said. "Prefer to watch football on my own, if you know what I mean."

They dived out into the cold water. The temperature had risen to just a few degrees below zero, and the March blackness of Oslo fjord had a film of oil that made the water seem warmer.

They climbed back out and hurried into an adjacent bar filled with divorced women in bikinis and an ageing nineties DJ in Hawaiian shorts.

Johnny bought two beers and handed one over. Ever since they had met, Sverre had liked Berg. Had been fascinated by him was probably closer to the truth.

"You wanted to talk to me about something?" Sverre said.

Johnny leaned on the counter and began to talk. About a topic that had long occupied his mind. A taboo topic. How people he knew from the best units in the army had begun to die. Not by bullets in combat but from heart problems, suicide and cancer, and in accidents.

"The immortal are mortal," Johnny said softly and reeled off some names. It was a long list, even if Sverre took only those of the people he knew into account. Several others were living with terminal cancer.

"I know," Sverre said, and was silent for a moment. "Do you think this has to do with radiation? There was a lot of talk about it at one stage. Depleted uranium in the bombs used in the Balkans and Iraq. Iraqi children with leukaemia, a suspiciously high incidence of cancer among soldiers who served there."

"Maybe in some cases," Johnny said, "but I don't believe it's that simple. I think it's more about the total burden. It's not healthy bottling things up, travelling back and forth between Norway and all these war zones year in, year out. Then they return home for good and many die from illness, in accidents, or from heart attacks in the middle of the night. And the rest of us veterans don't like talking about it. But it's real."

Sverre took a deep breath and shook his head. "That kind of thing freaks me out a bit. But I appreciate you sharing."

Why was Johnny telling him this? What did he want?

"I'd like to ask you something, Sverre."

"Fire away."

"When it comes to the veterans I was wondering if a foundation like SAGA could do something for them."

Sverre thought for a moment, staring straight ahead; he

liked what he was hearing. "Defence matters are popular, a lot more popular than media types in the capital realise."

"I agree." Johnny nodded. "There are more than fifty thousand veterans in Norway, not to mention their relatives. Most people have a veteran in their extended family."

"Berg," Sverre said, exhaling heavily as he turned to him, "I like this initiative. An award ceremony, or an endowment perhaps?"

Johnny nodded.

"I'd have to discuss it with the board, of course, but I feel sure they'll view it as a good idea, in keeping with the foundation's mission statement."

"Hans is the chair of the board now, right?" Johnny said, with affected hesitation.

"I thought you were writing his biography?" Sverre said.

"We don't have a lot of contact. He doesn't want to contribute. I think it might be a good idea to wait before involving him in this. Know what I mean?"

Sverre knew what he meant.

"Do you know Eliassen, the governor of Svalbard?"

Johnny pondered the question a moment and shook his head.

"He's known Hans for decades. Hans once joked that Eliassen knew his innermost secrets, long before they ever met."

He paused, wiped the beads of sweat off his forehead with his towel.

"Interesting," Johnny said. "Between us veterans, can we trust Hans?"

Sverre considered the question carefully. "I like Hans," he said at length. "But I wouldn't trust him as far as I could throw him."

Johnny finished his beer. "Another dip?"

34

THE DARK TRIAD

Cort Adelers gate, Oslo

In what had quickly become a morning ritual, Johnny was the first to arrive at the office in Cort Adelers gate, where he let himself into the winter-dark office space, made coffee and rolled a cigarette which he smoked out the window before starting work.

He spent the first part of the day going through those parts of Hans's biography he had already written. HK had prohibited him from spending time on it, but might there be any hints in what he had already obtained? He was certain there was something there that could shed light on Hans as a more plausible suspect. But what?

Restless, he wandered into the operations room in the centre of the workplace, where he glanced at a picture of Hans. The photo, in black and white, showed him dressed in scrubs under a white coat.

Hans shared clear biographical traits with Philby, Treholt and other notorious spies. Johnny scratched his scalp. A difficult relationship with his parents. Notions of greatness.

Line Mørk walked past and raised a hand in greeting.

Johnny looked up. "Have you got two minutes, Line?"

She shrugged and entered the room.

"What's the first thing you think of when you look at Hans's photo?" he asked.

Line thought for a moment. "Courage. Ardour. Compassion."

She hesitated momentarily, as though about to say something she should not. "Is he a bit of a narcissist too?"

Johnny nodded. "My ex is a psychologist."

A slight flush came into her cheeks, as if Johnny had crossed a boundary by bringing up private matters.

"There's nothing she and her colleagues don't know about couples' relationships," he said. "And every one of them is divorced."

Line let out an embarrassed laugh.

"Anyway, I asked her about the psychology of a double life. She told me about something she called the dark triad."

Line smiled. "Do I really want to know what a psychologist told her ex-boyfriend the spy about a double life?"

Reluctantly, Johnny had to admit he liked Line more and more.

"The dark triad consists of a trio of personality traits," Johnny said. "Psychopathy and narcissism are probably the most familiar to the man on the street. Lots has been written about psychopaths, but it boils down to people with a serious lack of empathy. You could say a traitor might have that deficiency, seeing how their actions can have direct consequences for the people they betray."

"And the third?"

"Machiavellianism, where other people are a means to an end and not an end in themselves," Johnny said. "While the two other factors are independent of intelligence – both smart and stupid people can be psychopaths and narcissists – people with a high IQ are over-represented among Machiavellians."

"What about him?" Line said, pointing at Hans.

"Hans is an extreme narcissist, even by to the high standards of the Falck family. A player. But he's *not* a psychopath.

If anything, Hans has too much empathy. Radicals often do, just think of Mao's Cultural Revolution. They are so empathic they want to punish those who don't have the same consideration as themselves."

"Cultural whatever," Line mumbled. "Lofty stuff the two of you talk about. Not quite like that where I'm from. What does that say about us? We eat meatballs and potatoes. We pay the bills before the due date."

"You check in luggage when you fly." Johnny grinned.

She smiled. "Is that also a no-no for the cool guys in intelligence?"

Johnny chuckled.

"You were talking about Sverre Falck's ties to websites devoted to the far right," she continued. "I checked with the team in Nydalen who work on right-wing extremist threats."

"And?" Johnny leaned over the table. "I thought you were working on Sasha and Mads?"

"Grotle had a lead on that angle, an American, I think he'll be here soon. But anyway, the alternative media. No matter how abhorrent they may be, there's little there to warrant intervention from Nydalen. They're dystopian but not violent. Wasn't that what HK was saying?"

Johnny sighed. "You're probably right."

"Unless you can prove they're intent on terrorism or are spying for Russia, which is not easy, we can forget about a court order."

When Line left, Johnny sat looking through the file he had put together on Sverre Falck; no one else could see it, illegal as it was. The year before, Sasha had spoken of her brother's anger and bitterness. His whole life he had been groomed to take over SAGA, only to be pushed out into the cold. On the face of it he had qualifications: a law degree, one year spent studying macroeconomy and political science at the LSE, and a spotless career in the military. What was it the men from his unit in Afghanistan had said? "Falck spent more time with the field chaplain than in the field."

Grotle and HK came through the door into the hallway. Johnny could tell by their voices that something important had happened. The older man made his way directly to the operations room. "Johnny, you here? Line, are you coming?"

When all four had gathered, HK informed them that he and Grotle had just come from a meeting with the CIA's top man in Norway. "The Americans have information that Mads and Alexandra Falck have applied for visas to enter Russia."

Line and Johnny both let out an audible sigh.

"Their applications were processed and approved unusually quickly."

Johnny scratched at his three-day stubble. "Do the service know anything about the purpose of the visit?"

"Only that they're apparently having a meeting at the Geographical Society in St Petersburg."

"It's not illegal to be granted a Russian visa," Line said.

HK sat with his arms crossed. "A geographical society sounds innocent enough," he said. "But anyone who's familiar with the history of European imperialism knows that explorers and surveyors were vital to that expansion. The same is true of the Russians. The Geographical Society is an instrument. For Russian imperialism. For Putin's ambitions."

"But why the hell are Mads and Alexandra Falck going there?" Grotle asked.

HK walked over to the photo of Mads and Sasha. "I'm not saying these are our people. But it's a lead, the best one so far."

35

UNIQUE PROPERTY – RARE OPPORTUNITY

St Petersburg, Russia

As the plane began its descent into Pulkovo International Airport outside St Petersburg, Sasha squeezed Mads's hand tightly.

She had had a dream about Johnny Berg, the first in a long time, as they had flown over the Baltic Sea and the Gulf of Finland. A very strange dream, as though directed by Eisenstein, with the Red Guard storming the Winter Palace, running through the ornate hallways, vandalising the renaissance artworks and rococo furniture, and pouring the contents of the tsar's wine cellars into the Neva. As the mob approached Sasha's hiding place, a man appeared and pulled her into the crowd.

It was Johnny.

"You were talking in your sleep," Mads said.

"Oh?" Sasha felt the sweat of her own palm. "I was dreaming I was Tsarina Alexandra during the revolution."

Didn't Johnny say that the best lies are those closest to the truth?

Sasha had been fascinated by Russia ever since she started reading the great Russian authors, no, ever since she found out her great-grandfather was a Russian Pomor merchant who got Vera's mother pregnant before making off.

Mads smiled. "Tsarina Alexandra. I'll remember that one."

They had a smooth landing, passed through immigration, and hurried across the modern arrival hall. Outside, Mads hailed a taxi and gave the driver some instructions in what Sasha perceived as very competent Russian. She was of course aware he spoke the language, but it had been a long time since they had travelled together to Russia. Mads gave the impression of being completely at ease. As a shipbroker, he had shuttled back and forth between Murmansk, Moscow and St Petersburg, or "Piter", as he called the city. If the meeting with Aliyev went according to plan, Mads was to travel on to Moscow for some more prosaic meetings with banks and corporate law firms, while Sasha would return home.

They drove out onto a broad boulevard decorated with marble milestones, immense palaces for the people in Stalinist style, triumphal arches and war monuments.

Normally, in her former life, Sasha could not have helped but be enchanted by this place. A city she had never visited before, where such great dramas between East and West, between rulers and the oppressed, had played out over the centuries.

Sasha forced herself to get a grip. What did she imagine? That the Falcks – with property and wealth that might be regarded as large by Norwegian standards, but a drop in the ocean in the maelstrom of history – could in some way be compared to the decadent haemophiliacs of the Romanov family, who had ruled the vast Russian kingdom for hundreds of years?

No, there was no comparison. Still, the fact that she reached for one just underlined why royals of the past continue to fascinate us: their triumphs and tragedies appeal to us precisely because their lives were such extreme versions of our own.

The taxi crossed three canal bridges and continued a few hundred metres up a pretty street with low buildings. The driver pulled up outside a granite facade.

"The hotel is a few hundred metres north towards Nevsky Prospekt," Mads said, pointing. "We'll check in after lunch."

They entered a bright lobby, were passed by security and welcomed by a heavily made-up receptionist.

"Mr and Mrs Falck? You're expected in the library. Please follow me."

The long-legged receptionist's high heels echoed as they followed her. Up a staircase with wrought-iron banisters and Romanesque church windows, past antiquarian world maps and portraits of landscape surveyors and officers during the Central Asian campaigns, as well as chairmen and patrons from Putin and Shoigu to a man Sasha did not recognise.

"See that guy there?" Mads whispered. "Paul Fredriksen, Danish billionaire and explorer. Few know the Russians as well as him. He's on the board of the Geographic Society."

"Please," the woman said politely, and held a door open.

The library was in darker wood than the lobby and staircase, and stretched over two storeys, a ground floor and a mezzanine, with desks and old-fashioned card catalogue drawers. The receptionist led them past some students and pensioners working there, and into a restricted section.

The door closed behind them. Sasha and Mads stood and looked around. The spines of the books in here were older and the maps were mounted behind glass.

A door opened and a powerful, slightly stooped figure approached them. His skin owed its deep bronze to a long life spent outdoors. His narrow, probing eyes had bags under them, and he had a long, thick grey beard.

He looks like a wizard, Sasha thought. He has the wise old eyes of Gandalf.

Artur Aliyev kissed her on the hand, in the French way; only his beard touched her skin. Then he placed his hands on her upper arms.

"You look just like your father, God rest his soul," he said in accented English.

It wasn't a compliment she was used to hearing, so she took a chance on answering him directly.

"Thank you, Mr Aliyev, I'm often told I resemble my grandmother, Olav's mother Vera, whose father was a Russian Pomor merchant from the White Sea."

Aliyev talked about her father in a way that made Sasha think he could probably have talked about thousands of people in a similar fashion, full of unbridled praise and name-dropping of prominent Norwegians.

"You know, dear Sashenka – is it alright if I call you that, by the way? – I just have to say a few words about my dear friend, Thor Heyerdahl. His *Kon-Tiki* expedition had such an influence on my becoming an explorer." He stared off into space with that affectionate look the past can evoke in old men. "As a little boy in Azerbaijan, I came across the *Kon-Tiki* book at one of our well-stocked public libraries in Baku in 1951."

"Mr Aliyev," Sasha said, "this is my husband."

Mads introduced himself in Russian, but Aliyev returned immediately to his own story, clearly finding it much more interesting.

"Of course you know, Sashenka, that Odin was a king from Azov, and that the Norsemen worshipped him as a god for his many triumphs."

"I wasn't aware of that," Sasha said.

"You must go and see the petroglyphs that demonstrate it, young lady! They prove that our beloved Azerbaijan was the centre of a great civilisation, on a par with Mesopotamia."

A woman carried in a tray with biscuits and poured them tea from a silver samovar.

"Well," Aliyev said, his tone now obliging, "my good friend Mrs Signy Ytre-Arna said we should meet. What can I do for you?"

Mads explained in brief how one branch of the Falck family had for many years owned a tract of land on Svalbard, in the Advent Valley to be precise, reserved for mining. The present owner now wished to sell the property, and he and Alexandra Falck had been tasked with finding the right buyer.

"Mr Aliyev, we're aware of your position within Russian society and political circles, as well as your directorships. You are the right man for the job."

The Russian sat deep in thought. His teaspoon scraped against the china cup.

"You know we Russians journeyed to Svalbard, or Grumant as we call the islands, long before official history would have you think?"

"I beg your pardon?" Sasha said.

"We were there first, then came the Dutch, the French and the Swedes. Finally, you Norwegians arrived. And claimed a God-given right to the polar regions."

Sasha could not help but notice Aliyev's interests revolved around the struggle over history and how it was woven into power and politics.

Almost in passing, he mentioned that representatives for Arktikugol, the Russian mining company in Svalbard, might very well be interested in meeting with the owner of the Advent Valley property.

"Have you given any thought to a suitable location where such a meeting could take place?" Aliyev asked.

"We have, Mr Aliyev," Sasha replied confidently.

The old man with the wizard-like beard nodded.

So far everything had gone without a hitch, but the hardest part remained.

"There is a 'but', however." Sasha cleared her throat. "Time is a factor. We need to have the framework in place for an agreement prior to a crucial family meeting that's scheduled to take place in a fortnight."

"A fortnight!" the Russian exclaimed. "You must know this is impossible."

Sasha looked at Mads. A worry line had emerged on his forehead.

"Well, Mr Aliyev," Sasha said, aware she had nothing to lose by rolling the dice now. "If that is the case, it's your problem. What is it estate agents say? Unique property – rare opportunity? This offer won't be on the table for long."

The old wizard chuckled. "You're fluent in the soulless language of property agents."

She nodded to Mads and they both stood up. "Thank you for taking the time, Mr Aliyev. You know our constraints. We have a discreet spot, a hunting lodge in the Norwegian mountains, that can be used for negotiations. We can be ready at very short notice."

She had turned to leave when she heard the Russian's voice behind her.

"So the rumours of a new Falck bud popping up were correct," he said quietly.

Sasha stopped. "I beg your pardon?"

"As you well know, Sashenka, every dynasty – whether a family or a civilisation – carries the seed of its own destruction.

After a few generations, usually no more than four, it all comes to an end. Crumbles into rivalry, decadence, infighting. I had heard this was the case with the Falck family. But after listening to you, I think the dynasty has a future. Your first time in St Petersburg?"

She nodded.

"Think about that when you visit our splendid palaces and museums. The Romanov family held power for a long time, then it was over. Everything is fleeting, Sashenka Falck."

36

THE FEELING OF TWELVE BILLION

Bø, northern Norway

The wind shook the helicopter lightly as Hans and Sverre began the descent into Bø in Vesterålen. A weather-beaten place, north of the tourist paradise of Lofoten, where the wind came in from the North Atlantic all year round.

The rugged coast came into view below low-lying clouds, then waves crashing against the rocks, before the helicopter flew low over a property dominated by a house perched on the edge of a cliff.

The house belonged to fish farm mogul Ralph Rafaelsen. Ralph's father had been in fish processing in a major way by the standards of his time, and married an American beauty queen, hence his son's English name. Ralph had grown up nearby and had established his aquaculture empire here, but the real reason he remained was the municipality's favourable tax policies.

They touched down on a large landing ground to the rear of the property. It was freezing cold and the wind was gusting. Crouching, they hurried out from under the rotors to be met by Ralph.

"No nerves about riding in a helicopter after the accident?"

Hans noticed that even though Sverre was the salmon tycoon's friend and drinking companion, he was not the one Ralph addressed first.

"I guess that's just not how I'm wired."

"Good," Rafaelsen said. "Welcome both of you. Sverre, first time for you too?"

Sverre shook his head.

They crossed a well-kept lawn.

"How do you manage to keep this so green?" Hans asked. "Is it artificial?"

"I can promise you it isn't," Ralph said. "But I suppose the climate mafia would say that lawns and swimming pools are the new diesel engines."

"The scientists I've spoken to are particularly concerned about climate change in the north," Hans said calmly. "It's occurring at twice the rate in the Arctic as in the rest of the world."

"You've just come from a meeting with them?" Ralph asked.

Before being flown out to Ralph's place in the salmon tycoon's own helicopter, Hans had been in Tromsø to discuss the upcoming Svalbard expedition with researchers from the Norwegian Polar Institute. As soon as the sea ice conditions allowed, they were going to sail north, with the Falck glacier on Kvitøya in the far north-east of Svalbard marked as their destination.

It was exactly a century since Theo Falck had set foot on the ice up there, and it would mean a lot for SAGA to plant the Falck flag on the family's land. The Polar Institute had been cooperative, offering to measure changes in the ice to reveal the direct effect of climate change in the Arctic.

"Expeditions aren't the forte of Norwegians," Ralph said. "The Russians do it ten times better. If you want to get to the pole, they have the logistics. They're the ones who can fix a short-circuited engine in thirty-five below, if you know what I mean."

"There's a political dimension here," Hans said. "My ancestors played a crucial role in Norway securing sovereignty over Svalbard."

Rich Norwegians not being like other rich people, the conversation soon turned to the acceptable social currency in their circles: ice-climbing in the Antarctic, kiting over Greenland and expeditions in the Arctic.

They entered Rafaelsen's living room, which looked more like a museum. It was decorated with contemporary art Hans did not recognise and which was no doubt extremely expensive. The room had a panoramic view of the Atlantic Ocean that occupied an entire wall. Ralph installed them on a group of low sofas.

"Now, gentlemen," he said, as a Montrachet was carried in by an Asian woman, "what can I help you with today? Cheers, by the way."

"It's about the coming extraordinary general meeting," Hans said, when they had lowered their glasses. "As you know, the branches of the family are at odds with each other. Sverre's sister Sasha against our side. Each coalition has approximately the same number of voting shares."

Rafaelsen did not seem particularly interested.

Sverre jumped in. "That is to say, until Constance Knarvik, née Falck, a peripheral figure in our family, pulled a rabbit from a hat. A convertible loan tied to a property in Svalbard. It can be exchanged for voting shares. She holds the balance of power and has let it be known she'll vote for whichever side buys her property."

"She'll hardly sell to me," Hans said, "but we imagine she might be willing to sell to you."

Ralph placed a pouch of snus under his top lip. "Why, what's the problem?"

"She doesn't like me," Hans said. "Some people just don't go well together."

The northerner got to his feet and went to the panoramic window. "Here's the thing. Fish farming is worth more than SAGA will ever be. Why would I spend my time on this? Convince me."

"Take a look at a map of the world," Sverre answered. "What proportion of your fish products are sold to the East Asian markets?"

Ralph hesitated. "It's a while since I last checked. About eighty per cent?"

"And at the moment that's shipped via the Suez Canal? Picture a time when the Arctic Ocean is ice-free in the summer. Then people like you will be cutting the journey by a third by using the northern sea route. And what's the last stop before Russian territorial waters? That's right, Ralph, it's Kirkenes, and Svalbard. And who owns the infrastructure there? SAGA."

"Oh, come on, spare me the bullet points of an overly optimistic mayor in Finnmark." Ralph was boorish but he was no idiot. "You know as well as I do that the Russians will do whatever they want with that route. People like me want *predictability* when it comes to shipping."

"If the ice keeps melting at the current rate," Sverre said, "the consensus is that the northern sea route will reach so far north that it avoids Russian waters."

"But the real reason for you to become involved in SAGA," Hans added, "isn't primarily about that. It's about being a part of something greater than yourself, than any of us. We're an instrument of Norway."

Ralph looked at his watch.

"Let's say I agree to buy the property," Ralph said, "that

would have to be regarded as significant support on my behalf. What do I get in return?"

He looked at them both in turn with a cold, penetrating stare.

"What do you want?" Hans said.

"What does the ownership structure look like?"

"Sasha owns around half," Sverre said. "Andrea and I have about the same between us. The rest is divided among others in the family, and then there's the share expansion we already mentioned."

Ralph's face broke into a smile. "Tell me more about this convertible loan."

The weather, as was clear to see through the panoramic window, was deteriorating, and when the formal part of the meeting was over, Ralph decided, in consultation with the pilot, that it would be unwise for them to fly to the mainland until the next day.

They were put up in separate guest rooms in a huge, unoccupied wing of the house. Everything seemed completely new, Hans thought, sterile and freshly painted, like in a newly built apartment no one wants to buy. He lay staring at the ceiling. What would young Hans Falck the communist feel about the person he had become? Contempt? Would he realise that the unsullied idealism of youth had to be tempered by necessity of compromise? Would he have understood that the Devil – Satan, Lucifer, Beelzebub, Mephistopheles – was no monster with horns but something we all had inside us?

No, young Hans would not have understood that. And even if he had, he would not have admitted it.

He could not sleep. He got out of bed and dressed. In the soundproofed house he did not notice how strong the wind was.

Hans had once heard that sense deprivation was one of the worst forms of torture. He went out onto the veranda and stood there for a while. Far below he could make out the foaming sea.

"Hans," a voice said behind him. It was Ralph. "Having trouble sleeping?"

"I wanted to smell the air in northern Norway. So many memories."

Ralph drew level with him and leaned on the railing. "Tell me something, Hans. Your politics are to the left of mine, to put it mildly, so how does it feel to have twelve billion land in your lap?"

"I think life is pretty much the same."

"Do you really mean that?"

It opened doors. Hans could not deny that. Wealth was *comfortable*. The bedding you slept in, furniture you sat in, cars you drove, your surroundings, the restaurant lighting, the hotel lobbies, the airport lounges – all more *pleasant*.

"I think so," Hans replied, thoughtfully. "The problem with money is that after the first million happiness stagnates. Success is relative, you never compare it to your own past, only to the success of others. Ronaldo earns millions a week and is worshipped by people all over the world. But he's still put out when the crowd chant 'Messi! Messi!' at him."

"What made a guy like you become a communist?"

"What do you mean?"

"You must have heard what Mao and Stalin were up to at that time? It annoys me how people go around in KGB hats on drunken weekends in Moscow, as though its fucking Halloween. I like you, Hans, but you socialists think you're so much better than the rest of us."

"We mean well," Hans said. "We want a good and just society."

37

WE HAVE NOTHING TO HIDE

Ustaoset, mountains of southern Norway

Sasha realised that calling the Falck hideaway in Ustaoset a cabin was equivalent to calling the grounds around Rederhaugen a patch of grass.

The place consisted of four buildings with sod roofs that surrounded a farmyard on a gentle slope in the valley. There was a barn and a storehouse, in addition to two farmhouses, each restored with four-hundred-year-old pine – leftovers from the trees transported to Bergen to rebuild the stave church at Fantoft, after Satanists had burned it down in the 1990s.

The place had stood empty for large parts of the winter, but to avoid further complications Signy Ytre-Arna was the one who had rung Hans to ask if she could use it for some business talks that required discretion. Hans had no objection. It was not an outright lie either. Together with Mads and Signy, with Connie in the background, Sasha had worked around the clock in putting together a formal offer for the Russians.

Sasha had spent the morning preparing the place, with the help of hired staff and cooks. Now she made out a small convoy of three cars climbing the winding road from the bottom of the valley. That had to be the Russians. Mads had obviously done a good job in Moscow. Business people from there usually had a penchant for private planes and cars with tinted windows. After they had discussed it between themselves, Sasha had managed to persuade Mads that that type of luxury would appear un-Norwegian and provincial. And the board of the mine from Svalbard were used to the Norwegian way of doing things, were they not?

In any case, that the Russians had agreed to meet them here on home turf was a big step in the right direction. Both Signy and Mads insisted it was a tremendous sign of goodwill that they were coming in person.

The hunting lodge was situated between the low birch forest at the bottom of the valley and the plateau at the top of the ridge. The small cavalcade drove into the yard and the car doors opened.

Mining director Sokolov, wearing a blue down jacket and aviator sunglasses in the harsh light, walked towards her, accompanied by a party of long-legged, model-pretty assistants and watchful men. Where Aliyev had been old and pompous, Sergey Sokolov was a handsome man about Sasha's own age, street-smart with a poker face. She had met him for the first time in Kirkenes.

"Sasha," he smiled, "a pleasure to see you again."

During their first meeting she had noticed he had the ability to put people at their ease. She found that unsettling, because who was this man really? Some kind of agent for the Putin regime?

"I don't want to see a single man from the Russian embassy up at Ustaoset," she had told Mads during the planning.

"Relax, Sasha," he had told her.

The woman from PST, Line Mørk, had come to mind. "We should inform the police that we're meeting the Russians."

He had sent her a despairing look. "We're only following the wording of the treaty on equal treatment. Notify them if you like, but don't be disappointed if the Russians cancel. And then the chances of success will be pretty much zero."

Mads and Solokov stood having a friendly chat.

Their acquaintance went back to Mads's time as a shipping broker in the Barents region, where the Russian worked in waste management.

"Same occupation as Tony Soprano," Sasha whispered, but the joke fell on deaf ears.

"Disposing of the Russians' waste in the Arctic is actually a very important job," Mads said humourlessly.

Behind them, Signy Ytre-Arna and Artur Aliyev, his long grey beard now resting on a red parka, formed the experienced rearguard.

"And the main character of the day?" Director Sokolov smiled tentatively.

A door opened. Connie had done herself up; her heavy make-up was very visible in the sunlight. Slightly stooped, she made her way over to them across the yard. "You must be Constance?"

The sight of Sokolov and his assistants seemed to surprise her. She had probably pictured a flock of geriatric Politburo types.

Sokolov wasted no time in showering Connie with attention. Blushing, she whispered to Sasha: "I hadn't envisaged such a *lovely* man."

Although at least a generation apart, Director Sokolov and Gandalf knew each other.

Mads clapped his hands. "Shall we have lunch?"

The food, prepared by a local star chef who had come fifth in the Bocuse d'Or, was fried mountain trout on a simple bed of caramelised leek and shallots, served with new potatoes and garnished with chives. The Russians – who in Sasha's experience often preferred decadent luxury in the form of champagne and Caspian caviar – were quick to raise their glasses and compliment the chef for the "sublime simplicity of the dish".

Sasha clinked a spoon against her glass. "Dear friends, thank you all for coming."

The people around the table nodded politely to one another.

"The purpose of this meal," she went on, "is to help us get better acquainted. And, subsequently, to find out if our shared interest in the Advent Valley property on Svalbard can be of mutual benefit. Allow me to stress once again, this is in effect a speed date."

Sokolov chuckled.

Aliyev had a certain trait, typical of men of a certain age: he believed that every occasion called for some "winged words" on his part.

"Thank you," he said, stroking his beard. "We're gathered today to discuss a property on Svalbard. But our presence here is important for another reason. In recent years, certain powers, and I'll refrain from naming names, have sought to diminish the friendship between our two nations and peoples. I want to propose a toast to peace, neighbourliness and coexistence."

The mining director may have been of a new breed, but these antiquated words could have been delivered at an embassy reception in the old Soviet Union.

Connie appeared slightly nervous and her words came haltingly when she finally spoke. This surprised Sasha, as she knew the woman had been engaged in solidarity work abroad.

But Connie's generation were not as accustomed to speaking English. She had studied French at university and that was probably the language she had used to communicate in Lebanon.

"As I'm sure you understand," Connie said, "this is a place of tremendous importance to me."

Until this moment she had come across as someone out of her depth, a random lotto millionaire in the presence of a portfolio manager, but now it was as though she had undergone a transformation. Connie straightened up, her eyes clear and focused. She fixed her gaze on each Russian in turn.

"Board member Aliyev and Director Sokolov, even though I'm very grateful to you for coming, I have no illusions about who you are and what you represent. I want to know your views on the Svalbard Treaty. It will weigh heavily when I come to decide who to sell the land to."

Mads shot Sasha an uneasy glance.

Gandalf cleared his throat. "We have nothing to hide," he said softly. "Our attitude to Svalbard is strictly informed by the treaty of 1920, an agreement to which both our countries have emphasised the importance of adhering. Yes, sometimes we have our differences with Norway, as all neighbours do. But that is regarding interpretation of the treaty, not whether we accept its existence. Does that answer your question, my dear Constance Knarvik Falck?"

Mads cleared his throat. "Our respective legal teams are going to address the technical aspects around a possible change in ownership of the Advent Valley property."

The others nodded.

"I need to draw your attention to one thing," he continued, "and that is that we will require a concrete offer in writing from you by the time the shareholders' meeting in SAGA takes place, in exactly one week."

This was and remained the critical point.

"If not impossible," Sokolov said, "such a deadline is both unreasonable and irresponsible. If our experts – both those carrying out an on-site survey in the Advent Valley and the lawyers examining the particulars of the sale – don't find any fault, we can commit to a purchase, but not to specifying an actual amount."

Sasha cursed under her breath; the sum was precisely what was needed to convince Connie.

Signy Ytre-Arna had been mostly engaging in one-to-one conversations during the lunch. "With all due respect, mining director," she said, her mouth still full of cloudberry cream, and in English which had not become more polished of late, "that is pure nonsense. We have arranged for the sale of a property that would otherwise never come into your possession. The last privately owned tract of land with a mining claim on all of Svalbard. We know what your country is capable of if you are really interested. We expect an answer within the time limit Mads has set."

Signy was a polished public speaker and her words did not lack force. It was refreshing to hear a politician get down to brass tacks.

"And one more thing," she said. "Connie Knarvik has already rejected an offer of 140 million Norwegian kroner for the land. Several other parties have made inquiries. That should give you some indication of the interest."

In the evening, when the Russians had left and Signy had retired to the storehouse where she was staying, Sasha stretched herself out on the double bed staring at the rosemaling on the ceiling. Mads lay beside her.

"What are you thinking about?" he asked.

The question was one he only posed when an uncomfortable silence arose between them. A sense of unease.

"I'm thinking how crazy it is," Sasha said. "When I was a little girl, I read about families who lost everything. People in Russia, or Cuba, or wherever. Families who had built up fortunes and property through generations. Suddenly it was gone. A revolution, a programme of nationalisation. Daddy often reminded me of it."

"Revolutions take place in countries with huge inequalities," Mads said, stroking her hair. "We've avoided that in Norway because everyone is better off. Well, almost everyone. And when people perceive they themselves have opportunities, they don't find the wealth of others so provocative."

Sasha turned to him, a tender look in her eyes, and rested a forefinger gently on his cheek. "You know, Daddy always said the same thing."

"Smart man," Mads laughed.

"But sometimes it gives me pause," Sasha continued, "to think I'm sitting negotiating with people probably working for Russian intelligence. Perhaps Vera was right. Perhaps those who say material wealth is ultimately meaningless are actually right."

"They're wrong," Mads said, his voice hard again. "Only people born into a life of plenty can say that. You're not doing anything illegal. Connie has asked for help in selling a property. You, *we*, are helping her. The Russians are allowed to buy land on Svalbard, just like everybody else."

"It's less than a week until the shareholders' meeting," she said, staring at the ceiling. "Do you really think we can get the Russians to commit to a binding agreement?"

"I think they can move very quickly when they want to."

"Do you think we'll win at the shareholders' meeting, Mads?"

He rolled over to face her. Kissed her. "We'll win."

She found herself thinking the same. And that the victory would be rooted in a majority vote. The thought made her surprisingly happy. She slept better that night than in a long time.

38

BEING A FATHER

Rederhaugen, Oslo

Two days prior to the general meeting, all the snow at Rederhaugen had finally disappeared. An endless Oslo winter – or so it appeared to a native of Bergen – was ending. In Hans's mind, winter in the east of the country was comparable to the course of a serious illness. It incapacitated you, temporarily relinquished its grip, then returned like a boomerang when you thought it was over.

But surely now this patient, this capital city, could be given a clean bill of health? The smell of the grass and buds, the sun warming at last and the chirping of the birds told Hans that was the case. He had opened the door of the boathouse down in Øksevika and pushed the wooden boat halfway out on the rails that led to the water. The boat was one of the first things he had brought from Bergen after taking over the property. First, he scrubbed the hull clean of barnacles, then went over it thoroughly with coarse sandpaper. The key to varnishing a wooden vessel was in the preparation. A blues number was playing on the portable radio he had placed on the ground. "And I went to the crossroad, momma. I looked east and west."

The crossroads was where Robert Johnson met the devil and sold his soul to become a skilled musician. It had been at a crossroads back in the 1970s that Vera Lind had told Hans he would gain more renown and wealth than he ever needed. At the price of a normal family life.

He heard footsteps from behind the boathouse.

"Daddy?"

It was Marte, wearing an oversized jacket that had to be far too warm.

"Good to see you. Would you like a cup of coffee?"

She nodded. Hans put on the kettle and spooned some instant coffee into two paper cups.

"Do you have time for this?" she asked. "It all kicks off the day after tomorrow."

"Practical tasks. There's always time for them. Relaxes me."

Marte ran a manicured finger along the hull. "I've always liked that you're handy," she said. "I can't handle men who aren't able to hammer together a bird box."

"You don't get far as a doctor in the field if you can't fix a broken engine or mend your own clothes."

She fixed her eyes on him. "Don't you miss it, Daddy? Life in the field, I mean."

"Everything has its own time, Marte," he said, placing his hand on hers. "I'm too old to be on the front lines. There were murmurings in the 330th Squadron: 'That guy Falck, isn't he a bit old?' I scoffed at the notion. But they were right. I *was* too old. I made mistakes. If they had sent a younger doctor, everything would have gone smoothly."

She was silent for a moment. "I don't know, Daddy. I've difficulty picturing you as a businessman. Drinking pricey wine served by Rafaelsen's help instead of saving lives."

Hans felt a pang of conscience. That twinge of self-reproach you experience when someone utters an obvious truth you have been denying.

"What do you mean?" he said. "They're not mutually

exclusive. Italian communists were renowned for wearing expensive suits."

Marte looked at him. "You can swear as much as you like that money isn't going to change you. But anyone I've known who became rich was changed."

Hans met his daughter's gaze and saw something in her eyes he had not seen before.

"You have changed, Daddy. Money makes you anxious, nervous. You grow scared of losing it. It makes a person less cool, basically."

"Cool?" he scoffed. "I'm finished with being cool! I've spent my entire life seeking the approval of others, of applause, chasing fame and women. If you only knew how liberating it is to let it all go."

He noticed his voice had started to tremble.

"God knows I had my doubts about demanding what was mine, Marte. Ever since reading Vera's will, I've been torn. But after the accident, I didn't think about myself for once. I thought about my children. About you. And Christian. Erik. Little Per. And the generation that will come after."

He fell silent. The rays of the sun fell obliquely across the cliffs; the surface of the fjord glittered like a crystal chandelier. For a moment Hans allowed himself to be overwhelmed by the beautiful light. Was this the old age he had feared so intensely? To bask in the beauty of nature rather than in the social great game? Perhaps it was not so bad.

At the hotel in Tromsø he had been sitting with a beautiful and, in her own words, "very newly single" Palestine activist in her late thirties, who had listened to his tales from the Middle East with stars in her eyes. The situation called for a tennis metaphor: it was a ball lined up for a smash. One drink later, after Hans had given her a chivalrous kiss on both cheeks and was making his way up to his room alone, he noticed the pleasure in what he could have done but had not.

No, these were new times. Memories of childhood, so long set aside, returned. Memories of when he had first become a father.

"I've made a lot of mistakes," he said. "But in this instance, I'm hoping I've done the right thing."

He could see that Marte was fighting back tears.

"Do you know I wrote the first draft of the anaesthetics manual with you on my lap?"

Marte smiled.

"There was no such thing as paternity leave back then," he continued. "I had just come home from Lebanon. Today I would probably be said to have been suffering from acute stress disorder. I began writing the field manual with you in the room, in a baby carrier beside the desk."

He had spent a lot of time away from Marte as well, of course. But in a strange way he had been there all the same. Like when he was district doctor in Sør-Varanger and took his daughter to kindergarten on a kick sled in minus 35°C. Or when she was thirteen, drunk out of her mind, and he had resolutely carried her out of a party in Fana. All these events that combined to form the fabric of fatherhood.

He looked at his daughter. "Is everything alright with you, Marte?"

"Connie rang," she said, her voice thick.

"She's just nervy before the general meeting, same as everyone. She's had a tough life, you know. Never been able to handle pressure."

"She said ensuring we lost the vote would give her no end of pleasure."

39

APRÈS-SKI

Oslomarka

It was the crack of dawn but the light in Johnny's office in Cort Adelers gate was already on.

"Johnny?" Line Mørk said, looking in. She was, of course, an early bird. "I need a little help."

He shrugged and followed her.

"We received a ruling for Mads Falck yesterday."

Persuading the public prosecutor to authorise the measures had not been easy, she explained. Only after they produced evidence of Mads Falck's extensive travels in Russia the week before, followed by his meetings with representatives from the Arktikugol mining company, whom counter-intelligence had on their radar, was communications surveillance granted.

"And look here," she went on. "Sergey Sokolov, mining director in Svalbard, is exchanging encrypted texts with Mads Falck on Signal."

Johnny leaned over her desk. On the screen it said:

Sokolov: *I would prefer to hand you our written proposal discreetly. Where in Oslo?*

Falck: *You're a skier – right?*

Sokolov: *Second place in 15k regional championship, Murmansk Oblast.*

Falck: *Don't worry. Organise skis and gear, train to Gjøvik, 0938, dep from Oslo S.*

Line looked up. "How are you at skiing, Johnny?"

"I'm alright. May not have won the regional championships in Murmansk Oblast, but I get by."

"We'll tail them," she said. "Where do you think Mads is planning to take the Russian?"

"The Gjøvik train covers almost all the forest and hills to the east," Johnny said. "The nicest skiing routes close to Oslo. Are you familiar with them?"

"Reasonably. More worried about getting hold of ski equipment. I don't have time to make it home."

At 9.36 on the dot, Line and Johnny ran into the departure hall at Oslo S. Rushing past the people on the travelator down to Track 8, they hopped aboard the train just before the doors slid shut.

Out of breath, they sank into a two-seater as the train pulled away from the platform. HK had equipped them with a good camera and directed Grotle to head north to approach from a different direction.

The old man's orders were crystal clear: they were to photograph any handover between Mads Falck and the Russian. Then follow the Norwegian back. If they found probable cause for an arrest based on the photos, the necessary measures would be taken.

"One carriage ahead of us," Line said. "Should be easy to see where they get off."

The train passed Kjelsås, continued along the eastern shore of Maridalsvannet and then on into the forest.

"I was thinking," Line said. "Almost everyone who follows the ski route along the Gjøvik line gets off at Gørja. I'm going to get off at Movatn whether they do or not. Then ski straight to Gørja sports cabin."

"What about me?"

A smile broke across her face under the tight-fitting Swix ski hat. "Your job is to follow them."

Soon after, the train glided in to a station next to a beautiful small lake surrounded by snow-laden conifers. Line grabbed her skis and poles and hopped off. There was no movement in the next carriage. She double poled over the frozen lake and disappeared into the forest.

Johnny's fear that he would be unable to maintain a suitable distance from the two men turned out to be groundless. They alighted at Stryken and made their way to the hilly scooter-made ski trail that followed the side of the valley upward in a southerly direction.

It did not take Johnny long to realise he was not on the same level as the two skiers ahead of him, not only the veteran of the Murmansk regionals, but also Mads Falck, who had clearly spent the winter making sure he hit top form at the right time.

After half an hour of tough uphill requiring a diagonal stride, the route fortunately levelled out into easy-going poling terrain. On flatter stretches he could see the two men ahead of him. They were moving with that leisurely assurance good skiers have when they're enjoying themselves, at a speed that would be the envy of most other people.

They poled across the icy surface of a couple of frozen lakes and began making their way uphill towards Gørja.

Johnny texted Line. She replied immediately: *I'm ready. Stay back.*

The glide on Mads's skin skis was good from the last time he had prepared them and they cruised nonchalantly down the final slope like contestants in a biathlon on their way into the shooting area. On the north shore of Store Gørja lake, smoke was rising from a red cabin. The sun was melting the snow on the pine trees. There was just one pair of skis wedged into a snowdrift. No more. That was good.

Sergey Sokolov's skiing skills had not disappointed. Mads figured he was in better shape after a formidable ski season, but the Russian made up for that with a basic technique you could only get from skiing competitively from a young age. It was as though he managed to inject a different level of energy into every kick. Not a single slip.

"The Russian relay team missed out on a natural," Mads called out, breathlessly.

Along the way the Russian had suggested that a skier behind was possibly keeping tabs on them, but Mads had laughed it off. It was probably an eager amateur trying to keep up. This was the cradle of skiing after all.

They planted their skis and ski poles into the snowdrift and went inside. The log walls were decorated with maps and old photographs. There was a serving hatch in one corner.

A smiling woman appeared in the opening.

There was something familiar about her, but Mads had been to Gørja many times this year, and she had never been here. She resembled someone . . . but who? One of the pretty brunettes on the national handball team?

Slightly flustered, Mads ordered two waffles and two cups of coffee. The director placed his lightweight backpack on the table. Regarded Mads with that poker face of his. Only his tired, smiling eyes suggested he was happier than he appeared.

"We've been thinking," he said. "And we're willing to make the offer you requested." He took a stiff, transparent blue plastic folder from the backpack. Pushed it slowly across the table.

At that moment the waitress arrived with two paper plates with waffles. "Would you like brown cheese or strawberry jam and sour cream?" she asked in Norwegian.

Sokolov merely gave her a friendly smile.

"One of each, please," Mads said.

She returned, spread the jam in a circle on one set of waffles, and put a dollop of sour cream on top. Using a cheese slicer, she cut a few slices of the goat's cheese and placed them on the other plate.

"I'm new to the job," she giggled.

"And the coffee?" Mads said.

She disappeared to get two cups of freshly brewed coffee. Mads opened the plastic folder and took out a stapled document, written in English. It took the form of a buyer's guarantee to the seller. Naturally Mads understood that the pages with attachments contained formulations detailing the circumstances in which they could opt out . . . if . . . if . . .

He paused.

The waitress appeared and placed two cups on the table. Mads blew on the scalding-hot coffee. Broke off a piece of waffle with jam and sour cream while he tried to gather his thoughts.

This was insane.

"I told you we were serious," Sokolov said, his face expressionless.

Mads sat staring at the number. As though he couldn't comprehend how much it was. Which he couldn't. It *was* incomprehensible.

When he and Sasha were newly-weds, he had often fantasised about saving her. He had felt so useless in the Falck family back then. As though his contribution was limited to being a sperm donor and stable father figure. Him, a man who had been both a youth politician and a shipbroker in the Barents Sea. Who had toiled so much harder than Sasha and the other Falck siblings.

Now he had saved Sasha, he knew that.

There it was, in black and white, an offer Connie Knarvik could not refuse. He put the contract in his backpack. He might as well have ridden in on a white horse.

Director Sokolov got to his feet. "So, I take it you'll be in touch after this shareholders' meeting?"

"Yes. This has been very productive," Mads said, as they exited the cabin.

"I'll find my own way back to the city." Sokolov nodded sideways in the direction of the cabin. "The waitress is watching us through the window."

"We're two good-looking guys." Mads winked. "You should ask for her number."

The sky was clouding over. He poled west along the groomed trail south of Helgeren lake at a furious pace, before following the snowmobile tracks that went all the way down to the elongated Myrtjernet lake, then further down to Skjærsjøen, where he propelled himself in a diagonal stride until he made it to the groomed Korsvoll trail. He avoided the busy trail down to Sognsvann.

Several times he glimpsed a figure further back. It couldn't be the same man who had been behind them all the way from Stryken, could it? No, Sokolov was a Russian and therefore paranoid. A characteristic that lay as deep in the Russian soul as guileless naivety lay in a Norwegian's.

He soon made it down to the buildings at the edge of the forest in Korsvoll. On really good winter days he liked to round off by skiing down the hill at Havnebakken. But now the snow ended where the forest did. He unclipped the bindings. It was early afternoon. The weather was mild. Passing the barrier, he decided to make his way down to the metro. He slipped slightly on the pavement as it had yet to be cleared of grit for the icy weather.

At that moment two unmarked police cars drove in from opposite directions and screeched to a halt. Armed personnel charged out. The sirens were wailing, the plain-clothes officers shouting. The last thing Mads had time to think as the operatives roared, pointed their weapons at him and pinned him down so hard on the tarmac that the gravel pressed against his cheek, was that spring had long since arrived down here and the pavements should have been swept ages ago.

Everything was as it always had been at the Palace Grill, located a stone's throw from Cort Adelers gate 17. The walls still smelled of smoke many years after the smoking ban was introduced, The Band's folk rock was playing on the jukebox and the crowd was an eclectic mix of nightlife rats, leather-jacketed Westside poets, hip art students and other sorry souls.

Johnny ordered two beers and found a corner alcove. Line Mørk slipped in with her back to the wall.

"Jesus," she said. "What a day."

"So, you've spoken to the people in Nydalen," Johnny said. "Tell me exactly what happened after the arrest."

"I don't know everything." She spoke quietly; this was not information she wanted overheard. "They took Mads Falck into custody with much fanfare, used the tactical unit. They took him to Nydalen and confronted him with the photos. All very Arne Treholt. Norwegian receives documents from suspicious Russian. It's a slam dunk."

"Your photos, Line."

She shook her head in disbelief. "The only problem is the document Mads Falck has been given by Sergey Sokolov is as legal as the right to roam. The Russians aren't idiots. Their offer was written by lawyers with expertise on the Svalbard Treaty and is one hundred per cent drawn up according to its terms."

"It's unbelievable," Johnny said. "Un-fucking-believable."

"As soon as Mads Falck realises this is just idiocy, he'll demand to make a call. To Signy Ytre-Arna."

"Of course," Johnny sighed. "Signy is helping Sasha and Mads."

"Anyway. When she shows up with the best lawyers in the country in tow to face the public prosecutors in Nydalen, it'll be men against boys. She'll explain matters and threaten a nuclear response if he's not released."

"So, Mads Falck will be a free man?"

Line nodded. Even after a day like this one she maintained her upright posture and interrogative gaze. Back straight, chest out. Line was not Johnny's type, but he had noticed she held enormous appeal, and that both a Stockholm-inspired party fixer and a drunken improv poet with a red bulbous nose were making eyes at her.

"We've been on the wrong track with Mads," Johnny said. He drained his pint of beer. "Confirmation bias. The human tendency to search for information that confirms our prior beliefs."

Line smiled ruefully. "I've also read *The Problem of Secret Intelligence*."

She got up, ordered another round, and placed the beers on the table.

"I've a favour to ask you, Line."

"You can ask."

"I've spent the bulk of my time looking at Hans Falck in relation to this case. I think the other suspects are noise without any signal. Hans, in my opinion, is the only one with the motivation, opportunity and personality profile to be a double agent."

Line fixed her gaze on the table. "What's the favour?"

"The case we're investigating ostensibly began when Governor Eliassen in Svalbard came across a Russian defector close to death. When I spoke to Sverre Falck, he told me that Hans and the governor knew each other from way back. Eliassen worked in the old secret service and I have a feeling he may have been involved in keeping Hans under surveillance. I think the key to the whole case may lie there."

"What is it you're asking for exactly?"

"Do you think you could find the file on Hans Falck?"

40

FIVE HUNDRED MILLION KRONER

Rederhaugen, Oslo

It was the day before the general meeting, and Hans – freshly showered and shaved – was standing in the doorway between the large stone patio and the conservatory. He would never become accustomed to Rederhaugen in the way Olav had been.

He had got a shock when he studied his reflection. He had become so much older! His mouth and jaw had slackened into that underbite characteristic of old men, his silver-fox hair was tinged with white. His upper body had lost more muscle mass. Well, that might be down to the accident, and the white hairs due to the stress of leadership responsibilities, though executives were supposed to go grey, not white, weren't they?

He had not got hold of Connie these past few weeks, despite repeated calls and voicemails.

By wearing a slimming vest with his tailor-made suit, however, he managed to conceal the worst. Georg Falck, "the bearer of tradition" and Connie's little brother, had arrived at the cattle show first, ruddy-faced and plump. Together with his children, he was standing in the foyer, not tempted by the rain and biting wind on the patio. Sverre and Ralf Rafaelsen also came trotting across the lawn.

"The young lions of the city," Hans said. "What are you

wearing, Rafaelsen? Were you partying late and neglected to change?"

The salmon tycoon was wearing a black shirt with a gold patterned brocade. That was bad enough. But he was also sporting matching shorts. He looked like he had wandered off the set of an eighties comedy.

"Limited edition. They only made ten of these," Ralph said.

"There's probably a reason for that," Hans said, drawing the northerner aside. "Ralph," he said seriously, "you're playing a crucial fucking role today."

Ralph shrugged.

Hans pointed to the corner of the house. "There's a basement entrance there. The door is open, go in, walk straight ahead, and you'll come to the door of the men's changing room. There you'll find one of my suits hanging up, dry-cleaned, along with a freshly ironed shirt and tie."

"What if I prefer my own clothes?"

"You don't," Hans said. "Connie, who's key to this whole plan, may not look it anymore, but believe me, deep down she's still a bourgeois Falck from the right part of Bergen with the name Constance on her birth certificate. If we're going to convince her, you cannot fucking look like that."

He nodded in the direction of the sunken entrance. For a moment they stood in silence, hackles raised, staring at each other. Then Ralph headed towards the corner of the house.

A black car came driving slowly down the avenue and stopped at the fountain. Connie emerged, dressed in a dark outfit, a mint-green shawl over her shoulders. He recognised her immediately. She was accompanied by another woman.

Sasha Falck. The two of them together was bad news. He composed himself.

"Connie Knarvik and Alexandra Falck!" he said, opening his arms wide. "Two generations of Falck beauties, you both look better than ever!"

Sasha smiled stiffly. "Being a womaniser is fine when you're young. When you're old, it's pathetic."

"Could I have a word in private?" Hans said, looking at Connie. "You've been hard to reach over the last couple of weeks."

"Maybe after the official portion of the programme," Connie replied coolly and continued into the house, leaving Hans to gaze thoughtfully into the middle distance. Was her old bitterness and enmity going to get in the way of everything?

Siri Greve clapped her hands to get everyone's attention. "I think we're all ready. Shall we?"

Georg Falck had difficulty negotiating the winding staircase past the director's office but eventually made it up to the main hall. Light refreshments in the form of coffee, fruit and mineral water had been laid out. Everyone took their seats.

"Let's get started," Greve said, and nodded to the accountant. "Are there any objections to this general meeting?"

Hans had often skipped the annual general meetings previously, voting by proxy. They had tended to be one-man shows for Olav. Now the energy was different, as though everything was in play.

Greve was chosen as chair and two shareholders selected to sign the minutes. Hans looked around. He was sitting across from Connie in a horseshoe-shaped seating arrangement; Sasha was sitting a little further down from her. Sverre and Andrea were seated either side of a corner.

"So, I would like to welcome you all to this extraordinary general meeting of SAGA Ltd," Greve said. "The statutes state that in the event of a chairperson's unforeseen departure, an extraordinary general meeting is to be held within three months, and a new chairperson and other board members are to be chosen by the shareholders."

There was a nodding of heads and she listed several more formalities. "With regard to motions, Connie Knarvik has let it be known she wishes to discuss the sale of a property – the so-called Advent Valley on Svalbard – and that the result of that discussion will be decisive for the last item."

Greve let her gaze wander around the table. She briefly explained how the property in the Advent Valley had been separated from SAGA Ltd against a so-called convertible loan dated June 25, 1965, giving the owner of the property the right to exchange the land for a five per cent stake in the company, equating to fifty shares in SAGA.

"It is this right shareholder Connie Knarvik is now exercising."

Although this was widely known, it raised murmurs just the same.

"The final item is the vote on the new board of SAGA. As the notice of the meeting states, there are two candidates for the position of chairperson."

She paused. "Those two candidates are Hans Falck and Alexandra Falck."

People nodded. After an external corporate lawyer had gone through various questions concerning the property and liquidity of SAGA, it was time for Hans's report on the state of the realm.

"Dear friends," he said, before fixing his eyes firmly on Connie's; she was the one he was speaking to, "in the wake of the tragic circumstances surrounding Olav's death in the winter, I was granted the opportunity to lead SAGA on an interim basis. It has been an honour."

Hans spoke, in vivid fashion, about SAGA turning its attention to the north, a strategy with deep roots in the Falck shipping empire, a plan with several components.

Firstly, the old board's decision to donate a vessel to the Society for Sea Rescue – *Falck III* – had been carried out. Prior to handover, the boat would function as a research vessel. A group from SAGA and scientists from the Polar Institute were going to travel from Finnmark to Longyearbyen, and their departure was only days away.

This matter, Hans told them, with building enthusiasm, pointed the way to the next. Thanks to climate change, no, that sounded wrong, *due to* climate change, the melting of the ice at the pole and a new geopolitical situation, the Arctic had become relevant with regards to new trading routes that would dramatically cut the distance to the large Asian markets. It would alter global commerce. Thanks to a successful visit to the north, SAGA had also garnered the political will.

"So it is we in SAGA who will be sitting in the driver's seat when the trade routes of the twenty-first century are redrawn. With our property in Kirkenes and with our long history in Svalbard."

He paused to make sure he had the whole room with him.

"And so to Svalbard. Connie Knarvik is sitting in this room. She is the daughter of my great-uncle Herbert Falck, former director of the Falck shipping companies and a key figure in shipping coal from Svalbard. Connie inherited the so-called Advent Valley property, which, among other things, comes with a right to mine for coal. For some time, she has let it be known that this is a property she wishes to sell. As interim chairperson, I've taken this wish very seriously. We want to buy it. We shall see."

There was silence in the room. Everyone was waiting for Connie's reaction. She cleared her throat and said, in a loud, clear voice: "That's all well and good, Hans Falck. Before I make any decision, I would like to say a few words."

Hans looked at Greve, who nodded. "The floor is yours, Connie Knarvik."

Hans studied her. Although she had aged significantly since he last saw her, it was as if her eyes had regained their revolutionary glow from the 1970s. He tried to read something in the way Connie was looking at Sasha.

"As the shareholders are no doubt aware," she said, "it's been a long time since I attended a general meeting of SAGA. My old holdings were limited to 0.2 per cent, the same as those of my brother Georg. With the conversion of the loan, I will receive a further fifty shares, thereby increasing my holdings to 5.2 per cent."

"Just to clarify," Greve added, "the number of shares will increase from 1,000 to 1,050 in such an eventuality, which will naturally mean a slight adjustment of shareholders' percentages."

She pointed. "Sasha, you've registered to be on the list of speakers."

"That's correct," Sasha said.

Hans had believed she would be more nervous, like when she took over after Olav's death, but she seemed calm, relaxed almost. "In order to find a good buyer for the Advent Valley property we have cast a wide net and spoken to several actors. However, the fact is there are very few interested parties who possess the combination of financial muscle, competence and experience to run mines on Svalbard. Especially since the Norwegian state, which operates the last mines there, has decided to close down its facilities. We did not, however, want to find actors from countries without a long-standing commitment to the islands."

Is this where she drags in the Russian mining company, Hans wondered.

"We've therefore spoken to our Russian contacts in Trust Arktikugol," Sasha continued. "As many of you know, that company has a long history of mining operations on Svalbard. The director, Sergey Sokolov, has, on behalf of the Russian authorities, given his guarantee for the acquisition."

"This means the Russians take over the property?" Greve said.

"Correct," Sasha said. "The Russians acquire the property, Connie gets the money, and SAGA holds on to its core business, which has made us one of the country's central commercial enterprises. As opposed to pipe dreams up north." She held up a document. "Anyway. This is our offer, Connie. The total sum is 500 million kroner."

Half a billion.

Hans sat with his mouth open, staring into space. A property on Svalbard with some subsidised coal mines worth 500 million Norwegian kroner? It was unbelievable.

All the same, Hans knew only too well what this meant. If Connie sold to the Russians for that astronomical sum, she would be putting her support behind the person who had facilitated this extraordinary sale.

Connie Knarvik would support Sasha.

41

AS NORWEGIAN AS THE MOUNTAIN KING

Rederhaugen, Oslo

When Sasha glanced in the direction of the corner where Andrea and Sverre were sitting, she noticed they looked glum. Hans sat motionless, his hand on his chin. This was going according to plan. Connie had done exactly what she had told Sasha she was going to do.

Sasha took her seat. Sverre had also registered to speak.

"I'd like to thank my sister for that rundown," he began, receiving an icy stare in return. He bore a strong physical resemblance to their father but didn't have a fraction of his charisma.

"The truth is that all so-called polar researchers or mining directors from Russia are in the pocket of the Putin regime."

He brought up a facsimile of a newspaper article on the screen behind him, with a photograph of a group of men dressed for polar conditions below a Russian flag fluttering in the breeze.

"In this photograph you'll see some of the lovely Russians you met at the hunting lodge," Sverre said, looking at Connie. "And who are they with, you might ask? Well, they're standing together with known Russian nationalists, people banned from entering Norway and other Western countries."

Sasha had been expecting this. She sat impassively, staring into the middle distance. Connie's face did not betray any clear reaction either.

"Consorting with these Russian actors," Sverre continued, "is the very reason the security services arrested Mads Falck two days ago, after he received documents from the Russian mining director during a secret meeting."

Sasha was baffled. Mads, arrested? He had been at home this past week. Was her brother making things up in front of the shareholders?

"This is beyond the pale!" Mads said. "I was subjected to harassment, based on unfounded allegations, and released after three hours. It was a total misunderstanding, and yet you dare to make these accusations at a general meeting?"

There were perhaps grounds for supporting her husband, but Sasha just sent him an angry look. Why had he not told her about this? Arrested and released, without saying a word. She shifted her focus to Connie, obviously the intended target of this vilification.

"I agree with Mads," Siri Greve said. "We can be spared that type of insinuation."

"Alright," Sverre said, with obvious satisfaction, as he could tell by looking at his sister that the damage had already been done. "But this is important all the same. As we're all aware, the property in the Advent Valley comes with mining rights. But what few people realise is that such a claim also includes the right to build a harbour, roads and other relevant infrastructure. Even an airport. And if we take a look at the area around the Advent Valley on the map . . . Can everyone see?"

"I don't know if Sverre was asleep when I was speaking," Sasha said. "I emphasised that our offer was dependent on the Russian purchase being in accordance with the treaty. Afterwards I will withdraw SAGA from Svalbard."

Sverre pointed. "You did mention the treaty. And I'm telling you, dear sister, that the treaty doesn't stop the Russians from legally building their own harbour and roads, and maybe even their own airport. All with the consequence of weakening Norwegian dominion over the islands. In the end, the result of such a sale – if it goes ahead – could contribute to undermining Norwegian sovereignty over Svalbard. If you sell to them, Connie, we may very well be on the slippery slope to our country losing Svalbard."

He was hitting his stride now. "I urge you, Connie, to consider an offer that ensures Norwegian ownership. Our bid, SAGA's bid, is less than that of the Russians, coming in at 450 million kroner. But it has something else. It contributes to Svalbard remaining under Norwegian control."

Now he delivered the coup de grâce. "It took a Falck to secure Norwegian sovereignty over Svalbard in 1916. Don't let it be a Falck who is responsible for us losing it."

Sasha went cold. She could see Mads was sitting still as a stone. Would Connie withstand the pressure? All eyes turned to the Bergen woman.

Without batting an eyelid, Connie got to her feet and walked over to the whiteboard at the end of the U-shaped seating arrangement. She picked up a black marker and drew a circle with a C in the middle.

"This is me with my fifty-two shares. I will be backing the candidate for chair of the board who looks after my interests. Sasha or Hans."

"And what decision have you arrived at?" Greve asked.

For the first time during the entire exchange she dropped the pretence. "Hans Falck is a liar and manipulator. I will not, under any circumstances, back a proposal allowing him to chart the course for a foundation that is a continuation of my father's work, a foundation that includes the property he held so dear. My answer to that is no. No."

Sasha could feel the burden she had been under all winter lift from her shoulders. Connie had stood firm. She had withstood the pressure. It was unbelievable. Mads, who had gone completely white at one point, winked almost imperceptibly at her. She could not resist sending a look of mild triumph in the direction of Sverre. He then whispered something to Ralph Rafaelsen, who took the floor, speaking in his refined Vesterålen dialect.

"Thank you for all the valuable input. As some of you are aware, Sverre has proposed me as a new board member of SAGA, as a replacement for Martens Magnus. Is that acceptable?"

"That is a formality we can vote on by a show of hands," Greve said. "Are there any shareholders who object to Ralph Rafaelsen becoming a new member of the board?"

No one raised a hand, so she continued. "Who supports the proposed candidacy?"

Somewhat hesitantly, all the shareholders raised a hand.

"Thank you for placing your faith in me," Ralph said, with a chalk-white smile. "I've read the articles of association and I want to invoke a clause. It states that a board member has the right to propose a chairman from the floor during the general meeting."

"That breaks with all SAGA conventions," Sasha fumed. Was Rafaelsen so shameless he would challenge the norms at Rederhaugen? Or was there something else behind this? "It's never been done that way."

"Well, the situation itself is unusual," Ralph said. "Both candidates for the role of chair of SAGA have severe shortcomings."

Sasha looked quizzically at Mads, who did not appear unduly worried.

"The accusations pertaining to Hans Falck's personal integrity are extremely concerning, from the perspective of a board member," Ralph said. "The same has to be said of your fraternisation with Russians with an interest in Svalbard. What I suggest, therefore, is meant to be viewed as a compromise."

Everyone was staring wide-eyed at the northerner.

"I have," he continued, "by virtue of my position in Arctic Fishery, been asked to act as the investor who ensures the Advent Valley property remains safely in Norwegian hands. A convertible loan, out of respect for SAGA's history, on which I will act as guarantor." Ralph smiled. "At the same time, I want your thoughts about the chairperson to be respected. We owe you that, Connie."

Connie sat motionless.

"Firstly, my offer will exceed the Russians' in financial terms. It amounts to 600 million Norwegian kroner."

A murmur went through the room.

"Secondly, it will ensure Norwegian ownership," he said. "Thirdly, it will ensure Hans Falck does *not* become chairperson. I would like to put forward Sverre Falck as chair of the board, a proposal I'm sure Hans will support."

Ralph winked at Sverre.

Sasha was at a complete loss.

"Sverre Falck has military experience," Rafaelsen went on. "He knows SAGA. He's a Falck. And he's as Norwegian as the Mountain King!"

Sasha noticed a shiver go down her spine. She felt cold. Her tongue went dry and she found it hard to breathe.

"Well," Connie said, with all eyes upon her, "so far as I can see, my criteria for sale are being met."

For a moment or two there was silence.

"I support Sverre Falck's candidacy."

Sasha froze, went rigid. Her skin was tingling. What had just happened? Was this a dream, a bad dream? A nightmare that had been going on ever since Hans turned up at Rederhaugen before Christmas with the will?

Ralph's motion was put to a vote.

All Sasha saw was white. Everything was a fog. Everything was floating.

"SAGA has a new chairperson," Greve said when the shareholders' votes had been counted. "Sverre Falck."

Sverre raised his arms in the air. Ralph Rafaelsen patted him on the back. Andrea hugged their brother. She had betrayed her, Mads had betrayed her. Sasha stood up. Took her jacket without saying a word. Brushed past people, walked down the winding stair in the rose tower, across the lawn with the statue of Vera, along the footpaths and familiar flagstones. She had to get away.

"Sasha?" Mads called, as he came running up beside her.

"I trusted you," she said, staring straight ahead. "I believed in you and in your fucking idea of selling to the Russians."

She sped up and he jogged to keep pace with her.

"You and your plan have made me a laughing stock. And when the PST *arrest* you for consorting with the Russians, you don't even have the fucking decency to tell me about it. You stick your head in the sand and hope it goes away."

"That's not how it was, Sasha."

She stopped walking. They had reached the crossroads. "I'll tell you exactly how it is, Mads. I'm going to Gimle terrasse. You find somewhere else to sleep tonight."

Sasha continued down the avenue towards the gate. Away from Mads. Away from Rederhaugen.

She was never going to return.

42

APPENDIX VERMIFORMIS

Rederhaugen, Oslo

After the shareholders' dinner there was a party. Connie left early but the others were intent on celebration. As Hans was still residing in the blue room, the festivities took place in the lounge with the fireplace and in the adjacent rooms in the east wing. Rederhaugen was in the possession of the Bergenites and would remain so.

Hans was relieved Sverre had been chosen. It was only when Sverre was announced as chair of the board that he realised just how much of a relief it was.

Sverre was surrounded by people. Hans had never seen him so happy, with Ingeborg radiant by his side and Ralph Rafaelsen as kingmaker. A number of friends were also there, keen to bask in the reflected glory of the new chairman and figurehead of SAGA.

"Friends!" Sverre shouted. "Today we're going to party. And as soon as the ice conditions allow, under Hans's eminent leadership, we're going to the north and beyond, to Svalbard, with our rescue vessel!"

Hans, standing at the back wall, nodded, looking slightly embarrassed. He turned and walked to the library. It was less noisy in there, something he had begun to appreciate.

He was standing pensively in the room when Sverre entered, poured them both a whisky and opened the door to the little balcony that looked out towards Vera's old cottage.

"I just wanted to say," Hans said, "that I think you deserve this, Sverre. I know how much you've wanted this position. How hard you've worked. And how much adversity you've encountered."

"You know, Hans, I've often wondered how I'd feel when this day came. Because Father really tested me, a school-of-hard-knocks approach. But I knew it would happen, sooner or later. The feeling is overwhelming."

Hans looked at him, curious. "What is the feeling?"

"Relief, mainly. Not euphoria, but relief. That I've become what I hoped I would."

"Interesting," Hans said. "I'm also relieved."

"All of you underestimated me," Sverre said. "First Father, then Sasha, and finally you. You were so preoccupied with one another and your rivals that you failed to see what was obvious: that I had a plan and an opportunity to carry it out."

"You've good reason to be proud," Hans said.

Just then Marte entered the room. "There's a man at the door who wants to see you, Daddy."

"Not now, Marte," he said, waving her away.

"He's from the 330th Squadron. He was with you when the accident happened. Says he has something for you."

Hans gave a little start. "Oh yes, of course."

"Giske." Hans smiled. "My word, it's been a while." He introduced the man to Marte and Sverre.

"The North Atlantic, the first of December last year, storm conditions," Giske said in greeting. "Good to see you've recovered, Hans. The boys in Bodø miss you. The story about the appendectomy on board a boat in those conditions is already legendary."

"The Russian surgeon Leonid Rogozov had acute appendicitis during a research expedition to the Antarctic in 1961. He was forced to perform an appendectomy – on himself. Compared to that, my efforts were rather modest," Hans answered. The others chuckled, and Giske was quick to apologise. "I can see I've wandered into a private party. I'll be brief."

He looked at the others. "When I was working with you last year, you told me we should preserve organs and tissue from patients, for research and such."

"That's right." Hans nodded. "You never know what you'll find."

"You probably don't remember, but when you were knocked unconscious, I was the one who hoisted you up to the helicopter. After that we got you to intensive care. Your personal effects were dealt with according to normal procedure. But in one pocket I found a sealed bag with what I knew must be the Russian's appendix. I gave it for safekeeping to a doctor in the squadron who promised to send it to you when you were better."

"Quite a story," Marte said.

"I didn't think any more about it for a while, to be honest. Until I remembered it last week and asked the doctor. But he hadn't sent you any *appendix vermiformis*, as he called it. It was still in the freezer, or whatever they use."

Giske took the diffusion-proof bag from his backpack. The seal was intact. The appendix was smaller and paler in colour than Hans remembered, understandably.

The two others took turns looking at it.

"Extraordinary," Marte said.

"Well, there you go, anyway," the rescuer said. "Something to remember it by, Hans."

Hans took leave of the party shortly afterwards. He followed the hallway from the lounge and the library on the first floor, away from the music and hubbub, past the oil portraits of the Falck patriarchs, to the blue room.

He let himself in. The fire was still smouldering so he got it going again and slumped, exhausted, into an armchair. Studied the appendix in the light of the flames.

Hans weighed the bag in his hand and smiled happily.

Happy, that was what he was.

43

REJECTION

Grieg Press, Oslo

Johnny was running late. He jogged past the fountain outside the offices of Grieg Press. Peder Grieg and Hans were waiting inside.

He had not worked on the biography since reading Connie's letter in early winter. That was prior to Medved's attempted defection and the establishment of the investigative team in Cort Adelers gate. Several meetings had been arranged by the publisher, only to be cancelled at the last minute every time, by either Hans or himself.

Hans, although recovered from the accident and spry once again, had a coolness and detachment in his eyes when he shook Johnny's hand, as if greeting a distant acquaintance.

Peder Grieg motioned for them to sit down. The serious look on the publisher's face put Johnny in mind of being summoned to the principal's office.

"Well, shall we make a start?" Grieg said, clearing his throat. Hans gave him a curt nod and the publisher produced a document.

"This is the contract we signed last year, Berg. It's crystal clear. We agreed on an authorised biography: Hans would make himself available and the resulting work would be based on his own experiences. Your last submission to us – the only so far this year, in fact – was instead a letter from a relative whom no one else brings up, but who claims to know the truth about Hans."

Johnny straightened up and looked at both men in turn. "There are two reasons for that. Firstly, Hans hasn't answered my requests since last winter."

"The rationale for that is obvious, it seems to me," Grieg said.

"But the most important reason is hanging on the wall out there." Johnny pointed in the direction of the corridor. "Wasn't Grieg the publisher of Vera Lind? Her mission as a writer was to provide a corrective to the history the men of the Falck family had promoted. We know how that story ended. In my view, Connie Knarvik is cut from the same cloth."

He stared at Hans, who held his gaze. "She tells the truth when others keep silent."

When Hans finally spoke, he had an exquisite softness to his voice that put Johnny on edge.

"There are a few things you don't know about *her*," Hans said. "She struggled with heavy drug addiction for many years in the 1980s and 90s. Many in the family, especially those closest to her, tried to help her out of the drug scene in Nygårds park. But that is what it's like having an addict in the family: betrayal of trust, broken promises and lies. Eventually her loved ones couldn't put up with it anymore. Just couldn't face it. There are limits to how much one can tolerate."

"Why?" Johnny asked.

"What do you mean?" Hans seemed almost annoyed.

"That's the question we always have to ask. In my job we do it all the time. Why do some people become terrorists? Why does someone betray their country? Why do others become addicts? Often there are common features, of course, but every story is unique."

"All well and good," Grieg said, impatiently, "and as interesting as that is, this discussion has little relevance to the biography and the contract entered into."

He looked at Johnny and swallowed. "We've considered the situation carefully, Berg. As the matter stands, with neither the subject of the biography nor the family willing to cooperate, and with questionable source material, well then, the terms and conditions that applied when the contract was signed are no longer in place. Unfortunately we see no other option than to terminate the project."

There was silence in the room. Peder Grieg appeared relieved to have put things straight.

"I'm sorry. But sometimes collaborating on a book doesn't go as one hoped."

Johnny turned to Hans. "I believed you. Thought you were different from Olav and the Oslo branch. But you're just the same."

Johnny left through the service entrance and came out into an alley. A failed writer, was that what he was now? The section chasing the mole was also staring down the barrel after the embarrassing arrest of Mads Falck. He had not spoken to Connie Knarvik in all that time, but he decided to send her a text and briefly explain the situation.

To his surprise she rang him almost immediately.

"I knew it," was the first thing she said.

"What did you know?"

"They're doing to me what they did to Vera. To anyone who dares to tell the truth."

"Vera's manuscript was burned and she was locked away in Blakstad. My biography of Hans was merely shelved. Not quite as heroic."

"Rubbish," Connie replied. "The reasons are purely political."

"But why?" Johnny asked. "That first letter contained startling information, but nothing that couldn't bear scrutiny."

"But there's a second letter," Connie said. "If you have the time to read it. The story has barely begun."

"Can you give me a hint?"

"I can," Connie said. "When I was a young journalist, Hans tipped me off about a sensational story. You can read the details yourself, but it was about Svalbard, secret intelligence activity and the Falck family. And the victims of this conspiracy."

"Is that so?"

"It's always the way, Johnny Berg. Powerful politicians, generals and social elites sacrifice the people at the bottom. They send them to war or on secret missions without warning them of the risks. It was Vera, you know, more than anyone, who inspired me to put pen to paper, and I hope it's written in her spirit."

"When can I see this letter?" Johnny asked.

10/9/1976

Dear Hans,

Chairman Mao died yesterday. I received the last letter I wrote to you marked return to sender the same day. Although I don't know where you are, these were two clear signs. I've given the newspaper my notice and resigned my membership of the party.

What a relief it was.

One of the first things I did afterwards was go to a record shop and buy an ABBA single. Previously I had only listened to it on the radio in secret. I have it on in the background here in Gimle terrasse as I write.

To think we dedicated hours in meetings to formulating resolutions condemning the "petit bourgeois" mentality of ABBA. From a distance I can now see how ridiculous we were. And how counterproductive. As though the way to win the working class over to our side was to gloat over their taste.

I could of course continue with an inventory of the party's tragicomic Sisyphean labours. But at one point our political edicts held life and death consequences. You know very well what I'm talking about, Hans. You will recall how my body changed in late summer, at the same time as we were putting the finishing touches to our story. You must remember I told you about missing my period, feeling nauseous and how tender my breasts were when we made love. A test confirmed my suspicions.

"You need to send in an application to the executive committee," you said.

"I'm pregnant and the first thing you talk about is a fucking application to the committee!"

"Connie, you know the rules," you replied. "The party are trying to turn *Klassekampen* into a daily newspaper and we're working on something with the potential to make headlines worldwide. We need to hear what they have to say about the matter."

That is exactly what you said.

I've been doing a lot of thinking about how I got mixed up in all this.

After the wedding I moved in with Mikael. His villa was only a short walk from the property where I'd grown up. To say I loved him would be an exaggeration. In secret I carried the memories of Provence with me.

Meanwhile you were headed for the stars, Hans. Even though you were a year younger than the others, you had achieved the highest marks in your year at Bergen Cathedral School. A fact that made my father so proud he decided to throw an impromptu party at our family home. The gathering took place on the gently sloping lawn running from the house down to the water. Cooks stood roasting lambs on a spit while the guests drank champagne and chatted.

I arrived with Mikael. As always, his tone became clipped and patronising when your name was mentioned. "Quite the fuss being made for this young lad," he said, looking around. "Is it really true that he supports Russia?"

"Russia?" I shook my head at his antiquated reference. "He thinks the Soviet Union is reactionary and social imperialist," I said, remembering a monologue you had given at the Christmas party. It was the last time I had seen you.

Mikael looked at me as though I were speaking a foreign language.

"He supports China and the teachings of Mao," I said seriously.

"I think I need a drink." Mikael smiled.

You had just turned eighteen. You made your way through the crowd, the men slapping you on the back and the women whispering compliments. Your open face, with those lively eyes and that crooked smile that rarely left your lips, was still boyish. All of us understood: for a brilliant pupil from our background the world was your oyster, and you would be part of shaping its future.

"There you are, Hans," called Father, beaming, and raised his glass in a toast. "As your godfather I've had the pleasure of watching you grow up. It seems like a long time ago but also like yesterday that I showed you Theo's stuffed polar bear, the thing that above all else symbolises our relationship to Svalbard, and thus our own history and that of our country. It's standing down there at the Falck offices. But actually there ought to be a statue of Theo and the polar bear in the public square at Torgallmenningen."

The speech was interrupted by applause and Father turned to praising your academic achievements.

"Not only are you the best, Hans, because any boring bookworm can be top of their class, but your brilliance is conjured with effortless ease. You are a great credit to the Falck name. I spoke to several of your teachers today, and every one of them said they couldn't recall ever having had a more gifted, charismatic and committed pupil."

More cheering and clapping.

"The family expects great things from you, Hans. People with your gifts are rare. And we have, of course, a present in mind for you," Father said, clearing his throat, "but it isn't of the material kind."

He winked at the people standing closest. "As you know, we always travel north to Svalbard in early summer, as soon as the ice conditions allow. This year's ship has already sailed. However, we have a new rescue boat under construction, and prior to it being put in the service of the Society for Sea Rescue at the end of next year, it will travel to Svalbard on an expedition.

"My gift to you, dear Hans," Father cried out, "is a summer of cold, seasickness, wild animals and toil on board *Falck II* next summer. In short, the best that life has to offer for a maritime family! You're going to become a man. You're going to Svalbard!"

You were presented with a watercolour of the Arctic Ocean.

"Would you like to say anything?" Father asked. "Any thoughts about what you're going to do on board *Falck II* and in Svalbard, for instance?"

You paused before answering. You already understood how silence could be a rhetorical device.

"Thank you all so much for coming," you finally said. "I'm overwhelmed."

You turned to Father. "I've actually thought a great deal about this journey. I'm planning to mobilise the sailors and the miners to fight against the ballooning cost of living for the common man and against monopoly capitalism."

Father and the assembled guests offered strained smiles.

"Against the cost of living and . . . monopoly capitalism," Father repeated. "It's great that you're bringing new thoughts and perspectives into the family. We can all do with that. Here's to you, dear Hans!"

After the speech, as I made my way over to you, I could feel my blood pumping fast.

"Hi," I said.

"Have you heard?"

That was the first thing you said. "Heard what?"

"Vera has had a breakdown. She's been admitted to Blakstad."

Although I didn't know Vera Lind that well, it was still shocking. "What are you talking about?"

"They're saying she's having delusions. Trauma induced."

"How tragic. Vera was a role model for us girls in the family," I said. "We looked up to her. She challenged the men."

You gave me a hard look. "But what they're saying is pure lies!"

I repeated what I had heard from Father and others in the family: "She's from a very humble background up north, and her mother did die when she was young. Maybe that played a part, and the ferry disaster on top of that?"

"The last time I met Vera," you said, holding back your anger, "she outlined the story of the new book she was writing. It was about just that, the Hurtigruten sinking. And about the lies our family told."

We wandered away from the gathering and towards the house, walking on the flagstones at the front. A waiter was smoking at the corner. You cadged a cigarette.

"Do you smoke, Hans?" I asked.

"Only today."

"Try to be a little happy," I said. "Father has put on a party and invited half of Bergen society."

You took another thoughtful drag on the cigarette.

"What about you?" you asked. "I never see you anymore, Constance."

"We've moved," I said and nodded in the direction of Fantoft stave church, further up the hill.

"Would you like me to call in one day? We could go for a walk."

"I don't think my husband would like it," I said, first looking away, and then over my shoulder, as if to make sure Mikael wasn't within earshot.

I changed the subject to try to lighten the atmosphere.

"I'm going to study at university," I said, breaking into a smile. "French, of course."

"What does your *husband* have to say about that?"

I shrugged. "He was against it at first. Raised the kind of silly objections the men in our family always have. But after I took the preliminary exams last year in secret, he's granted me his 'approval', as he puts it."

"I'll be at the university tomorrow night," you said quietly.

"But I haven't started yet," I said. "Neither have you, I imagine?"

"Study groups," you said, "organised by the Socialist Youth Union. We're having a get-together tomorrow. Say you're going to an information meeting."

I looked at you quizzically. "What for, Hans?"

"Because I want to convince you that everything that's ours, everything you see around you here, is based on the exploitation of the working class and needs pulling down when the revolution comes."

"I'm not sure," I said.

"It's a study circle for symps."

"Symps?"

"Sympathisers, Constance. And don't tell me you're from the upper class. There's a difference between class *background* and class *standpoint*."

I looked at you. Finally I felt I had the upper hand in the conversation. "But that's not actually why you want me to come?"

"Just come," you said.

The Maoists were everywhere at that time. The next day I found myself at a study circle arranged by the Marxist–Leninists. The meeting took place in a room at the university. The symps were students for the most part. Although younger than the others, you were the one who presided over the meeting and took the lead in speaking. You outlined the Maoist world view, based on the writings of Karl Marx, practised by Lenin and Stalin in the Soviet Union prior to the revisionist decline.

You described Lenin's theory of imperialism. I had problems keeping my eyes open when you spoke about the Marxist *dialectic*. It didn't speak to the heart, as you must have noticed, because you soon changed tack.

"Comrades, we can all feel powerless when faced with the world we live in. When confronted with the two imperialist superpowers, with all the pain, exploitation and wickedness that exist."

Is that it, I thought.

"But Marxism is not just prose, it's also poetry," you continued. "We are socialists because we dream of a better world. A world without capitalistic exploitation and imperialistic warfare, where people are free to do what they want, to love who they want."

A bearded philosophy student snorted at the banality of this but you went on.

"That's why I want to read you a poem," you said, showing a palm to the philosophy student, who was no doubt about to decry this bourgeois act. "And the poem is by Chairman Mao: 'Reascending Chingkangshan'."

That served to thwart the strict evangelists. No matter how bourgeois a poem might be, Mao Tse-tung was an ace up anyone's sleeve. You read:

I have long aspired to reach for the clouds
To again ascend Chingkangshan
I remember the merriment and triumphant songs.
Under this heaven nothing is difficult
If you dare to scale the heights.

"What did you think?" you asked, as we walked away from the campus after the meeting.

"I thought the concepts were a little hard to follow, at first," I said thoughtfully. "But they make sense too. Admit it, that Mao poem was something you made up to impress me."

"It's real. Chairman Mao really does write poetry." You laughed. "But I did recite it to impress you."

"I liked it," I said. "I've read my whole life and I like to write."

We sat on a bench, surrounded by purple rhododendrons, under a large birch tree. The colours were vivid; there was nowhere where green was as green as in Bergen.

"All people," you said, looking around before your eyes came to rest on me, "have a proletarian and a bourgeois side. Being a Maoist cadre is about acknowledging that. Without self-criticism we get nowhere."

I knew that for you talking about politics was just a way to avoid the core issue. So I asked: "How are you doing, really?"

You thought for a long time before answering: "I miss you, Constance, I can't stop thinking about you."

"I'm married, Hans. Mikael is kind and—"

"But you don't love him!" you said. "Why did you do it?" There was pain in your voice. "Why did you marry *him*?"

"What should I have done instead?"

You smiled. "Been with me. I want it to be the two of us, Constance." You purred like a cat, you had realised the power of words long ago. You stroked my hair, I felt butterflies in my stomach, you placed a rhododendron flower in my hand and closed it.

"What if I give up everything for us, something happens and we break up? Then I'm left high and dry," I said, gazing at the horizon.

"We won't break up. Anyway our journey together is so much bigger. To reach for the clouds, the ninth heaven, have you forgotten already? The personal is political."

"I'll think about it."

I leaned over and kissed you, then got to my feet. When I glanced back you were still sitting with your eyes closed.

I joined the party for you, Hans.

Once I had become a Maoist there was no stopping me.

When other girls from bourgeois backgrounds joined the movement they were soon given "class marks" immediately prior to their malign influences being driven out. It obviously takes one to know one.

Maoism was all-consuming. Everything was about the movement, the party whose establishment was secretly being planned, the struggle against the high cost of living and the EEC. Everything was political: I wore a long pleated skirt like a nineteenth-century peasant woman. I manned a stand selling *Klassekampen*, the Maoist weekly, a mouthpiece I read with ever-increasing interest.

The genius of Marxist doctrine was the combination of the complex and the strikingly simple. There were enough abstract concepts in Marxist–Leninist theory to satisfy a university professor for a lifetime, while at the same time the theories were based on a set of simple antipodes anyone could understand. Between the bourgeoisie and the proletariat, between imperialists and their progressive opponents, above all those in Mao's China.

I quickly graduated from the ranks of the symps to the regular study circles. I read Marx, first the polemic manifesto, then the intricate *Das Kapital*, as well as Mao's poetry and his Little Red Book. Mostly his book, perhaps. The Soviet Union was an old and rudderless supertanker; Mao's China was the future.

And yet I did not mention a word of this ideology I was brimming with to my husband. I was living a double life. Before arriving back at our villa, I took off the peasant skirt and traditional workman's shirt and put my pearl earrings back in.

One evening you and I were to face a so-called cadre evaluation at the apartment of one of the comrades in the party. A dozen or so of the Socialist Youth Union's most zealous members were packed together in the tiny living room to review our bourgeois aberrancies.

They started with you, Hans. These evaluations were unsparing affairs, and your bourgeois aberrancies were not hard to pinpoint, as you had grown up in one of the richest families in the city and had a flamboyant personality that provoked annoyance and envy.

You listened calmly to all the criticism, before clearing your throat and saying: "What is most important in self-criticism is to be ruthlessly honest."

Then you stared at your party comrades and said: "The problem is *your* criticism only scratched the surface."

The rest of the vanguard stared at you in confusion, but you continued. "As the son and heir of a shipping empire, I've grown up with privileges scarcely comprehensible and opposed in every way to the interests of the working class. We're talking about a luxurious villa with a private railway station on the Bergen rail line, a hunting lodge and cabins, properties from Oslo to Svalbard. When I went on summer holidays, it was with Jackie Kennedy, Evita Perón and Winston Churchill on Aristotle Onassis's yacht. The only thing I can say in my defence is that it is precisely because of my background that the reckoning I've faced has been far more fundamental than that faced by others."

Your judgement of yourself was so severe that even the puritanical Maoists were tongue-tied. They were used to softly spoken self-reproach from people weeping as they admitted having bought a new suit or having attended a bourgeois Ibsen play at the theatre.

I don't know if you were conscious of it then, but you knew instinctively that even among the Maoists the same principles applied as for the art of seduction: to lay bare your own weaknesses. The lesson being you could hide behind the magnitude of your own offence. The roué who admits *everything* is at the receiving end of less criticism than the moralist who admits *little*.

Then it was my turn to face the ordeal. I was dreading it. You had set a high bar for self-criticism, so what was I to do?

The first issue brought up was that I still went horse riding, "the very embodiment of bourgeois convention", as one of the members put it.

"That's correct," I said, "but out of class considerations I no longer ride my family's thoroughbreds and borrow a fjord horse from a neighbour instead. That breed is a hardy horse with its roots in the Norwegian smallholders class."

The cadres nodded. It was a valid point, accepted with reservations.

The inquisitors didn't go easy on me, but I was far from finished with my self-criticism.

I had had an idea that would put you in the shade.

"I was christened Constance Philipine Falck, and have since taken my husband's name and am now Falck-Dreyer. Seeing as Falck and Dreyer are distinctly bourgeois surnames, synonymous with extreme wealth and the exploitation of the working class, I shall go to the courthouse tomorrow and change it."

The cadres' eyes widened.

"I'm changing my name to Connie Knarvik. My grandmother was called Knarvik, and the forename is self-explanatory."

An impressed murmur rippled through the group. Even you, always so nonchalant, looked disconcerted, because many eyes inevitably turned your way. If I could take a proletarian name, then why not you? Hans was fine. But you could at least remove that ostentatious "c" from your surname. Hans Falk? Had you really taken a profound existential audit of yourself or were you merely a bourgeois silver tongue and poseur?

You grabbed me by the shoulder as we were leaving and whispered that we needed to talk.

We pushed our bikes along the fjord.

"Why didn't you tell the truth?" you said.

"I did. I am going to change my name!"

You stopped me.

"Are you going to tell your husband?"

"You know as well as I do that they'll never accept it."

"*They?* I'm talking about Mikael."

"You're not telling the truth either," I countered. "You're still just a bourgeois clown, an armchair radical, the sardonic outsider at family gatherings."

"Maybe, but you're a liar, who doesn't dare tell it like it is. I'm sure your name is Constance when you're with him."

Rain began to fall, a cold February shower.

"Do you remember the 'gift' your father gave me last year? The trip to Svalbard with the Falck rescue ship?"

"Of course. To set you on your way to being a 'real man'," I said with a laugh.

"I'm going to make that trip," you said solemnly. "I've spoken to people in Oslo. Maoists are becoming well represented in industry now, but we have hardly anyone at sea. The central members want me to work at recruiting sailors. Plus we need to show solidarity with the miners in Longyearbyen."

I nodded.

"You like to read," you continued, "and you're a good writer."

Although it might just have been cajolery, the words made me swell with pride. "Thanks. I dream about writing something for *Klassekampen* but I don't know if I'm good enough."

"Of course you are! I'll travel to Svalbard with *Falck II* and you come along as a journalist. You'll get some great stories in print, I guarantee it."

"Mikael has actually asked me to travel with him on a plane travelling north to Svalbard," I said. "I can't drop that plan."

"Fantastic," you said. "Don't change it. Imagine: we can finally experience Svalbard together."

*

You were already there when we landed at the provisional airport on the flat floor of the Advent Valley.

"Welcome," you said, greeting me, Mikael and the rest of the group. "How does it feel to plant your feet on your own property in the Advent Valley?"

At first glance, Svalbard, this mythical place from childhood, was a big disappointment. It was June, and due to the permafrost, the meltwater didn't penetrate the ground but instead formed large rivers.

The governor's people drove us the short distance to Longyearbyen, which seemed no more than a grimy, muddy cluster of shacks.

Indifferent as he was, Mikael had no qualms about "leaving me in the custody of Hans Falck" while he, the governor and the chief of the mine left for a two-day inspection of another mine.

"I can't believe we're here in Svalbard together," you said when the others had gone and we walked down the main street.

"Did you recruit any sailors on the voyage north?"

By your hesitant response I could tell it had been more difficult than you'd anticipated.

"But we had shore leave in Tromsø," you said excitedly. "The Maoists have a strong presence there. It turned out that, thanks to a symp who had studied at the Sorbonne, the party workers had come across an article in French from *Le Nouvel Observateur*."

"Go on," I said.

"*Un médecin accuse* it was called, and it was penned by a young French Maoist doctor. His name is Bernard Kouchner and he's an old friend of Fidel Castro. He's worked in the Nigerian province of Biafra. He's harshly critical of the Red Cross and of their failure to protect the civilian population from famine and attack: how can one belong to the political left and allow the massacre of millions of people, asks Kouchner. The left, if such a thing exists, is closing its eyes."

"Isn't that a rather reactionary viewpoint?" I asked.

"Apparently Kouchner is planning on starting up his own emergency relief organisation. Nothing against the social sciences, but I've been looking for something that combines analysis with practice. I'm going to study medicine, Constance."

"Connie."

You smiled. "Sorry."

"I've spoken to *Klassekampen*," I said, excitement in my voice. "They're interested in articles from Svalbard. I wonder what to focus on."

You shrugged. "Start with the mineworkers."

"The miners would be good," I said.

"I've got something else. Potentially bigger," you said in a secretive tone. "If you're up late tonight, come with me and bring a camera."

It was midnight and daylight all around us. We walked between the barracks and hangars down by the docks. An icy wind swept across the snowdrifts on Opera Mountain and into our faces. You took hold of my cold hand. *Falck II* was moored on the quay between other boats and ice floes. You looked around to make sure no one was looking at us, but it was completely quiet, on the sea and on land.

You climbed over the gunwale and held out your hand. We made for the wheelhouse. The radar was on a platform over the bridge, the dish curved like a sail in the wind.

I snapped some photos.

"What do you know about that radar?" I asked.

"It's strange," you said in a low voice. "According to the crew, it was installed before the boat came to Bergen. It wasn't used at all while we sailed up the coast. Not until we were leaving Tromsø. Then some American scientists and a couple of tight-lipped Norwegians came aboard to map the bottom of the Barents Sea. Parts of the vessel were declared off limits to crew members."

I felt a creeping fear. "This could be dangerous, Hans."

"The whole thing stinks," you said. "The chief engineer confronted the Norwegians. Asked what the hell was going on. If we were unwittingly part of a spy mission."

"The scope of this might be much more far-reaching," I said, and swallowed. "When my father was in the resistance during the war he worked with the Americans, and kept in touch with them afterwards, as well as travelling frequently to Svalbard. I have wondered if he worked for them. But I don't think he'll be very happy if we write about that."

"You have photos of a radar," you said. "Nothing tying Uncle Herbert to the Americans. But the radar will make for a good story. Very good."

I could feel the relief when we put our feet back on solid ground. Up in the shanty-town-like settlement of huts, mine-workers were staggering around looking for after-hours drinks. We followed in the direction many were headed and wound up in an overcrowded prefab, thick with cigarette smoke, clamour and the clinking of bottles.

One miner shouted: "Who are you two?"

"My name is Hans and this is Connie," you said. "We're from the Socialist Youth Union, the new communist movement in Norway. I've come to take a closer look at the exploitation and superpower rivalry here on the island, and when that's done, build a Maoist and revolutionary organisation among the miners."

The noise and clinking of glass ceased, and the twenty or so faces in the room looked seriously at you and at one another.

The oldest-looking of the men nodded. "Wake the shop steward."

Before long a mess cook with radical leanings made an appearance.

He was given a glass of spirits, soon perked up, and began to tell us about the conflicts with the employers in Store Norske coal mining. Particularly delicate was the matter of workers working on sites outside the mines. Many of the workers were incensed about the conditions.

You got up from the table, raised your glass and proclaimed: "A new generation of miners on Svalbard is ready to hit back!"

The men didn't laugh at you.

"We will build an organisation of struggle for the mineworkers in Longyearbyen and Svea," you shouted fervently, going on to rail against the two imperialist superpowers, each doing as they pleased on sovereign Norwegian territory on Svalbard. "To battle – against all superpower imperialism and for proper working conditions in the mines!"

The men applauded you. No, they cheered. You were soaring so high on this totally unexpected victory that you had the workers join in and sing along to an old Italian partisan song popular in the Socialist Youth Union. *One morning I awakened, oh bella ciao, bella ciao, bella ciao, ciao, ciao.*

We walked out into the midnight sun, drunk on the winds of revolution and each other, and went to your room. You sat on the bed; I stood in front of you. You undressed me, kissing me slowly and tenderly all over, but desire overwhelmed me and I pushed you down on the mattress, and whispered how long I had fantasised about exactly this.

We lay silently in bed afterwards. A gap in the curtains cast a sharp beam of light across our bodies.

"You'll stay here tonight?" you said.

I nodded.

"You realise you can't go on being with Mikael?"

"Yes," I said.

This time I didn't hesitate. Right after you had left Longyearbyen, I went to my husband and told him I wanted to separate. I told a shocked Mikael that yes, it was on account of another man, and no, I had no intention of saying who.

He said nothing.

"You're a good man, Mikael, but I don't love you and never have. That's the truth and I'm sorry. You know as well as I do that if our families hadn't pressured us we never would have married."

He was furious at first, flung the miner's helmet he was holding at the wall of the room at Funken Lodge, and for a moment I was afraid he would hit me. But his fury turned to reproach, then to self-reproach, and finally to tears and pathetic attempts to get me to stay.

I didn't look back as I left. One thing is for certain: I was no more convinced by his sentimental monologues than any other woman in the process of leaving her husband.

You had persuaded me to leave my husband, yet it was as though you didn't want to acknowledge us.

You moved from a student hall to a flat in the city centre that was practically rent-free. A spacious place with a communal toilet off the landing. I was often there, but your life was a non-stop whirl of medical studies, meetings, study circles, agitation and debates. And other women, of course. There was a lot of sex involved when the Norwegian working class were to be roused to revolution. Virile revolutionary males were everywhere to be found – in the party leadership, among the lionised writers, doctors, third-world activists, the newly proletarianised and, naturally, the real workers in the party, who were at the top of the food chain.

You had long since internalised Ekblad's words about life as theatre. You seduced me in the same way as you had seduced all the beautiful, radical girls at the university, in the canteen, in the lecture hall and on the street – preferably there, because who doesn't wish to touch the clouds? What female student with a sense of adventure didn't want to "reach the ninth heaven high to embrace the moon" or "dive into the five oceans deep" to capture a turtle with you?

It was during that time that Vera invited us to lunch at the venerable Theatercafeen. An orchestra was playing on the mezzanine as the liveried waiter led us to the table. Not perhaps the place for two Maoist cadres, but Vera had always walked her own path.

She was approaching her mid-fifties and was still very beautiful, even though the last few years had taken their toll. It was two years since she had been released from the psychiatric institution. She had since been trying to pick up the pieces of her life.

A smile spread across her face when she caught sight of us. "Constance and Hans!"

We sat down.

"Being an author entails the perfect level of fame," she said. "One is famous enough to get a table at a good restaurant, but still able to eat in peace."

"Do you still write?" I asked, surprised she still thought of herself as an author after everything that had happened.

"They refused to let me tell my story. So I don't actually know."

During the meal she related what had happened on the Hurtigruten ferry in 1940, when her husband Thor had died. In his position as director of the family shipping company he had made good money from the transport of German troops during the war. Which was completely at odds with the image of "Big Thor" the family had imprinted on his descendants: member of the resistance, recipient of the War Cross, hero.

"I have letters proving his collaboration," Vera said. "But that would be too much for the bigwigs of the resistance movement. After all, they're the ones running the country now."

We exchanged glances. I had had enough schooling in Marxist theory to know that the bourgeoisie would inevitably side with the fascists when a revolutionary situation arose and matters came to a head. But it was something very different when, as now, things entered the personal realm.

Vera, sensing the tension around the table, changed the subject. "How is university going?"

I hesitated to answer. My French studies had taken a back seat to my work for the party, and my time had also been spent writing articles for *Klassekampen*.

You, on the other hand, went on about how you had completed the first semesters of medicine at lightning pace, even alongside all your other activities.

"Let me tell you something," Vera said, fixing you with her gaze, oblivious to my presence. "For most people life is straightforward. They work hard and are perhaps rewarded every so often with a pay raise. For you, Hans, life will be different. You have charisma. And a distinctive quality that makes other people look up to you, want to follow you. It is so rare that the rules that apply to the rest of society won't count for you. Fame, status and of course money – you will have these in such abundance that you'll want to escape them."

Although she no doubt meant it as a warning, I could see your chest swell. If there was something you had always dreamed about, it was recognition and renown.

"I've been on the lookout for someone in the family who will change the world," Vera continued. "My son, Olav, accomplished as he is, is no idealist. But the two of you are."

I had a strong sense of being a fifth wheel in this conversation. "You write, Constance," Vera said. "And you, Hans, you're a dreamer, while at the same time you can get people to follow you. It's a gift almost no one is born with."

Then Vera placed her hands on yours, looked at you, and said: "But, dear Hans, this is a pact with the devil. Have you heard of Faust?"

Our eyes met for a moment. I thought about Ekblad the Swede. How everything was just technique. About your hand touching mine in the darkness of the theatre.

"The problem with people who want to accomplish great things in the world is that very often their moral compass in close relationships is affected. How minor must fidelity to a single individual seem to someone who wants to change the world? Believe me, I've known several such people – artists, politicians – yes, I even have a little of it in myself. Despite your gift, there's something you won't understand until you get older. That success in life is measured in how you've treated those closest to you."

One evening you and I were with some comrades in a draughty flat in the old town. The issue under discussion was the use of revolutionary violence in industrialised, developed countries.

Urban guerrillas in nations like Germany, Japan and Italy were severely criticised as revisionist and counter-revolutionary by the study leaders. As was Bernard Kouchner's aid organisation Médecins Sans Frontières.

Of course they were. There was no room for divergence.

In addition to the items on the agenda, there was discussion of a statement condemning the "petit bourgeois" appeal of the Swedish band ABBA, who everyone had started listening to. I sat lost in my own thoughts. I had read the story about the Norwegian-born member Anni-Frid Lyngstad, born outside marriage in northern Norway to a destitute teenager and a German Wehrmacht sergeant during the war, who fled to avoid abuse from the vengeful local population, lost her mother and grew up with her grandmother in Sweden.

What right had the party cadres, who often hailed from middle-class homes and had had good educations, to condemn the musical endeavours of a person with experiences like that as "petit bourgeois"? My thoughts turned to Vera. Her biography was not dissimilar.

After the meeting you and I wandered through the city. My split from the party was still long in the future, but doubts, however tentative, had begun to creep in.

I think you had similar thoughts, but you remained hard and uncompromising on the surface. You said: "The Red Army Faction in Germany and the Red Brigades in Italy are incapable of building the alliances with the population needed to seize power."

"But wasn't all that back there a little harsh on ABBA?" I asked cautiously. "I'm not so sure the way to building 'alliances with the population' is by ridiculing the taste of ordinary people."

"But admit it, Connie, ABBA are awful. You don't listen to *that*, do you?"

In secret, I was about to say, but I made no reply.

You switched to praising some articles I had written for *Klassekampen* concerning a strike at a hosiery factory. "You did a damn good job of getting the female workers to open up."

You obviously meant what you said and I was giddy with joy. "Do you think so?"

The *Klassekampen* editorial office was mostly stick and very little carrot.

"I'm positive that if you keep at the writing," you continued enthusiastically, "you'll do great things."

"I'm just a rookie journalist; you always think in such grandiose terms. Have you any suggestions though?"

"Did you read about the IB affair in Sweden?" you said.

"Not in detail, no." I had never quite understood what those espionage cases were all about.

"Jan Guillou and Peter Bratt, two radical Swedish journalists, exposed the existence of a secret intelligence agency abroad. Members of parliament knew nothing about it. The two of them were put in prison."

You gave a wry grin. "But they won all the same. The truth came out."

"Can't see myself ever having an exposé like that up my sleeve," I laughed.

"Don't say that!" you said, as we passed Our Saviour's Cemetery.

I loved when you were like that. Everything was possible for you. You had none of the puritanical and prosaic style that characterised the party cadres, who seemed to have wandered straight out of a Christian meeting house, mixing a comparable piety into the pot of Maoism. They had adopted all Mao's life-denying insights from the Cultural Revolution but nothing of the grandeur and poetry that allowed the cadres in the Chinese Communist Party to subjugate that vast country.

When you were like this, it felt as though we could fly to the ninth heaven.

"You remember the radar on *Falck II*?" you said.

I nodded. "Of course."

"I've been thinking about it. That reactionary American we met on Onassis's yacht, the one who had visited Herbert in 1952? His name is William Astor. And I'll be damned if he hasn't been appointed deputy director of the entire CIA. Do you honestly believe it's a coincidence they know each other? I don't. The Americans are interested in intelligence from Svalbard and the stretches of ocean towards the Soviet Union. To get that information they need a powerful radar."

I had my misgivings. "Vague suspicions and insinuation aren't enough. In journalism you need sources. You need documentation and proof."

We stopped to sit on a bench.

"You're talking and talking," I said, "but you're still avoiding the question."

You looked at me. "What question?"

I could feel my emotions beginning to get the better of me. "I joined the party for your sake, I divorced for you, no one in the family wants anything to do with me! And yet you won't commit to anything."

"It's just so . . . difficult," you said meekly. "The circles we move in are small, there's gossip, in Bergen, of course, but also within the party. About the incestuous relationship in the Falck family. Bear in mind we both start at a disadvantage as communists because of our class background."

"Surely you don't care about that kind of thing!"

"I've been thinking about going abroad when I graduate," you said in a low voice. "Solidarity work."

"So, what? Just venture ever further from Bergen?" Furious, I stood up to leave.

"The Middle East, maybe," you said calmly. "They speak French in many places there, Connie. I want you to come with me. Will you? I think we can be freer if we're somewhere far from Norway."

I didn't reply but you knew the answer would be yes.

"I have to go," I said at last. "I start work early tomorrow."

"Don't forget the big scoop." You smiled. "It'll happen sooner than you think."

When the scoop finally fell into my lap, I'd almost forgotten your words.

The workload at the *Klassekampen* office was extreme. We were expected to work every day, including weekends. Once or twice a fortnight we finished at a normal time. Other than that, it was constant pressure. On Saturday afternoons we were sent out onto the city streets to sell the newspaper. We had Sunday mornings off but were back at the office in the afternoon, working well into the evening.

One colleague, who developed ulcerative colitis from the stress, requested to be allowed to leave work at 8 p.m. on Mondays and Wednesdays. The committee's response was brutal: "We are of the opinion that our comrade's decline in health is a result of an unhealthy lifestyle in general, and that more leisure time will not solve the problem."

When the women on the editorial staff sneaked out to get a Wiener schnitzel for dinner before the last few hours of work in the evening, we often had harsh words to say about the male dominance of the party.

"You know what he said?" I imitated our male colleague: "'The revolution needs more fuckdolls.'"

The editor was a man, as was the rest of the AKP leadership. The overwhelming majority of the authors and intellectuals in the movement were also men. There were no limits to their progressive feminism in theory, but in practice they weren't the ones who were going to bear that particular burden.

As usual I was the first to arrive at work. I liked to get the odd jobs out of the way in peace and quiet, whether that meant answering correspondence or because it was my turn to wash the floors. Hiring a cleaner was dismissed as "bourgeois revisionism" but since the party leadership had decided to become a daily paper, the workload had become so strenuous that no one followed the washing rota and the premises stank of sweat and smelly socks.

I had just finished cleaning when there was a knock at the door. Who would knock? None of the staff anyway. I opened the door a crack. At first I thought the man on the doorstep might have been one of the lift technicians I had interviewed in connection with a strike, but there was something about him, as though he didn't belong in this city.

"My name is Bendiksen," he said in a northern accent.

I studied the lean, sallow man. "How can I help you?"

"I'm here about a story. I think it may be of interest to you."

In *Klassekampen* the articles came as decrees from the party leadership. Loud-mouthed men often got the exclusive stories while the women had to make do with lesser pieces. Our journalism was not exactly based on "walk-ins", and I was about to politely decline, when the man said: "I was chief engineer on the *Falck II* in 1971."

Did he know my family name? I suggested we take a stroll along the Aker river. The sailor walked with a stoop and wheezed like a nonagenarian.

"She was a lovely craft," he reminisced. "We were an experienced crew and had that whippersnapper Hans Falck with us as well. We were headed north. The boat was going to be a rescue vessel but had been leased first to the Polar Institute. We sailed around Svalbard and the entire Barents Sea."

The memories came flooding back and we sat down on a bench.

"A strange thing happened," he said. "Before we set out on the voyage, she was fitted with a huge radar down on the south-west coast, in Egersund. It was so big we had to put it on a specially built platform, and in the heavy seas along the coast I was worried the weight might tip the boat over."

That radar, I thought.

"But this is what I wanted to tell you." He paused. "The crew members who had been in close proximity to the radar over longer periods started to die. Inexplicable forms of cancer, every one of them. The captain, officers, seamen and engineers alike. So, we get in touch with the boat that had this radar fitted before us. *Skomvær II*, it was called. There are sailors on board her that also died from cancer."

"And now you want me to write about it?"

"Do you need to be spoon-fed?" the northerner said. "Sailors are dying like flies because of some mysterious radar. I don't have many months left myself. What's this radar doing up there in the Barents Sea? We're not morons, you know."

I began to fantasise about a big scoop.

But just then I thought of something else. "What about Hans? Has he been checked for cancer?"

"Dunno. But he should do it soon. Cancer doesn't make distinctions between people."

I immediately brought the story to the editor-in-chief, who discussed the matter with the party leadership. They were fired up. You had to have been involved in some way. And sure enough, it soon became clear that Hans Falck was the one who had pulled the strings that led to chief engineer Bendiksen knocking on the door of *Klassekampen*.

We devised a plan.

You had a key role. As a medical student you were to seek out research on radiation and cancer incidence, plus you had worked on *Falck II* for a season and could bear witness. It was pure dynamite.

We went to Bergen.

In the archives of the Falck shipping company we found the first clue: a contract signed by Johnson Radio Elektro Ltd in Egersund and Herbert Falck concerning the installation of the radar on *Falck II*.

Now we had evidence that Herbert had ordered the radar and had it installed. Given all the seamen sick or dead with cancer, this was a story in itself. But were there other, more powerful forces behind it?

We took a walk through Bergen, for the first time in years.

"This is the difficult part," you said quietly. "Locating evidence linking Herbert directly to Astor in the CIA. That's definitely not going to be in any open archive."

"Father has a safe in his bedroom," I said. "If he does have anything, it'll be in there."

"You're a journalist," you said sternly. "You can't just break into places, irrespective of what you might uncover."

I gave a wry smile. "True. But should you – in the role of whistle-blower on your own family – get hold of the documents without committing any crime, that would be legal. I believe you know the code?"

You looked at me with a crooked smile. "You're beginning to sound like a real journalist, Connie. Good thinking!"

Night had fallen when we made our way to the property in the Paradis neighbourhood. We crossed the bridge over the long-abandoned old railway line. I could clearly make out the silhouette of the magnificent villa in the moonlight and felt a pang of nostalgia. Not much seemed to have changed since the last time I was there. When was that? Five years ago?

The round moon was reflected in the large front window.

We moved along the foundation wall of the house. You stopped to listen carefully. It was completely quiet except for the faraway hum of traffic. The window of the potato cellar was slightly open. We looked over our shoulders one last time, pushed the window open to make room, and lowered ourselves down.

The cellar was cold and the air was stale. Nothing to see but empty wine bottles. The walls were white but looked grey in the darkness. Our shadows were enlarged in the moonlight. You cautiously opened the door to the basement hallway and we walked through the passage, the tiled floor dusty enough for us to leave footprints. Would the door to the steep staircase leading to the ground floor be unlocked? I tried the handle, causing it to squeak a little, and the door opened.

We ascended the stairs slowly, agonisingly slowly. You took a deep breath and opened the door at the top. We stood there smelling the air of Paradis, of childhood, of life as it had been.

A dog barked, the sound resounded around the house and was immediately followed by rapid steps. The sound of claws on the parquet floor.

Then I heard whimpering. Instead of attacking us, the dog rolled on her back with her forelegs stretched out.

"Arusha," I said, breathing in the smell of the guard dog's short coat, holding her strong head in my hands, "you remember me, of course you remember me."

The passageway led to a hall, with a wide stone staircase leading to the first floor, where the bedrooms were located. That was where Father kept his most treasured possessions. Had the barking woken him up?

Up on the landing we stopped.

"It's in there," I whispered, pointing.

"Are you quite sure?"

"Yes, Mother sleeps in the other bedroom. And that's my old room there."

Beside me, Arusha whined. "Go on now, good girl," I said, scratching the dog's ear.

I thought about the first time we kissed, in that very spot, after the performance of *Faust*. In secret that time as well. Call me melodramatic, Hans, but I experienced that same feeling of being on the threshold of something unknown. Only now did the implications of what I was about to do dawn on me: if my previous betrayals had not already ended my relationship with my family, this was the final nail in the coffin.

You entered the room, I waited outside. Everything was quiet, the door was slightly ajar. Dim moonlight shone into the room. Father was lying on his back, his even breathing culminating in a snore.

You didn't hesitate. In the top drawer of the bedside table, which scraped slightly against the wooden frame as you opened it, lay the set of keys. I could see the two of you so clearly, how Father was beginning to become an old man with bushy eyebrows and a potato nose.

Did Father open his eyes? Slowly shake his head? Or was that something I imagined?

The safe was, as it always had been, set in plain sight in the wall. Quickly and quietly, like a seasoned burglar, you opened the first lock with a key from the set you had found.

Then you were on to the combination lock on the dial.

The heavy safe door opened.

You took the documents out, put them in a bag, closed the safe, looked around and left. We were soon back outside.

We found more than we could have hoped for.

Among the documents you had taken was a contract. It turned out that when father purchased the property in the Advent Valley on Svalbard in the 1950s, he had done so with money from an American company called Arctica Inc., which on closer investigation was found to be a shell company of the kind an organisation like the CIA used. Who had signed the contract on behalf of the Americans? None other than one William Astor, who had gone on to be deputy director of the CIA.

And that wasn't all. You found a medal in the safe: an eagle with a name on the back and an inscription around it:

Herbert Falck

Central Intelligence Agency – for distinguished service

I had what I needed for the biggest exposé in *Klassekampen*'s history, proving collusion between Norwegian shipping owners and the intelligence services. And not only that: this secret cooperation had had devastating consequences for the health of sailors who had no idea what they were involved in.

I had their testimonies. And you had gathered expert opinions from doctors who had spoken in no uncertain terms about the dangers of radiation for anyone in proximity to such equipment.

You were elated. "Nothing in post-war Scandinavian journalism will ever have come close to this, if we do it right. It's bigger than the IB affair. This is going to cause a major political earthquake and the tremors will be felt at the very heart of the Kremlin and Washington."

"But Hans?" I said, hesitantly.

You could tell I was nervous.

"You do understand what we're about to do? Father is never going to forgive me, or you. Remember what happened to Vera when she tried to tell the truth about Big Thor's ties to the Nazis."

"Don't be afraid," you replied confidently. "Knowing Herbert, he'll be proud to be described as a Norwegian CIA agent. And anyway, Connie, we have each other."

I felt a surge of relief. "Do you mean that, Hans?"

"Of course I mean it. You and I."

But life is never that simple. It was around then that I started to suffer from morning sickness, and one day I was called in to the committee to discuss the matter. You didn't want to come with me, but I made you.

The editor and the leader of the committee, both of them men, were present at the meeting. The leader, his expression inscrutable, said: "The committee has considered your request carefully."

I nodded, my eyes on the tabletop.

"As you know, the workload at the newspaper is particularly heavy now as we transition to being a daily newspaper. This fact, as well as the spying exposé, means we can't approve your request to carry a child to term at the present time."

I stared at you, Hans, with a look that said: *Help me!*

You thought for a while before replying. "I think the editor is quite right. Given the situation, it would be completely indefensible to continue with the pregnancy."

It was two days until we were set to publish. Everything was chaos. You had travelled north on an "errand" and I was only too happy to be rid of you. I wasn't sleeping at night. The previous evening, I had put the finishing touches to the article. For once I came late to work. On entering the office, I could sense the excited, expectant atmosphere in the cramped newsroom.

It all came down to strategy now. We agreed to begin with a shock headline and a piece claiming that Norwegian shipowners had cooperated with the CIA. Their first instinct would of course be to deny the allegations as pure fabrication. Then we could present evidence that they were lying. Before going on to report on how a particularly sensitive part of Norwegian security policy – on Svalbard and in the Barents Sea against the Soviets – was being conducted without parliamentary knowledge.

When that part of the narrative had settled, we were going to run with the story of the mysterious radar. In the words of those whose health had been affected. That was when Bendiksen would get to tell his story.

I was sitting at my desk when the phone rang.

"It's Hans," you said, your tone cold. Something was wrong. You always used to say: "It's me."

"The line is bad, Hans, where are you calling from?"

"I'm in Svalbard. Longyearbyen."

"We have a lot to talk about," I said.

"Yeah."

"We're running the first part of the story the day after tomorrow," I went on, and explained the strategy.

"Constance?"

"*Connie.*"

"Constance," you said, "there is no story."

I wasn't fazed in the slightest. This had to be a misunderstanding. "What do you mean?"

"You have two main sources for your story," you continued. "First, chief engineer Bendiksen. He rang to let me know he won't be corroborating what he told you."

"I spoke to him the day before yesterday. He was all set."

"A lot of people have died, Connie, but as a doctor I can't vouch for a general claim of direct causality between the radar radiation and those deaths. It would be too simplistic."

I had an uneasy feeling in the pit of my stomach but tried to remain calm. "Let's say you're right, Hans. I doubt it, but let's say you are. We still have the documentation proving collusion between the Falck shipping companies and the CIA. That alone is a big enough story."

"You have two main sources for your story," you said again. "I'm the second. I was the whistle-blower who procured the information. I've spoken to people I trust. Do you really want to destroy the life of your ageing father for your own personal gain and aggrandisement? I don't. This is something I can't do."

My head began to spin.

"Then there's . . . no story? What are you going to do?"

"Finish my studies. Maybe travel to the Middle East. I don't know."

"But . . .?"

"I'm sorry," you said.

I gathered my things and left, without saying a word to

anyone. My time as a journalist was over, I understood that immediately. I was completely alone. You were gone and there was no one in my family I could talk to. Or was there? After some hesitation I called Vera. She realised immediately I was in a bad place. She picked me up in a cab, said she had made some calls and that one of the Falck family apartments on Gimle terrasse was empty. She accompanied me up the wide stairs, unlocked the door, got a fire going in the hearth and made some tea.

"So, they finally came after you too?" she said.

I nodded. "I just want to lie down and never get up."

"It may never quite pass," she said. "But there will be better days."

"What am I going to do?"

She looked at me for a long time. "Write. That helps. Write."

I began to write.

PART IV
DELIMITATION LINE

44

HISTORY REPEATING ITSELF

Gimle terrasse, Oslo

The doorbell of the apartment on Gimle terrasse was so loud that when someone rang it made a sound like you were trapped in a belfry.

Sasha opened her eyes. Had Mads come back? She had not been making idle threats after the general meeting. The next day she had filed papers for legal separation with the county governor. Her husband had fled to the mountains. Sasha had told her daughters that "Mummy and Daddy need a little time apart to think". Since their eviction from Rederhaugen, the nuclear family had been existing in a state of emergency. The startling news had therefore been met with the kind of shrugs that might greet an air raid siren in a war zone.

She listened to the peal of the doorbell ring out until silence descended on the apartment once more. Previous setbacks in life had filled her with horror and the desire for revenge, but what scared her the most this time was the apathy she felt. The money from her father's life insurance meant she could buy whatever she wanted. Should she purchase a small farm and become an artisan? Procure a Swiss chalet-style villa and pursue archival research as a hobby, surrounded by cats and antique furniture? Not even these disturbing notions, which would previously have caused her to shudder, had any effect on her.

No, her material situation would hardly arouse sympathy. But failure, just like success, is relative. Was it possible to conceive of a fall greater than the one she had experienced in the past few months? First you lose your job and your childhood home. Then your father dies. Your siblings turn against you. When you finally get your head above water again, you're tarred and feathered as a Russian collaborator. Which in turn shatters your nuclear family, the one thing you had left.

The ringing resounded through the apartment once more. Moving slowly, she got to her feet. She stopped at a mahogany-framed cheval mirror in one corner. Not even the stained grey jogging bottoms and Mads's T-shirt could hide the few kilos in weight she had gained. Her hair was greasy and unbrushed. Some angry pimples had broken out on her chin.

She pushed the button on the intercom. "Yeah?"

"It's me," a voice said. "Johnny."

Something in her wanted to hang up. Her palm grew sweaty.

"What do you want?" She hoped the intercom filtered the croakiness in her voice.

"I want to talk to you."

"About?"

"What we usually talk about, Sasha. The secrets of the Falck family. They actually lead to Gimle terrasse."

She tried to interpret his voice. Took a deep breath, buzzed him in, heard the slam of the door below, footsteps on the staircase. Was she still feeling as indifferent to everything?

Then he was standing in the doorway. Johnny looked the same as last time, in the department store. He leaned against the door frame.

"How are things with you?" he asked.

She did not reply.

"Sasha—" he began.

"I don't want to," she said.

He stared at her. "You haven't even heard what I have to say."

"It's not about you."

"Look," he said, pulling out two already opened envelopes. "You probably don't know what this is. Two letters, mailed in 1976 to Hans Falck, marked return to sender."

He pointed to the name on the flap in small writing crossed out. "Sent by Connie Knarvik."

"I can't take any more," she said quietly. "I lost almost everything. And when I tried to win it back, I lost even more. Sorry, Johnny, I often think about the trip with you and what happened afterwards. I had my reasons; you're due an unreserved apology. But there's a time for everything."

She made to close the door.

"There's more," Johnny said. "How do you think I got in contact with Connie? Your father put us in touch. We met at Dovrehallen."

It took half a second before she realised what he was saying. Daddy and Johnny Berg together? After Hans had thrown Vera's hand grenade of a will at the Christmas party?

"You spoke with . . . my dad?"

He nodded.

Sasha opened the door, let him in and followed him down the hall and into the kitchen.

"A few days before he died. He seemed somehow reconciled to his lot that day. He said the information he was going to give me was about saving the family."

She went to the sink and filled a glass with water from the tap, drank it, then filled another. When she turned back around her eyes were red and her voice was weak. "What did he say?"

"He knew I was still working on Hans's biography and that the Bergen branch of the family were unwilling to talk to me. So he told me that Connie Knarvik might be able to shed some light on the story in a more truthful manner than the main character himself."

Sasha eyed him sceptically. "Daddy didn't exactly have a close relationship with her."

"No, and he was upfront about that. Just like he told me that his reasons for contacting me weren't 'honourable'. It was all about destroying Hans and regaining control."

"Your story doesn't add up," Sasha said. Reluctantly, she acknowledged her curiosity had been piqued. "You hated my father and me. Why take our side and stab Hans in the back because he didn't pick up when you called?"

"I have an open mind and don't hate anyone. But Connie let me read the letters she had written to Hans in 1976. Letters from a scorned lover, telling the same story: about how Hans betrayed her, again and again. Connie lost everything. She left her husband, wasn't on speaking terms with her family and was denied the journalistic scoop of the decade, all because of Hans."

"Are you going to put this in the biography?"

Johnny laughed. "The book has been cancelled. What can I say? History repeating itself."

"I need to know what Connie wrote about the family," Sasha said and looked over her shoulder. "My eldest girl finishes school at lunchtime today and may be home soon."

"OK," Johnny said. "Read what I've got. Then get in touch."

He got to his feet, draped his jacket over his arm while looking at her. "I've missed having someone to work with. Haven't you?"

She stood by the window watching him cross the square

below until he was out of sight. Then she took a cold shower and cleaned the apartment. *Who am I?* Yes, who was Sasha and what gave her a sense of purpose? She was an archivist. Nothing had given her a greater sense of achievement than uncovering the truth about Vera's past. Sasha had imagined it had to do with the moral duty she felt towards her grandmother, as well as all the conflicting feelings she had towards Johnny. But it was about her.

45

BOOMER!

Rederhaugen, Oslo

The May sun moved slowly over Rederhaugen. In the morning it cast its copper glow over the cliffs in the east, across the lawns, hedges and colourful garlands of new-leaved trees, and, in the afternoon, into the boardroom at the top of the rose tower, where Hans was dazzled by its rays.

Siri Greve pressed a button on a remote control and the vertical blinds closed. Sverre was installed in the chairperson's seat at the head of the table, with Andrea next to him.

"The expedition is drawing near," he said with cold authority, looking at Hans. "What's the latest on the ice conditions around Svalbard?"

"The crew of the *Falck III* and I are in close contact with the Polar Institute and the meteorologists. According to the researchers, the volume of ice in February was at a record low in the wake of dramatically mild winter months, with temperatures hitting record highs in several places in the Arctic. The situation has stabilised somewhat, but the amount of polar ice is extremely low compared with historical levels."

"That's a good thing, right?" Sverre said. "I mean, in terms of the expedition."

Hans did not answer but said: "The captain believes we can leave for Kvitøya much earlier than anticipated barring any significant change in the ice conditions in the coming weeks."

"Where is *Falck III* now?" Sverre asked.

"In Tromsø."

"Can you travel north in advance, Hans? We've bought some of those cameras the state broadcaster used for that five-and-a-half-day-long live documentary on the Hurtigruten ferry's voyage along the coast. One crazy-expensive V14 HD camera to fit on the bow and another to place directly below the bridge. I'd greatly appreciate it if you could take responsibility for having those installed."

It was pure condescension, carefully wrapped up in consideration, something Hans immediately recognised.

"When are you coming to Tromsø?"

"I'm not," Sverrre replied. "I'll meet you directly on Svalbard."

"The chairperson should be on the voyage."

"Hans," Sverre said, "I know how much this expedition means to you personally. It's important to honour what's gone before."

An ominous opening to a line of reasoning, Hans thought. Although personally he was happy to be released from the role of chair, there was something about the look in *Chairperson* Sverre's eyes. His thoughts turned to the Stanford prison experiment decades earlier in which the college students role-played as prisoners and guards. Did they not have to call the experiment off because normal people had transformed into sadistic concentration camp commanders in just a few days?

Sverre had been boss barely a week.

"I also think the expedition is a fantastic idea," he said, looking at Hans in a way intended to convey sympathy. "But let's not have any illusions about the reasons for it. In terms of the SAGA Group's bottom line, it's worthless. Totally worthless. This trip is PR and nothing else. But in terms of PR it's important enough."

"Svalbard is a big hit on social media," Andrea said.

"Exactly. We have a dedicated website and a heavy presence on social media." Sverre's voice grew dreamy. "If this is done right, it could go viral and be transmitted live to viewers all over the world, on the website, on social media, under the hashtag *FalckArctic100*. Talk about setting the agenda!"

"Hash what now?" Hans said, clearing his throat.

"Haven't you seen this symbol online before, boomer?" Andrea said, placing two fingers at right angles to two fingers on her other hand. "It's a *hashtag*."

There was mild chuckling around the table. Everything comes to an end, and, as far as Hans was concerned, being shoved into the attic was preferable to falling to some dramatic scandal.

Women, ideology, neglect of family duties, questionable political bedfellows on foreign soil ... there was no shortage of charges to level at Hans, but he had been protected his entire life by his brazen behaviour and his aversion to moralising. The hypocrites were the ones the court of public opinion enjoyed seeing stew in their own juices. It had been the same during the cadre assessments in the AKP.

"Sverre?" he said, when the board meeting was over and everyone began making their way down to the ground floor to eat.

"Hans," Sverre answered, politely and correctly. "Anything in particular you were wondering about?"

Once again that condescending look, as though he were on the balcony of the royal palace, looking down.

"It concerns Ingeborg."

A flicker of uncertainty crossed Sverre's face. "What about her?"

"Has she started her new job?"

"No, not for a little while yet. Why do you ask?"

"I'll explain later," Hans said, starting to put on his coat.

"Aren't you going to eat with the rest of the board?" Sverre asked.

"Sorry. Lots to take care of."

Sverre held out his hand. "You and I will be in touch a lot going forward, but if I don't see you in the flesh before you leave, I want to wish you the best of luck in Tromsø and on the voyage to Svalbard."

Hans walked outside, just as the top of the sun was disappearing behind the forest-covered hills in the west. It was still chilly in the shade. He followed the avenue towards the gate with the engraved falcon. What would become of SAGA now? What would become of him? Hans was not a man for deep existential crises. Little good came of endless introspection.

The board meeting confirmed what he had thought since the shareholders' meeting, no, since the accident with the 330th Squadron: he used to spare a thought for all kinds of bankrupt TV celebrities, comedians and others who had at one time defined the zeitgeist but had now been left behind, complaining about a world they did not understand. Now he, the once immortal Hans Falck, whose mental age was half what was recorded in the church register, was getting old. An out of touch fossil.

He followed the side roads through villa-style neighbourhoods in the direction of the sea. Far away, he could hear the strains of a school band rehearsing for the national day, mixed with the low hum of electric cars. In the gardens he heard the excited squeals of children jumping on trampolines or playing football.

How long was it since he had been like that? Fifty-five years. It was fifty-five years since Hans began school in Fana. More and more, the amount of time that had passed made him dizzy, like the moment you come upon a precipice and find yourself staring down into eternity.

Hans took out his phone and stood holding it while thinking about what he was about to do. The number was not saved. He punched it in but did not press the call button. There was a car park in front of him, and parkland beyond. Through the elm trees he could see the fjord.

He called the number.

A long pause followed.

Finally, an unfamiliar voice answered. "Herr Falck, it's been a while. How can I help you?"

"I'm travelling north soon. I thought that might be of interest to you."

46

THE THERAPEUTIC GAZE

University of Oslo Library

The following day, Sasha walked out the door of Gimle terrasse, continued past the church and down the gentle slope of Bygdøy allé, before crossing the park in front of the Norsk Hydro offices.

The entrance of the National Library was just as monumental and the frescos just as sinister as she remembered from when it was the University of Oslo Library. She felt the throb of her pulse in her ears as she ascended the steps to the café on the first floor. There, a popular historian was drinking coffee with a high-profile psychologist, known for his trademark therapeutic gaze when offering the public advice on love and other matters.

What would he have said to her? That everybody makes mistakes in a long marriage, including Mads Falck? Or that some relationships are doomed to founder? That she would be better off following the heart's dark path into the arms of an enigmatic adventurer who once again was digging up skeletons in the Falck graveyard?

No, the celebrity psychologist would hardly have offered her that advice.

She placed her bag in a locker and went to the reading room. It was quiet there, apart from someone occasionally clearing their throat, the turning of a sheet of paper and the sound of a heavy law book being opened. The room was bathed in a greenish light.

Johnny was not to be found among the students and researchers sitting at the rows of desks. But she spotted him standing in the corner diagonally opposite, his back to her, in front of one of the shelves that stretched all the way around the room.

She walked across the middle of the room, between the rows of desks on either side, until she was a couple of metres away. He turned to face her, as though he had known she was coming the entire time.

"I've read the letters," she said.

"And?"

"I believe her," Sasha said, after a brief pause. "I'm impressed that you've unearthed the fate of yet another woman whose story changes the family narrative. Impressed, but also a little ashamed that none of us did it before you. I want you to know that."

She looked directly into his emerald-green eyes.

"Why has no one done it?" Johnny asked.

Sasha had wondered the same thing when reading the letters. She could blame it on Connie. But the truth was that Sasha had been a daddy's girl. She had let consideration for her father determine her actions. That was why she had hidden the truth about the will. And when Olav was gone, she had put all her eggs in her husband's basket.

"I'm thinking about the road ahead," she said. "So, it's 1976. Hans has scuppered Connie's big exposé."

"Right," Johnny said. "Why? Fire away, talk before you think."

"He wants the glory for himself."

"Definitely a possibility. Keep going."

"Someone tells him to put a stop to it."

"Bingo," Johnny said. "Who?"

"I've only read Connie's letter," Sasha said. "The AKP leadership is one option."

"*Klassekampen* was the party newspaper back then," Johnny said. "The editor was part of the leadership. And nothing of what Connie says indicates that."

"An intelligence service?"

He nodded for her to continue.

"My first guess would be Norwegian state intelligence, due to the incidents of cancer on the rescue boats putting Norway in a bad light. But suppressing something like that? It seems strange. I suppose that leaves us with the Russians?"

"But the AKP were strongly anti-Soviet," Johnny said, playing devil's advocate. "The Soviets after Stalin were *social imperialists*."

Sasha was hitting her stride now.

"Daddy said Hans always cheered on the Russians when there was sport on TV. Later, Hans used to say that the war scare was the AKP's biggest mistake. Remember, as time went on, he was mostly in the Middle East. Relations with the Soviets were at the forefront there and Mao's China far away. Moreover, he was familiar with Svalbard and Kirkenes. The two places in the country where ties with the Russians are closest."

Johnny looked at her. "Good, Sasha."

Sasha was sitting with her hands folded. She stood up. "This is a lot to take in. I need some air."

They walked down the staircase under the arches and Emanuel Vigeland's vaulted ceilings. It was a chilly May day, warm in the sun, cold in the shade. They crossed Drammensveien and sat down in Hydro Park.

"Will you roll me a cigarette as well?" she asked.

"I don't think Connie knows more about what happened in 1976," he said. "But through a colleague I managed to get hold of the Police Security Service file on Hans. Do you know who was carrying out surveillance on Hans in the 1970s?" He answered his own question. "Robert Eliassen, the current governor of Svalbard. Do you remember where Hans was when he rang Connie, according to her letter?"

"In Longyearbyen."

"I think something happened up there in August 1976. I wonder if the two of us need to take a trip north, Sasha."

She flicked the cigarette butt into a puddle as she thought of the chaos at home.

"I want to talk to Connie first. Can you arrange that?"

"I can try. But why?"

"Because I happened to think of that portrait interview you did with Hans in Lebanon. I'd never actually read it but came across a copy in the apartment in Gimle. He talks about the massacre in Sabra and Shatila. Describes young men with their genitals cut off and pregnant women with their stomachs cut open."

"And?" For the first time Johnny seemed unsure.

"When I was trying to persuade Connie to take my side during the shareholder meeting, she told me the same thing. The exact same images, the same injuries."

"Could be false memory, hearing someone else's story and making it your own. Connie has the personality for it."

"Maybe, but we know she did solidarity work in the Middle East. That she began to lose it after that. My gut tells me something happened there."

"What are you thinking?" Johnny fixed his eyes on her.

"Let's not beat around the bush," she said, her tone

assertive. "You and I know what this is really about. I was head of SAGA when that poisoned Russian collapsed in Svalbard. You've investigated the case. We both know there's a mole in SAGA and my family. Both of us want to find this person, albeit for different reasons. You carry out your assignment and I find out the truth. Sound like a deal?"

47

VILLA GRANDE

Rederhaugen, Oslo

Sverre believed victory was something to be enjoyed. Savoured like that first swig of beer after a long hike in the mountains, like a glass of freshly pressed orange juice after a drinking binge.

Walking into the kitchen in sky-blue boxer shorts and a white singlet, he opened the fridge and drank half a carton of juice in one go, then found some paracetamol and washed them down with more juice. Blast, he should have bought in fresh oranges. The hangover was manageable, but passing the mirror in the hallway he noticed how quickly drinking made him gain weight.

Once he had been younger than the footballers in the World Cup. That was a long time ago. Now he was older than Tony in the first season of *The Sopranos* and approaching the average age of a member of the Traveling Wilburys.

While also being childless.

On the other hand, he was no longer a lightweight. He was chairperson of SAGA. One of the richest and most powerful men in the country.

How had he wound up here? He had gone from being a bitter, perpetual singleton, whom people invited to dinner parties out of charity, to being surrounded by "an aura of self-assurance and success only a Falck could possess", to quote a fawning interview he had given after the vote.

Yeah, right. He was a phoenix. Suddenly *MSM-Lügenpressen* could write about SAGA chairperson and CEO Sverre Falck with the greatest respect – the decorated war veteran who had been groomed for the post in SAGA he was finally ready to claim, with a beautiful girlfriend from the legendary Johnsen family by his side.

He had signed a contract with Hans for the short-term lease of an apartment in the east wing of Rederhaugen. Situated above the dining room and furnished in the style of the national romantic movement, it was larger and the decor more modern than the blue room where Hans had stayed, which in any event was intended for prominent guests. The contract lasted until the expedition began.

Sverre and the Bergen side of the family might be natural adversaries, but circumstances had bound them together, Hans emphasised. Hans had to travel to Bergen for a while to see his family and take care of a few things. He was still the winner. The majority of the board were still behind him and no one had suggested challenging his ownership of Rederhaugen. That belonged to the Bergenites.

Craving something healthy, Sverre sliced up some fruit he found in the kitchen. Then he turned on the coffee maker. A pleasant aroma began to pervade the room and he tried to resist the temptation to prepare a salty brunch.

"You were screaming in your sleep again," Ingeborg said. "And sweating like a boxer trying to drop down a weight division in one day. You can't go on like this. Me not being able to sleep is one thing but it's worse for you."

If the Johnsen women were anything, it was *imperious*. The

more time he spent in her company the more apparent this trait became.

"Is this something that's happened before?" she asked. "I mean, after your last tour of Afghanistan?"

He stared down at the table and the mug of steaming coffee. Suddenly picturing that day at the fjord when he told Olav about the mission. How his father's eyes had lit up when Sverre had told him he was going to Afghanistan with the Marine Hunters. He had believed that Olav was genuinely proud of him then. Before he understood it was something his father had arranged behind his back. Were the night terrors because of Olav? Or the legacy of untreated episodes from Kabul, roadside bombs, the terrorists in Park Palace and other events?

"No," Sverre lied. "It's never been like this."

"You need to get help," she said, and had begun mentioning the names of psychologists she and her family knew when Sverre interrupted her.

"It's not about finding a therapist," he said. "You're always thinking in practical terms, in terms of solutions."

"Is there something wrong with that?"

He looked at her with sad eyes. "No, no, of course not. I wish I was like that. But it's about the meaningless of it all."

She looked out the window contemplatively; this was a frequency she did not understand, a colour she did not see. Instead she said: "Hans called, by the way."

"Oh?"

"He needs a Russian interpreter on the Svalbard expedition. Said he'd been considering a few people but I was his preference."

"I don't blame him," he said. "What did you say?"

"That I'm between jobs until the summer, doing nothing

besides being wife of the CEO at Rederhaugen until I begin at the Foreign Office. So I said yes. In any case, I'll see you up there. Date at the Red Bear Pub in Barentsburg?"

That night they held one final get-together to celebrate Sverre being made chairperson. Ralph Rafaelsen had been in Oslo for the last few weeks, holding court at Rederhaugen in the evenings.

Victor Prydz did not need asking twice and turned up at Rederhaugen with the adjutant to the chief of defence.

"Damn, Ingeborg," Prydz said, "You're going to be a political adviser. I'd completely forgotten. Congratulations!"

The two men, Prydz, corpulent and brash, and the adjutant, squeezed their way through the throng of people dancing to the rhythms of tropical house, many of them Ingeborg's blasé friends, who usually cursed the paucity of men in Oslo, and who were now being introduced to wealthy scions and foreign diplomats.

At the centre of it all: Sverre Falck.

It was as though part of him was taking to the air by helium balloon, while the other part was being pulled downward by a plumb bob.

Prydz finally succeeded in persuading the DJ to play "Les Lacs du Connemara" by French balladeer Michel Sardou.

"Listen, Sverre!" he shouted.

"What is this shit?" Sverre shouted back.

"An anti-Islamic, pro-colonial protest singer." Prydz grinned. "Only in France. A kind of *reactionary* version of the Village People. The French's unofficial national anthem after a few drinks. Enduring gay anthem in the basement clubs of Paris. *Santé!*"

In the middle of the floor, the adjutant was leading the others in a march perfectly in time to the song, when Sverre caught sight of someone attempting to get around the shrieking crowd. Johnny Berg was wearing a black leather jacket over a white shirt.

"Johnny," Sverre said.

Johnny nodded to Sverre. "Have you got two minutes, Sverre? To talk in private?"

Ingeborg was in the apartment, so Sverre led the way down the winding stairs and decided on the pool area. He unlocked the men's changing room.

The swimming pool was still and bathed in turquoise, only broken by the vibrations of bass from the floor above, making the surface tremble slightly.

They sat down on two plastic sunloungers.

"Are you drunk?" Johnny asked.

Sverre hesitated. Something about the other man made him feel sober.

Johnny pulled a document from a shoulder bag. "I have something important to tell you, Sverre. But I can't do that until you sign this."

Sverre had trouble focusing – so he was not completely sober – but he could discern a document bearing the stamp of the armed forces, making him a source for the Kingdom of Norway and liable in law should the classified information be leaked.

"And if I don't want to?"

"Don't be silly, Sverre," Johnny said. "If you've served your country once, you never stop."

Sverre paused for a moment before giving a brief nod and signing the confidentiality agreement. "What do you want?"

Johnny told him about their suspicions against Hans. That

he may have been recruited by the Russians during the Cold War, in August 1976, on Svalbard.

"You're both going to Svalbard," Johnny said. "Hans is going to receive an award from Russia. But I think what he's actually doing is handing over intelligence about the property in the Advent Valley, which the Russians have been drooling over for a long time."

Sverre sat for a while without responding. All at once he noticed the nausea. Without warning he leaned forward and threw up.

"Sorry, Johnny," he grunted.

The other man got to his feet, but remained standing, looking down at him. "I want Hans Falck."

He turned and disappeared.

48

I THINK IT'S TIME YOU BOTH LEFT

Lindeberg, Oslo

Johnny followed the stream of people down the slight incline into the underground entrance of Nationaltheatret station. After the mistake of arresting Mads, the investigation had come to a standstill. Johnny had been granted a "short, unpaid leave of absence" by HK to pursue the biography lead.

"You're sure Connie is OK with me coming along?" asked Sasha, walking beside him.

"She'll tell her story to whoever will listen," he assured her. "I've never been to her home, so let's keep our eyes open."

They had reached the platform for eastbound trains.

"At my secondary school there was a girl who was so embarrassed about taking the train to the east of the city she would hide behind those pillars there." Sasha pointed. "And sneak aboard so no one would see her."

"Line 2," Johnny said, as the train swept into the station. "That's us."

They sat facing each other in a four-seater as they headed east through the city centre. The metro exited the tunnel into daylight.

"You know this was where the AKP started?"

She shook her head.

"Next station Hellerud. Heartland of the Norwegian

Maoists. The affected way they spoke was an imitation of the East Side accent here."

It seemed like a long time ago. At every station further east the people in the carriage changed. The city had always been divided between east and west, poor and wealthy, employees and employers, but the ethnic dimension had been mixed in with social distinctions. City centre developments were gradually replaced by industrial areas and high-rises, and by the time the train pulled into Lindeberg metro station, Sasha was the only person in the carriage with Norwegian grandparents.

They alighted and followed the paths through the housing co-ops, mostly low-rises only four storeys in height, uphill to Lindebergåsen where Connie lived.

"Do you know this area?" Sasha asked.

"Not that well, but I've played football on most of the pitches around here," he said, his thoughts turning to the hard gravel pitches at Veitvet and Romsås, and the rare occasions they were allowed to play on the pristine grass pitch in Høybråten, which lay hidden in a labyrinth of quiet residential streets, so different from the high-rises associated with this area. Or the time they beat Stovnerkam in a penalty shoot-out and had to hightail it from angry spectators and hop on a metro back towards the city.

The memory bank was deep as an oil well, invisible to the naked eye. If you drilled in the right spot, it came gushing up.

"Here," Sasha said, pointing at a wide seven-storey block with woods on one side and the hazy valley floor on the other.

They located C. Knarvik on the list of names.

Connie buzzed them in immediately, as though she had been sitting waiting. The entranceway was dark and dank. She lived on the fifth floor. Her door was ajar.

"Just come right in, you don't need to remove your shoes."

The flat was clean. A large corner sofa in imitation leather occupied one part of the room and there was a big flat-screen standing on a TV table. A large print of the Virgin Mary dominated an otherwise bare wall.

Connie was sitting in the kitchen with a cigarette and *Klassekampen* open in front of her, looking pensively out over the valley. Johnny complimented her on the view. She welcomed Sasha with a peck on both cheeks and put on the kettle.

She placed instant coffee and teabags on the table.

"Let's pick up where we left off," Johnny said. "It's August 1976. You've been working around the clock on the exposé. About how the most reputable, the most Norwegian of companies is lackey to an intelligence agency, how the Svalbard Treaty is being broken, and how this has had fatal consequences for Norwegian sailors."

Constance nodded.

"Then the whole thing is just called off. Couldn't you have gone ahead with the story yourself even though Hans had pulled out?" he asked.

She lit up a fresh cigarette.

"I wrote about that in the letter. It was Hans who had given me the story and the sources. When he withdrew, Bendiksen and the others disappeared. Wouldn't take my calls. When the sources pulled out it fell apart. All you had was an unsupported claim that people from the intelligence services had been on board."

Connie looked down. "When Hans was with me, everything seemed possible. He had that effect on people. With Hans you could touch the clouds, as Mao said. After he pulled out I felt so alone. A young female journalist against NATO. Also, they threatened me with prison."

Sasha and Johnny exchanged glances. "*They* threatened you?"

She hesitated, a tremor in her voice. "*He* threatened me."

Dust was dancing in the air.

"He?"

"It was the same night Hans rang. I was sitting at Gimle terrasse. I'd bought an ABBA LP – my little protest against the party. I was devastated. The buzzer downstairs rang. I ignored it. Shortly after I heard steps outside the apartment door. Then knocking. 'We know you're in there,' a voice said. I opened the door. It was your father."

She looked at Sasha.

First Vera in 1970, Johnny thought, then this. A pattern was emerging.

"Did he threaten you?"

"Not in so many words. Olav was a ministerial adviser at the time and was always good at cloaking a message. He told me he had spoken to Hans in Svalbard and it was obvious the story was without merit. As far as cooperation between Herbert and the Americans on the Advent Valley was concerned, that was filed under NATO Cosmic Top Secret. I still remember that term. Talking about it could lead to years in prison."

"And then?"

"That's it," Connie said. "I didn't dare go further. Decided I was finished with journalism. I had failed."

"It's a human response," Sasha said, placing her hand over Connie's.

Johnny stood up to use the bathroom. The door to the bedroom was ajar.

Her bed was made. Some framed photographs stood on top of a bureau. Not many from the party days, the result, no doubt, of the secrecy around that. There was one of Constance in her younger days, wearing flares, on a runway. Where? The colours were pale, due both to the picture's age and the heat where it was taken. He looked closer. Beirut International Airport. So Constance had been in Lebanon. Like Hans.

He stopped at one photograph. It was of Hans as a young man, in khaki shorts and a headscarf, with two women, one of them in a black tight-fitting singlet, holding a Kalashnikov. He had seen it before, at Hans's house at Hordnes. Without knowing it was Constance Falck who was standing next to Hans's old flame Mouna Khouri.

He texted Sasha and returned to the kitchen.

"Don't worry, we're going to Svalbard to find out the truth about this," Johnny said, looking at Sasha.

"Which leads us to the next part of the story," she added.

"What are you talking about?" Connie's tone turned hard, closed.

"You were in Shatila during the massacres?"

"What makes you think that?" Her voice was that of someone about to lose control.

"When Johnny was a young journalist, he interviewed Hans about the scenes he had been confronted with there. When we spoke in the church you told me about the injuries. About men with severed genitals, pregnant women with their stomachs slit open. Exactly the same. It's grotesque, even for the Middle East. You were there, with Hans?"

"I . . . I . . . I think it's time you both left."

Sasha again placed her hand upon Connie's, but Connie withdrew hers. "I have allowed you to be privy to certain things in my life," she said, anger in her voice. "But I resent this prying."

She got to her feet and cleared the cups from the table. "You can leave now. You can leave."

49

THE ULTIMATE TERRITORIAL PISSING

Barents Sea, between Bjørnøya and Spitsbergen

Hans was stirred from his thoughts by the loud screech of a seagull.

The weather was cold, hovering around freezing, and he was standing alone in contemplation at the stern of *Falck III* while the wash from the propellers coiled behind the vessel into the wake. Contrary to what he had thought, the Svalbard trip had not cured him of his melancholy. It had only served to amplify the feeling. Of everything being in the past, Svalbard in particular. A place he associated with the demagogy of the seventies and the urge for revolution, and, prior to that, with Uncle Theo's mythological place from childhood. The nostalgia also made him self-conscious: *that Hans Falck, he's certainly aged since the accident.*

Since they left Bjørnøya, Bear Island – a misnomer, incidentally, as it was a huge fog-laden bird cliff – twenty-four hours earlier, they had not heard so much as a peep from the air. The days lasted forever and when he went to bed he lay twisting and turning behind the blackout blinds without getting much sleep.

But now screeching kittiwakes and other greedy gulls hovered around the boat.

"We're getting close to land," Hans shouted.

The sight had roused him. He hurried across the deck, issuing instructions and asking people to meet him on the bridge.

The islands appeared on the horizon, low at first in a thin strip of indeterminate colour, then as rugged mountains and vast glaciers snaking down between the mountains. The bow of the boat broke through green water and more and more ice; the drift ice in the Arctic Ocean had begun at 74 degrees north, and there was more of it than they had anticipated.

"Just a quick meeting," Hans said, rubbing his hands together before unzipping the neck of his survival suit.

He looked at Ingeborg, at Marte, Christian and Erik, Siri Greve and the research team from the Polar Institute, all wearing signal red.

"We set out from Tromsø a week ago!" he said loudly. "Like the crew of my ancestor Theo's expedition, we have, together with our foremost ornithologists, investigated the avian population on Bjørnøya. Of course, we're enjoying considerably more pleasant conditions than when Theo set sail for Svalbard in May 1916, or when Norwegian trappers travelled to the islands. Those were men who subsisted on what nature could provide of fish and wild reindeer, who couldn't hop on the first plane home should something go wrong. We are forever grateful to them."

He gave the floor to the two researchers, who summarised the alarming situation in the Arctic, how the permafrost was melting and the ice retreating, how birdlife was vulnerable and the polar bear's habitat was under threat due to the reduction of polar ice.

"Remember we are guests," Hans said and repeated a mantra often heard up in these parts: "This is the kingdom of the polar bear, the kittiwake, seal and reindeer."

He explained that the plan was to follow South Spitsbergen north, past Isbjørnhamna up to Isfjord Radio, and further on to the Russian settlement in Barentsburg.

"What are we going to do in Barentsburg?" Erik asked.

"Hans is being awarded the Order of Saint George for heroism for saving the life of the captain of that Russian trawler," Siri Greve said. "No small decoration. It comes from the president personally."

"From Putin?" Erik said.

"Every president needs to approve such a medal presentation. The general consul and the Russian mining director want to speak to us beforehand to arrange a suitable venue for the award. That's understandable."

Hans interrupted her with a wave of his hand.

"Yes, yes – after Barentsburg there will be a tour of the Advent Valley property. And after that, if fortune favours us, the Falck ice cap on Kvitøya. And that is *far* away." He nodded to the north-east. "In that direction, past King Charles Land, where the polar bears are born, and all the way along the enormous island of Nordaustlandet, until we're almost in Russia."

The *Falck III* headed slowly north, past dark mountains with white troughs of snow resembling zebra stripes and huge glaciers calving ice into the ocean with deep rumbles, making waves that rocked the rescue boat from kilometres away.

The cluster of people on the deck dispersed. Accompanied by Erik and Christian, Hans went up to the captain on the command bridge. Ørnes was an experienced sea dog and knew these waters well, which was why Hans had recruited him.

"Everything alright?" asked Hans, looking out at the greenish sea filled with drift ice as they slowly glided through.

"A lot of ice this year," the skipper said.

"A hundred nautical miles to Barentsburg?" Hans asked.

"We should be there this afternoon."

Hans got a beer from the mess and found somewhere to sit on the deck that afforded him a view towards land. The temperature had fallen to a few degrees below zero and the weather had cleared up. The evening sun was still high, and coloured the vast landscape, giving the dark mountains a rusty-red glow.

Those who said the landscape was barren only said it because they could not see: not the bears and walruses lying lazily at the water's edge, of course, nor the reindeer peeping out, the tracks from the foxes and grouse across the glaciers, the whales breaking the surface now and again, the fulmars, guillemots and little auks who dived down into the deep to hide from the fearsome glaucous gull, and the droppings from the nesting cliffs that made the vegetation below them green. All of this was to be found in the vast panorama.

He closed his eyes and must have nodded off because when he awoke Ingeborg Johnsen was in front of him, wearing an open survival suit.

"Hans, were you asleep?"

"Of course not," he said, clearing his throat.

"A school of narwhals just swam past."

He stood up and walked to the railing. Ingeborg came and stood beside him, her light blonde hair falling over her shoulders. It occurred to him that they had never had a conversation in private.

"Your family are fond of Russia," he said, rather out of the blue.

"We are, but we're not uncritical of what's happening there, for the record."

"Wenche Johnsen was brought down by her ties to the Russians."

"That was a smear campaign, dirt dug up by rivals in the party and the CIA. Everybody knows that."

"Perhaps, but the damage was done," Hans said. "You've been appointed a political adviser now, I hear?"

"Where are you going with this?" she said in a low voice.

"You're au fait with things Russian. Be careful you don't get tangled up in something you can't handle."

She left without replying. Hans stood there for a long time, staring at the towering mountains. They passed Isfjord Radio at the mouth of the fjord. The Russian enclave was not far now.

This was the last time he was going to carry out an assignment.

This time he meant it.

50

THE RED BEAR

Barentsburg, Svalbard

Sverre sped up the last hills towards Barentsburg. Then he cruised into the snow scooter parking area between the hotel and the red Arktikugol headquarters. The settlement was located high up on the hill, tubes and pipes leading from it down to the sea.

He looked out to sea to try to spot the *Falck III* but could see no boats at all. What time was it, anyway? He had no idea, nor did it matter. It was daytime. And daytime would last several more months.

He followed the road past the mining company in the direction of the consulate general. The place was smaller than Longyearbyen but the buildings were larger, and their monumental brutalism held a peculiar charm. In front of two large apartment blocks, newly refurbished and decorated in red and blue, stood a bust of Lenin.

Yes, these were definitely "weeks where decades happen".

Inspired by the powerful quote, Sverre had attempted to read some of the man's writings. The po-faced ruthlessness the revolutionary Russian displayed had both frightened and fascinated him. What would Vladimir Ilyich think of Svalbard? Well, he had been alive when the Soviet Union signed the treaty, if not when it came into effect several years later.

Some Russian workers passed Sverre as he walked back to the hotel and checked in. He had just managed to hang up the snow scooter suit and put on a pair of rubber slippers when the Norwegian retinue marched in.

He kissed Ingeborg and greeted the others.

"The voyage went well?" Sverre asked.

"We got here," Hans said. "I think everyone would agree with me when I say it was quite an experience."

Hans gathered everyone into a semicircle. "We'll eat dinner together afterwards. Siri, Ingeborg and Sverre, can the three of you come back down to the lobby in ten minutes, so we can all go over to the consulate together?"

A frozen iron gate swung open. The consulate general was decorated with bright marble-tiled flooring and cream-coloured leather sofas. Director Sokolov and the consul general received them. Greve and Ingeborg were the only women.

The consul was a red-faced man in his sixties who helped himself to the food laid on with the greed of a hungry gull. He did not chew the herring and streaky pieces of meat but held them over his mouth and swallowed them whole.

Sokolov clinked his vodka glass discreetly against Sverre's. Sverre smiled back.

"As I understand it, we have two things to discuss," the consul said. Ingeborg acted as interpreter.

"Two?" Hans asked in surprise.

"You've requested assistance from our icebreakers for a voyage to Kvitøya, Herr Falck."

"The latest assessments from the meteorologists and experts at the Polar Institute," Hans said, "suggest that at the moment the sea ice is between the 79th and 80th parallel, with considerable drift ice in the area, which in turn renders passage with vessels such as the *Falck III* impossible."

"Yes, yes," the Russian interrupted, his mouth full of a mix of roe and sour cream. "We can arrange an icebreaker for you, no problem."

"Is it so easy?" Hans asked.

"One of our icebreakers is in the area west of Franz Josef Land at the moment," the Russian said. "It will do the job, providing the Norwegian governor doesn't impose restrictions. Allowing the icebreaker into these waters is also important to us due to the other matter."

He produced a map. "Regarding the Order of Saint George. My government wishes the ceremony to take place on the so-called demarcation line, exactly 35 degrees east, twenty-eight kilometres from Kræmerpynten, the most eastern point of Kvitøya, and thirty-two kilometres from Victoria Island, belonging to the Russian Federation."

"Why there exactly?" Siri Greve asked.

"As a sign of our good neighbourly relations in the Arctic." The consul smiled. "Herr Falck has always been a bridge-builder between our two peoples."

So they keep saying, Sverre thought, as, following the consul's example, he ate another slice of rye bread with vendace roe.

"Our country will be represented at a high level. Doctor Aliyev himself, from the Geographical Society, hero of Russia, will likely be awarding the medal."

Sverre sat quietly on the sofa.

Hans turned and sent him a questioning look – *That's OK, right?* – and Sverre gave a brief nod.

"We need to discuss the details of course," Hans said, "but it sounds logical, since it involves recognition of a maritime endeavour. So long as our glacier walk on Falckejøkulen goes as planned. Would you gentlemen excuse us for a moment so we can discuss it?"

He leaned towards Greve. "What do you think?"

"I don't like it, Hans."

He sighed. "Why not?"

"The Russians wouldn't call in an icebreaker without good reason."

"All due respect, Siri, but in this matter you're way off the mark."

He turned back to the Russians.

"So?" the consul said.

"Yes," Hans said, looking first at him, then at Sokolov. "We're agreed."

The consul got to his feet and, breathing heavily, waddled across the floor. He thanked each of the Norwegians in turn and shook their hands.

A fat little hand took hold of Sverre's.

"We look forward to continued cooperation."

They ate an excellent trout dinner at the Hotel Barentsburg, after which Sverre went to the red wooden building housing the Red Bear. Ingeborg was sitting by the window. He ordered two beers.

She regarded him with a look which was either loving or distant, he could not decide which. Maybe both.

"What is it, darling?" he whispered, cuddling up to her.

"It's just—" She broke off.

"You can tell me, you can tell me anything," he whispered.

"No." She sighed. "It's nothing. At least nothing concerning us. It's just I had a dream that the same thing happened to me, to us, as happened to Nana. That we were hung out to dry as Russian collaborators."

Sverre chuckled. "You don't usually use your dreams as your guide in life, dear."

She took a sip of the frothy pint. Below them the surface of Green Harbour lay calm, and in the distance, to the west, they could see glacier tongues extending into the water.

"I don't want you thinking like that," he said. "Remember what we talked about when we first met? What we were going to become? I was going to be the head of SAGA. You were thinking even bigger. You're going to achieve your goal, Ingeborg."

"Sverre," she said, in a tired voice, "don't start with all that. There are too many variables in this equation."

"It's not by chance some people are lucky," he said. "It's the people who are trying, who are failing, putting themselves in positions where luck can play a part, who get the breaks."

She stroked his hair. "Sverre, Sverre."

"Do you know how the small migratory birds in Svalbard manage to mount a defence against the birds of prey hunting their eggs? It's because they cooperate."

51

THE HISTORY IS ALWAYS IN THE ARCHIVES

Longyearbyen, Svalbard

Sasha slept soundly on the flight north, not waking until the flight attendant tapped her on the shoulder to request that she open her window blind. In a half-daze, she looked out. The polar light burned her eyes. The sky was clear. The archipelago unfolded below her. Plateaus of glaciers spreading out between dark, craggy mountains, or sinking down into the glittering fjords.

"In danger of being bitten by the polar bug?" said Johnny, in the seat next to her.

"Bit early to say. I've always liked heat more than cold."

An icy wind from the north blew as they walked from the runway to the low terminal building. She had sent Governor Eliassen an email prior to departure. He had yet to answer, but she had received an email from Store Norske, the state-owned Norwegian coal company on Svalbard, welcoming them.

They wasted no time in driving towards Longyearbyen and checked in at Funken Lodge, situated on a small hill above the settlement.

The buildings in town followed the valley floor down towards the fjord. They took a walk down, arriving on a pedestrianised street surrounded by bars, shops and tour operators, like in a tropical backpacker resort. The temperature was around zero. New houses and apartment buildings were springing up. The town was growing. The surrounding mountains looked like enormous burial mounds, formed like pyramids, their sides adorned with cable cars for the coal.

"That's the emergency hospital Colonel Zemlyakov was brought to." Johnny pointed.

"Doubt we'll find anything there. Wasn't he dead on arrival?"

"I didn't mean it like that," Johnny said. "I just think we're getting close to the answer to all this."

Sasha checked her phone again. She had received an email from the governor's office, from the head of communications, informing her that "Governor Eliassen's schedule was full", but that she was available to answer any "general questions about upholding Norwegian sovereignty". Sasha cursed; she hated generic answers from people like that.

She showed Johnny the email.

"Little help forthcoming there," she said. "But I know where we can begin."

Store Norske Spitsbergen Coal Company was a shadow of the behemoth the Falck family had once done business with. The building down on the plain facing the Advent fjord might have been the premises of a mid-sized accountancy firm.

The building appeared almost empty. They were greeted by a receptionist, an elderly woman who eyed them sceptically. "Who did you say? And please remove your footwear."

"Falck," Johnny said. "I'm Hans Falck's biographer, and this is Alexandra Falck. We're working together on a book and we have an appointment."

Sasha added: "My family were closely involved with Store Norske throughout much of the twentieth century."

The receptionist nodded, became more amenable. "Yes, I met Hans and Olav Falck on several occasions."

"He's my father," Sasha said. Why was she still referring to him in the present tense? "Olav, that is."

"Anyway," the receptionist said, "we have an archive you can access. Is there something in particular you're looking for?"

"There is," Sasha answered. "We'd like to see the list of visitors to Store Norske between August 15 and 25, 1976."

The receptionist nodded and disappeared.

"Isn't that a long shot?" Johnny asked. "We have nothing to indicate that anyone from Store Norske was involved."

"Store Norske *was* Svalbard before the state acquired all its shares," she said. "We know that my father and Hans were in Svalbard in August. And both of them had strong ties, to say the least, to the private shipowners who owned Store Norske."

The receptionist beckoned for them to follow her. They went down into the dusty archive. Sasha had that sensation she so often had upon seeing old folders in alphabetical order, a mild feeling of excitement at nearing the goal, the sense that history itself lay hidden somewhere in this dry correspondence.

"Enjoy," the receptionist said.

There had been many visitors during the period in question, which was shortly after the government takeover.

"I can't find any of the people we're looking for," Sasha said, frustrated.

She sought out the receptionist. "Do you have a similar logbook for trips organised by Store Norske? The company must have had boats, snowmobiles, maybe even helicopters at their disposal?"

The woman searched and pulled out another binder.

It did not take long to find some familiar names.

"Look here," Sasha said. "Hans Falck arrives in Longyearbyen and requests a lift from the airport to the centre of town. The airport had just opened, you know."

Sasha read on. According to the correspondence, Hans had stayed at Funken Lodge. "The following day 'ministerial adviser Falck inspects the Svea mine and then Quade Hook'."

She continued reading.

17.08.1976
Tour of the so-called Advent Valley property. Requisitioning of helicopter: from Longyearbyen to Sallyhamna north on Spitsbergen.
Passengers:
Olav Falck, MOD
Hans Falck, MD
Robert Eliassen, POT (Police Surveillance Agency)

Finally, some luck. Sasha let out a loud "Yes!"

"That's the journey we've been looking for," Johnny said.

There was nothing more about the trip in the logbook. Sasha photographed the page and put the binder back.

"Wait," Johnny said.

"No," Sasha replied, "we need to talk to the governor and we need to do it now."

"It's eight o'clock in the evening."

"Listen. We know that Hans put a stop to Connie's exposé while he was visiting Svalbard during this period. We know my father was there at the same time. And now we have it in black and white that the two of them, along with Eliassen, travelled together to the north of Svalbard. Why would they go there?"

"It seems like a good place to get some privacy," Johnny said.

Eliassen was not to be found in the administration building or the governor's residence. They hurried past the cemetery to the church, an odd building, red at one end where the steeple rose up, with an adjoining lower building in white. They went inside.

Robert Eliassen was sitting in a lounge area on the first floor.

"Can I help you with something?" he said as Sasha stopped at his table.

"August 17, 1976," Sasha said. "Does that date mean anything to you?"

He thought about it for a few seconds. "Nothing other than it was a long time ago."

"I'll give you a hint," she continued. "You requisitioned a helicopter for yourself and two relations of mine. My father, Olav Falck, was one of them."

Eliassen studied her for a long moment. "Good heavens, are you Alexandra Falck?"

Sasha introduced Johnny and sat down on the sofa next to him. He had watchful eyes, like a bird of prey, and a reddish beard that was beginning to grey. She waited before answering.

"You never contacted me personally after you found Colonel Zemlyakov dead," she began. "I realise you were probably muzzled but I was actually a little hurt. Since it related directly to my family."

He opened his mouth to speak, but Sasha went on.

"But the Russian's last words are still relevant. And that's why I've contacted you."

"You no doubt understand there's a lot I can't tell . . ."

"I get that, Robert," she said in a considerate tone. She had him now. "Because what I wanted to ask you about was the helicopter trip in August 1976. A young, radical medical student, an officer from the Police Surveillance Agency and an adviser from the Ministry of Defence travel to Sallyhamna. An unlikely trio. What were you doing there?"

"The location was picked so we could have some privacy," he said quietly. "As you probably understand, Olav and I had things we wanted to discuss with Hans. We were concerned. An empowerment conversation, I suppose you'd call it nowadays."

"What were you concerned about?"

"I had worked with Hans as a newly minted officer in the Police Surveillance Agency, POT. We were complete opposites. He was from a shipping family in Bergen, I was a working-class lad from Hamar, and I was intrigued by him. At the same time, we realised early on that he might have a greater potential for violence than many of the others in the AKP."

"A potential for violence?"

"Our view was that it was down to class background," Eliassen explained. "Leftists from the social elite could be influenced to a greater extent by extremist factions in other countries, where the threshold for resorting to political violence to achieve societal change was much lower."

"Say what you like about Hans," Sasha said, "but he's saved lives, not taken them."

Johnny had been listening quietly. Now he spoke up. "I've read the file on Hans and I know you were the one keeping him under surveillance. But what if this was about something else?"

"Like what?" the governor said.

"Hans was the main source in a highly sensitive newspaper story," Sasha said. "The Maoist paper *Klassekampen* was about to expose a conspiracy between the shipowners and intelligence people. Civilian rescue boats leased to the Polar Institute were fitted with radar and other military equipment in direct contravention of the Svalbard Treaty. And this resulted in the deaths of Norwegian seamen."

She leaned back in her chair.

"That was an unintended and extremely unfortunate consequence," he said. "But are you aware of what might have happened had we not talked to Hans? We could have lost the place where we're now sitting. Norway could have lost Svalbard."

"That's a bold statement."

"Think about it: had it emerged that the CIA was breaking the treaty and using Norwegian civilian organisations to spy on the Russians, it could have set in motion a chain reaction with terrible consequences."

"Tell us about the trip to the north of Spitsbergen," Sasha said.

"Well, we flew Hans up there. It was surprisingly bare of snow and we opened the cabin. Ate a good reindeer dinner. We talked about responsibility. Your father spoke a good deal about loyalty and betrayal. About how the family had ties to Svalbard going back to when Norwegians first bought the mines in Longyearbyen. Hans understood. He's no fool, you know."

"Did you recruit Hans?"

He shook his head. "We talked to him. Aired concerns. A frank discussion, I'd call it, but I don't remember the details."

Sasha looked at Johnny. "I think I understand the implications of the exposé. How important it was. But what about the property in the Advent Valley?"

"That had nothing to do with Hans," the governor said. "When the state bought up the land on Svalbard, some remained in private ownership. Around one per cent, 0.8 to be precise. The Advent Valley was part of that. The owner, Herbert Falck, bequeathed it to his daughter."

"One last thing," Sasha said, pensively. "I presume you knew about the relationship between Connie and Hans if you were hiding in the bushes around that time. Do you know when they broke up?"

"I'd like to think I'm above that kind of speculation," Eliassen said.

Sasha stood up. "Thank you, that was very helpful."

The river dividing Longyearbyen was still frozen and covered in snow. They squeezed their way between tourists, researchers and young tour guides speaking English, French, German and Italian to one another at the bar in the Radisson. The drinks were cheap; all of Svalbard was tax-free. Johnny ordered two half-litres and placed the beers on the table.

"You believe what he said?" he asked.

"I don't think he was lying," Sasha said. "I'm just not sure how much of the truth he left out."

"Let's say he's telling the truth. That Olav and Eliassen have a serious chat with Hans in 1976 and he puts a stop to the Svalbard story. But Constance and Hans find their way back to each other. They were in Lebanon together – there's no other way to interpret the photo at her place, not that I can see."

He swallowed; his lips trembled ever so slightly. "One of the first things she said to me was my Arabic birth name."

"What did you make of that?" Sasha adopted a soft voice.

"That it was about Lebanon, of course. That was where I was found, after all. Chargé d'Affaires Berg brought me back to Norway before he died, tragically, the year after."

Sasha looked at him wide-eyed. "I never knew that."

"I spent years when I was younger trying to find out more. Before eventually accepting I was Norwegian."

He squeezed his eyes shut; she stroked him gently on the arm. "Can we talk about something else, Sashenka?" He smiled. "You want to go out?"

The midnight sun shone, lighting up the landscape in hues of gold and yellow. It was one o'clock in the morning, the early hours of the long day. Johnny walked towards where the snow scooters were parked.

"You have a rifle, I hope? Oh wait, you don't even have a snow scooter suit," Sasha chuckled.

"It's not that cold," he said. "Just hold on tight."

He warmed up the snow scooter, slung the rifle diagonally over his shoulder and took her hand. Sasha mounted the scooter. Put her arms around his waist.

"Ready, Sasha?" he said, turning his head.

"Ready."

They drove slowly down the hill past the university and the museum. He opened the throttle when the surface was level. The floor of the Advent Valley lay in shadow. Their speed increased. One hundred kilometres per hour; she held him more tightly. Could feel his pulse as she leaned against him.

"We're going up that slope." He pointed. "We need as much weight as possible on the front of the scooter, understand?"

Sasha nodded.

It was a wonder the scooter did not tip over going up the almost vertical escarpment, but after a few minutes the mountainside flattened out. Johnny made a sharp turn and stopped.

The weather was milder. Soon the winter season would be over. He produced two collapsible rubber cups, handed her one and poured them both a hot toddy.

The Advent Valley lay below them, flat and white. A trail meandered along the valley floor. Opera Mountain was bathed in midnight sun. Far off, the blue arm of the fjord went into the enormous Isfjord, and beyond that new fjords, new glaciers.

"This is what your family have been fighting over," he said contemplatively. He rolled a cigarette and gave it to her, then rolled another for himself.

"Well, I can understand that," she said, looking out.

"Svalbard is the Wild West of the Arctic," he said. "The vast distances. People wanting to live free, without interference from others. I get it. There's no social welfare office in Longyearbyen. If you live here you need to be able to look after yourself."

"Who are we?" Sasha said, gazing out at the valley. Nature on this majestic scale brought to mind the big existential questions. "Who are you, Johnny? Isn't it our disposition, actions and the choices we make that determine that? Not our name and who our parents are?" She took a drag of the cigarette. "Over the last few months, I, for one, have realised I can't base my life on the fact my name is Falck."

"Yeah, and 150 million might come in handy when you need to find yourself." Johnny smiled.

"I know, I know," Sasha said. "But here we are, sitting at the top of the world. The ice is melting and the superpowers are arming themselves around us. But . . ."

". . . right now . . ."

She finished the sentence for him: ". . . it feels kind of like we're free."

At that moment the midnight sun came into view behind the mountain, just a sliver, making them squint. They took each other's hands and leaned into one another. Then they went back to her hotel room.

"Wasn't it here at Funken Lodge that Connie and Hans spent the night together in 1971?" Johnny said the next morning.

She smiled.

52

SAINT GEORGE'S CROSS

The demarcation line between Norway and Russia, Barents Sea

The ice lay thick to the east of Kvitøya, and the Russian icebreaker made a metallic racket as it forged a channel through it. They were nearing the island.

Hans was standing at the bow. For some reason he had pictured the ice of the Arctic Ocean as a desert. One uses the tools at one's disposal and Hans knew the desert better than the poles. But the Arctic *was* a desert of sorts. And just as the desert broke with the sand dunes of tourist images, so did this ice. On the horizon to the north lay endless pressure ridges and treacherous openings, resembling, in monochrome, photographs of a city razed to the ground during a war. "Stalingrad Ice", one polar explorer had called it, and Hans understood what he meant. Even unaided by Russian environmental pollution, the Arctic was like an endless, snow-covered, monochrome scrapheap.

The edge of the Falck glacier came slowly into view, like a mountain cliff. Hans went to the starboard side and felt his heart beating faster. Had he returned home? No, that sounded too dramatic. He had returned to his childhood.

Ingeborg, Christian, Marte and Siri Greve, who was cursing the Arctic cold, were aft, with the researchers from the Polar Institute.

A long, fresh channel had opened behind them, and drift

ice rose up like small bluffs on both sides of the greenish polar water. Even in summer, Kvitøya was covered in snow and the enormous Falck glacier, which rose gradually up to almost 400 metres.

"We anchor here," said the captain, who had joined them on deck. "The Russians agree. And then we'll go on land on Andrée Headland, the ice-free south-western tip."

Hans began to tell the others about the balloon expedition of 1897, which ended with Swede August Andrée and his crew having to seek refuge on the island, where they perished, most likely from the cold or torn apart by polar bears.

"They were only found in 1930 by an expedition funded and equipped by Theo Falck," Hans said reverently.

"Was it Theo who found their remains?" Sverre asked in surprise.

"It was. Together with some sealers from Tromsø he knew. Which again goes to show that Theo was one of the most important, unsung national strategists in the polar arena."

He clapped his hands. "Shall we make our way onto the ice and over to the island?"

The others nodded.

"Well?" Hans said companionably to Marte and her sons, who were standing by the exit. "This is a big moment for me, planting the flag one hundred years after Theo. You're coming with us to the island?"

An elevation loomed in the endless white: L'île Blanche, White Island, Kvitøya.

Of course, they would be glad to.

Not long after, a delegation lowered themselves onto the ice and skied the few hundred metres to the Andrée headland.

They made their way up onto the barren, rocky tip where the memorial to the Swedish expedition was to be found. Some walruses lazed on the ice just beyond.

We're here, Hans thought, allowing himself to be overwhelmed by the splendour of the moment – of generations succeeding one another and the infinity of history. Theo Falck stood here in the Year of our Lord 1916, and now history had repeated itself, like at a birth, where you stare infinity in the eye.

As always Hans had an instinctive flair for the dramatic, and he sank to his knees on the glacier, leaned forward and kissed it, like a Muslim at prayer.

He got back to his feet and squinted at the horizon.

"You alright?" Marte smiled.

"It's emotional," Hans said. "Fucking emotional."

"What happens to the Falck name when the glacier melts?" his daughter asked.

"That's still a long way off," Hans said dismissively. "This glacier isn't like one in the Alps."

Hans eyed Marte for a long time from behind his sunglasses. "The day the Falck glacier melts away, the family dies with it. That's my prediction. Sorry to say."

The researcher from the Polar Institute chimed in. "Thanks to our satellite pictures from ICESat we now know more about how the glaciers on Svalbard develop. Overall, the glaciers show a clear decline over the past thirty years, especially in the south and west of the islands. Here, in the north and east, the situation is a little different. Like the Austfonna ice cap, the Falck glacier has accumulated more ice at higher altitude, about fifty centimetres annually. All the same, its total volume has been reduced by calving and the retreat of the glacier termini we see here."

Hans threw out his arms and addressed the gathering in English. "From here we can see all the way to the North Pole, eastward to Russian Franz Josef Land and southward to the Norwegian mainland!"

Which was not quite true.

"The point is," he continued, fired up. "A spirit of discovery and sense of adventure are not mere abstractions. They also mean power. When our ancestors, from Nansen onward, braved the forces of nature to survey and explore places no one had been before, they played a crucial role in these territories coming under our national control. The same way as Russian explorers brought the vast areas on the outskirts of their country under the control of the Russian empire."

Hans paused.

"In my younger days," he said, "I would have been the first to reject this kind of talk as a 'justification of imperialism'. But that was long ago. Svalbard was also different, a *terra nullius*, with no indigenous people to trample on. I'm proud of our history and I'm proud that we can share it with our Russian friends."

Before going back down, Hans and the others placed a picture in front of a flag with the words *Familia ante omnia*. He had brought a bottle of spiced vodka in his backpack and they stood and made a toast.

Getting from the edge of the ice down to the waiting boats was complicated, but the group abseiled down and were transported back to *Falck III* on inflatables.

As they approached the boat, Hans noticed that all the engineers, as well as what seemed to be every other crew member, were engaged in furious activity, both on board and on the ice around the hull.

"What's going on?" Hans shouted.

"Blackout," Captain Ørnes replied. "It's dead."

"No fucking way," Hans said. "Isn't there another system on board that kicks in if one short-circuits?"

"That's correct," the captain said in a bitter voice, and went on to explain how these systems operated independently of one another, like on an aircraft.

"Try again," Hans ordered. "In the meantime, I'll get in touch with the governor and the mainland."

After a ten-minute conversation on the satellite phone, Hans made his way down to his small cabin. Eliassen had told him that as long as this occurred in Norwegian territorial waters there was no danger. However, the ice made it impossible for the governor's boat *Polarsyssel* to perform a rescue operation. So he had spoken to the captain of the Russian nuclear icebreaker, who had agreed to tow *Falck III* back to Longyearbyen after the medal ceremony on the dividing line.

"The conferment is to take place in a lounge below the command bridge on the icebreaker," Siri Greve explained to the crew and guests on board *Falck III*. "I was on board for a little inspection and it looks like they intend to pull out all the stops. Russian delicacies galore, of course. The Russian VIPs came by helicopter from Kapp Heer an hour ago. We'll arrive at the dividing line in approximately three hours."

"The Russians gave us a lift as well," said Sverre Falck, joining the group. "They had room for me and another Norwegian."

Johnny opened a hatch and climbed a ladder down to the lowest deck on *Falck III*. Within minutes the icebreaker and the boat it was towing would be at the dividing line. The rest of the Norwegian contingent had been taken aboard the icebreaker; except for the crew, the vessel was empty.

The ceremony would be getting under way at any moment.

Johnny had spent the last few days at Funken Lodge with Sasha. They had left the room only to eat a meal and have a drink, before returning to make love again.

On the third day, Sverre Falck rang from Svalbard. Johnny had stepped out into the hall and, after a little thought, told him he was in the same place. Sverre had not forgotten the agreement they made at Rederhaugen and had asked Johnny if he wanted to join him on *Falck III*. HK had been in raptures at the thought.

He opened the door of a cabin. It was empty. Something was amiss. All the resources, time and energy channelled into the anniversary expedition and it ends on the windblown headland on Kvitøya? A new ship suddenly suffers engine failure and needs to be towed?

He came to the cabin furthest along. A sign read NO ENTRY. The door was locked. The corridor was quiet. Johnny jogged back the way he had come. In the engine room he grabbed what tools he could and hurried back. He wedged a crowbar into the door frame, working it back and forth until the door bent. He broke the door open. The cabin was bigger than the others.

There were analogue HF radios on a table along one wall. He recognised them as the type used for Morse code and normal communications. A screen covered the other wall. Johnny turned it on. The first thing he saw was a detailed satellite image of Svalbard and the surrounding waters. The routes of what he assumed were Russian trawlers were displayed. Yagry, Sevryba. The names meant nothing to him. What was this?

It was exactly what he had spent the last six months striving to understand. Johnny had the feeling of recognising something that had been right under his nose. How had he not seen it before? He had studied and written about how the CIA and Norwegian intelligence cooperated in utilising shipping companies and Norwegian organisations for the purposes of espionage. The Polar Institute. The Society for Sea Rescue. They had undertaken voyages in the Barents Sea and collected intelligence for the NATO countries at the same time. As Hans's biographer, Johnny knew all this.

But he had not realised that Hans Falck was operating in precisely the same way with *Falck III*. Apart from one small, crucial difference: he was using what he knew of this type of intelligence – but for the Russians.

Johnny grew afraid.

Why were the Russians towing this ship across the demarcation line into Russian waters?

Because they wanted access to whatever was on board.

That must not happen, under any circumstances.

He scampered up the ladder towards the command bridge.

A faint smell of cigarette smoke and old furniture hung in the room where the ceremony was to be held. A large framed photograph of the president of the Russian Federation held pride of place. Hans was greeted warmly and shown around. The view from the bow area was panoramic.

Large plates of rye bread, herring, cod's roe and smoked meats, with classic Russian trimmings such as dill, gherkins and sour cream, were carried in.

They were welcomed not only by Aliyev, but also by the

consul, Director Sokolov and a second secretary from the embassy.

"Hans Falck," Aliyev said, handing him a glass of sparkling wine. "We don't stand on ceremony up here in the Arctic, do we?"

"Cheers." Hans smiled.

"Very well," the second secretary said and clinked a spoon against his glass. "I suggest we move on to the official part of today's programme."

He picked up a note and read: "A few months ago one of our trawlers found itself in a critical situation when the captain became acutely ill in Norwegian territorial waters. Had it not been for the timely intervention of the Norwegian 330th Squadron and the resourcefulness of Dr Hans Falck in particular, the captain would not have survived. In extremely difficult weather conditions, and putting his own life at risk, Doctor Falck performed improvised emergency surgery on the captain."

Sverre noticed Aliyev had a small case next to him; he knew what was coming next.

"On behalf of the Russian Federation, I hereby award Hans Falck the Cross of Saint George in the rank of commander, the highest decoration for bravery that may be bestowed on non-nationals. President Putin has also sent a personal telegram of congratulations."

He opened the case and held up the medal. Everyone clapped.

"This is . . . overwhelming," Hans said.

A woman pinned the medal to his chest.

"Would you like to say a few words on behalf of SAGA?" the second secretary asked Sverre.

"I hadn't planned on saying much," Sverre began, Ingeborg simultaneously interpreting. "But as CEO of SAGA, the place where we currently find ourselves – the so-called dividing line – symbolises to me the peaceful relations between two neighbouring states. It also symbolises how two countries with contrasting histories and cultures can coexist in the far north."

He looked at Hans. "You carry the same contradictions in your heart, Hans. You are a shipowner's son and a radical, you're a Norwegian and a cosmopolitan. Now that you can add the prestigious Order of Saint George to your already well-stocked medal cabinet, I ask: what other Norwegian can boast of being the recipient of the Lebanese Order of the Cedar, honorary Kurdish citizenship and an honorary doctorate from the University of Florence? Congratulations. And *na zdorovye*!"

Johnny checked his watch again. They were only two nautical miles from the 34th parallel. After that the Russians could do as they wanted; they would be in their own waters.

He called HK on a satellite phone. His words came flooding out.

"Calm down, Johnny," the older man said. "You're saying you've discovered military communications equipment on board *Falck III*? And that Hans is cooperating with the Russians to bring the boat into their waters?"

"We're less than two nautical miles away," Johnny said. "We're being towed in that direction and there's nothing we can do about it."

HK sighed. "I think it's time to improvise. You know that yourself. I'll back you if you land in trouble. But no violence against the Russians under any circumstances, is that understood?"

Johnny hung up. Then he ran up to the command bridge.

"Berg?" Captain Ørnes said. "What are you doing here?"

He explained his purpose. The captain and second officer both shook their heads. "We can't give you any firearms."

"This is a matter of national security. Don't you understand why we're headed for Russian waters?" Johnny said, his voice low. "Then we'll just have to do it this way."

He pointed the gun at the captain, hoping the shock would prevent him from examining the weapon too closely, since it was a flare gun.

"I'm ordering you to find the rifle," Johnny said sharply, alternating between pointing the gun at the captain and at the second officer. They raised their hands.

"It's punishable by law to . . ."

"Do it," Johnny said. "For reasons I can't go into now that involve national security, I order you. Just consider it a hijacking. Quickly!"

The second officer held out the weapon carefully. Johnny seized it, checked if there was a round in the chamber and loaded it. Moving briskly, he made his way down and walked to the bow of the boat. An icy wind was blowing. Towlines were running through scuppers on both sides.

One nautical mile, then they would be in Russian territorial waters.

All around him the sub-zero wasteland of ice and snow stretched as far as the eye could see.

Johnny fired. After a series of shots, the rope between the icebreaker and *Falck III* was severed. The hawser was released from the winch and through the scuppers, the rescue boat slowed and the icebreaker glided away from them.

*

"What was that?" Hans asked, upon hearing three thuds from outside.

He noticed the Russians also looking around.

"As you've no doubt noticed, this vessel can often make a sharp sound as it breaks through the ice," Aliyev said, trying to maintain his composure as he whispered something to one of the guards.

"Could it have been someone encountering a polar bear?"

"Let me go out and check!" It was Greve's voice.

The Russians exchanged glances; the captain shrugged. "By all means, if you like."

Hans waved her over and looked at her admonishingly. "Siri."

"Sorry, Hans, but something strange is going on here. I'm taking a look."

She made to go out but two guards took up position between her and the door. "Who do you think you are to refuse me free movement on a boat in Norwegian waters? The impertinence!"

"Russian jurisdiction," the man said.

Hans, standing with his medal case in his hand, noticed how the ceremony had moved from the false courtesy of diplomacy to something else. The Russians were engaged in intense conversation on their mobile phones. The stunned Norwegians stood in the middle.

"What is going on?" Ingeborg asked with authority in Russian. "We demand to know what's happening."

"Of course," the second secretary replied. "You'll soon be informed."

Aliyev and the Russian VIPs were suddenly nowhere to be seen. The door to the lounge opened. The second secretary nodded to the two men who entered. Young, athletic types, probably military. And in that moment Hans had a realisation. He had always held that life hinged on certain moments, diverging paths into the deep, chaotic, impenetrable forest of existence. A signpost pointing one way, to a woman who became the mother of your child and was thus connected to you for life, another to an ideology, a country and a profession. Yes, life was of course *all these days that came and went*, as the aphorism went, but so were the big moments. The meeting with Vera in 1970. Shatila in Beirut in 1982. Sallyhamna with Olav and Eliassen in 1976. All those years since, living with the fear of being caught.

The two military-looking men produced ID cards, held them up in front of Hans, and said something in Russian. FSB, Hans made out.

"Ingeborg, can you translate?" he said calmly.

One of the Russians said in good English:

"We are in Russian territorial waters. You are under arrest, Hans Falck, suspected of acting as a secret agent for the United States under cover of providing emergency relief to people in need. You will be remanded in custody under paragraph 265 of the Russian penal code, the so-called espionage paragraph."

PART V
THE LAST MISSION

53

WE'RE THE MOTHERFUCKERS

Longyearbyen, Svalbard

Lawyer Jan I. Rana placed his feet on the ground at 78 degrees north and inhaled the polar air.

The snow-covered pyramid mountains around the airport in Longyearbyen were bathed in sunshine and the deep blue water in Advent fjord lay calm. The weather had been perfectly clear for the entire flight north and Rana had been seized by an acute feeling of patriotism. The sea was the royal road to praise and power. Wasn't it whatshisname Sverdrup who said that? Why had he remembered that?

Because he was a man who remembered things.

Still, was this Norway? In Tromsø he had had to show his passport to travel further.

He hailed a taxi and was driven the short distance to the governor's administration building in Skjeringa. Rana hurried in and presented himself.

"I represent John O. Berg," he said. "And wish to speak to my client immediately."

Annoyingly, they left him waiting for a long time before showing him downstairs, where he was placed in a waiting room. When the door finally opened, he saw only Johnny's silhouette at first. An officer let him in, then locked the door, leaving them alone. They embraced.

"Brother, have they treated you properly?"

Johnny nodded. He had grown a beard since Rana had last seen him. It made his narrow face rounder.

"I've been bitten by the polar bug," Rana said. "On the flight I familiarised myself with the Treaty of Svalbard and the mining code that applies here. As well as the legal objections the EU and Russia have raised against Norway's interpretation of the treaty."

He grinned. "Here was me thinking Norway was a peaceful little nation being pushed around by the superpowers on Svalbard. But we're not the ones being fucked over here. *We're* the motherfuckers."

"I see."

"You know we're on thin ice when the EU *and* Russia present a united front *against* imperialist Norway when it comes to interpretation of the treaty."

"But Jan—"

"This place must be the closest you can get to the Republican Party's dream society," Rana said, pointing to the floor above, where the governor had his office. "It's run by an unelected governor, weapons are mandatory, tax is below ten per cent, and there is no one on welfare as far as the eye can see."

"Always refreshing to hear your perspective on things," Johnny said. "But any chance you could get me out of my cell before we continue this discussion? You know . . . do things in the right order?"

He related in detail what had happened up until he "cut the string" between the icebreaker and *Falck III*. While Hans was, presumably, receiving his award on board the icebreaker, *Falck III* had remained behind on the demarcation line. Johnny and the crew had been evacuated by helicopter. Captain Ørnes had obviously told the governor's people about the "hijacking" because on arrival at Longyearbyen Johnny had been arrested.

Rana listened patiently before saying: "You're holding something back. If I'm going to help you, I need to know everything."

"What do you mean?"

"What was important enough to invoke defensive force and make sure *Falck III* wasn't towed into Russian waters?"

Johnny leaned forward over the table. "This is top secret, Jan," he whispered. "I searched the ship just before the 'hijacking' and had to break into a locked room. It was full of communication equipment. That was when I solved something I've spent six months trying to figure out. The man receiving an award from the Russians, Hans Falck, has been working for them. He's been using the same methods as his father before him, spying under the guise of research expeditions with rescue ships."

A worry line appeared on Rana's brow. "Hans Falck is a Russian spy?"

"If the Russians had towed the vessel into their waters, they would have been free to go through the catch at their leisure. They could also have interrogated me. I couldn't allow that to happen."

The lawyer scratched his scalp and looked thoughtful. "OK, Johnny. I think we have enough. Are you ready?"

The interview took place in a bare room one floor up, with Johnny sitting in front of the governor and a woman from the administration's PST department.

"I for one am unclear as to why we're sitting here at all," Rana began. "As far as I'm aware my client has acted in accordance with the law. He would like to return to Norway as soon as possible."

"We are in Norway," Governor Eliassen said.

"We've conducted interviews with the crew members aboard *Falck III*," the policewoman said. "Captain Ørnes and the second officer have both related how Berg seized a weapon, by force, which he later discharged several times, in an extremely dangerous and involved situation, while the vessel *Falck III* was being towed by a Russian icebreaker. This is a very serious matter. It falls under chapter 18, paragraph 139 of the criminal code concerning the hijacking of vessels and carries a sentence of up to twenty-one years."

Johnny sat motionless but Rana shook his head.

"Berg exercised the right to self-defence."

"We would remind you that the right to self-defence only applies if the crime being prevented is greater than the crime committed," the PST woman said. "I have difficulty in seeing that that was the case here."

"On board *Falck III*," Rana said slowly, "Berg discovered concealed advanced communication equipment. The investigation will no doubt throw light on who was using this equipment. But whether it was a Western operation directed against Russia or a Russian spy on board *Falck III*, Berg did the right thing. Did what he was trained to do. He defended Norwegian interests and will be commended for it."

Governor Eliassen looked in irritation at his colleague.

"But anyway, it's a secondary concern," Rana continued and took out a large, detailed map of the entire archipelago. "This is a map of the area. Do you have access to the rescue helicopter's log?"

They both nodded.

"I want complete and accurate coordinates," Rana demanded.

The log was located and examined against the map.

"As you can see," Rana said with a triumphant smile, "the

incident occurred at the meridian exactly 34 degrees east of Greenwich, in international waters, on the so-called dividing line. So, we can safely say there are no grounds for detaining Berg. Now, if you have what you need, you'll have to excuse us. My client and I would like to experience the midnight sun before returning south."

The entire scene reminded Johnny of when he had been remanded in custody the year before as a foreign fighter. Rana had run rings around the prosecution and forced his release.

Afterwards, Rana had a brief private conversation with Governor Eliassen, before he returned with a smile on his face. "Let's get down to the main street for a few units of tax-free alcohol, Johnny. That's an order."

It was midnight. The sun made them squint. "Why go to Dubai when you have Norway? Bjørnson, Johnny, have you read any of his stuff?"

"No."

The lawyer was in high spirits. *"They felt, as they sat there among the trees, with fjord and mountain lying before them deep in the evening sun, as horn and song sounded far in the distance, that this indeed was happiness.* Norwegians are lost in admiration when a foreigner can pull a quotation like that out of his sleeve. World's easiest parlour trick. This *evening* is on me!"

The temperature had dropped to a few degrees below zero and the snow had stopped melting. They trotted into the first bar. Rana went up to order and returned with a trayful of pints.

"Cheers," he said.

They clinked glasses.

Then they heard a patron shout: "Turn up the sound on the TV, it's about Svalbard!"

The conversations in the bar ceased. It was an international news channel.

"We're going to Svalbard, a group of islands between Norway and the North Pole," a news anchor with a British accent said, "where there have been reports of gunfire on board the Norwegian rescue boat *Falck III*. The vessel had become trapped in ice off Kvitøya and was being towed by a Russian icebreaker."

Rana cast an uneasy eye at Johnny.

"The *Falck III* was fitted with a Cineflex V14 HD camera to stream the voyage live, so we can now show you pictures of what unfolded in those dramatic hours in the Arctic Ocean," the news anchor said.

The camera must have been on the bridge, the angle showing the vessel's bow. On either side lay the Arctic Ocean's endless white scrapyard of pressure ridges and channels. The silhouette of the Russian icebreaker was visible above the prow. Then, from the right-hand side, a man entered the frame. He walked purposefully, placed a rifle in the pocket of his shoulder and fired a series of single shots at the hawsers, severing them. As the man turned in the direction of the camera, the TV channel froze the picture and zoomed in on the low-resolution face.

Johnny closed his eyes, as though meditating.

"Relax," Rana said quietly. "I'm sure there are bigger hooks in this story. Hans Falck, for instance."

Just then Johnny's phone vibrated.

"Don't take that," Rana said.

A cautious smile played across Johnny's lips and a slight flush appeared on his cheeks as he got to his feet. "It's private."

"Do you *have* a private life?"

"It's just . . . a girl I really like."

54

NORWEGIAN CELEBRITY DOCTOR ARRESTED ON ESPIONAGE CHARGES

Longyearbyen, Svalbard

Sverre and Ingeborg embraced outside the governor's administration building. They stood swaying back and forth, like an awkward couple on a dance floor.

"I'm so glad this is over," he mumbled into her Gore-Tex jacket.

After Hans was arrested the others were put ashore at a remote base on Franz Josef Land before being flown by Russian helicopter that same evening to Barentsburg, from where they were transported to Longyearbyen. On their arrival they were interviewed individually by PST people in the administration, who were attempting to reconstruct the entire sequence of events, from the engine failure aboard *Falck III* off Kvitøya, to the arrest of Hans. How had the power cut happened? Sverre shrugged and was eventually allowed to leave.

"This isn't over. It's just getting started," Ingeborg said at length, and took out her phone. "Look."

Sverre leaned closer but could not discern the Cyrillic letters, much less understand their meaning.

"It's from an investigative journalist I know in Moscow.

Always well informed. He's retweeting a tweet from the Rosbalt news agency."

The piece stated, in unambiguous language, that "a Norwegian citizen" had been arrested for espionage in Russian territorial waters the previous day and was being held in custody at the Nagurskoye military base on Franz Josef Land, awaiting escort to the Russian mainland.

"This isn't some misunderstanding," Ingeborg said. "At least not one that can be cleared up quickly. Hans won't be released anytime soon."

"This is going to be huge," Sverre said seriously. "This is the Treholt case all over again, maybe bigger. Remember, Hans is well known. Everyone is going to be placed under scrutiny. Me, you, Marte, Siri Greve, Johnny Berg. Where we were. What we were doing. What we were planning on doing. Are you ready for that?"

It is a false cliché that media storms come as "a bolt from the blue", even those that reach hurricane force. More often they begin as a breath of wind, a detail, something to all appearances quietly overlooked.

In this case the storm began with a telegram from an obscure news agency, hours before the dramatic footage of shooting at the demarcation line.

Sverre's phone rang.

Speaking with restraint and assurance, like someone clarifying the practicalities after the death of a parent, Marte told him she was at the Radisson in Longyearbyen.

"Have any journalists rung you yet?" Sverre asked.

"That's the reason I'm calling," she said. "I just got calls from two journalists. As well as some text messages. They know something happened on Kvitøya and at the demarcation line."

Ingeborg tapped him on the back. "The BBC's Moscow correspondent has just retweeted the story: *LIVE: Norwegian detained by Russia in the High Arctic over spy charges.*"

Marte's voice took on an anxious, disconcerted tone. "What will I do, Sverre?"

"We're on our way," he answered, and hung up.

They hurried to the Radisson hotel on the other side of Longyearbyen, glancing over their shoulders as they walked. Everything seemed calm.

"I don't think Svalbard is the best place for the family to be in the coming days," Ingeborg said. "It's too small, impossible to lie low."

Sverre became annoyed. "Well, why don't you suggest that to everyone then, if you're such an expert on crisis management?"

"Now you listen to me," she said angrily. "Both Mum and Nana were involved in things that make this look like a picnic."

"I wouldn't be so sure about that," he muttered. He scrolled on his phone. "Nothing in the Norwegian press yet."

As they entered the hotel they were blinded by the flash of a camera. One man took a series of photos of them while an older reporter in a khaki vest, equipped with a notepad, stepped forward.

"We're from *Svalbardposten*. Can you confirm you're aware of the arrest of Hans Falck?"

Bewildered, Sverre looked at the man. Yes, there were times when he used to fantasise about being famous, having a famous girlfriend and having to dodge the paparazzi outside Chateau Marmont or a casino in Monte Carlo.

"No comment," he said, guiding Ingeborg through the lobby.

The photos would look good, though, no doubt about that.

*

Hans's family came on the next flight and soon arrived at the Radisson hotel: Christian and Erik Falck, Synne with little Per on her arm. Marte organised the whole thing.

Although Sverre and the other Norwegians were of course shocked by the arrest, the atmosphere was relatively restrained. Surprisingly so, Sverre thought. The family was of course accustomed to Hans Falck's many escapades. Had he not been taken prisoner by the Turkish authorities in the Kurdish region as well as by rebels in eastern Congo on previous occasions? But Hans Falck, CIA agent? Surely this was a misunderstanding,

Only Erik Falck was beside himself.

"Fucking Russian scum," he shouted, gesticulating.

Christian tried to calm his little brother.

Marte placed the chairs in a ring and asked the others to sit down. She had dark circles under her eyes and her skin was pale, almost yellow, but it was obvious she was the one keeping the family together now.

Ingeborg and Sverre remained in the background, standing leaning against the wall.

Just then Marte's phone rang. She did not recognise the number.

"Don't take it," everyone said in unison. "Guaranteed to be the media."

Upon checking her voicemail, her face assumed an attentive, expectant expression, which was picked up on by the others. There was silence in the room.

"The Norwegian embassy in Moscow," she said quietly. "I'll ring them back."

Her call was answered by a man who introduced himself as First Secretary Klouman in Moscow.

"This is Marte Falck, I'm the daughter of Hans Falck. I'm

in Longyearbyen. I have you on speakerphone with the family, just so you know."

"I understand," the first secretary said, clearing his throat. "I'm calling to give you some practical information and tell you about what will happen moving forward. The embassy received a telegram from the FSB, the Russian security service, an hour ago. The Norwegian citizen, Hans Falck, was arrested in Russian territorial waters yesterday at 21.25 and transported to the Nagurskoye military base on Franz Josef Land. We aren't able to provide assistance at that location. According to the FSB, Falck will shortly be transferred to Murmansk. Whereupon our consul and a representative from the embassy will be allowed to see him, we've been promised that."

The usual, disappointing platitudes.

"I did talk to Hans for a minute over a bad telephone line," the diplomat continued. "He said he was OK but was sorry for the pain he had caused all of you."

"Sorry?" Erik exclaimed loudly. "I doubt Dad was sorry. Furious more like – these charges are baseless!"

"Those were the words he used," Klouman said.

"How long will it be before he gets out?" Marte asked. "Surely even the Russians don't hold innocent people for that long, especially if they're Western?"

"We're communicating directly with people at the highest level and working on several possibilities," the diplomat assured her. "But I want to inform you all of two things before this explodes."

There was silence.

"Yes?" Marte said.

"That we're taking this very seriously and will use absolutely every channel to secure the release of Hans Falck. The other . . ." he said, hesitating, "is that Hans has let it be known that he will be putting all his cards on the table. 'I'm guilty of the Russian charges,' he said."

The call cut out.

"Is Dad guilty?" Marte mumbled.

"Of course not," Erik said. "They've probably doped him with something to get him to admit to a crime he didn't commit."

Sverre moved to the window and opened a small gap in the Venetian blinds. At the same moment a dozen or so photographers sprang forward and snapped pictures of him.

Yes, this was going to be huge.

55

"ARE YOU A COUPLE?"

Oslo

There was no internet on board the direct flight between Longyearbyen and Oslo. Johnny slept dreamlessly until the captain began the descent.

Naturally Sasha had been shaken by the news when they spoke. Being aware of his presence on board *Falck III*, she had immediately put "two and two together" when the footage was publicised. The wider family were in emergency mode, she confided, fighting back tears.

"It's a lot, Johnny. Too much."

They agreed to meet as soon as he returned to Oslo.

"Look at this," Jan I. Rana said, as the plane was about to land and messages started coming through.

"Hans Falck arrested for espionage against Russia," he read.

"It has to be wrong," Johnny said. "Why would the Russians arrest their own agent?"

"This is official."

Johnny read.

> *The Ministry of Foreign Affairs can confirm that the Norwegian citizen arrested in Russian waters in the Arctic two days ago was Norwegian doctor Hans Falck (63). According to the Russian authorities, he is being held at Nagurskoye*

military base on Franz Josef Land. The ministry is treating the case as a misunderstanding and are working to find a swift solution.

A misunderstanding. It must be.

In the arrivals hall Johnny noticed people walking with heads bent over their phones. Not in the normal absent-minded way, but absorbed, as when a major event has taken place. The mutterings were audible throughout the airport: *Did you hear? And that Falck guy, no less. A super-spy, that can't be true, surely?*

They hurried to the airport express train, which was about to close its doors. On a large screen in the carriage the news coverage was constant, Norwegian and English ticker tape rolling across the bottom of the screen. The first thing they saw was a photograph of Hans. Then the grainy film of "the shots in the Arctic", as the incident was now being referred to, dramatic footage that was irresistible to online newspapers and social media.

"Rule number two in crisis management," Rana said, while he munched on a carrot. "When you think the worst is over, things are only getting started."

Johnny checked the foreign media. Where the story was mentioned, it only figured as a small item.

"This is going to make front pages all over the world," Rana said. "People accused of spying in Russia always makes for a big story, and in this case you're also talking an eccentric leftist doctor and heir to billions."

The fields of the district of Romerike slipped past the windows, green and glowing in the warm spring sunshine.

An expert in defence and security policy was being interviewed on the TV. The Falck arrest was the main story. That the Russian regime would imprison an innocent humanitarian doctor on clearly fictitious accusations of spying was an example of how far Putin was willing to go in provoking the West.

Then the interview turned to the shots on board *Falck III*. "What do you make of the man on deck?" the host asked.

"This remains speculation," the expert said, "but judging by his posture and his skill with a weapon it's tempting to think this is an individual with a background in the special forces. Which leads to the next question. What was someone like that doing on board?"

Johnny felt a tightening in his throat. "What do you think, Jan?"

"I don't know," Rana replied thoughtfully. "You could lie low in the short term. Look after your daughter, take long walks in the woods and hope it blows over. It really depends on what type of equipment was on board that boat."

The train was rolling through Oslo. Johnny received a text from HK in Kirkenes. He was granting Johnny a week's leave. After which he was to report to section headquarters.

"In the long term," Rana said, "I'm afraid that there's too much in your story for this to remain hidden from public view."

Johnny made no reply.

"There comes a point," the lawyer continued, "where you have everything to gain by taking control of the narrative yourself. You're a Norwegian hero and the events in the north only emphasise that. The offer I made in December still stands. The day you want to tell all, I'll be ready and waiting."

Warm, early-summer weather greeted them on arrival at the platform. "Thanks for all your help, Jan." Johnny gave him a bear hug. "I suspect this won't be the last time I speak to you."

*

Over the following days Johnny walked his daughter to school and collected her early from the after-school programme each afternoon. Rebecca had seen the footage from *Falck III*, and with the keen eyes of an ex must have recognised the mystery shooter. In any case, she was surprisingly kind and understanding.

The weather grew warmer and at the end of the week, Johnny texted Sasha to ask if she wanted to meet at the bathing area in Nydalen. Johnny cycled up with Ingrid after school. A crowd of Osloites were perched around the artificial pool, all still so pale that the scene resembled a bird cliff, and his daughter plunged into the cold water with a yelp of delight.

He sat deep in thought on the steps while keeping an eye on Ingrid. A hand tapped him gently on the shoulder.

"Hi," Sasha said.

He felt a tingling sensation through his body. She was wearing a vintage singlet and denim shorts that showed to advantage her well-formed legs, but there was an uneasy look in her eyes that had been absent in Svalbard. He asked if things were going alright, considering the circumstances.

"I don't know," she answered candidly. "It's good to see you, even though everything's chaos. We just act like friends here, OK? I don't think Mads would like to hear I've been spotted out with a new man already."

She sat down, leaving a little space between them.

"Free Falck," she said, shaking her head.

"What's that?"

"Aren't you following developments, Johnny?"

"As little as possible."

"It's Mayor Sibblund's slogan. Apparently half of Kirkenes turned out in the public square under the banner. There were demonstrations in Lofoten and Bergen too. The Kurdish minister for health has tweeted #FreeFalck. The hashtag has gone viral on social media."

He turned to her. "I've been thinking about you a lot, Sasha."

She swallowed. "What have you been thinking?"

Johnny could not find the words. Ingrid waved to him from the pool, he waved back. "That I . . . would really like to see you again. I like when we, er, work together."

She waited a long time before responding.

"Me too," she said, eventually.

There was a lull in the conversation. He laughed quietly to himself.

"Why are you laughing?"

"I don't know, Sasha. Feels a little like we're both sixteen years old, had a summer fling and are meeting again after the holidays."

"I've shared some of the most powerful moments I can remember with you," Sasha said, fixing her eyes on his. "It's just that everything around me is a mess right now. Have you spoken to Connie?"

He shook his head. "But I did get a call from none other than Peder Grieg about the biography. He apologised for ringing but stressed it was his 'damned duty' as a publisher to do so. Said the decision to terminate the project was 'premature'. As far as the advance is concerned, money is no object."

"Connie took the news about Hans very hard," Sasha said.

"Really? They're not exactly friends."

"I guess the water has been pretty muddied there. Unresolved, complicated feelings. She called me, was clearly high. Yelled about you having contacted her under false pretences and told me I was just as bad. Wanted to retract everything she had said."

"Christ," Johnny said, scratching his chin. "That means there's only one person who can give us the rest of the story. And he's sitting in FSB custody on Franz Josef Land."

"In Murmansk," she corrected. "Remand hearing took place there yesterday."

"Still difficult, I'm afraid."

Ingrid emerged from the pool and began wading towards them. She stopped, her feet still in the water, and stood a couple of steps below them, her head tilted to the side.

"Are you two dating?" she asked, laughing.

56

DEZINFORMATSIYA

Cort Adelers gate, Oslo

HK unlocked the door of Cort Adelers gate 17 and went inside. A stuffy smell had pervaded the rooms since he was last there. It was seven in the morning and he was the first to arrive. His relationship with his husband was currently frosty and until he managed to clear up his private life, he preferred to work round the clock.

He made some coffee and opened the windows facing the street while thinking about the meeting with the Russian intelligence official at the general consul in Kirkenes. The Russian's suggestion, or rather his offer, had been so startling that it had been the only thing on HK's mind as he passed the demonstrators showing their support for Hans Falck in the square in front of Kirkenes community hall.

Let suspected spy Hans Falck speak to a journalist in prison? The Russian was up to something, but what?

In the public sphere the "spy case" was rolling on, now at ministerial level. The Norwegian foreign minister had accused Russia of the "arbitrary incarceration" of a Norwegian citizen. "Falck must be released immediately," the minister stated. The prime minister had raised the issue with his Russian counterpart, who in turn had accused Norway of the "reckless use of a weapon" and the "dangerous escalation" of a situation whereby the Russian icebreaker had simply come to the aid of another vessel.

Among those few in the know within the secret services the tone was different. They were at pains to advise the Norwegian ministers to avoid being so cocksure in their statements. Hans Falck might well be guilty of the Russian charges.

Johnny Berg's manuscript had reinforced these suspicions. HK had had serious doubts about granting him a sabbatical to write. Once again the "kid" – his term for a man in his thirties who held the War Cross with Two Swords – had managed to uncover some interesting material. Both about Herbert Falck's relationship with the CIA in the 1950s and 60s, and the aborted *Klassekampen* exposé in 1976. True, the service's "empowerment conversation" with Hans in Sallyhamna was not news to him, but subsequent events were unclear.

HK always liked to get miscellaneous tasks out of the way before the others turned up. But no sooner had he taken a seat at the desk in the corner office than he got back to his feet to move restlessly around the office. What was going to happen now?

At 8 a.m. on the dot he entered the operations room and nodded to the three people already present.

"Morning," he said tersely. "A lot has happened since the last time we were gathered here. Johnny, I'd like to hear your version of events first. Everything alright, by the way? Those pictures of you have garnered attention worldwide."

Johnny took his time and related the events that occurred in the 1970s, as well as the conversation with Governor Eliassen in Longyearbyen, and the situation as it had unfolded on board *Falck III*.

"Well," HK said, when he finished, "what your account

doesn't throw much light on is the sort of equipment that was on board *Falck III*, and for whom the intelligence was intended."

The three others around the table leaned forward as Johnny continued.

"It wasn't a Norwegian intelligence operation. I have the word of the defence minister and the agency executive on that. So, I contacted our American friends. They were able to inform me discreetly that their technicians have been in Tromsø, where *Falck III* is currently docked, for some time.

"History repeating itself," Johnny said. "American intelligence operating in the north under the fig leaf of rescue vessels and polar exploration. Just like during the Cold War. I was so convinced Hans was a *Russian* agent that I was blind to any alternative. I'm sorry."

"Don't worry about it," Line Mørk and Einar Grotle said in chorus.

"Which brings us to the next point," HK said. "What we, and by 'we' I mean the people in this room, will do moving forward."

"If Hans has been working for the Americans that means we're back to square one," Johnny said. "The mole is still out there."

The older man took a deep breath. "I understand how that might seem like the most obvious path. But what if we've been wrong all along?"

No one replied, and he went on: "*Dezinformatsiya*, or *deza* for short. You're all aware of the term and know as well as I do that it's been a cornerstone of Russian intelligence doctrine, historically and since the break-up of the Soviet Union. What if the Russians have long suspected Hans Falck of being an American spy? What if they leaked us information to sow division and spread disorder in the ranks? They've done it before. And it would certainly be effective here, no?"

"That's absurd," Johnny said at length. "Zemlyakov died of poisoning in Svalbard before being able to reveal the identity of the informant. Medved was shot at the Russian border before he could say anything. Even the Russians wouldn't sacrifice two of their people in a disinformation operation."

"I agree with Johnny," Line said.

HK was not fazed. "You know as well as I do that Zemlyakov was involved in a power struggle within their intelligence service. Any manner of things might have happened. And people crossing the border from the Russian side into Norway risk a bullet in the back if they're discovered."

"No," Johnny said, anger mounting. "We can't give up now! What is this?"

"Sorry," HK said coldly. "The top brass has made the decision. We operate at the discretion of the politicians. We're done for the time being."

Johnny stared down at the plywood table and shook his head.

"So we're finished?" Grotle asked with resignation. "All that's left is to tidy up after ourselves?"

"Not quite," HK said. He had deliberately waited before playing this card. "As you know, I've been in Kirkenes, where I met with the Murmansk chief of the FSB. They're willing to allow Hans a visit. By a journalist."

"What?" the other three exclaimed, almost in unison.

"Naturally, I said we were interested. And that we might have a suitable man for the assignment."

"No," Johnny said, noticing everyone else's eyes turn to him. "Absolutely not. Anyway, the Russians are furious about the shooting incident."

"I've received guarantees that they won't be pursuing that case," HK said.

"Have you considered it might be a trap?" Line Mørk asked.

"Yes," HK said. "But it's too obvious for that. The Russians aren't idiots. There's a reason they want Johnny to come and not the family. Johnny is Hans's biographer. The only stipulation is that the conversation be recorded. It's against all the rules, of course. They're looking to hear Hans confess. They want carefully directed propaganda. A show trial – the Russians are good at that sort of thing. And we're going to help them. You'll take the manuscript of the biography with you. Is that understood, Johnny?"

57

CROSSROADS

Murmansk, Russia

The gate of Murmansk prison closed behind him. A guard with a stain on one epaulette of his shirt glanced at the voice recorder, then took a closer look at it, before his superior hurried him along and waved Johnny through.

His steps echoed in the long corridor. A stale smell of moths, sweat and boiled cabbage hung in the air. The guard stopped at a door, unlocked it and held it open for him. Johnny stepped inside. The visitors' room had grey walls with peeling paint, and a little opening high up through which the perpetual summer light of the Arctic fell.

Hans was sitting on a brownish rod-back chair, in a clean white T-shirt, and was leaning forward, his bare forearms resting on his thighs. His hair had been shorn, no doubt to avoid lice and for reasons of general hygiene. His complexion was a little matte, and he was pale and thinner, which made him seem older. Overall, he looked no worse than could be expected. Another guard in the corner gave a sour nod.

Hans stood up and embraced Johnny. They rested their hands on each other's shoulders and looked at one another.

"We're making an odd habit of meeting under such circumstances," Hans said. "Just over a year ago it was the other way around. I was the one visiting you in prison."

Johnny made no reply.

With a gesture that was supposed to be gallant, Hans motioned for him to sit. Johnny complied, placing his briefcase on a small plywood table.

"I've been given permission to record our conversation," Johnny said.

"You do know they'd never usually allow that," Hans said. "Not in a million years. So this is a show trial, just to play to the gallery."

"I've understood as much."

There was a shortage of coffee in prison, so Johnny scooped the instant coffee he had brought into two cups.

"How did they catch you?" Johnny asked. "Have they got incriminating evidence?"

Hans blew on the steaming cup while shaking his head.

"I showed my hand," Hans said. "During my final mission with the 330th Squadron last year I performed that appendectomy on the captain of the Russian trawler. I set the organ aside, and being badly injured I didn't think any more about it. Not until one of my colleagues from the squadron showed up with an appendix that had been sitting in a fridge in Bodø. I had always impressed upon him the importance of keeping organs for research purposes."

"A pretext on your part?" Johnny asked.

Hans nodded. "It was. I got hold of DNA from the captain's appendix and notified my handler, who made a mistake. The Americans mounted a search for the Russian, based, among other things, on the DNA profile I had obtained. For the Russians that confirmed something they had long suspected: that I was working for the other side. The captain had never travelled outside Russia, so the only place the DNA profile could have come from was me."

"It could have come from your colleague?" Johnny objected.

"No, my overseers had supplied me with a diffusion-proof bag and the seal was intact."

"What is the FSB saying as regards a possible sentence?"

He shrugged. "Ten to fifteen years, according to my lawyer. If I'm lucky, NATO may catch some Russians and there'll be an exchange. I'll manage."

He was putting on a tough front, but Johnny could discern a quiver in his voice.

Hans looked out through the bars. Murmansk in early summer. Johnny hated prisons.

"But that isn't the reason I'm here," Johnny said.

Hans nodded.

Did Johnny glimpse something in his eyes, a twitch in his face?

"I didn't do what you said. I wrote a draft about the first part of your life, based on what Connie told me."

"I knew you would." His voice was soft and resigned.

"I want you to read it in peace and quiet while I wait outside."

He placed the document in front of Hans, stood up and signalled to the guard that he wished to be let out. He sat down on a bench outside and waited.

Johnny had travelled to Kirkenes by plane, then been driven in the Norwegian consul's car across the border on the Kola Peninsula to Murmansk. The city had colour now. He had cast a look in the direction of the pastel-coloured Norwegian diplomatic residence. This time he was not posing as one Roar Kirkkoniemi but an important guest of the Russian Federation travelling on his own passport and receiving the best of treatment.

After an hour the guard opened the door and signalled for him to come back in. Johnny noticed he was suddenly nervous, as if he was being called in for an oral exam. Trying to hide it, he sat down slowly opposite Hans, placed the voice recorder on the table between them and folded his arms.

There was silence in the room.

"Well?" Johnny said, and cleared his throat.

A fan on one wall emitted a low hum.

"I'm impressed," Hans said.

Johnny's initial relief was soon joined by an uneasy feeling.

"Everyone is infinitely complicated in their own eyes," Hans said. "But perhaps our true selves, who we really are, is best revealed through the simplified version other people see. What do you think, Johnny?"

"I'm open to the thought."

Hans tapped a finger on the manuscript. "I could of course get lost in the details of events I remember differently, but that's beside the point. You've found the most important things. The motivations, the dilemmas. Those moments you only realise in retrospect were crossroads in life."

"I appreciate that," Johnny said. "But it's Connie you should thank."

Hans made no reply, merely stared up aimlessly at the opening in the wall.

"You know, I considered telling you everything at the hospital that time in Bodø?"

"Why didn't you?"

"When we tell a white lie we automatically feel a small pang of guilt, of anxiety, you know? But if we keep on telling it then it dissolves in the body, like an anticoagulant, until it becomes part of our constitution."

"The life-lie," Johnny said.

"The first time you interviewed me, you began by asking me about the infant I carried through Shatila. I never told you the background, about the mother I bid farewell to in the infirmary. It was Mouna Khouri, and I loved her."

Hans cleared his throat. "She was your mother, and I'm your father."

Johnny sat as though turned to stone for a few moments. Then broke out in snorts of incongruous laughter. "You're . . . my father?"

He uttered the last two words with awe, as though they were not in his vocabulary.

"Let's have no illusions about this being uncomplicated for us, for you," Hans said. "You're going to view this, if you don't already, as unforgivable. You're going to confide in someone close that it would have been better if you hadn't found out. You're going to cry at night, curse me when you're alone, hate me and maybe, at some stage in the future, make your peace with me. But know that I've always loved you. That I did as Mouna asked. Kept my word about never revealing your identity and about giving you a better life."

Johnny closed his eyes. Felt the weight of something heavy and wet pushing from inside his head, saw Hans's face dissolve in his swimming vision. It was like trying to see underwater.

"I'm not angry at you," he sobbed. "I'm so happy we're having this talk. Tell me about my mother. Tell me about the two of you. I want to know everything."

Transcription of Hans Falck's testimony:

I'll be honest, Johnny.

I'm not asking for forgiveness but for you to understand what happened. I became an agent. I had no choice.

The first time I went to Lebanon was in 1980. With Constance. We got off the plane at the airport south of Beirut, the tarmac shimmering in the heat.

Times had changed. The Maoist party had gone to the dogs, thanks to sectarianism and threat of war. Thatcher was in power in the United Kingdom and the USA had just elected Ronald Reagan as president. If there was anything left of the radical zeitgeist, the remnants were there in war-torn Beirut. In the Middle East, in the global south. The front lines were shifting, one ideology replacing another. In Iran, Ayatollah Khomeini had overthrown the Shah and introduced theocracy. A number of our old comrades from the Maoist party had converted to Islam; the old leftist doctor Trond Linstad had taken "Ali" as his middle name.

In speeches, the ayatollah called the USA the "Great Satan" and a "wounded snake".

I was finished with my studies and had a couple of years of my medical residency behind me in northern Norway. I had the impression Constance's path had been harder for her to find. Much trial and error. I was happy when she decided to become a nurse and accompany me to Lebanon.

Constance was wearing khakis and had a shawl pulled halfway over her head. She squeezed my hand.

"Are you apprehensive?" I remember asking.

"I've never been in a war zone before."

"Me neither," I said.

We made our way to the meeting point we'd been given in the throng outside the terminal and were picked up by a young driver who sped the short distance to the nearby Palestinian refugee camp. On the way in we were stopped by some youngsters in a militia group at a checkpoint.

I tried to explain our business in English, but they looked at me blankly.

"*Nous venons de Palkom*," Constance said in her schoolgirl French, explaining we worked for the Palestine Committee of Norway.

It was a white lie. We had deliberately steered away from the Norwegian solidarity factions who, as was their wont, had split into tiny groups with microscopic differences and implacable enmities.

Eventually the youngsters waved us through with sour expressions. The camp was overcrowded. Little children were running around the filthy alleyways. This was Shatila, its inhabitants stateless Palestinians.

At the hospital there was no time for introductions.

We finished our first night on duty and had just sunk onto a sofa with cups of sweet tea when we heard a commotion outside: angry voices.

A group of people barged into the break room: "*Yalla, yalla!*"

"Doctor, doctor!" shouted one of the men. I could see both fear and anger in his face. He wore a keffiyeh on his head and had three-day stubble. They were clearly militiamen. Another of them pushed Constance aside.

They were carrying a makeshift stretcher with a young woman on it.

The first thing I noticed were her military boots, half covered by combat trousers belted at the waist. No visible injuries, so far as I could see, but when I looked at her chest, I could a darkish brown stain coming through the uniform.

The colour when military green meets blood. There was obvious trauma in the chest area.

The woman was pale and unconscious. Without hesitating, I checked her airways were unobstructed. Her pulse was weak and unsteady. I examined the entrance wound.

Constance came to my side. "Christ, she's been shot in the heart."

"Doctor, you must operate!" the militia leader cried.

Fear and anxiety washed through me. I was no expert in field surgery. During my two-year residency in Lofoten, the fishermen had taught me a lot about hypothermia and fishing lore.

But nothing about operating on gunshot wounds to the heart.

"What are you waiting for, doctor?" the man said.

"I'm waiting for the chief surgeon," I said.

The man took a step towards me, I could smell his tobacco breath on my face. "Doctor. You're going to operate. Now. Do you understand?"

The other men in the militia also moved closer, forming a circle around me.

The woman lay motionless on the stretcher.

The thought of what they would do to me if I did not manage to save her went through my head.

I took a deep breath and looked at the man. "I'm going to administer an anaesthetic," I heard myself say. "Then I'll try to open her up. I'm going to ask you to leave the room while we do that."

Helped by a Palestinian nurse, Constance cleaned the area of blood. Then I began. I didn't think. I acted. I quickly made an incision below the sternum. Even without knowing what had happened, I immediately realised the bleeding was originating from where a bullet had lodged.

I could see it next to one heart valve. Constance's eyes met mine over her face mask.

"We need to remove it," I said.

She nodded.

While she held the incision open, I moved the forceps down towards the valve. On the flight down I had tried to picture how I would react under this kind of pressure. When it did come, I was completely calm. As though the world around did not exist. All that mattered was taking hold of the bullet with the forceps, causing the least possible damage to the surrounding tissue.

After a few long seconds had passed, I felt the tip of the forceps meet something hard. Moving extremely slowly, I tried to take hold of it, but it slipped away. Making contact with the bullet again, I eventually managed to grip it with the pointed ends of the forceps. Moving almost imperceptibly, I began to extract the bullet. I knew this was the crucial juncture: if I was careless, the strands of connective tissue would tear, resulting in internal bleeding.

I pulled my arm slowly back.

The bullet along with it.

I held it up to the light. Constance hurried to get a tin cup and to this day I can still hear the clink of the bullet as I dropped it in.

After I had finished stitching, Constance dressed the wound and covered the patient.

I leaned against the wall with relief. I remained there for a time before opening the door carefully. The men outside got to their feet. The militia leader gave me a questioning look.

I nodded. "The operation was successful. The chances of her making a full recovery are good."

He studied me for a long moment. "Thank you," he said. "I owe you a great debt."

Constance and I left. Her hands were shaking, as were mine. Outside, in the temperate evening, I took the bullet from the cup and held it up to the light.

"Do you have a cigarette?" I asked.

"You haven't started smoking, have you?"

"Just give me one, please."

I took a drag on the cigarette as I looked over the rooftops of Beirut and out at the black ocean. I put my arm around her shoulder.

We stood like that for a long time. Then I returned to the patient. Inside the room I could study the young woman, lying wrapped in light fabrics, from a distance. Her dark hair was thick and cascaded over her neck and shoulders. She was young, very young, hardly more than twenty, if that, and around her neck she wore a cross.

That was your mother, Johnny. She was the one I operated on that night.

I removed a bullet from her heart.

I remember those first months in Beirut as a happy time. Constance and I rented a flat in the west of the city and were a proper couple for the first time. I had apologised for what happened in 1976 and was under the impression she had forgiven me. Far removed from Bergen gossip and the party rumour mill, we took long walks along the Corniche and ate fattoush and grilled meat from cafés. We would stop to watch the anglers on the craggy cliffs and kiss. We would make love in the warm apartment, row, and make up over a drink, just like other couples. Once, on a rare occasion we had time off, we drove out to the vineyards in an old convertible I had borrowed from a shifty Shia Muslim businessman.

Constance wanted to get pregnant because now no party edict could get in her way. But she wasn't able to. A dark cloud hung over our relationship.

The man who had pressured me into performing the operation turned out to be the patient's brother. He wouldn't stop thanking me for saving his sister's life.

"How is she doing?" I asked.

"Better. Much better," he told me.

After a few months confined to bed, the young woman slowly recovered. Although my workload was heavy, I often checked in on her. She had begun to sit up.

One day when I entered the room she was convalescing in, she looked at me. "I thank you for my life every single day, Dr Hans. You and Our Lord."

She squeezed the crucifix in the hollow of her throat. "You're a Christian?" I asked.

"My name is Mouna," she replied. "Mouna Khouri. Do you know what Khouri means?"

I shook my head.

"It means 'priest' in Arabic."

In my ignorance of the Middle East, I was about to ask why a Christian was active in the Palestinian resistance. She beat me to it. "You look surprised, Dr Hans. Do you not know that Christians have always been a large minority among Arabs? In Lebanon, of course, but also in Egypt and Palestine."

I nodded.

"Many of the great leaders in the fight for Palestinian freedom are Christian, did you know that? My family goes back to the first Christians."

"You look better," I said. "I can accompany you outside, if you like, so you can stretch your legs a little."

It was the first of many walks in the hospital garden, among the cypresses, olive trees and landscaped areas. Mouna talked incessantly about Paris, where she dreamed of studying, about the writings of radical thinkers like Franz Fanon, about her home town on the West Bank, which her family had to flee during the Nakba – the catastrophe – in 1948.

Your mother was so beautiful, Johnny, and in her face I read both innocence and toughness. My privileged upbringing was one thing, but what was worse was that everything Constance and I could bring to the table as communists – the years in the AKP, the cadre evaluations, the strikes, the sedition – all of it struck me as so incredibly irrelevant compared with the urgency of the existential, political struggle Mouna was involved in.

One day, as we walked behind a shady cypress, she took hold of my hand and kissed me. I offered no resistance.

"I don't think this is a good idea," I said.

I was with Constance. Mouna came from a place where premarital relations were not viewed favourably, to say the least, so shrouded in honour and shame was the culture. And yet we began. Of course we did. Taking ever-longer walks in the grounds of the hospital, and in time arranging illicit rendezvous around Beirut. I was going behind Constance's back. On the surface we were still together. I'm not proud of it, Johnny. I lied and deceived. Mouna and I met in bars in East Beirut and made love in cars and cheap hotels with hourly rates.

It was a story that could hardly end well.

A year had passed since we arrived in Lebanon and we still had not travelled home. The previous week Mouna had whispered to me that she was pregnant.

Constance had some business at a solidarity clinic in the south and for the first time I took the risk of bringing Mouna to our apartment. That night there was a noise at the door. Isn't all infidelity discovered in such banal fashion?

"Hello," Constance called out, "the meetings were cancelled so I came back early."

Mouna and I were lying in the bed.

Constance opened the door.

Mouna's crucifix hung over the white sheet she had wrapped around her upper body.

Constance just stood in the doorway. "You call yourself a Christian? Fucking hell. And you, Hans? I don't know where to begin."

Then she turned and left.

One day in the winter of 1982, I received a call from the UNIFIL force in the south of the country. They had urgent need of anaesthetisation training, they said, and wondered if I could come. Frankly, I had no real desire to; I had steered clear of the UN forces.

In the end, though, I decided to travel down to the UN battalion. It would benefit poor Lebanese and Palestinians, I told Mouna.

As I drove south my thoughts turned to Constance. I knew I had the ability to put things behind me; it was one of my great strengths. She was still in Lebanon, but I had no idea what she was doing. We weren't on speaking terms.

I conducted an intensive two-day course in bullet wounds and basic field surgery, and when I was finished a driver was standing ready to take me back to Beirut. The Blue Helmets waved our car through a checkpoint.

But we didn't drive in the direction of the main road.

The driver took me to a place called Falcon Heights. I was shown to an observation post. Two men were sitting inside. One was Robert Eliassen from POT, now the police liaison in UNIFIL, and beside him was an older man who introduced himself in English as William Astor.

"Hans Falck!" Astor said. "Do you know when I met you for the first time?"

Already sensing something was very wrong, I stared down at the table without answering.

"In Bergen in 1952. I was working for the company back then and was visiting my old friend Herbert Falck. You'd just been born, Hans, imagine that."

I was too shocked to speak.

"And the last time we met was in Svalbard in 1976," Eliassen said. "When you chose to heed our call and put a stop to the story about Svalbard and the rescue boats."

I stared at Eliassen.

"That was the first and last time I do you a favour, you can be quite sure of that," I said.

"Israel," Astor said, pointing south over the hazy landscape. "Galilee. We're worried about a full-scale invasion by the Israelis. We talk to them on a regular basis, their intelligence people are good at what they do and are well informed. Irrespective of what opinion one might have of their security assessments, it's easy to understand that having militant Palestinian groups on their doorstep is unacceptable to them."

I was about to object and say the answer to the question was simple: give the Palestinians their land back. But I refrained.

"I don't see what this has to do with my work as a doctor," I said.

Eliassen produced an A4 envelope from his briefcase and pulled out several photographs. They were of me with various friends from the Palestinian militia, including Mouna.

"From my own perspective," the American began, "I'm not opposed to giving repentant sinners who make a mistake in their youth a second chance. Stealing a moped when you're sixteen shouldn't destroy your prospects in life."

He gave me a mildly patronising look.

"However," he continued, "there's no doubt that your links to militant elements among the Palestinians is deeply problematic, from our perspective."

"I'm a communist." I had to say something. "I support the struggle for Palestinian liberation. If the choice is between the USA and Palestinians in the Middle East, it's a simple one."

"Excellent," Astor said, "that's my assessment too. But that's not why I mention it. We could use some information on your Palestinian friends. Mouna Al-Khouri for example?"

I felt anger rising from the pit of my stomach as I got to my feet.

"I'm going back to Mouna. The two of you can go to hell."

"When is she due?" Eliassen asked.

I felt an ice-cold hand grip my heart.

Astor sat back in his chair and left the talking to Eliassen.

"As your compatriot on foreign soil, I'm not sure it's such a good idea to return to Mouna and the Palestinians without doing as we say."

"Why not?"

"You're not naive, Hans Falck," Eliassen replied. "POT has been watching you for a decade." He nodded to Astor, who reached for a new dossier. They were obviously well prepared.

"What do we see here?" the American said. "Yes, your great-uncle Herbert Falck with a young American. Norway, is it 1944 or 1945? And that young American is me."

"They're not my sins," I said.

"True. Nor is it illegal to be photographed with the Aga Khan and Eva Perón on Aristotle Onassis's yacht."

He placed the picture in front of me. I thought about Constance, the Riva and the trip back to Antibes.

"But where it does begin to get difficult, if you insist on preserving your independence, are the photos of you as a deckhand aboard *Falck II* in the early seventies."

He placed the pictures of me and the other sailors on *Falck II* on the table. A grainy image, taken off Bjørnøya, with me standing between the cook and Bendiksen.

"They're dead, all of them," I said in a low voice. "It was your fault, with that radar you fitted, as well you know."

"Maybe," Astor replied, "though our specialist here . . ." he pointed to a man in the photo I didn't know, "Jim, is still alive. Retired now. If you don't do as we say, it's possible he'll have to tell your Palestinian friends in Beirut about your activities. You're not just starting to work for us now, Hans Falck. That damaging newspaper story you put a stop to in 1976 wasn't a one-off incident. No, you've been working for the company – or let's cut the bullshit and call it the C-I-A – ever since that voyage on *Falck II* in the summer of 1971. You're our man. You're an American agent."

They were the words of Shaitan.

Maybe the Ayatollah was right. Maybe the USA was the great Satan.

Now the devil had made me an offer I couldn't refuse.

I had no choice, Johnny. I reported on your mother for Western intelligence. I hated myself for it. But I still did what they asked. Winter turned into spring and spring turned into summer. The Israelis invaded Lebanon to destroy the Palestinian bases in the country. The leadership fled.

Then September 1982 arrived.

I hurried towards the run-down hospital in Shatila, past what was left of security at the door. The few doctors that were left were already overwhelmed by patients turning up with gunshot wounds.

"Dr Hans!" I heard someone cry out, but I paid no heed, not now. I continued down a grubby corridor and flung open the door of the maternity ward.

Supported by pillows against the barred headboard lay Mouna with a baby in her arms. It was you, Johnny. Carefully, I lifted you up. You were as light as a doll. An infant has something unborn about it, I had time to think, your eyes were barely open.

The sounds of shooting grew closer. Like an evil echo they reverberated through the streets towards the hospital building.

I looked at Mouna, your mother. Her dark curls falling over the blue bed sheets.

"Come on," I said. "We need to go."

Mouna didn't respond, just lay there staring at the ceiling. As bursts of machine-gun fire sounded outside, she closed her eyes, like someone going to sleep for the night. Like someone about to die.

"It's too late," she said.

"There's always a chance!" With you pressed against one shoulder, I tried to lift her from the bed. "They wouldn't dare stop a Western doctor. No way. Come on."

"They'll stop anyone," Mouna said. Her voice sounded resigned and she had a distant look in her eyes, as though she had already been shot.

"Please," I begged.

"Don't worry about me, Hans," she said calmly and slowly sat up in the bed. "I've done my part."

I was lost for words.

She fixed her eyes on me. "I want you to give the boy a decent life, understand?"

I looked at you, Johnny.

"I want him to be called Yahya. Never allow our enemies to find out who he is. Will you promise me that?"

As the flares streaked across the sky, I ran outside with you in my arms. And you know this story, Johnny, you told me it that time you interviewed me. I stopped. Between heaps of rubbish, boxes of war rations and spirit bottles lay the dead: young men with their genitals hacked off, pregnant women with their stomachs sliced open, children, babies. Some twenty metres away to the left, I caught sight of a cluster of women shielding their children, men in tight embraces, each with a small bullet hole in their forehead. All had been executed at close range.

I was surrounded by the smell of gunpowder and excrement. Then I heard the quiet, penetrating sound of your cries.

I took shelter behind a dustbin, sank to my knees and tried to rock you.

Could anyone see me? No, I was well hidden.

I remembered that in a side pocket of the large first aid bag there was a bottle of Johnnie Walker Black Label. I opened the bottle and dipped a finger into it. Then let you inhale the fumes before poking my fingertip into your little mouth. You went quiet, Johnny.

I walked through the camp, towards the iron cordon of soldiers surrounding it.

The militia soldiers stank of alcohol from several metres away. The young men, eyes swimming, kerchiefs over their noses, pointed their guns at me. Behind me I heard a series of shots, screams, then silence.

You were in the first aid bag, Johnny.

Sedated by Johnnie Walker.

I put the bag gently down on the ground. Carefully opened the zip. The militiamen leaned over me. Your face was covered but the blanket moved a little with your breathing. I took out the bottle of Johnnie Walker and held it up to the officer.

"You need this more than I do," I said.

The officer grabbed the bottle. "Get lost," he said.

My hands were shaking so hard I could barely close the zip. I felt weightless and numb as I walked the gauntlet between two lines of Phalangist soldiers, towards freedom, reassured by the fact that if they fired now, they would shoot each other.

Constance was standing outside the iron cordon. We didn't say a word to one another. Her eyes said it all. She had been there, had seen women and children being shot by the Phalangists, heard the screams, the awful screams, encountered the stench of excrement and cordite that hung heavy over the camp.

None of this was said but we both knew.

We drove off.

"What are you going to do with the baby?" Constance asked.

"I promised his mother never to reveal his identity. It could be dangerous. Do you understand what I'm saying?"

Constance nodded.

We drove back to her place.

That same evening the Norwegian chargé d'affaires in Lebanon, a middle-aged and carefree diplomat by the name of Bjørn Berg, showed up at Constance's apartment. Even though Berg was experienced, he was shaken by the news that had begun to seep out about what had happened in the Palestinian refugee camps.

He arrived with orders from the highest authority. All Norwegian citizens were to be evacuated from Beirut as soon as possible.

I sat there as though turned to stone. I hadn't smoked since I'd operated on Mouna Khouri, but now I lit up a cigarette.

"We've been given guarantees of safe passage out of the country tomorrow," Berg said. "I would strongly recommend you take advantage of the offer. The consular assistance we can provide otherwise is very limited."

I looked at Constance.

"I'm staying," she said.

"Likewise," I said.

"You're staying?" The diplomat seemed stunned.

"There's too much to do here," Constance said. "There's no end of suffering. I couldn't forgive myself if I left."

"There's a matter needs taking care of," I said, clearing my throat. "I rescued a baby boy from the massacre today. His mother is dead. We don't know anything about him. He's asleep in the next room. He needs to get to Norway."

Constance looked at me and shook her head.

I went into the room where you were lying, Johnny, lifted you up and looked at you for a long time.

"Take good care of the boy," I said.

Bjørn Berg carried you out. The next day you were on a plane to Norway.

But that isn't the end of the story.

After the massacres at Sabra and Shatila, Constance and I found our way back to one another, yet again. Mouna was dead. Nobody else could understand what we had been through. Nobody else could understand what those people screaming for their lives sounded like. Sometimes we made love, morbid as that might sound, but people still make love in times of war, in times of slaughter.

We didn't talk about the baby boy Chargé d'Affaires Berg had taken with him. Nor about Mouna Khouri. On the whole, we reacted very differently. I was a born optimist, but even I was more irritable and in lower spirits during that period than usual.

Constance fell apart. Her tendency towards self-destructive behaviour, when she drowned her sorrows in alcohol and other substances, came to the fore. If she didn't have any artificial means of escaping Shatila, she said, she would rather die.

"You're pregnant," I said to her one morning.

I'd had a suspicion for a while. It was like reliving that first trimester with Mouna over again.

She nodded, her eyes downcast.

"You understand as well as I do that this is an impossible situation. I know a good doctor in Hamra . . ."

"No," she said. "No, I can't do it."

"You're constantly high."

"It's my body and my choice, Hans. I'm going back to Bergen."

I began to feel deep unease. "It's our child, Constance. This is completely irresponsible. And I need to stay here until next spring."

"Everything will be different, Hans. If I can just get home."

So, she left. I stayed behind in Beirut and buried myself in work, not that it helped the anxiety fade. I should have been there, for her and for the unborn child. Because trauma doesn't recognise borders. She rang me sometimes, in the early hours. Told me she had been wandering through Shatila when she tried to sleep. How every night a flare flamed bright across her retina. How in the silver-grey light it cast she saw young men with their hacked-off genitals stuffed in their mouths, pregnant women with their stomachs sliced open, children, babies. How every night she stumbled over the piles of corpses.

The sound of gunfire, the screaming, the stench.

After not hearing from her for a while I called her several times, but got no answer. In desperation I rang a social worker I knew in Bergen who told me Constance had been observed in Nygårdsparken buying heroin and other opiates, while pregnant.

Eventually I travelled to Bergen. I was tortured by feelings of guilt, Johnny. I had already let you down. I couldn't do the same again.

In May, as the rhododendron blossom was coming out, Constance was in labour at Haukeland hospital. Just before midnight she gave birth to a baby girl.

Soon after, I entered the room. The doctor on call informed me that the child was healthy, if somewhat premature. Constance lay with the baby on her breast, still terrified, still with a glint of the infernal in her eyes, but also joy at having brought a child into the world. She began to speak, her voice groggy.

"She's to be called Marte. Marte Harriet Falck has a nice ring to it, hmm?"

I stood there, stock-still, in front of Constance and the girl.

"Do you remember, Hans,' she said, "that time we were at the theatre together?"

"Constance," I said.

"I've loved you ever since that day," she continued, smiling at the memories her words evoked. "Even when I was married to Mikael I loved you. Every day."

"Constance," I repeated. "Traces of heroin have been found in your blood."

She swallowed. "I've made mistakes. I've been so terribly down after what happened."

"You're not the only one who was in Shatila. You're not the only one who can't get those images out of their head, Constance. But no matter how awful it was, we have responsibility for a child."

I was shaking with anger as I looked at the little girl. "You could have damaged her for life because of what you did. Do you understand that, you selfish, self-pitying idiot?"

"But . . ." she said, her voice cracking.

"You must get your life back in order, Constance," I said. "Until that happens, you can't do this."

Calmly, I leaned over the hospital bed and took the girl from Constance's embrace.

"No," she wailed. "Don't do this to me, please, Hans, don't do this to me!"

She tried to rise from the bed but fell back in exhaustion.

"Don't take my daughter!"

I carried the girl out of the room and shut the door behind me.

Epilogue

YOU AND ME

Oslo

Summer came early in Oslo that year. A high lay over the city and the inhabitants sought out the swimming areas in the fjord. Temperatures continued to climb throughout June, the sunshine interrupted only by monsoon-like thunderclouds occasionally rolling in between the gently sloping hills. The jetties in Sørenga, the islands, the large sea-smoothed rocks along the shore, and the beaches were teeming with people, their skin bronzed as though in the Mediterranean, before they withdrew into the city, filling the outdoor areas of cafés and bars on those endless summer nights.

One evening, Ingeborg and Sverre cycled through the shimmering heat of the city streets. Despite the weather Sverre was dressed in a dark blazer and tie, causing amusement to some of those they passed along the way, not that it bothered him unduly.

They had been gearing up for the summer party at Rederhaugen the next week by attending a garden party at one of the large villas in Valleløkken, sitting at a long table cluttered with bottles of red wine with arty types talking loudly under the birch trees. But they only had eyes for one another, in the way stolen glances between lovers are stronger than any words spoken.

He felt secure. Naturally he loved her, insomuch as he understood the meaning of the word. What was more interesting, however, was that he felt loved in return. They truly were a couple. After Svalbard it had been clear to him. The strength in being together, how he became a better, wiser version of himself.

His years of wandering were over; he wanted to write a story with Ingeborg. Of course, make a blunder and the structure of the relationship could become a prison. But if you built it right, and Sverre believed that he was doing just that, with the interlocking double-notch joints of a traditional cabin, nothing could be more confidence-inspiring than marriage for a restless cosmopolitan like Ingeborg. And there were powerful people who wanted him to succeed.

"Where will we go?" Ingeborg asked, leaning over the handlebars. "We could get a drink in Torshov or Grünerløkka?"

Sverre smiled and shook his head. The streets teeming with people east of the city centre were hers. They were not his, at least not tonight. Although it was midnight, the sky, which never really darkened at this time of year, was still pale. They cycled down the wide, almost empty streets towards Bislett Stadium and followed the beautiful streets west, past Hegdehaugen, before pedalling up to the old substation at Briskeby and north along Gyldenløves gate.

"Did you know Queen Maud used to ride her horse on the grassy median there?" Sverre said, pointing.

Ingeborg leaned forward and kissed him. "You sound like my nana now."

"Any wonder I can't find a gentleman at my age when I have to ride on a sledge to the cabin," Sverre said, doing a passable impersonation of Wenche Johnsen. "Come on, Ingeborg."

He could feel his heart beating harder. After a few minutes they turned through the massive wrought-iron gate to Vigelands Park.

"I haven't been here since . . ." Ingeborg said.

Sverre made no reply, but after locking the bikes he took her by the hand and led her towards the back entrance of the outdoor Frogner swimming pool. The gap cut in the barbed wire on the top of the gate was still there. Sverre climbed up, then helped Ingeborg.

"Really?" she said, when she was sitting astride it.

"Really," he replied.

The diving tower stood silhouetted against the night sky, like an X.

They were alone. The pool lay abandoned, the surface of the water like oil. They walked past the one-metre diving board, then ascended the steps past the twin platforms at three metres. The stairs were steep and the treads slippery, just as Sverre remembered. Ingeborg was ahead of him.

"The five-metre one?" she asked.

"Keep going," he ordered.

When they reached the seven-metre platform, Sverre went in front and climbed the last steps to the tower's highest platform. Up on the ten-metre platform he could feel a little breeze, and it was as if the city had opened up, the clouds drifting high in the sky. From the dark wooded ridge of Holmenkollen the ski jump rose up like a lopsided obelisk.

"Do you dare jump?" Ingeborg said, squeezing his hand harder. "I've never really liked heights."

He nodded. Recalled all the days spent here with Prydz, Frölich and the others, the girls they had tried to impress – with little success. The pain when you landed wrong with a "death dive", when you landed wrong in life. Sverre thought about all these things, glimpses from the past, a different time. But most of all he thought about the future, about the woman gently stroking his forearm.

"Will we sit down?" he asked.

He sat down carefully on the edge of the platform and she followed his example. She dangled her legs, gingerly at first, then laughing gleefully.

Sverre took off the bag he had been carrying on his back. He produced a bottle and two plastic glasses, handing her one. The champagne opened with a sigh. He filled the glasses, noticing his hands were shaking slightly. That sharp taste in his mouth. They toasted. His heart began to pound and he found it hard to speak.

"Everything alright?" she asked, leaning her head closer.

"I . . . I . . . have something for you," he heard himself say.

There was no way back now. Was this one of the big moments in life? Yes, undoubtedly. He might not have a family in the conventional sense any longer, but he was in the process of building something, something else.

The small leather box had the Falck coat of arms embossed on it.

He held it half hidden behind his back. Then handed it to her. He held her other hand tightly while staring into her eyes.

"Will you . . ."

While he was talking, she got to her feet and stood on the edge.

Ingeborg held the box between them. Without hesitation, she took out the ring.

"Yes," she said, slid it on to her ring finger and kissed him.

How much does a proposal weigh? A lot. Sverre felt as light as a bird on the wind.

"I will," she said, taking hold of his hand. "I want to jump with you."

"Ready?"

He was about to take off his suit, but stopped. Had an idea. Why not jump with their clothes on? Ingeborg kept on her summer dress. A light wind caught her hair. The first light of morning was glowing behind the hills to the east.

They ran hand in hand. Then jumped, two flailing silhouettes against the pale blue June sky.

Johnny left the summer party at Rederhaugen early to meet Sasha. The weather was still glorious, so the party was held on the lawn in front of the main building, where an eclectic collection of the Falck family's old contacts in shipping, culture, business and politics mingled with the new guard.

As he rounded the corner of the house, Ingeborg and Sverre were walking towards him, hand in hand.

"Johnny, leaving already?" Ingeborg asked.

"A lot on my plate."

"We haven't had a chance to talk," Sverre said. "In fact, we haven't really talked since everything that happened up north. That was a pretty crazy business."

Johnny shrugged.

"The pictures of you have gone all around the world," Sverre continued.

Ingeborg cheerfully pointed her thumb at her fiancé. "He has more footage from that fateful trip," she said jokingly.

"I was wondering if you recognised any of the people standing in the background here?"

Sverre took out his phone and searched for the video.

"I did the filming," Ingeborg said.

The video showed Hans receiving the Order of Saint George from Artur Aliyev, alongside a diplomat from the Russian embassy and an unknown woman, Ingeborg explained. "But take a look at these two people in the background."

"Now that you," Sverre said in his speech, "can add the prestigious Order of Saint George to your already well-stocked medal cabinet, I ask: what other Norwegian can boast of being the recipient of the Lebanese Order of the Cedar, honorary Kurdish citizenship and an honorary doctorate from the University of Florence? Congratulations. And *na zdorovye!*"

Johnny stood deep in thought. There was something here that was not right.

"Sorry," he said.

At that moment he felt a chill spread through him. How had he not realised it before? How could he have been so blind?

Sasha was waiting at the bay in Frognerkilen. Her Riva Aquarama, moored at the jetty, was newly waxed. Tanned and in light summer clothing, she waved to Johnny when she caught sight of him. They kissed. He had confided in her after his meeting with Hans in Murmansk. They had cried together.

Her smile faded as their eyes met. "What's wrong, Johnny?"

"Let's get out on the fjord," he said. "Then I'll explain everything."

He clambered down into one of the speedboat's cream-coloured, sports-car seats. She started the Lamborghini engine and reversed slowly out.

"Are you going to tell me what's going on, Johnny?"

"A few months ago, last winter," he began, "Hans caught a Moldovan in the act of breaking into the blue room at Rederhaugen. He restrained the guy and called for help from someone we both know, my old boss from the service. It turned out the Moldovan wasn't after gold or jewellery. He wanted to photograph Hans's medal collection."

"His medal collection?"

"Why would someone take a photo of a bunch of medals, do you think?"

"To see where their loyalty lies? Where they belong."

"Exactly," Johnny said. "And he immediately suspected that a burglar interested in photos of a medal collection was working for someone. For professional intelligence people. My old boss saw to it that the Moldovan was able to complete his assignment – take the pictures and leave, apparently undetected. There was one catch. The intelligence man left an honorary doctorate from the University of Florence behind in Hans's collection."

"Hans must have a lot of honorary doctorates?"

"He does, so many it's hard to keep track. But he doesn't have any awards from the University of Florence. That one belonged to my old boss, whose first name is also Hans, by the way. Anyway, we managed to track the delivery of the photos to a Russian businessman. The bait had been cast. The honorary doctorate from Florence was a trap. A classic in my line of work. You plant a lie your opponent thinks is the truth and sit back and wait. For someone to repeat the lie, that is – and in so doing give themselves away."

"But hang on," Sasha said. "Wasn't the point that you suspected Hans of being a Russian spy?"

"No flies on you," Johnny said. "Of course, that was what we wondered. We thought the Russians might suspect him of being a double agent. In any case, while Hans was our main suspect, we worked on other leads. But when Hans was exposed as a CIA agent it made me think of this again."

"Smart," she said, leaning back in her seat.

"Earlier today Ingeborg and Sverre showed me footage from the ceremony at the dividing line, where Hans is presented with his Saint George's medal and is then arrested."

"And the Russians mention Hans's honorary doctorate from Florence?" she said.

"You're a bit too quick on the draw," he said. "Sverre gives a speech. He pays tribute to Hans for being the recipient of the Lebanese Order of the Cedar, honorary Kurdish citizenship and an honorary doctorate from the University of Florence."

She looked at him in disbelief. "You're absolutely sure?"

"Why else would he say it?"

"Christ." Sasha sat completely still. "That's crazy."

Johnny touched her gently on one shoulder. He did not say anything.

"What are you going to do?" she asked.

"I've no idea," he replied. "The investigation has concluded that the whole mole scenario was Russian misinformation. It's no longer ongoing. Hans is in prison in Murmansk, Ingeborg Johnsen is part of the apparatus of government and Sverre is running SAGA."

She was quiet for a long time. Then she turned to look at him with a black gaze, filled with sorrow.

"Every time I've been knocked down over the last six months, I've thought it had to be rock bottom. And every time I've kept on sinking."

"When I was in the army," he said, "we had a test called 'drown-proofing'. You're bound by your hands and feet. Then you're pushed into a three-metre-deep pool. You're supposed to hold out for five minutes. The more you try to keep your head above the water, the more likely you are to panic and need saving from the pool. The trick is to let yourself sink, then kick off calmly when you reach the bottom, and your motion will take you to the surface. You then take a breath, sink back down and repeat the process until the time is up. In principle you don't even have to be able to swim. On the contrary, it was often the best swimmers who failed the test."

He looked out over the fjord before his gaze met hers. "You're going to be alright, Sasha. We're going to be alright."

The Riva's Lamborghini engine rumbled.

She glanced in the direction of the cliffs at Rederhaugen. "What about SAGA?"

"No one can save SAGA now, Sasha."

She moved the throttle to max, allowing the boat to plane across the fjord. She turned to him.

"Not even you and me?"

ACKNOWLEDGEMENTS

This book is dedicated to Kjetil Anders Ely Hatlebrekke. Not only did he write the international standard work *The Problem of Secret Intelligence* (Edinburgh Press, 2019) and become the first Norwegian to be awarded the Intelligence Service Medal of Merit; Kjetil was also a warm human being and intellectual powerhouse who shaped the thinking of a generation of Norwegians with an interest in security policy and intelligence.

He did all this while suffering from serious heart problems and, later, terminal cancer. In his last years our conversations often centred on death. Around us many members of the Norwegian Armed Forces' best units died – of heart problems, in accidents, by suicide and of cancer.

We had no empirical evidence, but it aroused the unspoken fear that burdens so many veterans. That we had travelled to foreign war zones without understanding the health costs or being adequately informed about them. Both directly – in the form of exposure, for example, to depleted uranium – and indirectly, by failing to appreciate that the total burden over time of travelling to war-torn regions was greater than we understood when we were young and immortal.

This made a strong impression on me when I came to edit Geir Jan Johansen's *CIA i Norge. Den hemmelige historien* (Kagge, 2016), a book which among other things documents how the intelligence services equipped fishing boats and rescue vessels with powerful radars during the Cold War without the crews being informed. Many of the people working on the Norwegian Society for Sea Rescue's *Skomvær 2* and *Sjøfareren* later developed cancer. Although the cases have been publicised in the media, they have not, in my opinion, received the attention they deserve.

Many people are owed a debt of gratitude for this book seeing the light of day. In Kirkenes I stayed several times at the home of Rita Stenersen and Arne Harald Wartiainen, and spoke to, among others, Rune Rafaelsen, Inger Blix Kvammen, Luba Kuzovnikova, Evgenij Gorman, Frode Berg, Felix Tschudi and Arne Ulvang, who generously shared with me his memoir *Skisamarbeid med Sovjetunionen på 60- og 70-tallet* (self-published, 2013).

In Svalbard, I offer heartfelt thanks to Arnstein Skaare, who both loaned me his apartment on several occasions and allowed me to draw upon his encyclopaedic knowledge of everything from mining regulations on the archipelago to shipowners in Bergen in the post-war period. I would also like to thank Robert Hermansen, Bjørn Fjukstad, Dag Drevvatne, Arnt Angell, Inge Solheim, Petter Nore, Ildar Neverov, Christian Mikkel Doubloug, Harald Skaare and Ian Gjertz for their input in Svalbard.

Klassekampen newspaper editor Mari Skurdal provided me with free access to their archive. The descriptions of relations within the editorial office in the 1970s are on the whole taken from former *Klassekampen* journalist Bente Thoresen's article "Å søke om a bli gravid" (*Klassekampen*, February 12, 1994) and from conversations with the author. My parents Bibi Nore and Kjartan Fløgstad have been a useful sounding board and a great help in recreating the historical colouring of the 1970s. As has my job as editor of *Jon Michelet: A Hero of the People* (Kagge, 2021) by Mímir Kristjánsson. Thank you also to Jostein Gripsrud for his contributions on the Bergen of the 1970s.

I am grateful to Geir Woxholth for his legal opinions, Odd Karsten Tveit for his stories of Lebanon, Charlotte Lunde, Lars Wabø and Karim Sayed for medical corrections, Trond Elden for inside knowledge of the 330th Squadron, Ingvild Andersen for professional input on the psychology of double agents, Arne Borchgrevink for expertise on Russia, Petter Skavlan for discussions on plot, Alicia and Catherine Vaisse for their hospitality and insight into the running of the Haras du Coussoul estate, and Ole Jakob Sunde for highly creative suggestions as respects ownership, management and company structure.

My friends in the secret services shall remain anonymous.

At Aschehoug Publishing House, I would like to extend my thanks to Nora Campbell and Marius Fossøy Mohaugen, for reading and commenting on the manuscript with an enthusiasm that matched mine in writing it, and to Ruth Lillegraven, for her literary sensitivity and intelligence. I would also like to thank Åse Ryvarden, Mads Nygaard and Trygve Åslund for their readings and facilitation.

Finally, I wish to thank Anne-Laure Albessard, whose contributions to the story and the characters in it have been crucial, and who has endured our travels to the cold coasts.

ASLAK NORE grew up in Oslo. Educated at the University of Oslo and the New School for Social Research in New York, he then served in Norway's elite Telemark Battalion in Bosnia. A modern-day adventurer, Nore has lived in Latin America and worked as a journalist in the Middle East and Afghanistan. He has published several non-fiction books and three novels, including *Ulvefellen*, which was a bestseller and won the Riverton Prize for best crime novel in Norway in 2018. *The Sea Cemetery* is an international bestseller. He lives in Provence, France.

SEÁN KINSELLA was born in Dublin and holds an MPhil in literary translation from Trinity College Dublin. He has translated works by Åsne Seierstad and Stig Sæterbakken, among others. His translations have been longlisted for both the Best Translated Book Award and International Dublin Literary Award. He lives in Norway.